CONFRONTING DARKNESS

Book Seven

I0680395

Salvaggio's Light

An Epic Contemporary Romance Serial
By C. L. Cattano

VAGARY PUBLISHING

Confronting Darkness
Book Seven
Salvaggio's Light

A Vagary Publishing Book
Copyright © 2018 by C. L. Cattano
Cover Art, Title Page Art and Typesetting Copyright © 2018 by Chynsia Hinesley

Published by:

VAGARY PUBLISHING

www.vagarypublishing.com
inquiry@vagarypublishing.com

Rogena Mitchell-Jones, Independent Literary Editor
RMJ Manuscript Services LLC *www.rogenamitchell.com*

ISBN: 978-1-947852-05-1
First Edition

WARNING

IT IS SUGGESTED readers of this story be adults over the age of eighteen.

This dramatic romance series has many scenes describing sex as well as intense emotional scenes and acts of violence.

This is a serial story with themes that flow from one book into another with lots of twists and turns. Reading this series from the beginning is highly suggested, or the reader may not be able to follow all of the story lines.

Go to the Salvaggio's Light Facebook page to join other readers who are talking about the series.
www.facebook.com/SalvaggiosLight/

Join the C L Cattano mailing list and check out my website at www.clcattano.com

Acknowledgments

Thank you to those who have supported me in my endeavor. I know this has been a long ride but the end is nigh! Only three more books to go! You keep reading, and I'll keep writing!

Dedication

For Marie — who guides with her light

Salvaggio's Light

An Epic Contemporary Romance Serial

Coming Soon

How long in woman lasts the fire of love,
If eye or touch do not relight it often.
—Dante Alighieri, The Divine Comedy

1

Almost two weeks later. . .

INSIDE THE STARK hospital room in Mexico, Rafe Salvaggio was packing her things. After intensive therapy sessions, along with medication, Dr. Baker determined Rafe had stabilized and agreed there was no longer enough justification for her to be held any longer. Rafe was very aware of how patient Kate and the staff had been, and together, they worked through many of her smaller issues. She knew there were some things to work out and not all of her issues could be resolved in such a short time period. However, she didn't want to deal with them in the current environment, or in Mexico. She was still skittish and unsure about what she wanted to do and where she wanted to go. She just knew she wanted out of the hospital and never wanted to return.

"Hola, Rafe. Are you just about ready?" asked Nurse Rosita as she entered the room.

"Yes, I don't have much to pack," she said and forced a smile for the nurse who had sat with her and taken good care of her when things were at their worst.

"We'll miss you around here," said Rosita then laughed. "You've certainly made our jobs more interesting. I can't ever remember actually wanting to get up and come into work for a patient! And I know we've never had a patient who turned our hospital upside down in just under two weeks like you did!"

Rafe smiled indulgently. "Well, I was just trying to help."

Rosita laughed. "And you did!"

"I was getting bored, and they were getting on my nerves," Rafe confessed, chuckling along with Rosita, though no humor was in her eyes.

"Yes, well, our volunteer staff has never been more organized, or so enthusiastic!" she said happily. "You really lit a fire under them."

"I knew they'd come around to my way of doing things," Rafe said with a firm nod. Rosita laughed again thinking Rafe was being humorous. Rafe couldn't tell the nurses how much being in their hospital had disturbed her. She felt she had to do something about what she saw. She had never stayed in a hospital for a long period of time, and to her, it seemed like a prison without humanity or feeling.

"Well, I have to say, watching them paint decorations on bedpans was the funniest thing I've ever seen!" Rosita smiled as she looked at Rafe's chart and then took Rafe's vitals for the last time. "Then, when you ordered all those plants to put in them," she added, "I think up until the moment the project was finished, they thought you really were crazy! But the patients loved them!"

"I'm glad," said Rafe managing to keep the slight smile on her face. She allowed Rosita to unwrap the blood pressure cuff from her arm. "The rooms were so stark. They just needed something nice in them to make them bearable." She didn't understand how they could allow the patients to live in such unkind surroundings. The experience had added to the guilt she felt for leaving her father to die in a place like this alone.

Dr. Kate Baker walked in and took the chart from Rosita. "Good morning, Rafe. Are you ready for our last session?"

"I guess," said Rafe as she waved goodbye to the nurse.

"Everyone here adores you," said Kate as she closed the door. "Greer said you were a force. I didn't know just how much of one though."

"Greer is a force herself." Rafe smiled slightly at the thought of her. It was her first genuine smile of the day. "She's great. I love her very much."

"Here's your money from the safe." Kate handed her a package along with a small box. "There's a little gift there from the staff, too."

Rafe put the package on the table and opened the gift. "Oh, it's beautiful." She pulled a fine silver chain from the box. "They didn't have to do this."

Kate chuckled. "If you were anyone else, they probably wouldn't have. Delores said it would look good with your skin tone. Her husband made it at his silversmith shop."

"It is a real piece of art," Rafe said as she pulled the chain up so she could look at it closer. "I love it."

"Delores said she remembered how you admired hers." Kate waited for Rafe to finish admiring the chain. "Do you have everything you need? Plane ticket, luggage, money, medication," she said, ticking off a list. "Are we forgetting anything?"

"No, I think it's everything," said Rafe as she put the envelope with the money and the gift in her duffel bag. She sat down with her bag beside her then looked at Kate uneasily. "Will I see you when I get to the States?"

"I wish I could continue with you after this," said Kate earnestly. "I hate to leave a patient in such a vulnerable state, but I won't be in California.

"I see." Rafe couldn't hide her disappointment.

"Have you made a decision about what you're going to do," Kate paused, "about Eden?"

"No," Rafe said flatly.

"You know you don't put her in danger, right?" Kate reminded her.

"I know," said Rafe pushing away her discomfort.

"You love her," added Kate. Rafe didn't respond so she went another direction. "You love your daughter."

"Yes," Rafe agreed quietly.

"You'll have a lot of help, Rafe, when you go back," Kate reminded her.

"You mean a lot of babysitters."

"A lot of people who love you and want you back," Kate assured her and smiled. "So many things were, and may still be, mixed together in your mind and associated with your PTSD. It is going to take time to sort everything out. With your medication and therapy sessions, I think you'll be fine. You need to talk to people when you're feeling bad if you can."

"I don't want to talk to them."

"They're there to listen when you're ready to talk." She watched as Rafe crossed her arms in defiance. "You need to talk when you can. Try to find at least one person you feel like you can share with, even if it's only the therapist. It's not good for you to hold so much inside. You don't have to handle everything alone."

"I don't know where I'm going," Rafe confessed.

Kate hid her surprise. "I thought you said you bought tickets," Kate said calmly, wondering if she should keep her here longer or make her go to Baltimore with her. "We talked about all of this. Why don't you know where you're going now?"

"I—" Rafe sighed. "I bought three tickets."

Kate tried not to show emotion. "Three?"

Rafe nodded. "L.A., Baltimore, and Florence, Italy. My friend Gabri is there. It's my childhood home. I feel like I should go back there."

"I need you to stay in the States," Kate said firmly. "You need to continue with your treatment sessions. I need you to cancel your ticket to Italy. If you don't, I think I may need to keep you here longer."

Rafe thought about it and knew she couldn't stay in this hospital another day. She reached into her bag and gave Kate the ticket information to Italy. "You should give it to Rosita. It's transferable, so I'll transfer it. She wants to go."

"It's one way," said Kate in surprise as she looked at the first class ticket information then back at Rafe. "Okay, I'll give it to her. Maybe she can exchange it for an economy class round trip. Forward me the transfer instructions, and I'll help her."

"Thank you."

"So, you may go stay with Greer?" she asked calmly.

"I'm thinking about it," Rafe admitted. "She has certain requirements though." She sighed and looked away.

"I remember, you told me," said Kate carefully. "Do you think you can give her what she's asking for?"

"I think so." Rafe shook her head. "I'm not sure."

"You're not sure," she said softly. "Tell me, why did you make your timeline and the list of reasons for leaving Eden?"

Rafe frowned because she had told Kate she didn't want to talk about Eden.

"I can tell you think I'm breaching our agreement, but this isn't about Eden. This is about why you behaved a particular way. Maybe knowing the answer will help you know where you should go." She waited for an answer as Rafe scowled. "Letty said you told her she should show the timeline and list to *them*. It seems like you wanted both Eden and Greer to see what you made. Why was that important to you?"

Rafe rubbed her temples to calm her frustration. "I—" she paused, "I don't know. I don't remember everything I said to Letty. It was late, and I was tired." She didn't want to admit the whole night was lost to her, and she couldn't remember any of it.

"Let's back up," said Kate. "Just tell me why you made them."

Rafe leaned her head down and stretched her neck. "I made them so I could remember everything." *I can't outrun death, but I can keep track of when death was close,* she thought.

"But," Kate started, "the timeline was incomplete. Did you want them to forget about what had happened at the school?"

Rafe groaned and ran her hands over her head. "I don't know."

"Are there other things missing?"

"I don't know."

"You left two copies for Eden. Why was it so important to you that she had both things? What are you trying to tell her?"

As Rafe just sat and didn't explain further, Kate made some notes and decided to redirect. She knew talking about relationships, especially about Eden, was a sure way to get Rafe to close off if not careful. She would have to hope the therapist she was recommending in L.A. could probe further as Rafe dealt with, and would hopefully overcome, other more pressing issues. "You know what to do when you start feeling panic or if you have bad dreams, right?"

"Let someone know about it, no matter how hard it is," Rafe said mechanically.

"Right," said Kate knowing Rafe hated repeating the phrase over and over again. "If you continue to hold these things inside, you'll continue to have problems," she said. "And when you feel those phantom sensations—the pain on your temple and chest, and your throat, the one making it feel like you can't swallow."

"Tell someone," Rafe groaned.

Kate opened her folder and took out another envelope then handed it to Rafe. "I'm recommending a doctor I know who agreed to take you. I think you'll be comfortable with her. Here's the information on Dr. Conrad in L.A. She's expecting you. My card is in there too," she paused, "in case you go to Baltimore."

"Thank you," said Rafe as she put the envelope in her bag. Fear started bubbling through her again. "Kate?"

"What is it?" asked Kate with concern.

"I'm scared again," Rafe admitted with difficulty. "It's like I'm walking back into a life that," she fought for her words, "I don't really—" She shook her head. "It just doesn't seem real," she finally got out.

"You've had a hard few months," said Kate calmly. "It's hard to deal with knowing a lot of things you thought were true and real were really just delusions mixed with lies."

"Figuring out what's true and what isn't—" She closed her eyes and took a deep breath. "It's difficult."

"It's why your friends are there," said Kate calmly, "to help you deal with these problems. Remember, Rafe, don't lock your bedroom door anymore. They need to get in to help you if you need it, okay?" She watched Rafe nod. "Talk to them when you're ready. They aren't going to lie to you, Rafe. They seem like they care about you and want what's best for you."

Rafe looked at her doubtfully.

"Have you forgiven Letty? She did what she had to do to help you."

"I know," said Rafe. "She did the right thing. It's what I would have done." Rafe looked at her hands knowing it was a lie. She would never send anyone to an institution to be forgotten.

"You've made a lot of progress and the medication is helping you." Kate smiled wanting to pull Rafe back toward a positive attitude. "You're lucky. Sometimes things don't work out as well as this situation. You made the right decision to stay after my emergency time limit had expired."

"Well," Rafe said sadly, "I really just didn't know where to go. But I think I made the right decision, too."

Kate smiled reassuringly then looked down at her chart and back up at Rafe. "So, how did you sleep? Nightmares again?"

Rafe shrugged. "Not a really bad one," she revealed. "Not as vivid as some I've had. It's like they're fading, but slowly.

"Very good," said Kate trying to encourage her. "Your mind is working out everything, and your fear and stress are reducing."

"I guess I just needed some medication."

"Remember, you may have some small setbacks when you get home if you get into any stressful situations. Make sure you take your medicine, without fail," she said firmly. "Just keep working the way you have been and things will be fine."

"Okay," said Rafe softly and looked up at Kate. "I'm glad Greer knew you."

"I'm glad I know Greer too." Kate smiled brightly. "She's an incredible woman."

"She is," said Rafe as she studied Kate closely. "She told me that she was seeing someone," she said calmly. "Whoever it is. . . she's very lucky."

Kate smiled again. "I think you may be right."

2

A TAXI WAS speeding through the chaotic highway traffic carrying its passenger to her final destination. Rafe Salvaggio closed her eyes and breathed deeply, hoping she had made the right decision. Her mouth was dry, and her chest felt as if it was being squeezed. She took a sip of her bottled water and thought it wasn't too late to turn around.

She opened her eyes, stared at the back of the taxi driver's neck, and said nothing. She rubbed her temples, sighed, then looked down at the beautiful silver necklace she had been given and decided to wear. *So fine and intricate*, she thought. *Just like life. Just like relationships. Just like love.*

So many little details made up all of those things. They were almost innumerable. For them to work, be successful and last, everything had to be there, every detail. If just one was missing, it was no longer a perfect piece of art. She laughed at herself. *Perfect*, she thought. *Who knew what perfect was?* She certainly didn't anymore. She just knew what she felt. She knew what felt perfect even if it was flawed, even if she was flawed.

All those intricate details were taking her where she could see the most perfection. Where she had felt loved before, where she felt she could heal, where she hoped she could start again. A jolt of fear rushed through her, and she took a deep breath. Could she do this? Would this really work? Not knowing the answer terrified her. She hated doubting herself, doubting her life, but she remained silent in the taxi.

The nerve-racking ride finally came to an end. The driver got her bags out of the trunk, and she paid him. After watching him drive away, leaving her abandoned with her decision, she picked up her duffel bag and turned toward her final destination. Pulling the small suitcase behind her, she slowly made her way up the sidewalk and to the stairs. She hesitated for a moment then put her foot on the first step.

She had to go on. No turning back now.

She made her way up the stairs, stood in front of the door, and took a deep breath. This is it. This was where she was drawn to so it had to be right. She lifted her hand and knocked three times.

Rafe stood nervously in front of the door she had just knocked on, waiting. She sighed, hoping she was not making a mistake, hoping her feelings were right. She had been so unsure of things for so long. The thought terrified her. She swallowed back the sudden rush of fear running through her. Was she knocking on the right door? Would this life she was choosing really work? Everything would be so—different, so new and unknown, yet in many ways, familiar and comfortable. She knocked again. She waited again. She was getting impatient, and this time, she pounded harder.

Nothing.

"Fuck!" Rafe shouted frustrated.

3

MAKING THEIR WAY out of the Johns Hopkins Hospital Cafeteria, Greer Noble and Beth Westbern were leaving the staff brunch they had attended. They were stopped every once in a while by someone who wanted to talk about a case or other matters. Finally, they made it to the lobby and out the door, and then to the parking lot and their cars.

"Thank god work is over," signed Greer. "If I have to listen to one more of those stories about how 'god-like' Dr. de Blois is, I'll blind myself."

"Well, at least you don't have to hear his boring voice," Beth signed back and laughed as Greer smirked at her amusing observation. "He does just happen to help a lot of people.

"Yes, and it's a good thing, but so do a lot of other doctors, and they don't demand special speaking time to tell about it every month," Greer signed. "You're right. I suppose I should be thankful I can't actually hear him."

Beth chuckled as she signed. "So what are you doing today?"

"She's coming back today," Greer signed then glanced at her watch. "I need to get home to meet her. I promised I'd talk to her about everything."

"I'm glad she's back," signed Beth. "Have fun. Don't do anything I wouldn't do!" She laughed then got into her car.

Greer opened her car door, smiling, then tapped on Beth's window. "Is there anything you wouldn't do?" she called out teasingly then got in her car before Beth could answer. She made her way home with a smile of anticipation on her face.

4

ACROSS THE COUNTRY in Los Angeles, Eden Kingsley was inside The Kiki Bistro where she had met Abby Van Falkov and their friends for lunch. Eden was trying to settle an upset and unhappy Bronte while the others were enjoying food and talking.

"What's the matter with my little B Girl today?" asked Letty in baby talk as she walked up and saw the fussy toddler.

Eden tried to calm Bronte. "She's been like this every morning, and she's been just as bad when Lydia brings her home. It seems like I can't make her happy." She sighed. "Sometimes she's fine but—" She stopped as Bronte began crying. "Shhh, baby, it's okay. Let's get you a drink. Here, let's wipe those tears." She looked at Letty as she got Bronte a drink. "She gets up and wanders around the house. I know she's looking for Rafe. It's just," she shook her head at a loss, "I don't know. It's killing me to see her want Rafe and not be able to do anything about it. I never realized just how close they were until she couldn't see her."

Letty reached out for Bronte. "Let me take over for a while. I'll take her back to Ephraim and see if he'll take her for a walk." She tried to calm Bronte. "Yes, Ephraim will take your mind off Mama, and you can stop crying," she said to the little girl. "This baby would act the same way if she couldn't see you," she said reassuringly to Eden. "She's just missing her mama, and so is everyone else." She took Bronte and went to find Ephraim.

"So, Eden," said Abby hesitantly, "have you heard when she's coming back?"

"Yeah, have you or Letty heard from Dr. Baker?" asked Jude with concern.

Eden started to tear up but controlled herself. "Letty talked to her last night."

"What?" Jude asked with worry. "Is she okay? Does she have to say longer?"

"Should we call Katheryn to change the court date? How many times can she do that?" wondered Abby under her breath. She jumped when Jude kicked her under the table and gave her a scowl.

"She—" Eden choked up but pushed through her emotions, "she said Rafe bought three plane tickets."

"Three?" screeched Abby in surprise. "What the—" She shook her head.

Eden nodded, confirming they had heard right. "Italy, Baltimore, and here."

"Italy? She can't let her go to Italy!" Abby complained in frustration.

"She didn't," Eden assured her. "Dr. Baker made Rafe give her the ticket." She looked up at Abby sadly. "So she is either coming here or—" She couldn't finish the thought.

"She'll come home," said Jude and rubbed Eden's back. "She has to. She loves you and Bronte, I know it."

"She may love us but—" Eden broke out into the kind of tears she found were much harder to stop.

"I know it's been hard waiting to hear about her," said Abby as she hugged her. "It's been hard on all of us, especially you. But remember what the therapist we talked with and Dr. Baker said. We just have to be patient with some things. We shouldn't treat her any differently unless she's showing signs of stress."

"Abby, I can't treat her anyway if she doesn't come home," said Eden as she wiped away her tears. "I need her here, Bronte needs her here. Look at her," she said as she pointed toward Letty, Bronte, and Ephraim. "It's like she knows something's wrong, and she wants Rafe." She turned her tear-stained eyes on Abby. "I want Rafe," she said and wiped her eyes again.

"Oh, Eden," said Abby with sympathy. "You two have just..." she shrugged, "screwed up so bad over the past two years."

"Thanks, Abby," Eden said wryly as she calmed herself.

"Well, you have," Abby said as she sat back in her chair. "But at least one of you knows what she wants now."

"Abby, you're just..." Jude hesitated in frustration, "so insensitive."

"I am not," said Abby then took a sip of her drink. "I'm right, aren't I, Julia?

"I'm staying out of this." Julia sat her cup down gently and thoughtfully changed the subject. "At least work is going well for you, Eden. I was meeting with a client who works at the studio, and he was telling me you just finalized everything for the production of a popular children's book."

"Yeah," said Eden as she pulled herself together glad for the change of subject. "It all fell into place well."

"He said the script you helped with was great, and apparently, the director actually turned in a decent shooting schedule."

"Even the author is happy," Eden said proudly. "Turning a children's story into a movie is so hard because kids know how the story is supposed to go, and you have to be very careful when you make changes or leave something out."

Rafe walked into the bistro with just her small duffel bag over her shoulder. She saw the group sitting together and headed toward them.

Julia was glad she could take Eden's mind off Rafe. Hearing the same worries continually repeated over the past weeks had been beleaguering. "Yeah, he was saying if you do it wrong, it'll be a disaster when it's released."

"It's why I like original screenplays for children's films," Eden admitted. "But the work on this one is amazing."

"Rumor is it'll have a lot of special effects," said Julia as she ate more of her lunch.

"With the technology we have now, we can pull off the things the author has imagined," said Eden as she nodded then took a bite of her salad.

"Wow! Great, Edy," said Abby impressed. "Hey, maybe I can write something up about it for L.A. Magazine."

Rafe frowned as she stepped closer to the table and heard Abby's offer. "I don't know if I'd let her write anything," said Rafe sarcastically. "The last person she wrote an article about ended up leaving the country."

"Who the hell," Abby said as she snapped her head around. "Rafe!" she shrieked.

Everyone jumped up from the table to greet Rafe. Abby was the first to assault her with a bone-jarring hug. The commotion alerted Letty and Ephraim who brought Bronte over with them. As everyone hugged Rafe, Eden just looked at her and was unable to react.

"Someone's been missing you real bad, Cugina," said Letty as she hugged Rafe.

"There's your mama," said Ephraim as the crying Bronte reached out to her.

"What's the matter, B Girl?" said Rafe as she put down her bag and hugged Bronte before sitting down with her at the table. Bronte clung to Rafe, rubbing her face into her, and then started to calm down. "Let's just relax," she said softly to the tiny upset girl. "It's okay. Everything is fine. *Ti voglio bene,*"[1] she said. Bronte took a shuddering breath and snuggled into Rafe, holding her tightly. "Has she had a bad day?"

"More like a bad week," said Letty fretfully. "She's been missing you, Rafe. Eden said she's been wandering around the house looking for you."

"*Oi, mi spiace,*" Rafe said to Bronte and kissed her then looked over at Eden. "I'm sorry."

"We're so glad you came home," said Eden as she held back tears of relief and happiness that Rafe chose to come home.

"Cugina," Letty said nervously, "I'm sorry I had to do it. Sign those papers," she hesitated, "I just wanted what was best, and the way you were acting," she let her words fall away.

"It's okay." Rafe smiled reassuringly. She didn't tell her one of the first things she was going to do was remove her as power of attorney. She would not go back there or any place similar. "You did the right thing. Thank you."

"Well, this calls for a party!" Abby said happily.

"Maybe we should give her time to relax in her own space," Jude interjected.

"Whatever," said Abby and waved Jude's words away. "We'll arrange the whole thing, won't we, Julia? Tonight, at Rafe and Eden's house."

"Only if Rafe has nothing to do with the planning." Julia smirked playfully. "The last time, she changed the plates three times!"

---

[1] I love you,

"She'll be too busy catching up with everyone to get in the way," said Abby spiritedly.

"Rafe, I didn't get to jump off the bridge," said Jude with disappointment.

"It was a crazy stunt, Rafe," Abby burst, remembering her anger. "You scared the shit out of us! We almost died of a heart attack!"

Rafe smiled slightly. "Well, now, thinking about it, it's probably best you didn't do it, Jude."

"Ya think!" said Abby disgruntled.

"It was really fantastic, though," Rafe said as she grinned at Jude. "If you want to do it maybe you should do it with some professionals."

"I want to!" Jude nodded excitedly. "I will!"

"You're not really?" Abby shook her head in disbelief.

"So, Rafe, how are you feeling?" asked Julia as Abby argued with Jude.

"I'm. . ." Rafe started as everyone gawked then stopped not feeling like sharing anything with them. "I'm feeling okay." She nodded. "Okay."

"You're not feeling crazy or anything?" asked Abby as she looked closely at Rafe.

Rafe smiled as she tried to be tolerant of Abby. "No."

"Abby!" said Jude annoyed. "Stop saying those things!"

"How'd you get here?" asked Abby and ignoring Jude.

"I had to take a cab from the airport," said Rafe as she rubbed Bronte's back. "I had to leave my suitcase and camera case on the back patio because I didn't have a key to get inside."

Oh, yeah, I forgot," said Jude. "You put your car in storage and used Eden's keys to get into the house. Do you want me to take you to get your car?"

"It's okay," said Rafe appreciatively. "Maybe later. I figured if I came here, I'd eventually see Letty or someone."

"You found us all," Abby exclaimed. "You know, Rafe," she said, showing the jealousy she felt, "you should have taken me. I'm loads more fun in Mexico than Jude."

"Eden, you're awfully quiet," observed Julia as Eden sat quietly gazing at Rafe.

"I, uhm," Eden cleared her throat as Rafe looked over at her. "I'm sorry I wasn't home."

"It's okay," said Rafe as she stroked Bronte's back and held Eden's gaze in silence.

"So," said Abby breaking the silence, "party tonight, right? Julia, you make a list of the food and things, and let's do this."

"I'll bring the deserts and some wine for all of you," Letty offered happily.

"Great! So, it's all set," said Abby looking to Eden then Rafe. "Is it okay, guys?"

"Sure," said Eden as she tore her eyes from Rafe. "Sure Abby.

"It's fine," said Rafe with a shrug. "I'd like to get home. It looks like B Girl needs to have a little quiet time." She stood up with Bronte and grabbed her bag. "I think I'll just walk back with her." She turned toward Eden. "I'll need a key."

"Oh, no problem," said Eden awkwardly when she realized Rafe was talking to her. She stood up and pulled her keys out of her pocket then began removing the house key. She got the key loose then turned to Jude. "Jude," she said shyly, "will you drive my car home?"

"Sure." Jude happily took Eden's car keys. "Sure, no problem."

"See you all later," said Rafe as she turned and headed out of the bistro with Eden close behind her.

"So," said Abby dragging out the word as she watched them leave. "I'm betting some mind-blowing makeup sex is going to be happening very soon." She looked knowingly around the table. "I mean, did you see the way Eden was looking at Rafe? I think she wanted to jump her bones right here on the table!" She laughed at her own words.

Jude shook her head in annoyance. "Abby, sometimes I think you should be the one seeing the shrink!"

5

THE WALK HOME was quiet and uneventful, which was fine by both Rafe Salvaggio and Eden Kingsley. Eden offered to carry Bronte for a while or put her in the stroller they had retrieved from Eden's car, but Bronte wouldn't let go of Rafe. Bronte got upset when they tried to trade her off, so Rafe carried her all the way home. She needed the contact and comfort from Rafe that she had been missing. Eden convinced Rafe to let her at least carry her duffel bag. By the time they got home, Bronte had drifted off to sleep, and sweat covered both she and Rafe. Eden unlocked the front door and followed Rafe closely as she carried Bronte to her bedroom.

Rafe chuckled as she laid Bronte down. "I guess this is what happens when you use those attachment parenting techniques."

"Yeah," said Eden quietly and smiled as she watched Rafe tuck Bronte into bed. "She's very attached." Rafe looked up at her and gave her a small smile. "I am too," said Eden nervously.

"I—" Rafe looked away from her and took a deep breath. "I'm kind of thirsty." She walked out of the room and into the kitchen.

Eden closed Bronte's bedroom door quietly then followed Rafe to the kitchen where she found her looking in the refrigerator. "Rafe," Eden said cautiously, "will you sit down and talk with me for a while?" She saw Rafe hesitate getting her drink. "It's," she stumbled, "I mean there's no pressure. I just. . . I need to talk to you about. . . things."

"Oh," said Rafe feeling a bit nervous. She knew she would have to talk to Eden, but she had expected to have more time to get herself ready. *Maybe it's better to get it over with quickly*, she thought. "Okay. I'll bring you a drink." She quickly poured two drinks before following Eden into the living room.

Eden motioned to the couch. "Sit down," she said and smiled anxiously. She took one of the drinks as Rafe sat down then she sat next to her. "I'm glad you came home."

"What. . ." Rafe started then took a sip of her drink. "What is it you need to talk to me about?"

"I need to talk to you about where I'm going to live," said Eden as she watched Rafe avoid looking at her.

Wh—" Rafe tried to speak and hide her panic. "What do you mean?"

"Well, right before you left," Eden said warily, "you wrote a letter dissolving our cohabitation agreement and gave a copy of it to Katheryn." She waited to see if Rafe would respond, and when she did not, she continued. "I haven't really had a chance to look for anywhere to go." She looked at Rafe desperately. "Rafe," she said anxiously, "I don't want to go, Bronte doesn't want to go. Will you let us stay?"

"I think you should. . ." Rafe whispered shakily then swallowed. She remembered the talks with Kate and her assurances Eden was not going to be hurt if she was close. "Stay, please," she answered.

"Thank you, Rafe." Eden sighed with relief. "I'm so sorry about everything."

"I know I said some things," said Rafe uneasily.

"I know," Eden nodded, "some true things." She was prepared for Rafe to make a lot of new rules for her.

"No, no." Rafe frowned as she watched Eden's body tense. "I mean, I said some hurtful things to you. I'm sorry. I—" She shook her head hoping Eden could understand she had been in a very bad place in her mind.

"It's okay," said Eden as she put her hand on Rafe's leg. "I know."

"Things just seem so..." she paused looking at Eden's hand on her leg, "unreal right now. Being here with you," she said softly, "knowing some of the things I was thinking were..." she hesitated, "flawed. I just—" She stopped and moved her leg away from Eden's touch. "I'm home, but I just need some time to take it all in now."

Eden pulled her hand back and ran it through her hair nervously. "I'm sorry. I know you need time. I didn't mean—" she stopped short and swallowed her anxiety. "The adoption court date is Tuesday. Katheryn says everything looks good. There's nothing in the way anymore." She looked into Rafe's eyes. "Do you still want it? Will you take back the letter you wrote to her?"

Rafe leaned forward into her hands and tried to hide the tears attempting to form. She thought this wasn't going to happen. She had been convinced Eden was going to take Bronte, and she would never see her again. Now it just seemed so unreal Eden was actually going to stay and go through with the adoption. She looked up at Eden and saw her waiting for an answer. "I do want it," she answered softly. "I want to be Bronte's parent so much."

Eden reached out to touch Rafe but stopped. "I'm glad you want it. Bronte is your daughter. Just look at what we went through when you weren't here." She forced a laugh of relief. "She loves you and needs you."

"I know." Rafe nodded with a small smile. "I'm sorry."

"I need to talk to you about a lot of other things too," said Eden cautiously, "but let's not do it now. Why don't you just relax? The gang will be here later, and I'm sure they'll be a handful."

6

IN HER BALTIMORE studio, Greer Noble was working on a painting when the light flashed indicating someone was ringing the doorbell. She put down her brush, covered her work and paints, and then went to answer the door.

Once downstairs, she opened the door and smiled at the person standing in front of her. "Kate!" she said happily.

Greer had only been seeing Kate for a short time when Rafe called asking Greer to come to Los Angeles. Kate wasn't happy about her leaving, but she understood Greer needed to have some kind of closure with Rafe. When Kate dropped everything and flew to Mexico to help with Rafe's medical issues, Greer saw Kate in a renewed light. She realized she was a woman who was ready to offer everything and give her the relationship Rafe just couldn't ever give to anyone other than Eden. Now Kate was back, and Greer was ready to begin a new chapter with her.

"Did she show up here?" Kate signed uneasily.

Greer shook her head. "No. I told you Rafe's bond with Eden was too strong for her to resist."

"Are you," Kate hesitated her signing, "disappointed?"

Greer smiled and took Kate by the hands, pulling her inside. "No, I'm just so happy you decided to show up at my door. I was worried I had pushed you away."

Kate smiled back and signed to Greer. "You may be a force like Rafe says, but you're not a strong enough one to keep me away."

Greer raised her eyebrows and signed. "She said I was a force?" Kate nodded. "Well then," Greer signed and grinned. "Let's see if you can resist this force." She leaned in and kissed Kate passionately.

She did not resist.

7

LATER IN THE evening, the party at Rafe Salvaggio and Eden Kingsley's house was in full swing. Everyone enjoyed the food Julia and Abby had prepared, and the deserts and wine Letty brought. Flynn was helping Letty and Ephraim clear things up, and Julia, Eden, and Rafe were relaxing in their loungers. Abby and Jude were playing with Bronte in the pool when Bronte decided she wanted out, and Jude helped her up onto the edge of the pool.

"Watch out," called Jude as Bronte took off away from her. "Wet girl coming!"

"God, Jude!" Abby laughed hysterically. "When will you watch what you say," she asked as she rolled her eyes. "And you tell me I'm bad!"

"I didn't even think," said Jude, chagrined as everyone laughed. "I'm sorry."

"It's okay, Jude," Eden consoled her. "We know what you meant." She got the towel off the back of her seat to wrap up Bronte. Bronte climbed into Rafe's lap before Eden could catch her.

"Oh, now I'm all wet too," she said as she pulled Bronte up and everyone laughed. "Just give me the towel."

"There ya go, babe." Eden handed Rafe the towel.

"Thanks." Rafe wrapped up Bronte and hugged her.

Abby climbed on top of a reclining float. "So, have you turned on your phone yet?"

Rafe quirked her lips and shook her head at Abby. "It's charging inside."

Jude pulled herself out of the pool and sat on the ground next to Rafe. "Hey," she said hopefully, "can I ask you a question?"

"Does it have anything to do with being wet?" Rafe asked and smiled at Jude.

Jude laughed. "No!"

"Oh, my god! Jude," Abby interjected. "You're not still thinking crazy are you?"

"What?" Rafe asked with a frown.

Jude gave Abby a hostile look then turned to Rafe and hesitated. "I... I just wanted to ask you about something we talked about when we were in Mexico."

"What?" Rafe asked as she leaned back on the lounger with Bronte.

"Well, when we were going to stay in Mexico, you said I could be an artist," Jude reminded her. "I just wanted to know," she paused, "do you really think I can?"

"Or was it just your crazy talk," Abby interrupted. "Jude, you can't be an artist. You'll starve!"

"Was it?" Jude asked Rafe. "Was it just... talk?"

"No," said Rafe, "I was very lucid. I think you're a natural artist. I think with time and some training, you could do something great."

"See, Abby," said Jude smiling smugly.

"I told you, Jude. Rafe knows about this stuff," Eden added. "You should take some classes and see what happens."

"Classes?" asked Jude surprised.

"You know," Rafe said thoughtfully, "Annie is finishing with her graduate project. Maybe we can use the studio for something different now."

"Like what?" Jude's eyes were bright with interest.

"Well, I'm going to have to find a new teacher for Bronte," Rafe said as she tickled the little girl gently making her giggle. "I don't know if the new teacher will want a big group like Annie had. Maybe I can split the studio. We can use part for Bronte's lessons and part for you to use for your art projects—

if you take some classes. I'll keep the studio supplied as long as you continue to make progress and want the opportunity."

"So you'd still be my patron?" asked Jude to clarify.

"Well, Mexico is a lot less expensive than L.A.," Rafe explained, "so you'd need to keep your job. But I will be your patron as far as supplies and things for the studio. You need to talk to me about what you want and what you're doing."

"I'd like to try it," Jude said unable to hide her excitement, "I really would. The more I think about it, the more I think I can do it."

"You can do it," Rafe encouraged her. "But it does take dedication and a lot of time. You can't expect to be great overnight. Though it has happened," she admitted with a smile.

"Let's do it," said Jude eagerly. "I can't wait to get started."

"Just go online and get a class schedule," suggested Rafe. "Let me know what you want to start with, and I'll help you enroll. Maybe we can get you some federal grant money too. We can talk to the financial aid department."

"This is so great!" said Jude as she stood up then ran and jumped in the pool with a shout of happiness.

Eden laughed. "She's excited!"

"Do you really think she'll be good?" Julia asked curiously.

"Yes," said Rafe, "if she sticks with it." She turned to Julia. "What about you?"

"What about me," Julia asked confused.

"Yes, are you going to continue to subject yourself to financial boredom?" Rafe teased. "Or are you going to do something about it? Your father told me you talked with him about continuing to work for him when he was here."

"Boredom is right," Julia scoffed, hiding her annoyance that father and Rafe had been discussing her "I've been working on it, Rafe. Since Eden took me to her studio, I've really enjoyed dealing with the film industry people. I have some ideas I am looking into, a couple of them Daddy's actually considering. "

"Well, then they must be good ideas," Rafe encouraged her. "I'm glad you're trying to put yourself in the position to do something on your own and that you love. Just don't let Abby write about it in L.A. Magazine or do a blog about it," Rafe said mischievously. "I'd like you to stay in town."

Abby sat up and fell off her pool float. "I heard your crack, Salvaggio!" she sputtered as she splashed around.

"Let me know if I can help, Julia. You never know," Eden said as she stood. "I'm going in the water." She slipped off her wrap then picked up Bronte from Rafe's lap. "Are you ready for another dip? Let's go," she said to the little girl then turned and walked to the pool.

Julia saw Rafe go pale. "Are you okay?" she asked with concern.

Rafe watched Eden walk away now wearing only her bikini. Her eyes focused on the fading bruises covering Eden's body. "I. . ." she said shakily. "Excuse me. I need to—" She stood quickly then went into the house.

"Rafe?" called Julia worried. She looked from Rafe to where she had been looking. "Oh, shit." She groaned when she saw Eden. She moved to the edge of the pool where everyone was laughing and splashing. "Eden, Eden," she called insistently.

"What?" Eden asked while laughing. She looked up and saw Julia's serious expression then looked for Rafe and saw she had gone. "What happened? Where is she?" she asked panicked. She climbed out of the pool with Bronte clinging to her.

"I'm not sure. She was fine when she was looking at you and Bronte," said Julia troubled, "then suddenly she turned very pale and said she had to go inside."

"Shit, Eden!" Abby hissed. "Your bruises!"

"Crap!" said Eden mad at herself. "I just forgot! Everything was going so well." She closed her eyes upset.

"Great, Eden!" Abby admonished her. "You just forgot! You have them all over you!"

"Stop it, Abby!" said Jude defensively.

"How the hell are we supposed to act normal when this kind of shit happens?" asked Abby. Upset, she got out of the pool and gathered her things to leave.

"Abby, don't go," Eden pleaded. "I'll go talk to her," she said hoping to fix everything.

"No, I'll go," said Julia as she held Eden back. "Put your wrap back on. At least now we know this is still an issue and can watch ourselves."

"You mean I can watch myself," said Eden as she teared up. She sat Bronte on the lounger and picked up her wrap. "It's all my fault," she said as she put on the wrap and watched Julia walk into the house.

Julia found Rafe in the kitchen talking to Letty and joined them. "Rafe, are you sure you're okay?" Julia asked with concern.

"I'm fine," she said calmly and smiling. "Here." She handed her a small bowl. "Try some of this gelato Letty brought for me." She walked into the living room and sat in one of the chairs with her bowl of gelato.

Julia followed her into the living room and sat on the couch near Rafe's chair. "This is good," said Julia as she swallowed a bite. She waited to see if Rafe would say anything about what had happened by the pool, but she just ate her dessert in silence. "So," Julia said wearily, "did you let Greer know you were back?"

Rafe looked up from her desert and pain shot across her face. "No, I'm sure she knows I'm back, though."

"Really?" Julia asked confused. "How would she know?"

Rafe looked at her intently then looked back down at her dessert. "She's with someone now," Rafe revealed. "Since I couldn't give her all of me, I just thought she would be happier if I didn't go see her."

"Someone in Baltimore, you mean?" asked Julia surprised.

"Kate," said Rafe softly.

"Kate? Kate who?" Julia asked curiously.

"Kate. Dr. Baker, my doctor in Mexico. I think they'll be happy together." She set her desert bowl down on the coffee table.

"So, your doctor and Greer got together down there while you were in the hospital?" Julia asked appalled.

"No," said Rafe. "They were together before I called her and asked her to come here."

"How do you know they're together?" Julia wondered if Rafe really didn't want to be here with Eden.

"I figured it out," said Rafe with a shrug. "I talked about Greer a lot, and Kate," she hesitated, "she changed when I did. Then she let it slip she was from Baltimore, and I confirmed it when I saw her card. So," she shrugged again, "I knew."

"So, you're okay with it?" asked Julia hesitantly. "You do want to be here, don't you?"

Rafe looked up at Julia, her face shadowed with sadness and her liquid gray-blue eyes shining with torment. "Yes," she said softly, "this is where I think I need to be, where I belong. For now anyway."

8

MIDNIGHT WAS FILLED with nightmares haunting and tormenting Rafe Salvaggio, making her toss and turn in her sleep. Her face and body covered with a thin layer of sweat, she mumbled incoherently in her slumber. She made a sudden lunge in her sleep and landed hard on the floor, coming awake from the impact.

"*Merda!*"[2] She groaned as she shook with fear. "Shit!" She held her head and chest and rocked on the floor, taking deep breaths until her body stopped shaking. She had lost count of how many nights she had woken this way before she lost control. She did her best to hide what was happening and to stay in control, but it all became too much. Now everyone knew, and she had to tell someone when she had a nightmare. She hated the thought of them knowing she was not in control of her own mind.

When she could, she got up shakily and walked quietly to Eden's room. Rafe slowly opened the door. She did not see Eden at first and started to panic. Then she realized a pillow was hiding Eden, and only her arm was visible, draped over the pillow. She called her name softly, but Eden didn't stir. Rafe started to call louder but changed her mind. She closed the door and walked back to her room. Inside, she sat on the floor in front of the bed and held her head and chest, covering the places where the phantom pain was pressing against her.

"This is not real," she whispered and closed her eyes against the pressure she was feeling. "It was only a dream. This is not real." She recited the mantra repeatedly, fighting the panic wanting to storm inside her.

Eden had heard her door close and got up knowing it must have been Rafe. She walked quickly to Rafe's room and tried the knob. Relief surged through her at finding the door unlocked. She opened the door and saw Rafe on the floor.

"Rafe?"

---

[2] Shit!

Rafe looked up in distress, "Eden, I..." she whispered shakily.

Eden rushed over and knelt next to Rafe. "It's okay," she said, worried. "You should have got me up, babe. Are you feeling it?" she asked as she stroked Rafe's hair. Rafe nodded, and Eden placed her hand on Rafe's heart where the gun had been placed. "It's okay," she said trying to stem off her own anxiety, and at the same time, remember what the therapist had told them to do to help.

Seeing Rafe so terrified unnerved Eden and brought the reality of her pain to light. "Right now, it's just my hand, okay? It's my hand," she said and kissed Rafe's warm temple. "All you feel is my kiss right there, okay? It's just my kiss," she whispered. "I love you. It's okay."

"Okay," said Rafe her body shaking. "Okay."

"Everything's going to be fine, babe," Eden reassured her. "Nothing's going to happen. You're at home, and you're okay, and I'm okay. We're all together again. I love you," she repeated. "You're going to be fine."

"I was ready to die, Ede," Rafe whispered. She looked at Eden intensely wondering if she knew how close the bullet had come to her and the fact she had only been an inch away from dying.

"I know," Eden said softly, remembering what Greer had told her about the day Rafe had been held at gunpoint. "I know, babe," she said, and tears started to fall. "I'm so glad you didn't. I love you. I don't want you to leave me," she said and kissed her temple again.

"It was so close," said Rafe as she looked far away remembering the dark voice in her nightmare. She could almost hear it while awake sometimes. "Death."

"No, Rafe, don't think about—" Eden could not bring herself to say *death*. "Look at me," she said and pulled Rafe's face up so she would look at her. "It's all over now. Okay? It's over," she said through her tears.

"What if it's not, Ede?" Rafe asked frantically her eyes burning with fear. "I still feel it. The shadow of death," she said and clutched Eden's shoulder tightly.

"No, no," said Eden wiping her tears away quickly. "It's just my hand see," she said as she put her hand on Rafe's chest again, "and my kiss," she said and kissed her temple. "Come on," she said and pulled her up off the floor. "Let's sit somewhere else, okay? Let's get away from all of this."

She led Rafe to the living room and sat on the couch with her.

"Okay, now," she said softly, "this is better. Come here and let me hold you, okay? Just put your arms around me. It'll be okay," she said and started to pull Rafe to her.

"I—" Rafe choked out in fear, "Ede," Rafe resisted Eden's pull, "I can't!"

"What, babe?" Eden said in confusion.

"I can't," Rafe swallowed, "touch you!"

"Sure," Eden sobbed, "sure you can. It's okay," she said in misery.

"No," Rafe said panicked, "your bruises. I can't!" She looked at Eden with agony in her eyes. "Ede," she said and pulled further away, "I'll hurt you again. I can't take it." She shook and slid down off the couch and onto the floor. "I can't."

"Oh, Rafe," said Eden overcome with guilt about what happened by the pool. "I'm so sorry. Babe, it doesn't hurt if they're touched anymore. They are still healing, but I'll be fine. You won't hurt me," she said as Rafe shook her head no. "Okay," she said and got down on the floor with her. "I'll just hold you instead, okay?" She put her arms around Rafe and pulled her close. "Rafe, I love you. Everything is fine," she whispered and kissed her temple again.

"Ede," Rafe said shakily. "Ede, I'm slipping. I've been slipping, and I'm terrified," she whispered.

"Why," said Eden her heart beating hard, "Why are you afraid, babe?"

"I'm terrified because. . ." Rafe swallowed, fighting the fear inside her. "What if I fall in love again, and you start to have feelings," she looked at Eden in misery, "and they aren't for me?" *What if I touch you and the darkness covers you like in my dreams*, she thought.

"Rafe," said Eden and caught her breath then fought her tears of guilt. "I only love you. I won't have feelings for anyone else," she promised, "I won't."

"Ede," Rafe said looking far away again, "I'm terrified of losing control again," she whispered as blood-filled dreams played out before her in her mind. She didn't understand why they were so vivid. Confusing images of Eden's bruised body and memories from her childhood flashed in her mind. "Ede," said Rafe softly, "slipping hurts." She held her hand to her head again. "If I do," she let out a shaky breath, "I know I'll never make it out of the darkness again," she whispered fearfully.

"It's okay, babe," said Eden as she stroked Rafe's hair and back, and then moved her hand and kissed her temple again. "If you slip, I'll be here to help you. I love you."

Rafe squeezed her eyes shut at the pain in her head. "Everything hurts. It's hard to think. I don't know if I can do this. I'm not sure of anything anymore."

"I'm sure. We can both be sure. Rafe, we've both hurt so much while we were apart. I know I don't ever want to hurt like that again," she said and held her closer. "I never want you to hurt again, either. I love you," she whispered with all her intent into Rafe's ear. "Dr. Cathcart and Flynn kept asking me to tell you everything, but I couldn't do it. I was afraid you wouldn't love me again and of so many other things. But now, I don't think you ever really stopped loving me. Everyone kept telling me you loved me, and I just couldn't hear them. I'm so sorry for doubting you and for doubting myself and how I felt about you. I don't have any doubts now. I'm so sorry for everything. I love you. We can do this," she said as she held and kissed Rafe and calmed her, hoping she heard and believed everything she said.

"Ede," Rafe said shakily, "I'm just so beat up inside."

"It's okay," she said and kissed her head again. "I think we're both pretty bruised and battered. But we're healing, babe. Come on, lean back. Let's see if we can sleep."

After a while, giving in to emotional exhaustion, they fell asleep together on the floor in front of the couch.

9

MONDAY MORNING WAS clear and bright. Rafe Salvaggio had just finished her first session with Dr. Conrad and was in a great mood. Kate had been right about the new doctor, and Rafe was relieved. They were able to go over everything Rafe did in Mexico and make a new treatment plan. Because Rafe had reported such a hard time over the weekend with nightmares, Dr. Conrad gave Rafe a different prescription.

After the session, Eden drove them to the drugstore to drop off the script, and then they headed to Katheryn's office to talk about the adoption.

"It looks like you're still in a good mood," said Eden as she drove. "Did you have a good session?"

"Well, she asked me if there was anything, in particular, giving me problems, and I told her no," Rafe said casually.

"You told her about your nightmares?" asked Eden warily. She was happy Rafe felt good during the day but worried about her at night.

"Yes, she meant besides those," Rafe said with a shrug. "It's why she prescribed a different medication and says if the dreams start getting more intense, she can give me something even stronger. But, back to what I was saying."

"You were saying nothing else was bothering you," said Eden relieved Rafe was doing so well today.

"Right," acknowledged Rafe. "Well," she paused, "there is one little thing."

"Rafe!" said Eden getting upset as she looked over at her. "You have to tell her, or me, or someone," she admonished. "She said you have to talk about everything."

Rafe laughed and shook her head at Eden's interpretation of what the doctor said about talking to people. The doctor certainly never said she had to talk about everything. She only had to talk if and when she was ready. "I'm talking to you," she said pragmatically. "Do you want to know what's bothering me?"

"Yes," Eden said concerned. "Please, tell me what's bothering you."

"Abby," Rafe said flatly.

"Abby?" Eden repeated. She looked over at Rafe confused and then back at the road.

"Yes," said Rafe as she grinned. "I owe her one."

"What are you talking about?" Eden asked wondering what she could owe Abby.

"You don't remember?" Rafe asked in disbelief. "She accused you of forcing me to use a strap-on."

"Oh, my god!" said Eden and laughed even though she was angry Rafe had worried her. "Please don't go there!"

"Oh, I think I have to," said Rafe firmly. "She's been a pain in my ass calling me crazy and things. I owe her," she said mischievously."

"Rafe, she doesn't mean anything," said Eden in Abby's defense. "She's just worried and overcompensating. What are you going to do?"

"Well, I can't tell you unless you're in," said Rafe with a smile and crossed her arms.

"Unless I'm in? You're not supposed to be keeping secrets," Eden warned her as she maneuvered the car through traffic.

"Too bad." Rafe scoffed at the fact Eden was telling her not to keep secrets after all she kept. "If you're in," Rafe shrugged, "I'll tell you. If not," she grinned, "well, if not, just be warned. You may be getting another visit from Abby."

Eden saw Rafe's smile and was glad to see her so happy and playful. "Well, if I'm getting into trouble anyway," she said with an exaggerated sigh, "I'm in."

Rafe smiled wickedly. "Good, very good."

10

RAFE SALVAGGIO CARRIED Bronte inside Katheryn Hardam's Law Offices and walked straight into Katheryn's office without stopping. Eden gave a small apologetic smile to the secretary as she followed them. Rafe sat in one of the big leather chairs and put Bronte on the floor with her toy to play. Eden sat in the chair beside her and looked up at Katheryn.

Katheryn walked around her desk and stood in front of them. "I'm glad to see you back, Rafe," said Katheryn as she shook her hand and Rafe nodded. "I didn't file your letter with the court. Like I said before to Eden, you were uninformed when you wrote it. Now, I'm presuming you would like me to disregard it," she stated calmly.

Rafe nodded. "Yes, and the letter dissolving the cohabitation agreement with Eden."

Katheryn looked both women over. "You're sure?"

Rafe searched Eden's face as she considered her answer. "Yes, I'm sure," she finally replied.

"Okay." Katheryn took an envelope from her desk and handed it to Rafe. "The letter and the check you gave Eden are in the envelope. It never happened."

"Thank you," said Rafe looking at the envelope in her hands. She opened it and took out the check, looking at it for a moment. She handed it to Eden. "You can use this to cover your expenses for Mexico and buying Abby and Jude's tickets and the hotel costs."

Eden looked at the check then up into Rafe's eyes. "You don't need to pay me back." She pushed Rafe's hand away gently. "It's too much anyway."

"Okay." Rafe nodded. "Then just take whatever you spent off the rent and send the receipts to Katheryn."

Eden wasn't sure if she should feel hurt or not. "I didn't ask you to pay me back." She would have paid ten times as much to get her back, a thousand times.

"You don't have to ask. You spent the money because of me, and I want to make sure you're paid back. I want to pay my debts."

"Your debts?" Eden watched Rafe nod and was not sure why she was doing this now. "I don't consider anything I spend on you a debt."

Rafe could see Eden was starting to get upset. She frowned because it was not her intent. "Listen, I know you spent a lot to get everyone there, and I just want to pay you back. You and Greer. I don't understand why you're getting so upset."

"I'm upset because you made it sound like you just didn't want to be indebted to me like I was some kind of creditor and not the person who loves you."

Rafe looked at Katheryn who didn't look like she was interested in helping at all. She looked back at Eden. "I'm sorry if I sounded impersonal. I was just doing what I thought was the right thing."

"Fine," said Eden with a frustrated sigh.

"Fine?"

"Yes, fine. I'll send Katheryn the receipts for Abby and Jude's part." She did not want to lose the balance in responsibilities she felt she and Rafe had. She made the decision to go to Mexico, and if she let Rafe pay for her part, then she was just letting Rafe take care of everything again.

She didn't want to go back into the kind of relationship with her they had before.

Rafe sat back in her chair with a frown, not understanding why Eden was making such a big deal out of repaying travel expenses. "Fine, if it's what you want. It's fine," she repeated.

Katheryn saw their little issue was settled and made her way back behind her desk to sit down. She opened a file on her desk and looked up at them. "Family Court is at ten in the morning, Courtroom B on the second floor," she informed them. "Don't be late. Everything's in order so there shouldn't be any problems."

"Great," said Eden in relief. "Thank you, Katheryn. Thank you for everything."

"No problem." Katheryn smiled as she closed her file. "I'll see you two in the morning."

11

TUESDAY MORNING, THE courtroom on the second floor was filled with petitioners and lawyers. Rafe Salvaggio and Eden Kingsley were surrounded by friends showing support on this important and long-awaited day in family court. The adoption petition for Bronte L. Kingsley-Salvaggio was on the docket. The judge had deposed several cases and finally reached their petition. The clerk read off the case name and number.

"Will all parties for the case please come forward?" asked the judge as the clerk handed him the file. Katheryn, Rafe, and Eden holding Bronte approached as the judge looked over the paperwork. "Everything seems to be in order," he said and looked up. "Ms. Kingsley?"

"Yes," said Eden as she stepped forward with Bronte.

"You understand the ramifications of what you are doing here and the impact this will have on your daughter's life and your own?" he asked formally.

"Yes, I do," she said and kissed Bronte's head.

"And this second issue," he said looking at the file. "You're resolved about its disposition and understand its impact on the situation?"

"Yes," said Eden and stood up straighter in determination.

"Okay," said the judge and wrote something in the file. The judge turned to Rafe, "Ms. Salvaggio?" Rafe acknowledged him with a nod. "You understand the obligations involved and the ramifications of what you are doing here, and the impact this will have on Bronte's life and our own?"

"Yes, I understand," said Rafe reservedly.

"Very good," said the judge and signed the petition. "Let it be known Jayne Eden Kingsley and Rafaella E. Salvaggio are hereby equally and in all ways the parents of Bronte Lijia Salvaggio." He struck his gavel and handed the file to the clerk.

Rafe looked up in surprise then at Eden. "What? Bronte Lijia Salvaggio?" she repeated in confusion.

"Yeah." Eden smiled shyly as she held Bronte close, "I hope you don't mind."

"Eden," said Rafe dumbfounded. "I. . ." she stumbled, "no, no," she shook her head, "not at all."

"Come on," said Eden as she took her arm and started dragging Rafe out.

"Why didn't you tell me?" she asked confused as she let Eden pull her along. "When did you decide to do this? I thought you wanted to hyphenate."

"Well, you weren't available," said Eden happily. "I talked to Letty, and she liked the idea," she shrugged, "so I just had Katheryn make sure it was all done at once. I think being a Salvaggio girl makes you special." She smiled shyly. "I know they're special to me."

Rafe just watched as Eden joined their celebrating group of friends with Bronte, still in a bit of shock.

12

LORENA MARIE DEPAZ had not used the name Trouble for weeks, and it felt good. She had used her real name to book a few hotels the day before and told everyone else to call her Maria Lorpaz. She knew she would be changing her name soon anyway, and she liked the idea of keeping a name resembling her real name subtly. She thought she looked more like a Maria than a Marie anyway.

Today was the date on the instruction document Mason had given her. She knew by now he was out of the country and working at his new job. It was time to try to make a new life for herself. Using the computer and portable printer she bought on the Conservatory campus, she had read all of the documents on the USB drives. They were straightforward and, most surprisingly, open-ended. She thought Mason would be more of a control freak. She opened the document on the computer and read it again.

Here are your instructions.

After the date on this doc name, I'll be gone, and other important parts of the plan should have been taken care of by this time. You should execute this part of the plan as soon as possible.

Hopefully, you still have all the USB drives in a safe place. If you haven't figured it out yet, here is my plan.

The Red USB is for a certain lawyer. Her name and address are below. It's important you give this one to her first. Stash the others before you go see her so she can't talk you into letting her see them. Lawyers are tricky, and she's a very good one.

Use this USB drive to negotiate getting protection and a new life in exchange for one of the other drives. You should look at it and add anything you want. DO NOT let the lawyer know where you're staying. This is where having several hotels booked and making sure the USB drives are somewhere you can get to them at any time will be useful. This may be tricky because once the FBI is involved, they could follow you. I trust you'll figure out how to deal if anything comes up.

Now for the final play—the other USB drives. I'm leaving it all up to you. You get to choose.

Black USB Drive: If given everything you want, then you can give them the Black USB drive. If you do this, they'll have hit the jackpot.

All the information they could ever hope to have on the Stewards and everyone in the group is there. Also, everything I found on Tony and his associates and their crimes is included.

Blue USB Drive: Use if treated badly and they offer nothing of value. Or if they give you something, but not what you really want, or if you think they're going to fuck you over. It gives them a starting point, but they have to do their own work. I'm sure they'll want to work with you because, if you do the Exodus Plan, they'll look like idiots.

If they don't want to give you the deal you want, then keep the Black USB and follow the Exodus Plan in the instructions.

Exodus Plan: Create an email account at the site below and copy the document in the folder titled 'Exodus Plan' into an email. Send it to the news reporters' email addresses listed below. The document asks for money to be sent to an account I set up in the Cayman Islands. You'll need to email in the signature card saved to this drive so you can have access to the account. When funds are verified, first buy a ticket wherever you want to go, then give whoever sent the money the instructions on finding the Black USB drive. Leave it somewhere or have it delivered to them so they can get it once you're on the plane. Do not meet anyone in person.

With the Exodus Plan, you don't get a new name from the government, but leaving the country rich is almost as good. I suggest going somewhere warm, California girl.

Trouble scanned the information at the bottom of the page. She had already made an appointment with the lawyer for today. She closed the instructions, picked up the Red USB drive, and slipped it into her pocket. The others were well hidden, and she was ready to go.

She looked over at the twin bed and Carson. He turned out to be more help than she had intended. Instead of staying in hotels, she had been staying in his dorm room. There was no way Tony would be looking for her on a college campus. She still had a lot of cash left and hadn't used the credit card until yesterday when she booked the hotels. She didn't think, after talking to the lawyer, it would be a great idea to return to the dorm.

Trouble quietly packed her computer and all her other things in her backpack. There was not much, though she had bought a few more things to wear. The most expensive thing she bought was the business pantsuit she was wearing along with the blouse, shoes and other bits she needed to look professional. She wanted the lawyer to take her seriously and not treat her like a kid off the street.

When everything was together, she walked out the door without looking back. There was no way she could know if she would ever see Carson again. She warned him someday she would just be gone. He thought she was joking, even though she assured him many times she was not. She walked out of the dorm and made it across campus to the bus stop. The bus was right on time and would take her close to the lawyer's office for her appointment.

Living on the campus had been a lot of fun. She liked the school and, with Carson's help, got to be a guest and visit some classes. She even showed some of her artwork to one of the professors who seemed to like what she saw. The biggest disappointment was not getting to meet the one person she had hoped to meet. Dean Salvaggio was out on administrative leave and had not been back to campus. Trouble did get to see her from a distance at a big party put on by the Conservatory she attended with Carson. She was able to watch her speak and then watch as everyone congratulated her and shook her hand.

She had been tempted to join the line but decided, because of the information she had and the plan, it would be better not to approach her. At one time during the evening, she was watching her, and it seemed like Dean Salvaggio looked straight into her eyes. It spooked her, so she took off and hoped she was lost in the group of students. She knew it was dumb to be spooked because the dean had no idea who she was, but the way she stared at her made it seem like she recognized her.

The way the students talked about Dean Salvaggio only made her jealousy grow. She wanted someone in her life to help her like the dean had helped Mason and all those students. The problem was she did not know if she was worthy of her help, so she would just have to help herself. The more she thought about everything, she realized, in a small way, maybe Dean Salvaggio had helped her. The dean had helped Mason, and now Mason had opened this opportunity. *I'll take it,* she thought. She smiled because for the first time in a long time she had hope. Then she let go of her jealousy.

13

KATHERYN HARDAM HAD just pulled out a fresh legal pad when the receptionist opened her office door and led in a potential new client. She stood up and walked around her desk holding her hand out to the young woman.

"Ms. DePaz," she said politely, "please, have a seat. Can we get you anything? Coffee or water?"

"I'm fine," said Trouble softly. Trouble was more nervous than she thought she would be for the appointment. She sat down in one of the luxurious leather chairs.

Leaning against the front of her desk, Katheryn sized up the young woman. She had straight, long, jet black hair and was nicely dressed in a new pantsuit. She was thin but seemed healthy. She was definitely nervous, but most clients were the first time they visited a lawyer.

"I understand you need representation for legal matters with the government. My consultation is free, and I have a new client package outlining the firm's fee schedule." Katheryn handed Ms. DePaz the packet then went around and sat behind her desk. "How did you hear about my law office? Was I recommended by someone?"

"You could say so," said Trouble with a solemn nod. "You're handling a relevant case."

"I see." Katheryn was intrigued. "Why don't you start by giving me a basic overview of the situation," she said and picked up her pen to take notes.

Trouble liked how down to business this lawyer was being. She thought Mason was right. She was very good. "Actually," Trouble started, "I have everything already together on this USB drive." She pulled the red drive from her pocket then leaned forward and put it on the edge of the desk. "If you could just take a moment to look at it, I think you'll understand the situation perfectly."

Katheryn pursed her lips and frowned. This was a very unusual tactic for a client who wanted help. "Very well," she said and picked up the USB drive.

She pulled a laptop from her bottom drawer. Once it was on and ready, she plugged the USB drive into a port. The laptop was not attached to either the office Ethernet or the Internet. She was always wary of viruses from things people brought into the office, so her security people recommended having a secure way of looking at possibly high-risk media brought into the office. When the drive was recognized, a small list of files came up. She clicked and opened the first file 'Document 1: Introduction and Facts' and waited for the document to open.

"Holy shit," Katheryn mumbled as she read the document. She regarded the young woman in astonishment. This girl had been in the hands of the *Stewards* cult and, according to the document, had incriminating evidence about the entire organization and the people involved. "How did you escape?"

"I didn't," said Trouble. "Someone let me go. You'd call them a whistleblower, except they needed me to blow the whistle. This is why I need protection and the things on the list. I have to start over where no one can find me."

"What about this whistleblower?" Katheryn asked. "Do they need help getting out too?"

"No," said Trouble firmly.

Katheryn waited for the young woman to say more, but she stayed silent. She wasn't sure if it meant she was afraid to say more or if she knew nothing more. "Okay," she said finally. "Do you have a child in danger?"

"No, I'm the minor in danger," she said softly.

"Right," said Katheryn with concern. "Is your mother in danger?"

"No, she's complicit," she said evenly. "It's why emancipation is one of the things on the list of demands." She also knew she would need it to get a passport to leave the country. A passport was another item she had added to the list when she found Mason hadn't thought of everything.

Katheryn scrutinized the young woman then took a breath and let it out slowly. "Okay." She scanned the document again. "So, how firm are you on these demands?"

"Firm," said Trouble. "No deal if I don't get them all."

"The FBI is not an easy agency to negotiate with," she informed her.

"Using the information or not is up to them," said Trouble with confidence. "I have a backup plan if they don't want to make a deal."

"Oh, what is it?" Katheryn asked Ms. DePaz. The young woman gave a small smile but said nothing. "They'll want to see proof of the information you have."

"Proof is on the USB drive. If they want anything more, they have to agree to all the demands." She considered all her options that did not include Katheryn and knew it was time. "I need your answer now. Will you represent me?"

Katheryn gave a small laugh at Ms. DePaz's cheekiness. "Damn right I will," she said with a smile.

14

NEGOTIATING INSIDE THE offices of the FBI was not ideal in Katheryn Hardam's mind. She would much rather have been on neutral ground or in her own offices. The only reason she agreed was because she didn't want them to give her the old excuse about having to go 'talk' to someone and take forever getting back to her. Showing up on a Friday was another way she hoped would put pressure on them to work out a deal quickly. Since she was here, in their offices, they had everyone available, and if someone important was out, she could play hardball until they contacted them.

At the moment, they were reviewing the information her client had provided along with the list of things she says she can provide if her demands are met, and they guarantee her protection.

Agents Foster and Brewster walked back into the conference room.

"Well?" Katheryn asked. "Pretty impressive, don't you think?"

"It was interesting," said Agent Foster showing no emotion. "What we find more interesting is the fact your client didn't come with you today."

Katheryn chuckled. "My client values privacy. There's risk here, and we're mitigating it by me coming to you alone." She did not want them to know her client was a minor before she could push through the emancipation, therefore allowing her to legally sign a contract.

"When will we get to meet your mystery client?" asked Agent Brewster.

"I don't know if you will," said Katheryn with a smile. "Do we have a deal?"

Agent Foster tapped her fingers on the table. "The thing is we have another informant. You remember Jake Thompson.

The information he could give us may be enough for our investigation."

"I remember," said Katheryn with a scowl. "You wouldn't have information from him if it weren't for my help, either. I'm the one who contacted you about the messenger."

"Right," Agent Brewster nodded. "The information in the package was a full confession tying Thompson and the *Stewards* to the Kingsley case along with supporting documentation." He watched the lawyers face and had to hand it to her, she knew how to keep her cool. "We're trying to hammer out a deal for him right now *if* he agrees to give us more information. So, you see, we aren't sure we need your client's information."

Katheryn leaned back in her chair to consider their argument. She wished that right now she knew exactly what her client had so she didn't feel like she was negotiating blind. Her best option was to assume the whistleblower who gave DePaz the information had a really big whistle. They sent a young girl with the information and, she assumed, they took off for parts unknown or were prepared for the fallout.

"Here's the thing," said Katheryn confidently, "I know how the Agency likes to spend years and years running down leads only to get a handful of arrests and even fewer convictions." She smiled cockily. "What my client is offering is a golden ticket. You just have to buy the chocolate." She glared at them until Brewster shifted in his chair.

"Yeah, see there's a problem." Foster smirked. "We feel your client should hand over the information like a good citizen. Then, if anything comes of it, we'll give any recognition due."

Katheryn laughed. "Recognition due?" She gave them a stare of steel. "Listen, you already have evidence this group is kidnapping and trafficking in children. Who knows exactly what they're doing to them. You know they're doing many other illegal things like internet stalking, invasion of privacy, criminal trespass and who knows what else in the name of their cult. Right now, you have one case and the smell of hope for more." Katheryn leaned forward looking at each of them in turn. "What my client is asking for is reasonable considering you'll be saving millions in taxpayer dollars. Not to mention the time and shoe leather you'll save. The way I see it having two sources is better than one anyway."

Agent Foster glanced at her watch. "Well," she said as she stood, "we still have to run this by a supervisor. Why don't we meet back here next week after we talk to the brass?"

"I don't think so," said Katheryn as she leaned back in her chair. "I've been instructed not to return to the FBI if I leave without a deal—this deal submitted, today."

"We could detain you for obstruction," threatened Agent Brewster.

"You could," Katheryn agreed, "but I don't have access to the information being offered, and right now, I don't even know where my client's staying. Even if I gave you my client's name, there's no guarantee you'd find them to force the information from them, before they offered the information to someone else or used the information another way." Agent

Brewster could not hide his shock. "My client isn't stupid," Katheryn said brazenly. "Both your agency and my client have needs, and my client's life is on the line. This is not a game."

"We never said it was a game," said Agent Foster trying to hide her anger at Agent Brewster for putting the lawyer on the defensive. Defensiveness always made negotiations harder. Hardam had given away nothing so far, not even the gender of her client, and now the lawyer knew she had the upper hand on Brewster's emotions.

"Good," said Katheryn firmly. "Go talk to those who control your puppet strings and get me an answer," she said watching the heat of anger run over Agent Brewster's face. "While you're at it, I'd like to see old Jakie-boy's confession. As you know, Ms. Kingsley and Ms. Salvaggio are also my clients and, for certain courtesies, I'm sure they'd be willing to help with your case against him and the *Stewards*."

"We'll see what we can do," said Agent Foster evenly then turned and walked out the door. She controlled her ire over the lawyer now making even more demands. *Fucking Brewster!*

Agent Brewster glowered at Katheryn hard then followed Foster, closing the door hard behind him. *Fucking lawyers!*

"Nothing like a nice game of hardball," mumbled Katheryn as she took a sip of her water. She settled in for a long wait.

15

RAFE SALVAGGIO WANDERED through the house making sure she had not missed anything while cleaning up from the toddler's birthday party held earlier in the day with all of Bronte's friends and their parents. While Bronte napped, Rafe had taken the opportunity to shower and slip into her pajamas. Eden had gone to the store because the party guests had gone through more food and drinks than they anticipated and she wanted to replenish before the workweek began.

Rafe had spent most of the week at home with Bronte unless a therapy session was scheduled. Rafe was doing better during the day, but she still had trouble with her phantom pain and nightmares. She was hoping the new medication would kick in and help soon.

When Rafe looked out the window, she saw Abby getting out of her car. Eden had called to let her know Abby was on her way over, so she was expecting her. Rafe smiled then went into the living room and sat on the couch.

Abby had not seen Rafe all week and was worried. Eden called and asked her to stop by to check on Rafe until she could get home because she was running late. Apparently, Rafe was not answering Eden's calls again.

Finding the door unlocked, Abby walked into the house and found Rafe sitting on the couch in her pajamas and holding her head in her hands. "Rafe," said Abby concerned, "Rafe, what's wrong?"

"Nothing." Rafe sighed heavily. "I'm okay."

"Okay," said Abby worried, "it seems like something's wrong. I mean, you're sitting here, not dressed. Is it," she looked wearily at Rafe, "is it the stress? Eden's worried about you."

"No," said Rafe with her head still in her hands.

"Listen," said Abby as she sat down next to Rafe, "whatever it is, you have to talk about it. The therapist said so," she reminded her. "You have to talk!"

Rafe almost scoffed at the fact they all interpreted the doctor's words the same way. The wrong way. She had another issue to take care of now, so she let it go. She looked pointedly at the box at her feet. "I can't figure out what to do with. . ."

"What is it?" asked Abby as she eyeballed the box.

"It's nothing," answered Rafe and pushed the box so Abby could not see it. "I can't talk to you about it," she said shaking her head. "You already think I'm crazy." She forced a laugh then bit her lip. "This'll probably make you think I've really lost it."

"I won't," she promised. "Please, let me help you," she begged. "What is it?"

"Eden," she said sadly. "Eden told me what you thought," she faltered and looked up, "about her comparing me to Jake."

"She did?" asked Abby nervously. "But, but," she started and couldn't help remembering what Eden had said about Rafe's hands being better than anything of Jake's.

"Yes," Rafe said softly, interrupting Abby's reflections. "She thought it was so funny," she said as she looked at Abby in misery. "Why did you tell her, Abby? You said you wouldn't."

"I'm sorry," she squeaked and gawped at Rafe's hands. "She... she told me your hands were better than, than anything," she said shakily. "She said you had magical, flexible fingers," she blurted desperately. "I... I don't understand!"

Rafe looked away from Abby and tried not to laugh or let her see the surprised look on her face. She took a breath to regroup then gazed at her again sadly. "Well, I guess it's not enough anymore," she said in despair. "She found it, and she thinks I used one with you and some other women. Now she's angry because I'm telling her I didn't, and she thinks I'm lying."

"So, what are you saying?" Abby reeled in confusion as she realized what Rafe was talking about and what was in the box,

"Abby, I can't do what she wants!" Rafe insisted. "I don't want to do what she wants!" she said and turned away from Abby.

"But," stammered Abby as she saw Rafe in misery, "but she told me she'd never make you do anything you didn't want to do," she said frantically, putting her hand on Rafe's back.

"Of course she did," said Rafe in mock frustration turning to face her again. "She's convinced I do want to do it! She thinks it's the reason I bought it, and I just don't want to with her! She accused me of using it on the others after we split up." Rafe reached out and held Abby's arms. "She thinks I'm keeping part of myself from her," she whispered frantically, "I'm not, Abby! I never used it! I never!"

"I know!" said Abby stunned. "Shit! I. . . I'm sorry Rafe!"

"Don't tell her I told you," said Rafe as she released Abby. She stood and began pacing then looked outside and saw Eden walking to the door. She looked away quickly and continued to pace. "She says she's in charge of everything now, so I have to do this before she finds out. You have to keep this a secret," she said desperately as she turned suddenly toward Abby. "Can you help me? Will you take it out of the house so she can't make me use it?"

Eden walked inside and saw Rafe standing over Abby who was on the couch with a small box next to her. "What's going on here?"

Rafe looked at Abby pleadingly then turned toward Eden. "I can't, Eden," she said frantically, "I just can't do it! Just ask her," she said as she pointed toward Abby. "Ask Abby!" she said and picked up the box.

"Rafe!" Eden growled menacingly. "So, has she convinced you to lie for her?" she asked angrily. "You were just supposed to be checking on her! I'm in charge here now. She'll do whatever I say!"

"Help me, Abby," Rafe pleaded. "Help me, please," she said fearfully. "Tell her!" She gave Eden a sly wink, and it was all Eden could do not to smile.

"I. . ." said Abby as she stood up, "she. . ." she stammered freaking out at the surreal situation. "Eden, we never," she shook her head, "I mean, she wouldn't!"

Rafe shoved the box into Abby's hands and screamed as Eden charged forward. "Run, Abby! Take the strap-on and run!"

Frightened Abby jumbled the strap-on box. "Shit!" she screeched as she got it under control. She took in Eden's angry face then at the box. Dodging Eden, she ran out the door with a high-pitched scream.

Eden watched Abby run out, and then Eden fell onto the couch laughing. "When. . .when she finds out," she said laughing, "you. . . you're dead meat!"

Rafe laughed with her and looked out the window at Abby trying to figure out exactly what she was supposed to do next. "So are you!" she joked with a grin. "Come and watch." Eden went to look out the window with her. "Will she throw it in the trashcan or put it in her car?"

"Surely she'll throw it away," said Eden with tears of laughter in her eyes.

"Well," said Rafe trying to control her laughter, "she knows it's never been used!"

"Oh," Eden exclaimed as she seized Rafe's arm and watched Abby. "Oh, my god, Rafe! She. . . she put it in her car!" They both fell on the couch laughing. Eden looked at Rafe's smiling face as love for her swelled inside her. She put her hand to her head and caught her breath. "Oh, man," she sighed, "what's she going to start telling people about me?"

"I don't think you have anything to worry about," said Rafe as she smiled. "She's probably still talking to everyone about

Cattano

whatever you told her about my magical, flexible fingers." She waved her fingers in front of Eden.

"What?" Eden asked in surprise then remembered the night she was on pain medication drinking wine. "Oh, no," she groaned, "I'm so sorry. In my defense, I was drugged up, and she gave me wine." She worried because she knew Rafe didn't like her talking about personal things with Abby because she was such a gossip. "Please, don't be mad at me."

"Oh, I'm not mad," said Rafe as she lifted herself up and rolled herself on top of Eden pressing her hips into her.

Feeling a tingling rush run through her, Eden smiled up at Rafe. "Well, maybe we should buy a new," she raised one eyebrow, "you know. Then we can really see how magical you are."

"Oh, I know how magical I am," she said and winked. She leaned in close, and Eden lifted her face in anticipation. Rafe put her lips close to Eden's ear. "I hope you didn't tell her about all my magical powers," she whispered. "You didn't, did you?"

"No," Eden breathed her heart beating hard imagining what Rafe could do to her if they had a strap-on. She loved feeling Rafe over her and couldn't wait to make love to her.

"Good," whispered Rafe. "I'd hate for anyone to know about my magical tongue," she said and licked Eden's face from her cheek to her ear then jumped off her laughing.

"Rafe!" Eden shrieked in surprise at the wet lick. She sat up and wiped her face with the back of her hand. "Gross," she grumbled as Rafe disappeared into the kitchen. She shook her head and smiled at Rafe's payback before she jumped up to join her in the kitchen. She hoped Rafe was happy all night.

16

EDEN KINGSLEY ANXIOUSLY made her way inside the law offices of Katheryn Hardam. She was very aware Rafe had not been included in the request to meet. Katheryn called and said she had some important news about the FBI case against Jake and the *Stewards*. Eden didn't know if this news was good or bad. She just knew it made her nervous to keep another secret about Jake from Rafe

She left Rafe at home watching Bronte, telling her that she was running errands. Rafe had only been home for a week, and Eden felt everything seemed to be going well. She didn't want anything to mess up the ground they were gaining. Eden made it to the reception area, and the receptionist showed her into Katheryn's office.

"Eden," said Katheryn warmly as she made her way around her desk. "Thank you for coming. Have a seat."

Eden sat in one of the leather chairs and looked up at Katheryn. "What's going on," she asked unable to hide her nervousness.

"Before we get started, I want to give you this," said Katheryn as she handed Eden a professionally wrapped gift. "I don't know if you've had the birthday party for Bronte yet, but I wanted to give her something."

Eden took the gift. "Thank you," she said. "Her kid party was yesterday. We're having another party for her tonight. We're going to the Kiki. It's friends and family, and you're welcome to come."

"I appreciate it, but I have a lot going on right now," she said as she went back to her chair behind the desk. "I have a feeling my firm is going to be very busy for a long time." She turned her focus to the reason for calling the meeting. "I have some good news and something to show you," said Katheryn with a tight smile. She turned the laptop on her desk around so Eden could see the screen. "I wanted you to see this evidence and hopefully put your mind at ease about Jake and the *Stewards*," she said and used the mouse to open a file.

"What is it?" Eden asked as she watched.

"Jake's confession," she said and pressed the play button on the video.

Jake's face appeared on the laptop screen. He had a dark smudge on his forehead, and he looked scared and angry. He took a breath and began to speak. "My name is Jake Thompson, Soldier 5th Tier, California Regiment in the organization *Stewards to the Protection of the Innocence and Morals of Youths*. I am speaking to all who see this video documentation freely and out of my own conscience for what I believe is the good of all innocents and mankind. We must root out the evil residing within the Stewards, beginning with the evil within myself. With this in mind, I feel it my obligation to confess the evil corrupting me and, by default, this organization, so it may be purged.

"After reflection, I have come to regret my actions and the harm they have caused. With the understanding justice must be done, and with the acceptance punishment must be doled out, I beg for mercy and forgiveness. I hope this confession shows the depth of my sincerity.

"Along with this video, documented evidence will be provided, and you will see it is indisputable. I will cooperate in all ways, to the best of my ability, to put an agreeable end to this dark threat."

The video Mason had edited stopped, and Eden looked up at Katheryn in shock. "How—" Eden managed, but then didn't know what else to say.

"The FBI speculates Jake has been looking for a way out of the *Stewards* and was planning to turn his confession over to them on your court date," Katheryn explained. "Obviously, something happened to make him snap and attack you, which lead to him being shot. We don't know why it happened yet, and we may never know." She saw Eden's bewildered look and continued. "Now he wants a deal in exchange for turning over evidence and testimony."

Eden's face paled with the thought of Jake being able to make a deal that might lead him back into their lives. "So, what does this mean for us?" asked Eden with confusion. "I mean, the case was thrown out, and the adoption went through. Why am I here? "What about Flynn? Will he be okay?" Eden asked with worry. What does Jake want from me?"

Katheryn clicked her tongue in a slight self-admonishment for feeding Eden's anxiety. "Jake is not in a position to ask anything of you," she assured her. "I had a meeting with the prosecutor last week," Katheryn said calmly. "I've made my case, and the FBI has backed it up, so I think he will be excused to self-defense and the defense of another. I don't see any problems where he is concerned."

"Thank you," said Eden, glad her friend and rescuer would be okay. She bit her lip nervously and her heart beating rapidly in her chest as she waited for Katheryn to continue.

"You're here because, based on your testimony, the FBI wants your cooperation," Katheryn paused, "and Rafe's, with building their case against this cult and Jake. I told them I represented you, though technically, I only represent Rafe. I understand if you want a different lawyer, but I don't think you should go in unrepresented. They'll tell you everything will be fine if you talk to them, but you need to be given certain safeguards, and you need to be aware of the fact you don't have to answer any unnecessary questions."

"Safeguards? Unnecessary questions?" Eden repeated. She looked at Katheryn thoughtfully. "But I already told them everything I know."

"Maybe." Katheryn nodded. "But they have new questions now." She closed the laptop.

"Well, if I need a lawyer, I'd like it to be you," she said earnestly.

"I want you to understand I'll only be your lawyer for this matter and, since I'm representing Rafe too, there could be some overlap. However, for all other matters, I am Rafe's lawyer. For any agreements or litigation between you two, I will be representing her."

Eden nodded. "I understand."

"Okay, but I'll say it one more time, you need representation for this, and I can recommend other lawyers. I want you to know you don't have to hire me to help you."

"I understand," Eden repeated. "I think you'd be the best though because you know Rafe's case, and you know me. I trust you, and I think you'll do what's in my best interest. I won't ask for anything else."

Katheryn frowned. "I don't want you to think you can't come to me for help if you need it, Eden. I just can't risk client conflict of interest. I can't represent you in any litigation against Rafe. She's one of my biggest clients, and I've represented her since she moved to California."

"No, I get it," Eden assured her. "I know it's just for this FBI thing and nothing else."

"Good," said Katheryn. "I'll get a client packet for you before you leave." She wished she could tell Eden about Ms. DePaz, but her hands were tied for now on the matter. She would be able to tell her once things were finalized and the young woman was in a safe place. For now, they needed to discuss other things. "So," she started, trying to be upbeat, "like I said, the FBI wants to make a deal with Jake. They want to let him agree to a plea bargain. This means no trial. Part of the deal is you don't take him or the *Stewards* to civil or criminal court."

"Me?" asked Eden. "Why would I?"

"Well, the evidence proves they did a lot of illegal things causing you and your child direct harm. Normally, you would have the right to sue for damages and might even be eligible to receive compensation from a victim's fund."

"I don't want their money," said Eden feeling sick at the idea of touching anything coming from them. "I just want them out of our lives."

"I understand," said Katheryn and tapped her pen on her pad of paper. "The thing is that you're lucky. You don't need the money, and you still have your life and your daughter. What you need to understand is other victims aren't as lucky." She watched Eden think about her words. "Technically, you'll be the first victim to file charges against the *Stewards*," she explained. "This means your settlement agreement can set precedence for any future victims. So, if you get compensation, they have a good chance of getting it too."

"But like you said, I don't need it," said Eden.

"So, you put it in a trust or some other instrument and give it away or do something good with it," said Katheryn. "It's not about needing it for yourself. It's more about making sure those who need it have a chance to get it."

"So, what am I supposed to do?"

"As part of Jake's plea bargain, and in exchange for your cooperation in not suing, we can ask to have a victim fund set up. There are probably formulas for figuring out who gets how much, but if we need to, we can come up with one. Once they start seizing assets, the agreement will stipulate proceeds go to the fund, and then victims can apply. The details will be pretty standard."

Eden shrugged. "Okay, I guess. I wouldn't want to make things harder for anyone."

"How do you feel about possibly not having your day in court for the assault against you?" asked Katheryn.

Eden thought about the question. "I don't know. They want me to drop those charges too?"

"Yes," said Katheryn gravely.

Shaking her head, Eden looked up at Katheryn with growing aggravation. "So he walks away from everything, and we're left with what? Nothing?"

"He's not walking away," Katheryn assured her. "He will be held by the FBI. I don't know all the details of his plea bargain yet, but I do know if he doesn't follow through, he'll be in prison for a long time."

"So! What if he does follow through?" she asked shakily. "Does it mean he can come back?"

Katheryn could see Eden's anxiety and fear building, and it was not what she wanted. Good decisions could not be made under those conditions. "He won't be coming back," she said firmly. "But to ensure it, we can stipulate a restraining order in your conditions. If he is released, he can't go near you, Bronte, or Rafe."

"Do those things really work?" she asked doubtfully.

"Nothing is guaranteed. But even if you went to court, and he spent time in prison for assault, eventually he would get out," Katheryn reminded her. "At least, this way, you have something on record."

"I don't know what to do," she said and ran her hand through her hair. "Maybe I should talk to Rafe."

"Is she in a place where she'll be okay talking about this?"

"She's been doing well," Eden assured her and sighed. "But you're right. It could cause a setback." She leaned forward and put her face in her hands. "God, why is this so hard?"

"Eden, who did you hire to represent you in the assault case?" asked Katheryn.

Eden looked up at Katheryn with a frown. "Hire? I didn't hire anyone. I just talked to the prosecuting attorney's office."

"Oh, boy," sighed Katheryn. "I should probably submit myself as your attorney for it too then. Sometimes it's good to have an intermediary between two government entities," she mumbled as she made a note on the legal pad. She looked up at Eden and folded her hands on her desk. "This is what I need you to do. Think about what we've talked about. If you want to cooperate and give the FBI your testimony by answering their new questions, it may be the best way to help yourself and other victims. If you don't do this, they could just pull jurisdiction and leave you with nothing. There will be other victims, but who knows if a lawyer will represent them or not," she said with a shrug. "Get back with me by Friday. We can't afford to drag this out."

"Okay," Eden nodded wishing she knew what to do. "Katheryn, I don't want to make a mistake."

"I know," she said sympathetically. "Think about this. If you go to court, you would have to face him again, and so would Rafe. You would absolutely get a conviction. The question is, would the conviction and facing him in court help you and Rafe feel better or would it add to the stress you already have. If you go with the FBI option, he will be held by them, and even though there's no trial because of his confession, he will be pleading guilty in his plea bargain to his crimes. We can see if we can include the assault. Believe me, the FBI won't let go of him until they are one hundred percent sure they have everything out of him."

Eden thought about Katheryn's words and nodded. "Okay," she said softly, "let's do it. Let's work with the FBI."

"Great. Now that we've talked, we'll meet again with Rafe," said Katheryn with a nod. "Would you like me to inform Rafe we need another meeting?"

"No," said Eden as she clasped her hands together. "I'll tell her."

17

THE BIRTHDAY CELEBRATION for Bronte was a happy event at the Kiki Bistro. While Bronte ate birthday cake, Eden Kingsley and Rafe Salvaggio were laughing about the joke they had pulled on Abby the day before. They both tried to hold in their mirth when they saw Jude and Abby had arrived at the table.

"Hey!" said Jude as she pulled up a chair. "You guys look happy tonight."

"Is, uh," Abby swallowed nervously, "everything okay?"

"Rafe, I can't do this!" Eden burst out laughing. "Tell her, please! Don't make her suffer!"

"What?" Abby asked anxiously. "Tell me what? What now?"

Rafe gave Abby a serious look. "Thank you, Abby, for taking care of my little problem yesterday," she said and could not help herself as she joined in Eden's infectious laughter.

"You... you," stammered Abby with her mouth hanging open. "You two were messing with me! I'll get you back for this, Salvaggio!"

Eden watched Rafe as she laughed and talked with their friends. She felt herself pulled toward her and wanted to reach out and touch her, but she stopped herself knowing Rafe still needed space.

It was so good to see Rafe smiling and happy. Eden found herself dreaming about her again, even though they were in the same house. So much had happened, and she knew now this was where she needed to be, for herself as well as for their daughter. Rafe was back now, and it was as if a weight had been lifted from her. It was a marked difference from the way she felt when she was away from Rafe. It reminded her of how she felt when they first met, and all her issues with anxiety seemed to disappear.

Now her anxiety was aggravated by knowing, for the next couple of weeks, they would be talking with the FBI again and not knowing how it might affect Rafe's progress and their relationship. Katheryn set up a date to meet with Rafe again in two weeks. The biggest issue on Eden's mind was that they hadn't told Rafe about her decision not to take the *Stewards* to court for everything they did and not to take Jake to court for the assault. Just the mention of Jake still set Rafe off.

She had already told Rafe they had to meet with Katheryn, and they may be speaking to the FBI. She knew Rafe was planning to go to the meeting ready for a fight. Rafe was technically being considered a witness, not a victim, so Katheryn advised her just to let Rafe say what she needed to say. Eden worried because it seemed like, even though they were in the same house, the whole situation with the FBI and Jake was still forcing a distance between them, and she did not know how to bridge it. Coupled with Rafe's PTSD, she knew it would be a lot to overcome.

"Hey," said Rafe with a smile, "are you okay?"

Eden looked up into her blue-gray eyes and smiled. "I'm fine," she said softly and could not stop her words. "I love you." She never wanted to stop telling her. She hoped it would help build the bridge of love they needed to find each other again. She knew she was so in love with Rafe and always would be in love with her.

18

KATHERYN HARDAM HAD been playing hardball with the FBI since Eden first gave her the information on the *Stewards* several months ago. What started out as a bogus adoption injunction then turned into a full-blown sting operation, affecting thousands of innocent victims. Finally, it felt like she was getting somewhere with the FBI, and she owed a lot of her progress to her newest client, with the new name of Marie Lorpaz. Having the leverage of the USB drives helped not only Ms. Lorpaz but helped make significant progress on behalf of her other clients, Rafe Salvaggio, and now Eden Kingsley. The meeting with the FBI went well. She talked to Eden many times over the past few weeks about her situation with Jake and the *Stewards*, so some things were resolved. Now they have to get through today and telling Rafe about Eden's decisions. Then, there was what was in the files sitting on the floor beside her desk.

Both Rafe and Eden were on their way in for their ten a.m. appointment and, as Katheryn regarded the large file in front of her, she knew she had to give them the information at her feet. She was obligated because Rafe was her client. She wished she didn't have to give it to them, especially since Rafe had been back home from her treatment in Mexico scarcely a month. She was very concerned about how it would affect their relationship since they seemed to be getting along and the adoption had gone through. She hoped they would find something positive about what she was about to reveal.

The buzzer on her phone went off, and she knew Rafe was on her way. Almost immediately, her office door opened and Rafe walked in with a smile and sat down in the leather chair across from her desk.

"It's good to see you again, Rafe," said Katheryn as she made her way to the door to close it. "Is Eden on her way?"

"Nice to see you too," she replied. "Eden should be here soon. She's coming from work."

"Good," said Katheryn as she sat back behind her desk. "I want you to know everything you set up for Bronte is filed and all taken care of for you. She's a lucky little girl."

"Great," said Rafe with a nod. "Thanks. Oh, and thank you for sending her a birthday gift. She had a lot of fun with all of her friends." She smiled as she remembered the celebration for Bronte's second birthday. "We had a family party too. Letty made Ephraim bake a mini cake for her." She tried not to think of Bronte's last birthday, the one celebrated in Canada, and everything they had gone through afterward.

Katheryn wondered if she should just tell this information to Eden and let her decide if Rafe should know. The problem was, Rafe had been her client long before Eden, and their cases were intermingled since Rafe was also filing suit against Jake the *Stewards*. The content of the large files on the floor was evidence and could be used in both cases.

The buzzer on her phone went off, and her question was answered as the secretary showed Eden into the office. She could see by their interaction that there was still some tension between the couple, but she knew they were both working on their individual issues. "Eden, thank you for coming. Please, take a seat."

Eden smiled at Rafe, happy to see her, and sat down in the chair next to her. "Hi," she said quietly, touching her leg for a moment, and then looked up at Katheryn. "What's going on? Is everything okay?"

Rafe saw the thick file on Katheryn's desk and thought she knew why they were really there. "Katheryn," said Rafe as her leg shook revealing her agitation, "what's happening with the Stewards group? Did our statements help the FBI shut them down?"

"They have made some progress," Katheryn confirmed as she put her hand on top of the file on her desk, "and from what I understand, Jake is going to testify for a more lenient sentence."

"What? Lenient?" Rafe repeated angrily as she stood up and leaned over Katheryn's desk. "You mean he's not going to jail? What about what he did to Eden? He needs to be put away! All of them need to be put away!"

Katheryn glanced at Eden then back at Rafe. "Rafe, he will spend some time in jail. I'll make sure of it," she said firmly. "But if he cooperates with the FBI, they'll be able to catch the ringleaders and make more of an impact." She could see it was not enough for Rafe. "Sit down, Rafe," she said calmly and waited for her to comply. "I've discussed this with Eden. If he agrees to a plea, then she doesn't have to face him in court, and neither do you."

"You've discussed this with Eden?" Rafe frowned at Eden with suspicion. *More secrets, more lies*, she thought and turned back to Katheryn. "I'll face him," Rafe said angrily. "I kill him!"

"Please, Rafe," said Eden as she put her hand on Rafe's leg to try to calm her anger. "This is exactly why I agreed to work with them. I just don't want to cause you, or us, anymore stress," she reasoned. "If I do this, the FBI may be able to shut down their whole operation, not just Jake. I know you're angry with him and everything," she paused, "and so am I, but think about it. Do you want anyone else going through this?"

"No," said Rafe as she scowled and moved, so Eden's hand slid off her leg. She was angry Eden hadn't talked to her about this and was keeping secrets from her again. Eden did not know what Jake had said to her and what their group thought about gay women. Eden didn't understand Jake was insane, and he was a threat to them and everyone. She tried to tell the FBI when she gave her statement. But they didn't consider her a victim and disregarded everything she had said, and it made her angry. It was the main reason she was suing them on her own for all the things they did to her from the interference in her relationships to the libel and loss of her job.

"Well, then," said Eden pleadingly, taking her hand back as Rafe moved away. "I think this is the right thing to do. It's what Katheryn recommends we do. Can you be okay with it?"

"Only if they also put a lifetime restraining order on the guy so he can't come anywhere near us, or make him leave the state permanently," said Rafe as she crossed her arms. "I don't ever want him around us again."

"I don't think it'll be a problem, Rafe," Katheryn assured her. "He won't be in any position to bother anyone. He'll be in FBI custody for a very long time." Katheryn could see Eden's relief and Rafe's dissatisfaction. She hesitated and faced them sternly. "There's something else you should know, Eden."

"What?" she asked nervously as she watched Rafe attempt to control her anger. It seemed lately Rafe was angry a lot. She tried to hide it, but Eden could feel it always just below the surface.

"The FBI has figured out who the source was who gave you the information," she revealed. "I can't reveal a name, but an informant came forward with some new information. With the information she provided, we were able to find your source. The FBI gave her my name, and she reached out to me. I'll be representing her. She wanted me to give you a message."

"A message?" repeated Eden curiously.

"Yes," said Katheryn. "She wants me to tell you," she paused, "both of you—thank you. She would be in a much worse place if not for everything you went through. If you'll allow it, and after her case is decided, she'd like to meet you."

Rafe glared at Katheryn with anger. "Who the hell is she? Why didn't she do more? If she had, then there would have been no attempts to take Bronte, and Eden wouldn't have almost been killed. I don't think I want her near my family."

"Rafe," said Eden softly. "If it weren't for her, things may have been worse. Maybe we should thank her for taking the risk to help us. Who knows what she's been through," she said with sympathy.

"Things were very bad for her," Katheryn confirmed. "But now, with mine and the FBI's help, she'll be able to start a new life." She could see Rafe wasn't convinced to meet the woman.

Rafe crossed her arms denying any sympathy to the woman or anyone she felt was part of the problem

"The other informant," Katheryn continued, "a young woman who risked a lot to get this new information to me, would like to meet you, too, if you're willing. She somehow knows a lot about you both. She's a tough cookie. I suppose she had to be with all she went through. To get the information to me, she took a big risk, and it could have meant her life. We made a deal to get her a new identity. She's decided to leave the country for a while, and once she leaves, she may not have the opportunity to meet you. She'll come back when the FBI needs her, and she may move back permanently once she feels safe. She's actually a terrific artist." She hoped Rafe would take some interest in the girl. Ms. Larpaz had asked a lot about Rafe, and she even went so far as to say Rafe was an inspiration to her.

Rafe frowned and shook her head unsure why those people wanted to meet. She didn't trust anyone who was part of the Stewards. She did not want to have anything to do with them or possibly be pulled into dealing with the people she felt were criminals who should be behind bars. Sure, she felt empathy for both the women, but it didn't mean she wanted to be reminded and relive everything. She did not want Eden near anyone who was part of the group responsible for trying to kill her and take their daughter. It would be like inviting Death back into her life, and she couldn't face it again. Maybe if it were a few years down the road when it was safer, and the FBI had arrested everyone, she could do it. But not now. "I can't," she said softly.

Eden couldn't understand why Rafe wasn't more sympathetic to these women. They had obviously gone through much more hardship than they had experienced and for a longer period of time. She wanted to thank both of them for being so brave. "Let's think about it before we give an answer," she suggested. "They deserve our thanks for the risk they took." She looked up at Katheryn. "Is it okay if we take some time to think about it?"

Katheryn could see what Eden was doing. She was trying to give Rafe time to calm down so she could think more clearly about the matter. "Sure, think it over. I'm sure they can wait for your decision." She steeled herself for the next order of business. "Something else has come to light," she said evenly and opened the thick file on her desk. "Like I mentioned before, the informant came forward with new information about the Stewards." She wished again she could tell them about Ms. Lorpaz and how the FBI was about to pull one of the biggest sting operations ever done on a religious cult.

Because of Ms. Lorpaz, the FBI had enough evidence to arrest and convict the highest leaders in the organization.

"This informant will be instrumental in the FBI's investigation. Because of the information provided, I was able to obtain the file the Stewards had on you, Eden. Some of what I have has been redacted by the FBI, but, with what's intact, you'll still get an idea of what was happening."

Rafe looked up at Katheryn with confusion. "File on Eden? We already know what happened. Jake took advantage of her, and he lied to me about her."

"Actually, Rafe, there was more. Much more," said Katheryn with a sigh.

Eden could see Rafe getting agitated. "What more?" Eden asked anxiously. "I know they found me online because of what Flynn found." She stopped herself and looked at Rafe. She didn't want to remind her of what she had done online. Rafe was already angry, and she did not want a setback.

"Sadly," Katheryn sighed, "there was a lot more to it."

"Just get to the point," said Rafe impatiently. She could feel her anger rising and prolonging things did not help.

"Fine," said Katheryn. She reached down, picked up two thick, bound files off the floor beside her, and dropped them one at a time on her desk. Each file was heavy and about as thick as her forearm was long. She stood and handed one to each of them. "This is a copy of the file the Stewards kept on Eden. There are almost three years of information."

"What the hell?" asked Rafe. She took the thick file she was handed and started thumbing through the tomb. She had been expecting something bad from the file she saw on Katheryn's desk, but nothing like this.

Eden went pale as she took the thick file. "I don't understand."

"Eden, this group had been watching you since the first time you went online to discuss your insemination experience three years ago. According to what's in the file, once they designated you as one of their missions, they made it their business to influence you and groom you to do almost exactly what you did."

Rafe looked through the file with frustration then looked at Eden incredulously. "You told them all of this? I knew you talked to Abby but—" she shook her head in disbelief. "I was right. You were telling strangers about us." She was not sure how to react now as her anger began to flair and fight for release.

Eden watched Rafe anxiously. She looked back at the file and was at a loss. She knew from what she had received anonymously about Jake, and from what Flynn found, they wanted to take her and Bronte away. But she had no idea all the friends she thought she had made on the artificial insemination sites she visited and a few others were members of the *Stewards*. She thought that maybe the one person she talked with online and had a sexual exchange with was with them, but none of the others. "I don't understand," she said nervously as she watched Rafe tear through page after page of the file.

Katheryn looked at Eden with sympathy. "Eden, these people systematically profiled you and assessed your vulnerabilities. Then they proceeded to bombard you with so-called 'online friends' and even sent spam emails and other online encouragements to influence you with advice and prey on your fears. Then they went as far as influencing you directly. According to the file, they talked to you in grocery store lines, at doctor's appointments and many other public places. Originally, they worked to stop the pregnancy by discouraging your decision and sabotaging your personal relationship with Rafe. They hoped being without the support of a partner would change your mind about having a baby. Only after they found you were pregnant and had Bronte did they add Jake into the picture. His mission was to remove you from what they deemed an 'ungodly' lifestyle."

Rafe stopped thumbing through the file. She read the open page then looked up at Katheryn. "They're the ones who sent her to therapy?" She glanced at Eden. "I don't understand. I know you insisted on going to therapy, and you were lying to me back then about why we were going! I knew I was right about the therapy you forced on me and it only made things worse! I knew you were going for you and your feelings for fucking strangers! But now you're telling me, on top of everything else, you were letting strangers choose our therapist?" she asked shaking her head in disbelief.

Eden began to shake at Rafe's words. The information was so overwhelming and damning. They knew everything. Every complaint she had about Rafe, every doubt of herself, every negative thing she said, they collected and used against her. She looked at Rafe. "I'm sorry," she said shakily. "I meant it to be for us, I told you, to make sure we were good."

"It sounds as confusing now as it did then, Eden," said Rafe. "If you—" she started and Katheryn cut her off.

"Rafe," said Katheryn interrupting her, "you have to understand. They influenced Eden to choose their therapist. He, in turn, was part of their attack on your choice to have a child. The therapist's goal was to break your relationship apart." She saw Rafe's anger building, but she had to make her understand the big picture. "Rafe, there was nothing Eden could have done to stop them after her first contact with those websites once they decided to target her. No one who has gone up against these people could stop them or prove anything against them until now. They're not some small group, apparently. They have a large infrastructure, and it includes online teams, research teams, live contact teams, a group they call Soldiers, and a hierarchy protecting the top members of their organization."

Rafe shook her head. "No, she could have stopped talking to them. She could have talked to me instead of strangers. Even if they tried to influence her, it would have been harder to influence us both. It was her choice to talk to them and keep secrets from me," said Rafe evenly as she put a shaky hand on her head.

Watching Rafe nervously, a wave of fear and nausea ran through Eden. "I... I tried to talk with you," she said as her anxiety grew. "You weren't there. I just thought," she swallowed, "you were busy, and I knew you weren't happy about how things were going. I thought I could get some advice and things would be okay."

Rafe held in her anger and tried to speak evenly. "If you tried to talk to me, Eden, then why didn't I know about this until after Bronte was born? Why didn't I know you were having feelings for men while we were going through the insemination process? Why didn't I know the therapist was for you, and the fact strangers recommended him? You didn't tell me anything, you didn't try to talk with me, you left me out and kept leaving me out. For all I know, you still are. You told me you didn't have any more secrets, but it looks to me like you have a lot more," she said as she threw the heavy file on the floor in front of Eden. "There are the people who know your secrets," she said as she pointed at the file, "the people you trust more than you trust me."

"I don't trust them more than you," Eden said as she fought her tears. "I didn't."

"You did," Rafe snapped. "It's probably why those people want to meet me!" she raged. "To tell me what a fucking fool I am!"

"No," was all Eden could force out because it felt like the breath had been knocked out of her.

"What I don't understand is why?" Rafe fumed. "We were good then. I hadn't done anything to hurt you. I was working so hard to make sure you were happy and could be home and relaxed like you needed so we could start our family. I may have been gone a lot, but it didn't mean I wasn't there for you. I may have been upset about how things were going, but it was because I loved you and wanted everything to be perfect for you."

Katheryn watched their exchange aware the situation could escalate at any moment. She knew it was necessary to mediate and hoped she could keep things amicable between them. "Rafe, none of this was in Eden's control. Thousands of people go onto websites and into chatrooms every second. There was no reason for Eden to think anything of this magnitude would or could happen."

Rafe looked at Katheryn and then at Eden. She got up, grabbed the file from the floor, slammed it onto Katheryn's desk, and flipped through the pages. She stopped and ran her finger down the page then began to read each line aloud.

"'R is far away again at work. I feel so alone here.' 'Our second insemination failed. I really needed her to hold me before she left, but she was busy getting her things ready.' 'I'm feeling disconnected from her. I don't know what to do.' 'I'm not sure I can do everything on my own here. I wish I could have gone with her.'"

Rafe turned to Eden, her anger on the brink of bursting out as she fought for control. "All of these were sent to a stranger. There are tons of messages like this you sent out! How many of them were sent to me?" She waited for an answer. "Exactly," she said when Eden just stared at her with wide red-rimmed eyes. "None! None were sent to me! Am I a fucking mind reader? No, I'm not! You can sit for hours—hours!" she yelled, then fought to control herself. "You could spend hours with them, but you couldn't take even one minute to type those things in an email and send it to me. I'm pretty sure you had my email and my phone number!" she said as she slammed the file closed angrily. She looked at Katheryn then at Eden again. "That was under your control!" she seethed. She took a breath and fought to restrain her fury. "I have to go," she said and walked out the door.

"Rafe!" Eden called out and started after her, but the door slammed before she could get to it. She looked back at Katheryn with worry and guilt. "Katheryn—" She gasped as she fought to breathe and sank into her chair.

Katheryn saw Eden struggling and knew she was having an anxiety attack. She made her way around her desk and grabbed a bottle of water for Eden. She set the water down and took Eden by her shoulders. "Calm down, Eden. It'll be okay." Eden continued to struggle and began to cry. "She'll calm down, and we can talk to her again," Katheryn reassured calmly. "Just take deep breaths. You'll be fine."

Eden worked to control herself using the breathing techniques she had learned in therapy, and finally, she was able to calm herself. "She's right," she sobbed. "I didn't tell her anything. I could have prevented everything if I had told her."

"You can't know for sure, and neither can she," said Katheryn firmly. "Even if you had sent her emails telling her those things, just by being in those chatrooms, things still might have happened, and you would have been targeted," she said as she stood up and handed Eden the bottle of water. "You were the very definition of one of their missions. We can't know if things would have been better or worse if they had started targeting you both, instead of just you."

"Katheryn, I don't know what all of this is going to do, what Rafe's going to do," she said shakily as she picked up her section of the file off the floor. "We were doing so well." She stopped and took a breath then a sip of her water. "I just don't know how to fix things anymore. I don't know what's going to happen or how Rafe is going to react. I love her, Katheryn. I don't want to lose her again. I'm still fighting against things I did, mistakes I made, choices I made—not just being in chatrooms."

19

DRIVING AIMLESSLY AROUND downtown Los Angeles, Rafe Salvaggio was trying to figure out what she needed to do. She felt what she knew were phantom pains in her head and chest and knew she was supposed to talk to someone, tell someone, but she didn't know where to go. She certainly didn't want to talk to Eden so she couldn't go back to Katheryn's office. She definitely did not want to talk to Letty or Abby. They would just push her toward Eden or call her crazy again. She just felt like driving. Maybe just driving would help.

She turned her car around and headed toward her private garage. When she got there, the attendant smiled and waved her inside and leaned into her car window.

"Hey, Ms. Salvaggio!" he shouted happily over the noise in the garage. "We had your car detailed like you asked. Are you taking it out or storing this one again?"

Rafe smiled back at him hiding her torment. "Hey, Rick. I'm taking out the Spyder. Can you bring it out and go ahead and put the top down for me?"

"Sure, no problem," he said excitedly. He loved driving the car even if it was just to the entrance and back. "Just give me a few minutes. Go ahead and park and fill out the log book."

Rafe parked while Rick got the keys to the Spyder. Then she went into the small office and helped herself to the logbook behind the counter. She found her page and looked over all the check-in and checkout dates logged with mileage and instructions. Since her father gave her the car, Rick had always done the detail work. She was lucky he had a long-term storage space for rent when she sold the building along with her business. She heard the familiar sound of the car engine startup somewhere in the garage and smiled at the feeling it gave her. Quickly, she entered the date and time then stepped out of the office with the book.

Rick pulled the blue Maserati Spyder up to the office door, with the soft top already down, and shut off the engine. He checked the mileage and got out of the car. "Thanks," he said as Rafe handed him the logbook. He entered the mileage and showed her the book. "So, there are five miles on it from moving it to detail and gas up," he said. "I also took it to the shop for the tune-up, so she should be good to go for a while. Sign here."

"Sounds good," she said as she signed out the car and gave Rick the keys to the car she was leaving. "Will your night guy be here in case I want to bring it back tonight?"

"Yeah, it'll be Andy tonight," he said as he tucked the book under his arm. "I'll tell him to keep a watch out for you. Gotta take care of my best customer," he said with a smile.

"Thanks." She gave him a false smile as he tossed her the keys. She went to the back of the car, opened the trunk, and looked inside. She saw her mother's easel and the box with her father's ashes as well as other things she kept there. When she was satisfied everything was still as she had left it, she closed the trunk. "I may take her near the ocean, so mark me down for another detail," she said as she got in the car. She took her father's cap out of the glove box then put it on. "My father would roll over in his grave if I left salt on his baby for too long." She turned over the engine and smiled in appreciation of the smooth rumble promising speed.

"No problem!" called Rick, watching Rafe give a wave as she pulled out of the garage and took off down the street.

Rafe loved the powerful feel of the car as she maneuvered through the streets. She also loved the envious looks she got at the stoplights. Before she met Eden, it was one of her favorite ways to pick up dates and meet women after her father had it shipped to her in California. Now it was a portal of solace. She rarely had anyone in the car with her anymore, and she found she could think better alone.

As she downshifted and slowed for another stoplight, Rafe sighed. Driving in the city was just not satisfying. She looked over and realized she was near Julia's office. She pulled through the light then eased over into a parking space along the sidewalk and cut the engine. If she had to talk to someone, maybe Julia would be a good bet right now. She smiled at the thought of the wagers she made with Julia then picked up the phone and dialed.

"Yes, this is Rafe Salvaggio for Julia Hawthorn." She held the line as the call was transferred. "Julia, what are you doing right now?"

"Order memos. I hate them," she said with a groan.

Rafe laughed. "Can you come out and play? It's adventure time."

Julia sighed into the phone. "I don't know. There's a lot going on today."

"Well," Rafe hesitated, "what if I need to talk to you about financial stuff? Will money get you out? I promise to move a lot and make it worth your while."

"Is everything all right?" she asked wondering why Rafe was really calling and not wanting her to cause more work. "Where are you?"

"No, things really aren't all right," she admitted reluctantly. "I'm outside your building."

"Okay, I'll be down. I'm on my way."

"Great, I'm in my father's car. Bring a hat or a scarf if you have it." She hung up and smiled at the girl who was admiring her car as she walked by. She got out of the car for a stretch and leaned against the door to wait for Julia.

A few minutes later, Julia walked out of the building and spotted Rafe. She walked up to her with a smile. "Don't you look jaunty," she said nodding to Rafe's hat.

"Thanks," said Rafe with a chuckle. "It belonged to my papa. Let's go," she said and got in the car. She waited for Julia to get in and settle, then watched her put on sunglasses and then tie a scarf over her silver hair. "You look like a movie star," she said, and Julia laughed. Rafe started the car and headed out of the city.

20

PUSHING THE SPEED as she drove up the Ventura Highway, Rafe Salvaggio made it through the road construction then veered off at Malibu Canyon Road. The radio was loud, and the engine raced as Julia teetered between fear and exhilaration. Rafe maneuvered the car skillfully through traffic when they met it and curves as they appeared before them. They made it down to the 101 and headed to the Malibu Bay Restaurant and Bar. Rafe pulled into the parking lot and cut the engine.

"I love this car!" said Julia with a giddy laugh. "I can't believe you kept it and you haven't taken me out in it before today."

They made their way inside where the hostess led them to a table with a beautiful view of the ocean.

Rafe gave a nod of approval as they sat and the waiter appeared to take their order. "Let's start with the oysters on the half shell and give us both *Gueuze Tilquin*, please."

"Would you like a half or a full dozen?" asked the waiter.

"A dozen," answered Rafe then looked over at Julia. "Do you want to add anything?"

"No, we can see where we are after," she answered. The waiter left to put in their order, and Julia looked at Rafe somberly. "Okay, adventure girl. What's going on?"

As they ate oysters and drank their Belgian beer, Rafe filled Julia in on what was happening with Eden, and the file Katheryn obtained from the FBI. Julia could see how angry Rafe was even though she was attempting to hide it by acting blasé about the situation. Julia watched as Rafe's hand shook when she talked about Eden and knew more was going on in her mind than she was admitting.

Julia recalled the group session that they had with the psychologist on how to handle certain things they might see in Rafe. She was worried she was seeing some of the signs they had discussed. On the other hand, she understood Rafe's anger and hurt at what she was revealing. It was hard to hear. After all they had been through, Rafe was finding out Eden hadn't been honest with her for almost a year before they first split. It seemed like Rafe fought so hard to get Eden back into her life and now things were falling apart again.

Rafe had finally gone quiet and was gazing out at the ocean as she sipped her *gueuze*. Julia noticed Rafe had only eaten a few of the oysters. She suspected drinking with her medication wasn't allowed, but it looked like the beer had a calming effect. She was relieved to see Rafe less agitated.

"All of this is hard for me to hear," said Julia as she refilled her glass with the last of the beer in her bottle. It was hard to hear because, as a friend, she wanted Rafe to be happy, but deep down she had always wanted to be who Rafe ended up being happy with. It just never seemed like Rafe felt the same way. "Do you think it means, even without the whole Jake thing, you two would have split?"

"I have no idea," said Rafe with a ragged sigh. "I want to hope we wouldn't have, but I can't know she wouldn't have still needed to leave to deal with her feelings about being with a man. She keeps saying she loves me, but how do I know it all won't change again? I feel like I'm always on edge waiting for more shit to happen."

Julia knew she had to tread cautiously. Despite her feelings for Rafe, she had to remember she had been relegated to friend zone and couldn't say anything about her feelings. Rafe had already made things clear, but Julia could not help hoping. Maybe this time, if Rafe decided to leave Eden, they could revisit the possibility of a relationship. After all, they had been close since their school days and were compatible. She pushed down those thoughts and forced herself to help as just a friend.

"Well," she began gingerly, determined to say things a friend would say. "You made it through something worse than her talking to strangers. You two found each other again with all the chaos caused by the *Stewards*. Do you think you should take it into consideration when you're figuring out what you want to do?"

"Did we find each other again? I don't know," said Rafe as she took the last sip of her *gueuze*. "Sometimes I wonder what I got myself into. I don't regret becoming Bronte's parent. I love her and want to give her a good life. I just wonder if all the fighting I did for Eden and bringing us back together was worth the effort. I wonder if I should just go back to Italy and get away from all of this."

"Wait, Rafe," said Julia concerned, but her heart gave a hopeful thump at Rafe's doubts, "I thought you loved Eden. I don't think you should look at the fight for her as not worth it. If you hadn't fought, where would Bronte be now? If you had just let go, they might both be in a bad place like the woman you said gave Eden the information on Jake."

"I know, I know," said Rafe softly. "There's just so much to sort through. All those what-ifs and could-haves just build up and make me so angry. I have all these questions I don't think can be answered. For a start, how could she be so thoughtless, so careless?" She gave a sharp laugh. "The worst part is not how thoughtless she was about me, but she didn't even think about herself or Bronte. And now I have to reconcile the reality she started doing this before she was even pregnant."

Julia glanced at her watch not sure how much more she could listen too without encouraging her to leave Eden and move in with her. "Let's get out of here," she said wanting to get Rafe in a better mood. "Take me on another fast ride in your car back to the office." She knew taking another drive would please Rafe because she loved adventure. "I need to try and get something done today. And please, Rafe, don't make any more paperwork for me. Just leave things alone for a while," she pleaded with a laugh and Rafe gave her a small smile. Rafe's smile, full of hurt, made Julia want to comfort and care for her.

21

AFTER LEAVING THE lawyers office, Eden Kingsley called in and took a personal day from work. She immediately let Letty know Rafe was upset again, and she was looking for her. They tried calling Rafe, but she wasn't picking up her phone. With Ephraim's help, she spent most of the day driving around the city looking for Rafe. They searched for her at home, at the bistro, at several parks and other places she might go, but they still couldn't find her. Finally, Eden decided to drive by the house again, and she saw Rafe's car.

Relief flooded through her. She called Letty to tell her Rafe was home. Letty agreed to take care of Bronte for the night so Eden could help Rafe if she needed it. After ending the call, Eden sat in her car for a while to calm herself and figure out how to handle the situation. She knew Rafe was angry and they needed to talk about what had happened at Katheryn's office. She didn't know how to make things right again, but she had to try.

Eden made her way inside the quiet house. Walking to the back of the house, she found Rafe's bedroom closed and knew she was inside. She took a deep breath, steeled herself, then knocked on the bedroom door. "Rafe? Rafe, can I talk to you?"

"Can I stop you?" she said sarcastically, annoyed she couldn't lock her door and keep everyone away.

Eden put her hand on the door handle hesitantly and pushed back the anger flaring inside her. "Rafe, we need to talk, and I don't want to do it through a door."

"Maybe you can send me some messages, or wait, I know, let me set up a chatroom. Maybe it will make things easier for you."

She knew Rafe was trying to push her away, so she took a breath to calm herself. "I want to talk to you in person," she said as she gripped the door handle. "Can I come in?"

"Well, since I'm not supposed to lock the door anymore, I guess you can do whatever you want."

Eden turned the handle and pushed the door open but stayed just outside the room. She looked inside and saw Rafe sitting on the floor. She was in her meditation position on her yoga mat with her back to the door. "I don't want to invade your space. I just," she hesitated, "we need to talk."

"I'm really not sure what you want to talk to me about. It seems like you've said it all to a bunch of strangers. Maybe talking to them will help you now too. I have no idea what to say to you."

"You don't have to say anything. I'll talk," said Eden nervously. Rafe gave no response. "I'm sorry I didn't talk to you about what was going on with me back then. You're right. I should have told you what I was going through instead of talking to strangers. I should have been talking to the person I love. I know I made another mistake, Rafe. I've made so many," she said and sighed softly. "I don't even know if I deserve your forgiveness, but I hope you can give me some, even a little." She watched Rafe roll her shoulders and take a breath. "Will you turn around and look at me, please?" Rafe turned, but Eden could see she was very angry. "Can you forgive me enough that we can work through things?"

"What exactly am I supposed to forgive you for?"

"For the mistakes I've made with you and with Bronte," she said shakily under her stare. "I'm sorry."

"You didn't make mistakes. You made choices. Mistakes don't last for years! Choices do! I have no power to make you feel better about your choices. So, why do you need my forgiveness for the choices you made? Do you need it so you can feel better about them?"

"No, it's not what I want," she said softly. "I was just hoping you could forgive me."

"It's not my job to confirm or deny your choices were mistakes and dole out some kind of forgiveness. Forgiveness doesn't fix mistakes or bad choices. So, there's really nothing I could possibly forgive."

"Rafe, I'm telling you I know my choices were mistakes. Without forgiveness, how can we fix mistakes or bad choices? We have to forgive each other," she insisted. "I forgive you! I forgive you for not being here when I needed you and dropping everything here at home on me while you were gone all over the world working. I forgive you for being so angry when I was having problems conceiving. I forgive you for," she hesitated and let loose her anger, "for cheating on me! I forgive you for putting me through hell right now when I'm trying to tell you I love you and want to be with you! I forgive you for every fault I ever told you I thought you had! For being controlling, for being stubborn, for being an asshole, for thinking you're the only perfect person in the freaking world!"

"Well, thank you, fucking Saint Eden!" Rafe yelled back. "I never asked for your precious forgiveness. You can't fucking forgive me for being myself and doing my job, for caring about you and for supporting my family! It's who I am! It's not going to change! When I made a mistake, I stepped up and admitted it! I didn't keep doing it and expect you to forget all about it! I hope you don't forget! I cheated on you, and I apologized! I promised I wouldn't do it again, and I didn't! I told you the truth about it and took the fucking years of punishment you heaped on me, and I did it without complaint! I left my door open for you to show you I still fucking cared about you. I never left without saying goodbye! I never cut you out of my life! That was you! If anyone has been walking through hell, it's me! You haven't even started the fucking journey!"

"I don't want to walk through hell, Rafe!" Eden yelled back. "I don't want you to feel like you're walking through hell, either! I want us to be happy. I want us to love each other again! I love you, and I want you to love me back! I want you to love me," she sobbed, "I need you to love me!"

Eden could see by Rafe's face that her words had little effect except to make her angrier. She sat down in the doorway, her hands clasped together to keep them from trembling. She wished she could take everything she had done wrong back. Everything causing Rafe the pain she was seeing in her, everything keeping them from being happy together. She looked up and saw Rafe was looking at her with those gray-blue eyes, so full of hurt and fury.

"I wish I could take everything I did wrong back, but I know I can't. I want to fix things," Eden said desperately. "I really do love you, so much." She sighed heavily. "Rafe," she hesitated, "since you've come home, you haven't," she paused and looked away from her eyes, "you haven't told me you love me." She looked up. "Do you?" she asked shakily. "Do you still love me?"

Rafe sighed and looked away. "I don't know if it matters anymore."

"It matters," she said softly then swallowed back the hurt as it rose up in her.

"I just don't feel like I know you anymore. I'm not sure what we are or even who we are anymore."

Eden nodded her head, remembering all the things she had talked about with Greer. "We've both changed a lot over the past few years," she acknowledged. "We have a lot more pieces to our puzzles."

Confusion crossed Rafe's face. "Puzzles?"

"Yeah, it's something I talked with Greer about before you left. She talked about how people are like puzzles except we can grow and add pieces making the pictures of ourselves change."

"I see," Rafe said surprised Eden had been talking to Greer about anything except finding her in Mexico.

"I learned about a few more of your pieces, the things making you who you are. Things I never knew."

"Really?" she asked, uncertain of what Eden was talking about.

"Letty told me more about your mom," she paused, "and your friend Brettito," she revealed. "I learned you think they, and your father, kept some secrets from you. I think it's why," she paused, "one of the reasons why, when I had secrets, you had such a hard time."

Rafe's mind reeled. She wondered what Letty told her and if she really knew all the secrets surrounding their deaths. "She knows about their secrets?"

Rafe had asked her question so softly that Eden almost had not heard it. "She didn't know what the secrets were," said Eden shaking her head. "She just said you told her they were keeping secrets from you."

Rafe furrowed her brow thinking about what Letty might have said but couldn't remember what she had told her.

"She told me about them when you left and went to Mexico." Eden watched as Rafe rubbed her temples. Eden stayed silent and then took a deep calming breath. "I have an idea," she said suddenly, and Rafe looked over at her warily. "Since we're both so different now," she shrugged and bit her lip, "maybe we should start over and get to know each other."

Eden held out her hand toward Rafe. "Hi, my name is Jayne Eden Kingsley. Please, call me Eden. I hate hate, my first name. Mean kids at school used to call me Plain Jayne, so when I got into high school, I started using my middle name."

Rafe watched Eden as she sat on the floor and held her hand out toward her through the threshold, wondering if she was going crazy again. "Eden, I don't want to play games with you," Rafe said surly.

"I'm not playing a game. I'm serious," she said regarding her intently. "I want you to know exactly who I am now, and I want to know who you've become too." She held out her hand again. "Come on."

Rafe closed her eyes and rubbed her temples because she already knew the story of why Eden didn't use her first name. Eden told her the story the first time they went out together. It was not really a date, it was a brunch, the day after a party Eden's boss had thrown.

When she opened her eyes again, she saw Eden's determined look, so she moved to the doorway and sat in front of Eden in exhausted exasperation. She took Eden's hand and shook it. "Rafaella Salvaggio," she said and held on to Eden's hand as if it were the first time she had met her. "Please, call me Rafe. I'm sorry to hear you were teased in school. You're definitely not plain." She released Eden's hand.

Eden could feel the heat of Rafe's hand, warmed by her anger, surge into her own skin. She missed her touch as soon as Rafe let go. "Thank you," Eden said softly and smiled. "You're the most beautiful woman I have ever seen. Actually, until you touched me, I thought maybe you were just a vision in my mind."

Rafe gave a short laugh remembering when she told Eden the same thing when she was trying to convince her to sit for the painting. "I think I've heard your line before," she gave a small smile.

"Really?" Eden let a small amount of humor show in her smile. "Then you probably knew my ex. I should probably tell you I really messed up my relationship with her. I mean, really messed it up."

"Well, I've done some things I'm not proud of either."

"Whatever you did, I'm pretty sure it can't compare to the things I did. But I think, no," she shook her head, "I know, I've learned from my mistakes. But now, I've just changed too much for her to love me. I can't give her back the woman she first met, so I have to start over again."

"I see," said Rafe not knowing what else to say.

Pain washed over her because Rafe had not denied those words were true. "I think you should know, though," said Eden, "I still love her. But she says she's changed too." Eden watched Rafe play with the hem of her pants. "She was my first kiss," she cleared her throat, "my first kiss with a woman." Eden moved so she was lying on her stomach and propped up on her elbows but still didn't cross the threshold of the room. "I gotta tell you, it was life-changing." She smiled remembering their first kiss. "When was your first kiss?"

Rafe watched Eden spread out on the floor and couldn't help notice the curve of her body and the cleavage peeking through the opening of her shirt. She got up and pulled the pillows off the bed. If she was going to play her game on the floor, she wanted to be comfortable. She gave a pillow to Eden, put one on the floor for herself, and faced Eden, reflecting her position. "My first kiss was a secret," she confessed.

"A secret?" Eden asked and watched as Rafe's eyebrow arched in confirmation. "Secrets have got me into a lot of trouble."

Rafe frowned. "Me too."

"So," Eden said cautiously, "will you tell me about your secret kiss?"

As Rafe studied Eden, her mind went back to when she was twelve years old. She wasn't sure if she wanted to tell Eden about the kiss or the secrets surrounding it. It was so long ago and it had taken a long time for her to get past the pain and chaos caused by the kiss. If Eden knew the secret about the kiss, there was no way she would see her as good again. Maybe she never would see her as good again anyway. She cleared her throat. "I was twelve," she started.

"Wow," said Eden softly. "You really did start young," she smiled. "What happened?"

"I was on an adventure," she hesitated, "with my friends Gabri and Brettito."

Eden saw how uncomfortable Rafe seemed and wondered if her first kiss was someone taking advantage of her—someone who made her keep it a secret. "Was your first kiss with one of them?" she asked hesitantly.

"No," she said softly. Rafe looked into Eden's eyes as she decided if she wanted to tell her about the secret kiss, the kiss the led to so many other secrets. "Can I trust you? If I tell you, it's a secret. No one else alive knows about it—just me. No one ever talked about it if they did know about it. You can't tell anyone. Not your shrink, or Abby, or Letty, or a stranger, or anyone. Ever. If you do tell, and I find out," she glared at her threateningly, "you will never have the chance to regain my trust again. Never."

Eden listened to Rafe nervously not sure what to make of what she was saying. "What? Are you serious? Are you joking with me?"

"Dead serious," said Rafe evenly. "If you tell anyone, ever, there will never be any possibility of the precious forgiveness you crave given to you. You will never be able to gain my trust again, and you will never see me again—ever. Are you sure you want to know about my secret kiss? Are you trustworthy enough to take everything I tell you about it to your grave, even if it means walking through hell the rest of your life? Even if it means you lose everything by knowing it. Even if it makes you change your mind and walk away from me?"

"Rafe," Eden said concerned. "I don't understand how a kiss can be such big of a secret."

"I knew you didn't trust me," said Rafe as she smiled sadly. "You don't trust I'm telling you the truth and it needs to stay a secret."

"Why?" she asked nervously, hoping she was not destroying her chance to fix things. "Why do you have to keep it a secret?"

Rafe just stared at Eden for a moment. This woman, who never had to keep a real secret in her life. How could she have ever thought a relationship with her would work? She thinks she is walking through hell just having a fucking conversation. She doesn't have any idea what things should be kept secret and what should not. She kept all the information about all her fucking feelings and about Jake a secret and created a fucking nightmare. If she doesn't know the difference between what things should and shouldn't be kept a secret, maybe she should not know hers. "I'll tell you about a different kiss. One that wasn't a secret," she said. "I was fourteen," she started.

"Wait, wait," said Eden nervous from watching Rafe's eyes shift back and forth as she thought. "I trust you. I just wanted to know why it was a secret and why I have to keep it a secret." Dread ran through her at the possibility she had pushed her too hard. She watched Rafe feeling guilt and fear, wondering if Rafe was breaking down again.

"I can't tell you about it or why it has to stay a secret—unless you swear never to talk about it and understand what will happen if you do." She shrugged indifferently. "All I can tell you is it's very important to me that it's kept secret. You'll be the only other person alive who knows about it. Can I trust you? Do you really trust me like you claim you do?"

Eden looked away from Rafe's gray-blue eyes and took a deep breath. She couldn't let her stop talking, and if somehow knowing this would help her, she had to know. But if she promised not to tell, how could she get help for her? If she told, and Rafe found out and left again—she could not finish the thought. She looked up into Rafe's eyes and made her decision. "Okay, I promise," she said softly.

"No, you have to swear on your life," said Rafe calmly watching Eden closely. "Swear with your name, *lo giuro sulla mia vita prendo questo segreto nella tomba.*"[3]

"Rafe, I don't know Italian," she said hesitantly. "What am I saying?"

"It means you swear on your life you will take this secret to the grave," said Rafe solemnly. "Say it, *Americano e Italiano.*"

Eden swallowed and took a breath. "I, Jayne Eden Kingsley, swear on my life I will take this secret to my grave," she swore then Rafe helped her with the Italian, and she swore again in *Italiano.*

Rafe gave Eden a small smile after she said the words. She felt a little sick that she was going to tell her, but now she had no choice. She had to tell her the story. "Don't forget," she said, "if you ever tell anyone, don't come looking for me." She watched Eden nod and lick her lips anxiously.

With a soft voice, Rafe began telling Eden about her secret kiss.

---

[3] I swear on my life I take this secret to the grave.

22

TWELVE-YEAR-OLD RAFE SALVAGGIO ran through the streets of Florence, Italy, with her friends Gabri and Brettito. Rafe's dark hair was hidden under the cap Brettito had given her with the *Fiorentina* logo. They had been on a school trip to the Palazzo Pitti and decided to skip because they had been there many times with Rafe's mamma who gave free art lessons for kids there sometimes. They deliberately, and easily, lost their group in the garden behind the palazzo and made their way to the bridge—Ponte Vecchio. With their school bags on their shoulders, they made it to the tourist-crowded bridge. The tourists were milling around all of the shops and food vendors taking pictures and admiring goods. The three friends weaved their way in and out of the crowds and took a shortcut through an alley leading below the bridge.

The trio decided to get close to the river and see what kinds of things they could find. Tourists were always losing things off the bridge or throwing different things like stones or coins for reasons that eluded them. Once they saw a college student throw a bicycle off the bridge. Another time, one threw all the art he had created into the river.

As they walked down the alley to get under the bridge, they saw a girl walking toward them. The girl smiled at them as she approached. Rafe thought she was beautiful. She stopped in her tracks, looking at the girl as she walked by and Gabri and Brettito kept walking. Rafe was entranced and couldn't take her eyes off the girl. When the girl passed the trio, she whistled shrilly. It was then they knew the girl was *zingara*, gypsy girl.

From the side streets, some *zingari* boys appeared and ran past Rafe. They pushed Gabri and Brettito down, and they took Brettito's school bag, stripping it from his shoulder. Rafe was stuck in place and could only stare as the girl slid Rafe's bag from her shoulder. Gabri and Brettito took off after the boys, and as soon as Rafe came to her senses, she ran after the girl.

The girl was fast, but so was Rafe. She chased her down the ally and under the bridge. The girl made a mistake, or maybe it wasn't, but Rafe cornered her between the bridge and a drop off into the river. She turned, flashing a smile Rafe found fascinating.

"You're a beautiful boy," said the girl, breathless from running.

"I'm not a boy," said Rafe with a laugh as she took off her cap revealing her curly, dark, shoulder-length hair. Rafe scrutinized the girl again as she smiled, happy she had cornered the *zingara*. "You're beautiful too," she said returning what she thought might be a compliment, but still determined to get her belongings back. "Give me my bag," she demanded.

The girls just smiled at Rafe brazenly. "I took it, so it's mine," she said. "The only way you can have it back is if you take it from me or if you trade me something for it."

Rafe ran up to her and grabbed the bag from her hands, and the girl let go easily. *"Grazie,"* said Rafe with a triumphant smile.

The girl leaned back against the bridge and sighed then smiled again as Rafe turned to leave to go find Gabri and Brettito. "I see how you look at me with burning eyes," said the *zingara.*

Rafe turned and scrutinized her again. The girl was dark everywhere, dark hair, dark skin, dark eyes all enhanced by the bright colors of the scarves in her hair and her clothes. Rafe knew she was older by maybe two years or three. Rafe didn't speak. She wasn't sure what the girl meant.

The dark girl took advantage of Rafe's silence. "I cannot go home with empty hands. I will trade with you."

Rafe laughed because the girl didn't have anything to trade unless it was one of the scarves wrapped in her hair, and she did not want those. "You have nothing I want," Rafe told her.

The girl looked down, very sad, and then lifted her head slightly as Rafe turned away. "I can trade you *mistici segreti,"* she called out.

Rafe turned back intrigued. What twelve-year-old would not be stopped in their tracks at the possibility of learning mystical secrets? It was an adventure Rafe couldn't resist. She turned back to the girl. "Okay, I will trade my bag for *mistici segreti."*

The girl smiled and beckoned Rafe closer. Rafe put the bag behind her back. She wanted to make sure the girl was not going to trick her and take the bag again. She stepped closer, and the girl grasped Rafe's shoulders. The girl pulled her, turning her and then pushed her against the bridge. Since Rafe was holding her bag behind her back, her arms were pinned.

The dark *zingara* smiled and moved her face closer, then Rafe felt the girl's lips on hers. At first, in her surprise, she fought the kiss. But as the girl held her against the bridge, and as Rafe tasted her, she stopped fighting and let the girl kiss her.

The girl pulled away and smiled. "Now you know the *segreti di la magia ragazza amare le ragazza,*"[4] she said heavily into Rafe's ear.

Rafe didn't really understand what she meant, and she wasn't able to speak. Once again, the girl kissed Rafe, and this time, Rafe couldn't stop herself and kissed her back. As Rafe's head spun, the girl reached behind her back and easily took the bag from her hands. She pulled away and laughed beautifully then walked away as Rafe stared after her frozen in place. The girl turned back and smiled again, then disappeared around the corner. Rafe took a deep breath and shook her head to clear it, then ran after her. But it was too late.

The girl was gone.

---

[4] mystical secret of the girl loving the girl.

23

RAFE SALVAGGIO COULD see the scene, and the beautiful dark girl from her childhood, in her mind perfectly, even though it was so long ago. She smiled sadly. "It was my first kiss, my secret kiss."

Eden looked at Rafe with wide eyes. "Your first kiss was with a gypsy girl, under a bridge, in Italy," she said softly then licked her lips and swallowed. "It's so romantic," she said in astonishment.

"I guess," said Rafe with a small smile and a shrug. "I don't know if she was really what I know now are Romani or if she was just part of some transient group. I just know what the adults at the time called them."

"So, you knew you were gay then and kept it a secret?"

Rafe turned over and lay on her back. "Not exactly." At the time, she didn't have a name for what she felt or what loving a girl meant. Not until later, when she learned others considered her feelings *amore morboso*.[5] She took a deep breath and sighed. "It was a secret leading to other secrets. It also led to the death of my mamma and Brettito."

Eden sat up with concern. "You think your first kiss caused their deaths?"

"I know it did," said Rafe as she tried to keep memories and images of their deaths from her mind.

---

[5] morbid love

"Well," she hesitated, "how? How could a kiss lead to their deaths? I don't understand."

Rafe rubbed her temples, closed her eyes, and ignored Eden's questions. "You wanted to know about my first kiss. Now you know. What was yours?"

"You know mine, Rafe." Eden chuckled. "You were there."

"No." Rafe shook her head with her eyes closed. "I wasn't your first kiss. I was only your first kiss with a woman. I can't claim to be anyone's first kiss anymore." Rafe sighed. "After high school, practically everyone has had a first kiss. So, tell me." She really didn't need to hear because she already knew about Eden's first kiss. Eden told her a long time ago. She just wanted her to stop asking questions so her head would stop hurting.

As she bit her lip, Eden looked across at Rafe. She needed to know why Rafe thought her first kiss led to her mother and her friend's death. She wondered if it was part of her PTSD or something else. She remembered Letty telling them about the death of Rafe's mother, and then Brettito's death and how Rafe was found covered in his blood. She remembered the horror she felt for her when she heard what she had gone through.

She lay back down over the pillow and propped herself up on her elbows. "I was sixteen. It was behind our church," said Eden as she thought back to her first kiss. "I was very nervous. His name was Levi, and he was very sweet. I remember wondering why everyone was so excited and talking about kissing. After we kissed, I didn't see what the fuss was," Eden admitted and shifted her body. "After the initial nervousness, it was kind of anticlimactic."

Rafe chuckled because the story was much shorter this time. She left out how everyone thought the two would marry until his family moved away. "Well, not everyone's first kiss is earthshattering."

"I did have an earthshattering kiss, though. The one I had with you," she declared.

"You've never kissed me," said Rafe softly and turned over to look at Eden. "We've just met."

Eden smiled back at Rafe. "Oh, yeah. Well, then, it was with my ex. Her kiss changed my life. If it had been my first, I'm sure I would have understood exactly what the fuss was when I was sixteen. Whenever she kissed me, I felt like I could float away and nothing else mattered."

"She sounds like a really good kisser," Rafe said with a small smile.

"Oh, she was." Eden nodded. "She is! No one has ever kissed me and made me feel like she does."

"Too bad you messed up so bad with her," Rafe said wryly, "but there are plenty of fish in the sea, as I hear people say."

"No, not like her." Eden shook her head. "Not for me. I don't think she can be replaced by just anyone. It's going to take someone very special to be able to take her place," she said softly.

Rafe watched Eden as she shook her head and her golden hair fell forward. Rafe reached out and pushed it away from Eden's face. "Sometimes, I feel the same way."

A rush went through Eden as she felt Rafe gently move her hair. "I would do anything to have her back," she confessed. "Could you take your ex back?"

"I don't know," said Rafe as she looked into her eyes. "I gave up so much and fought so hard." She sighed. "So much was lost. In the end, it turned out to be all for nothing. Nothing except for my daughter, who I love very much."

Stricken, Eden pulled her gaze away and closed her eyes to keep her tears from falling. "It sounds bad," said Eden when she got her voice back. "I'm sorry you had to give things up and lose things. Maybe you can get them back someday."

"I don't know," said Rafe. "It would be hard, impossible for some things. Others, I'm not sure if I want them back."

"What don't you think you can get back?"

Rafe looked unwaveringly into Eden's eyes. "Trust mostly. I think it would be the hardest thing to get back."

"So, you can't trust her?" Eden said trying to hide her misery. "I agree. Trust could be hard for you to find again."

"No," Rafe shook her head, "for both of us. I don't think she trusts me either anymore. I think she stopped trusting me a long time ago. I'm not really sure why she stopped, but for some reason, I'm not worthy of her trust."

"You're worthy," Eden said softly, "I trust you."

"No, you shouldn't trust me," warned Rafe. "I'm a stranger. You should make me earn your trust. Just like you have to earn mine. Don't tell my secret," she reminded with a slight rumble.

"I hope I can earn your trust," she said softly. "I won't tell your secret." Eden tried to swallow, but her throat was dry. "Hey," she said with a forced smile, "are you thirsty or hungry? Maybe we can go talk in the kitchen, and I can make you something." She wanted to get her into a new place and hoped the new surroundings would help her.

"You go ahead," said Rafe as she sat up. "I think I need to stay here in my room."

Eden watched Rafe stand and stretch her body. "Well, you have to eat," she said knowing Rafe was not eating much lately. The evidence was in how thin she had become over the past month. "What if I made something and brought it to you?"

"You don't have to," said Rafe. "I had lunch with Julia today."

Eden watched as Rafe turned her back on her, went to her meditation spot, and then sat down. She didn't want them to stop talking. She got up and went into the kitchen knowing Rafe needed to eat even if she did say she ate with Julia earlier. She started making dinner thinking about Rafe, wondering how she could fix things between them.

24

IN THE KITCHEN, Eden Kingsley opened a bottle of red wine to let it breathe. She put a pan of water on to boil then began making her homemade Alfredo sauce to make chicken Alfredo. As she cooked, she smiled remembering the first time she made the dish for Rafe. Rafe told her how she had never eaten fettuccini Alfredo before she came to America and how strange it was to her when she tried it at the insistence of one of her father's clients. Rafe said she had been surprised it tasted good, and when she tasted Eden's, she said it tasted even better.

Everything came together, and she had two plates heaping with fettuccini noodles and chicken, garlic bread and a salad.

Eden put the plates on a tray along with silverware and wine glasses. She carried everything through the house to Rafe's door. At some point, Rafe had closed her door, so Eden sat everything on the floor then went back to the kitchen and got the bottle of wine. When she had everything set up, she knocked on Rafe's door.

"Rafe?" she called and put her hand on the handle. "Rafe, can I open your door?"

"It's not locked," Rafe said from inside.

Eden opened the door and saw Rafe still in the same position. "Rafe, I don't really want to eat alone, so I brought you some food. Will you eat with me?"

Rafe had been suffering through the delicious smell of the food wafting through the house. She knew whatever it was Eden had made, it would be very good, and her body was betraying her by wanting it. "Sure," she relented. She got up, went over to the doorway, and saw what Eden had made. If it were true, the way to a person's heart was through her stomach, Rafe would have no choice but to fall in love with Eden again for cooking one of her favorite meals. She sat down in front of the doorway where Eden had set out the food. "This looks really good, thank you."

"No problem. I used to cook for my ex all the time," she said as she sat on the floor and handed a plate to Rafe. "She always said she liked my cooking."

"She was very lucky," said Rafe as she took her plate and sat down across from Eden. She used her fork to swirl a small amount of her pasta into a bite-sized portion and began to eat. She did like Eden's cooking, and her version of this dish was the best she had tasted because she knew it was always made with love for her.

Eden watched with a smile as Rafe ate then began to eat her own food. They ate in silence for a while, and Eden tried to think about how to get Rafe to talk with her more. She knew they could not fix everything in a night, but if they could just get through tonight, well, maybe they could fix things one day at a time. She wanted to earn back Rafe's trust and show her she could be trusted too. "So, Rafe, tell me about yourself. Where do you work? What do you do?"

Rafe put her fork down as she lost her appetite. It looked like Eden still wanted to put her through the 'starting over game' she was playing. "Right now, I don't do anything," she said then took a sip of wine. "I just go to my stupid therapy and then screw around all day, unless I have Bronte here." She didn't want to share what she did all day. It was her time, and the things she did should be of no concern to Eden. She knew Eden didn't really want to know about all the things she had to take care of with her father's properties and investments. She was just asking to fill the silence. "Where is she anyway?"

"Oh, she's with Letty and Ephraim tonight. Ephraim said it was cookie night."

"Oh," said Rafe, "maybe she'll be able to cook for herself soon. Hopefully, he'll teach her to cook things besides cookies."

"I think it'll be awhile before she cooks for herself. She's only two," Eden said with a smile. "She likes to help when I make dinner. At my old place, we used to make pizza. She really liked making it, and we had a lot of fun. I haven't had the chance to make pizza here." She waited for Rafe to respond, and when she didn't, she changed the subject. "But you have a job still, with the Conservatory. Right?"

"Maybe. I don't know. I'm on a paid leave. I don't know if they're going to take me back or not. I don't know if I want to go back."

"What will you do?"

"I don't know, Eden," she said annoyed. "I gave up doing the job I loved the best with the company I built with my father. I gave it up so I could be home more with the woman I loved and my daughter. I didn't mind selling it because I thought I would be here with them, and we would be happier having more time together—but I came home one day, and they were gone. So, instead, I got to come home to an empty house after every trip I had to go on to finish projects and sign paperwork to sell it because it was too late to back out of the sale. I barely got to see my daughter for almost a year, and I had no idea why my ex started letting me see her again until I found out she was being targeted by some fucked up religious group."

Eden tried not to cringe at her words but failed. "I'm sorry. I'm sure it must have been very hard," she said shakily and took a sip of her wine. "Do you really think she started letting you see her again because of the..." she hesitated, "the group?" She was afraid mentioning the *Stewards* by name would upset Rafe even more.

"I've had no other explanation."

Eden put her plate down and stood up. "I'll be right back." She went into the guest room then came back and sat down. She unfolded a wrinkled piece of paper and put it on the floor in front of Rafe. "This is why I started making sure my ex was able to see our daughter more. I let someone convince me I was doing the right things when it came to them seeing each other. When I read this, I knew the things we were doing were wrong. I know now she never did anything to cause me to doubt her intentions with our daughter, and I was wrong to keep them apart." Eden watched as Rafe just stared at the piece of paper. She could tell Rafe knew exactly what it was. It was the letter she wrote to her mother. "I read the letter every time I had to have a confrontation about the subject. It gave me the strength to fight against him harder."

"I feel sorry for your ex and your daughter," said Rafe flatly.

"You," Eden stammered. "You do?"

"Yes, I do. Don't you?" she asked evenly.

"I–I don't know what you mean."

"What I mean is, when it comes to them, you don't have a mind of your own. You let other people hurt them. You stood by and allowed it until you found some pitiful letter your ex had written after they both had already suffered so badly. A letter not even meant for you. Only then did you think about how they must be feeling. You seem like a person with a lot of empathy," said Rafe, her words dripping with doubt, "but maybe, you just didn't have any for your ex. Maybe, it was because you never really loved her. Maybe, you were just becoming unhappy with the situation you were in, so you used the letter for yourself more than for her."

Eden looked up at Rafe, her heart cut by her words. She shook her head in denial. "No," she said softly. "I know I always loved her, and I still do."

Rafe pushed the letter back toward Eden. "Maybe you should keep this so you can look at it and remind yourself your ex is human, she has feelings, and she has suffered because of you." She took a sip of her wine to cool her temper. "I guess those are hard things for you to remember without a note."

Tears burst from Eden's eyes, and she couldn't stop them. She wiped them away with the back of her hand and took a deep calming breath. She glanced at the letter and then at Rafe. "I told you I really fucked things up," she said hoarsely. "I know it's no excuse for hurting you, but I was going through a lot too. I had a lot of anger, fears, and anxiety problems that I'm just now able to reconcile and sort out. It's hard to think about other people when you can barely even think because of what's going on inside yourself. I have better tools to cope now, and a good therapist helping me."

"Great," said Rafe unfazed by her tears. "Hope it all works out for you."

Eden picked at her salad feeling defeated. She wanted things to go in a different direction for a while. "Why do you say your secret kiss caused your mom and your friend's death?"

Rafe was silent for a while as she scowled. "I just do." She didn't want to talk to her about the past. It was too painful to dig up. She rubbed her temple and sighed. "I don't want to talk to you about those things. You're a stranger, remember? You haven't earned all my trust yet."

"Okay," Eden relented. She could see Rafe was digging in, and Eden knew, if pressed, it would just get worse. "Why didn't you ever talk to your ex about it?"

"Let me tell you about my ex, the woman I loved," said Rafe sadly avoiding the question. "When I met her, she was so open and saw everything in such a positive way. It was so different. She would just tell me everything on her mind without even thinking about what she was telling me. It felt good to be so trusted. It felt good knowing no matter how silly I might have privately considered her thoughts to be, she would share them because she could trust me with all of them. When she was hurting or feeling anxious about something, she would tell me everything through her tears, and she never left anything out. She actually completely trusted me with everything. It made me feel good to be the one she came to, even if I couldn't help with what she was going through. She had to make a lot of hard decisions when we met. Ones I never had to make. Sometimes, it was agony watching her fight through her feelings and not being able to tell her what I thought she should do. I had to trust whatever decision she made, it would be the right one—even if it meant she had to walk away from me. I trusted her, and when she stayed with me, I thought she knew she made the best decision for herself. Now, I wonder if she did. I wonder if her decision was based on something more arbitrary than being in love with me and knowing herself honestly."

Eden was confused though she knew Rafe was talking about when she was having problems with her parents and had to make the decision to break from them and stay with Rafe. "Arbitrary? I stayed because I was in love with you and wanted to make a life with you."

"Are you sure?" Rafe asked skeptically. "Maybe it was just easier for my ex to stay with me than continue to deal with her parents. She seems to have a habit of taking the easiest way out, even if it wasn't the best way, and it put her in danger. It seems like now, talking to me, has turned into a very hard path for her. Now, it looks like I'm in the same category she put her parents in. I'm left behind and rarely thought about."

"Not fair," Eden said softly. It hurt, and she was trying not to cry. "You're not the same as my parents. If you think hearing the things you're saying to me is hard for me—you're right. And I'm still here. I haven't left you behind."

"Sure. It must be very hard for my ex," said Rafe with a shrug. "So, I'm sure some other stranger will make things easier for her, and she'll go with them, but when it gets hard, she'll probably leave them too."

"I'm not leaving," Eden insisted as tears of anger and hurt slid from her eyes.

"Today," said Rafe. She got up and put her pillow back on the bed then picked up her wine glass. "I'm going outside. I need some air," she said and walked past Eden then making her way to the patio.

Eden watched her walk away and shook angrily as she picked up all the dinner things then took them to the kitchen. "What am I doing?" she asked as she put the dishes in the sink and leaned over it. She had no idea if she was dealing with Rafe or with her stress issues, or both. She thought things were getting better and now she may have pushed her back into a bad place. "I don't know what I'm doing," she said to herself. She heard the music outside turn on, so she took a breath, picked up her glass of wine, and then headed out to see what Rafe was doing.

Outside in the dark, Eden found Rafe on one of the loungers holding her wine glass and looking up at the stars. She sat down on the lounger next to hers then leaned back and sighed.

"You don't have to follow me everywhere," said Rafe churlishly. "I don't need a babysitter or a mother, even though you think I do."

"I know," Eden said shakily. "I heard the music and just wanted to come outside. I don't want to fight with you."

"Good."

"You exhaust me sometimes," said Eden and closed her eyes.

They sat silently for a while then Rafe turned to Eden who was sitting back with her eyes closed. "Are you still hurting?"

"What?" Eden said as she opened her eyes turning her head toward Rafe.

"Are you still in pain? From what he did to you," she said not wanting to say Jake's name.

"I'm fine. I still have a little soreness. All but the worst bruises are gone." She wanted it to be clear she really had recovered from the injuries Jake had caused. "I really am much better now. You don't need to worry."

Rafe looked away and out at the pool. She drank the rest of her wine in a single gulp and then sat the glass down. She stood up and started to strip off her shirt.

Eden watched as Rafe took her shirt off then unbuttoned her pants, pushed them down, and then kicked them off. She took in a sharp breath at seeing Rafe in just her underwear and bra in the soft low pool light. It was so hard being close to her and not being able to touch her. She watched as Rafe walked to the edge of the pool, dove in and then swam to the end of the pool and back.

When she got to the edge of the pool, Rafe lifted herself out then went back and sat down on her lounger. "Your turn," said Rafe.

"What?" Eden said as she took in Rafe's wet, more than half-naked body.

"I said your turn. The water feels good, and it's a nice night for a quick swim."

"Oh, no thanks."

"Don't worry, it's dark. No one will see you with your clothes off."

"I'm not worried. I've swum naked in the pool before, Rafe. You were there."

"No, we just met. I've never seen you swim naked in the pool."

Eden gave a short laugh. "Well, then, I'd have to say, since we just met, I'll pass. I've learned it's best for me to go slow and think things through before I take my clothes off."

"Ah, playing hard to get. Good move," Rafe purred and grinned at Eden.

Eden smiled back glad she seemed to be in a better mood. "You look great without your clothes on and dripping wet. Makes me wish I knew you better," she said, aching for her.

"The dark hides a lot of flaws."

"If you were my ex, I'd tell you I love all your flaws."

"If you were my ex, the woman I loved so much I told you about, I would have already had your clothes off and be having my way with you."

"She would be lucky."

"I would be lucky," said Rafe as she sat up in her chair. "I'm going inside. I need some sleep."

"Rafe, you really do drive me mad sometimes," said Eden frustrated at Rafe's teasing. "Good night."

25

JERKING AWAKE FROM her nightmare, Rafe Salvaggio sat up and rubbed her temple to make the phantom pain go away as she shook slightly in panic. Following her doctor's orders to tell someone when she was feeling the phantom pains, she got out of bed and walked to Eden's room. She knocked, but there was no answer. Opening the door, she looked inside, letting her eyes adjust.

Eden's bed was empty.

Panic ran through Rafe again as she stepped into the room to look closer. She looked in the bathroom and Eden wasn't there. *Where is she*, Rafe thought to herself as her heart raced. *Has she left me again?* She frantically started looking through the house and still couldn't find her. *I knew this would happen*, she thought as her body shook. *I knew she would leave again.* She stopped and took a calming breath then noticed the patio door was still open. She went outside to continue her search.

Relief ran through her body as she saw Eden asleep on the lounger. She knelt down beside her. "Eden, you should wake up and come in the house," she said softly. Eden didn't respond. Hesitantly, Rafe touched her shoulder and shook her gently. "Eden, wake up," she said a bit louder.

Eden opened her eyes slowly, and she looked up at Rafe. "Are you okay, babe?" she asked sleepily.

"Yeah, I went to your room, and you weren't there," she said shakily.

She could see the panicked look on Rafe's face and sat up. "Oh, I'm sorry. I'm here, babe."

"Let me help you get inside." Rafe took Eden's hand and helped her up. Gripping her arm, she started walking her inside.

"I'm fine, Rafe. I'm awake now," she said as she let Rafe lead her inside. She realized this, other than their handshake, was the first time Rafe had touched her purposely for any length of time since she got back home and they played their joke on Abby. "Are you okay? What did you need?"

"I just. . ." said Rafe as she maneuvered her into the guest room, her whole body shaking. "I just needed you to be in your room," she said and led her to the bed. "Here, get in," she said and started helping Eden into bed.

"Rafe, I still have my clothes on. I need to get into my pajamas," Eden said and tried to get back up. Rafe ignored her and pushed her back on the bed, so Eden just let her put her to bed with her clothes on.

Rafe put the sheet over Eden, then stood up and licked her lips, and wiped her hand over her face. "Okay, I'll go lock all the doors," she said and left the room.

Eden sat up in bed and listened as Rafe made her way through the house closing and locking the patio doors then walking through the house checking doors. When she heard her in the hallway, she called out softly. "Rafe, are you okay?"

Rafe did not answer, and Eden saw the bedroom door as it pulled closed. She listened for a while, then got out of bed and put her pajamas on. Worried, she slipped out of her room quietly and went to Rafe's room. She opened the door, peeking inside, and saw Rafe lying on the floor with a pillow looking up at the ceiling. Eden walked carefully over to her. "Rafe, why are you on the floor, babe?"

Rafe looked up at Eden and turned over. She got up and got the other pillow from the bed and sat it above hers then lay down again on her back.

Eden realized the pillows were set up like they were when she was outside Rafe's threshold. She knelt down beside Rafe. "Is this pillow for me?" she asked surprised Rafe wanted her to stay in her room. Rafe nodded. "Okay."

As Eden got on the floor, Rafe turned over on her stomach, so Eden lay on her stomach too. As they faced each other Eden worried as she noticed Rafe had a light layer of sweat around her hairline. "Rafe, did you have another bad dream? Are you okay?"

Rafe looked in Eden's eyes and moved a little closer to her. "I'm not a stranger," she whispered. "I belong here."

"I know. It was just a way to help us know each other again," said Eden anxiously under Rafe's fevered gaze.

"It hurts me, you needing to pretend I'm a stranger to tell me things," she said then turned over onto her back. "Go to sleep."

Eden felt like she'd had the wind knock out of her. She just wanted to be able to talk and not fight. She turned over and lay on her pillow, feeling guilty and sad. Rafe's scent surrounded her, making her want to hold her and kiss her, but they were lying head to head. She wanted to say so much more but knew she couldn't right now. She shook as tears ran quietly down the sides of her face. "Goodnight, Rafe," she said softly.

"Keep my secret," Rafe whispered.

"I will," Eden promised again softly.

She lay there listening to Rafe breathe. When she could tell Rafe was asleep, she got up and pulled a cover from the bed. She put it over Rafe then went back to her room. She climbed into bed, closed her eyes, and quietly cried herself to sleep.

26

JULIA HAWTHORN SURVEYED all the paperwork on her desk, glad it didn't include anything new added by Rafe today. With all the extra time on her hands, Rafe had been creating a lot of work. Some of it, Julia's father was looking into to do for some of their other clients. Julia wasn't looking forward to the additional workload.

Julia sighed and took a sip of her office coffee. The coffee was terrible. The new intern had no idea what she was doing. Its only redeeming quality was the bitter taste kept her from falling asleep on the job.

She thought about yesterday and the adventure she went on with Rafe. Remembering Rafe's shaking hand, she wondered if it meant anything or not. Rafe seemed to be better when she came home from Mexico. Now, after going through her therapy here at home for almost a month, it seemed there should be some measurable progress. Julia worried Rafe needed more support than what she was getting. She hated to admit it, but she may have to talk with her father about Rafe.

Julia picked up the phone, punched in a number, and waited. "Hello, Emma. It's Julia. Is my father available? I'll hold." Julia waited on the line until her father picked up.

"Julia?" Ian Hawthorn's voice came through the phone. "What can I do for my girl today?" he asked, happy to hear from his daughter.

"Daddy, I saw Rafe yesterday, and I'm worried about her."

"Worried? Is she still sick," he asked with concern.

"Yes, she's still sick, and I'm not sure if things are going well for her. She apparently had a big setback yesterday."

"I'm sorry to hear that. I thought Rafe would be getting her life back by now."

"Me too," she said feeling helpless. "She called me for an adventure and we drove to Malibu in her father's car," said Julia. "Her driving is still as precipitous as ever."

Ian chuckled. "Sounds like the Rafe we know. That could be a good thing. Maybe she just needs more time."

Julia wasn't sure if it was a good thing. "It's more than her driving," she said. The suddenly leaving town, dangerous antics, high-speed driving, and the sometimes cruel 'I don't give a fuck' attitude—she knew these were not just part of her PTSD. She didn't know how to tell her father she thought Rafe was turning back into the person she was before she settled down with Eden. "I think she might need more help than she's getting."

"Have you talked with anyone there about your concerns?"

"Not yet," she admitted. "I was considering calling Greer for help and checking on getting her placed somewhere again."

"Placing her sounds serious. Is Rafe still seeing a doctor?"

"Of course," answered Julia. "I just think Greer could handle her better. Rafe might listen to her." It seemed like Greer did the best at managing Rafe—much better than Eden was doing.

"I met Greer, you know. She's a very interesting person. I've taken an interest in some of her work. I can contact her if you'd like."

Julia frowned wondering exactly what type of interest her father had in Greer. He already held Rafe on a pedestal and now it seemed he had another person taking up his time and attention.

"It was just a thought. I don't want to do anything before I have more facts," Julia said. "I'll let you know if I need you to call her." It was frustrating because now she knew she would have to talk with Eden. Working with Eden would be easier than dealing with Rafe, but it seemed like it was just as hard. She thought by now Eden would grow up and start taking Rafe more seriously, but she was still like a child who had to be told what to do. Julia had visited Eden so many times without Rafe's knowledge to tell her what was going on and how she needed to take some sort of action. She wondered how many times she'd have to warn Eden she was getting close to losing Rafe.

"You know I'll help Rafe in any way I can, pumpkin. Tell me what you're thinking."

"Well, I'm thinking about taking some time off," she said. "I think Rafe needs someone there to help her. I wonder if she might need more than just the therapy she's getting. Like I said, she may need to be placed. I hope not. It would be a last resort. I'm just worried."

"I hope you're wrong. This is hard to hear because Rafe's always been very strong."

Julia closed her eyes and bit her lip. "I know, Daddy. She is strong, but I don't think this has to do with strength. I think it has to do with all her loss. She really hasn't dealt with it, and apparently, before she went to Mexico, she had been bringing things up about her mom and her friend in Italy. You remember what her dad was doing to her. He punished her with her mother's death every time she got in trouble."

"I remember. She's been through a lot," agreed Ian, "but it seems she's always come out stronger. She had to be strong to survive her father." His voice was filled with disfavor. Ian had never really liked Ettore.

Rafe's father was a real son-of-a-bitch and was the most ruthless person Julia's father had ever dealt with. The article written about Rafe was not far off about how Ettore Salvaggio, Rafe's father, had dealt with the acquisitions of important properties or big contracts for restoration, not just here in the States, but all over the world. The guy had Italian politics down and used all his knowledge learned from dealing with the sometimes corrupt and volatile systems to deal with his business interests. Julia's father tried to deal with him for years, and finally, just stopped returning his calls—personal and business. However, for some reason, Ian Hawthorn thought Rafe was something special and remained in contact with her throughout her life, even if it was just in the wings.

Julia leaned back in her chair. "If all those things are surfacing, and she's going back to her old mindset, she really will lose everything she's built."

"I know you'll do your best to take care of Rafe. She's been your best friend for a long time. Take as much time as you need. Just call me if you need anything."

"Okay, Daddy. I'll will. Thank you, Daddy. I love you too." She hung up the phone.

It was clear, no matter how frustrating, she would have to talk with Eden. Rafe didn't want Eden to know how she used to be before they met, but some of the old Rafe was surfacing. Julia had witnessed the dramatic change in Rafe after meeting Eden. She knew Rafe loved Eden. But still. Sometimes, she thought she should just convince Eden to leave. Rafe might be more open to letting her help, and things would be less complicated. It might even open the door that always seemed closed between them. It was difficult to balance friendship while wanting more. But right now, she knew Rafe needed her as a friend.

Julia gathered her things together and told the girls she was taking time off and blessedly gave them all the work on her desk. She headed out wondering if she would ever be as important in her father's eyes as Rafe seemed to be. Maybe, if she and Rafe ended up together, her father would think of her as worthy of the same attention he gave Rafe and Greer.

27

IT WAS FRIDAY, and after a lot of consideration, Julia Hawthorn called Eden to arrange to meet for a long lunch at Julia's condo to try to talk with Eden about Rafe. She hated to betray Rafe, but, at this point, she thought it was time Eden knew some things about her. She knew Rafe thought everything would be different and none of the stuff before Eden mattered. But with the trauma that happened to Rafe, it looked like it all mattered again. If Eden left again after learning about the 'real Rafe,' then Julia knew she would just have to be there—hopefully, as more than a friend.

Julia wanted to tell Eden to take off the rest of the day rather than a couple of hours, but decided to see how their conversation went. Pulling into her condo parking lot, Julia saw Eden was already there waiting. She got out of her car, a shopping bag with their lunch in hand, and walked over to where Eden was parked.

"Hello," said Julia as Eden got out of her car. "It looks like you found the place well enough."

"Thank god for GPS." Eden smiled, though she was wondering why Julia wanted to meet at her condo. "I don't get to this side of town much. Why didn't you want to meet at the bistro?"

"I need to talk to you without all the others around," she said as she led her toward the building. She unlocked the door and they went inside.

"Wow, this is a great place," said Eden as she looked around the condo and then out at the ocean view.

"Thanks." Julia sat the shopping bag on a side table and took the bag with their lunch to the kitchen. "It took a bit to find, but it's a brilliant place. It's further from work, but it has more amenities than my old flat." Julia pulled out pre-cut vegetables, hummus, and flatbread from the bag. "Rafe filled the place with art and a few unusual pieces of furniture for a housewarming. It's all just on loan, of course. She thought some of this stuff would help me impress women." Julia laughed and arched her brows suggestively.

"Well, I'm impressed," admitted Eden with a short laugh. She recognized some of the art from Rafe's collection on the walls and strategically placed on small tables. She raised her eyebrows at the fact Rafe had loaned Julia her sculpture by Pasquale Delor of two women kissing but didn't say anything. It wasn't the most expensive or the most erotic sculpture Rafe had, but she and Eden had picked it out together.

"As soon as I have time, I plan to hire a decorator," added Julia as she got drinks ready. "But I'm never one to turn down Rafe's generosity."

Eden sat down at the kitchen table. "So, what is it you need to talk to me about?"

"Rafe came to see me after your meeting with Katheryn," said Julia. When she had everything for lunch on the table, she sat down across from Eden. "How do you think she's doing?"

Eden shifted nervously and took a sip of her iced tea. "I don't know. Rafe's been angry a lot," she revealed. She didn't want to go into detail about the angry words, slammed doors, and the outbursts that left things like dishes or some of Rafe's many projects broken. "She's been controlling herself better, so I thought things were going well. There were times when she was very sweet, especially when Bronte is home. Then we saw Katheryn. When I got home, after looking for her half the night, I found her in her room. Things were scary at first, then just upsetting and sad. I don't know what to do, and now it's like I can't do anything right. I called her therapist and told her what happened with Katheryn." She looked down trying to carry the burden of the secret Rafe made her promise to keep. One she couldn't even tell Julia. "Now Rafe's avoiding me, and I don't know what to do or how to talk to her without causing her stress or anger. Her moods change so quickly, I don't know from one moment to the next when it's Rafe and when it's her PTSD."

"She picked me up in her father's car for our adventure after your meeting with Katheryn," Julia told her. "Letty was right thinking Rafe still had it. We drove it out to Malibu for a long lunch."

"I'm not surprised she kept it," said Eden as she ate. "I am surprised she didn't tell anyone."

"I think she has started taking it out a lot. Eden, when she drives the thing," she paused, "I don't want to say she's reckless, but she's not exactly a model for safety. She's taken to wearing her father's cap too. It was an exciting ride, but I felt like I was hanging on for dear life most of it."

Eden put her hand to her head and pushed her hair back as she sighed. "I can't take it away from her. I don't even know where she keeps it. I can ask her, but I have no idea if she'll tell me or not."

Julia shook her head and frowned. "This is about more than taking her car keys away. She clearly isn't doing better. As a matter of fact, I've seen her regressing into—" She stopped herself.

"Into what?" asked Eden concerned. "Julia, what did she do or say when she was with you Tuesday?"

"This is not just about Tuesday," said Julia firmly. "It's been since before you left her the first time and you two were going through all those issues. Some things have been subtle, but other things have escalated to the obvious. I'm worried how much more they'll escalate." She looked at Eden, hoping she was doing the right thing. "Eden, you can't depend on Rafe just to take care of you anymore."

"What?" Eden asked in surprise. "What do you mean, take care of me? We split everything. I contribute just as much as she does."

"This isn't only about financial things," said Julia trying to clarify. "It's everything—financial, emotional, physical. . . everything. You're going to have to grow up. You're going to have to learn some things about Rafe and the way she was before she met you. When you do, you may even have to learn to live without Rafe in your life, too. She may not consider me a friend either," she said under her breath, "if she decides I've betrayed her by telling you things."

"What are you talking about?" Eden asked anxiously. "You're scaring me, and Rafe already scares me enough right now!" she said trying to control the volume of her voice. She wondered if Julia was talking about the secret from last night or if Rafe had another secret only Julia knew.

Julia watched as Eden fought to control herself. She considered leaving Eden out of the whole thing. Rafe would probably be less angry if she did. She didn't know if Eden was capable of handling what might be coming. Even Rafe complained Eden had always been bad in stressful situations. She remembered Rafe holding Eden together when she was dealing with her parents and other issues through the years.

"Eden, you have to understand something. Rafe was a different person before she met you. Not a bad person, just. . ." she hesitated, "more adventurous." Eden started to speak, and Julia held up her hand to stop her. She leaned toward Eden. "I don't know how you can be so dense. Fucking Abby is always going on about Rafe and her 'wildling ways,' and you always ignore it while Rafe is doing her damage control," she said with frustration. "I kept silent because it looked like Rafe had grown out of her old behaviors and was making a good life with you."

"Well, I guess I am dense, Julia," Eden said bewildered. "I get it, Rafe used to date a lot of women, one of them being Abby, and some were hurt by the way she treated them, but what it has to do with anything going on right now is beyond me! So, please, explain it to me!"

Julia took a sip of her tea then sat it down carefully. "You have to understand..." she hesitated again, "Rafe hasn't had the kind of life you or I have had. A lot of things have happened to her. And now a lot of things are happening again." She gave a short nervous laugh. "I always thought I had such a hard life until I met Rafe."

"What are you talking about?" asked Eden unable to imagine Julia ever had a hard life.

Julia scoffed. "It seems like a miracle she's lived this long."

Eden looked up stunned and upset. "Why is it a miracle? What happened to her?"

"Calm down. I just mean she's done so many crazy things. Like when she jumped off the bridge in Mexico. You said it looked as though the thing was about to fall down and she jumped anyway. She used to do similar crazy things all the time, but around the time she met you, it all seemed to stop."

"She's told me about her childhood, how you two met and use to go on adventures," said Eden. "She took me on some adventures too. She took me to St. Croix, and she took me to Point Udall, the place where the sun first hits the United States. It's where she asked me to live with her. We also went to Italy and to France and a lot of other places."

"No," Julia shook her head, "it may be her definition of an adventure with you, but just going on a vacation was not her definition of an adventure when we would have them," she explained. "When Rafe was young, she didn't need a mother— she needed a prison guard. She was fucking criminal in a lot of things she did and was as wild as Abby describes, but more so than even she really knows. If my father didn't think he had some sort of bond with Rafe and wanted to help her, I'm sure he would have kept me far away from her. I'm still not sure exactly why Daddy is so partial to her, but I do know he hated Rafe's father."

"Whoa, Julia, slow down," said Eden overwhelmed. Julia was calling Rafe wild and criminal. . . It sounded crazy to her. "I can't believe Rafe was some sort of criminal, and her father was a very nice man. Rafe loved him."

"Yes." Julia sighed at Eden's naivety. "She did love him. But he was not a nice man. Haven't you ever heard Letty talk about him? She hates him. My father called him a ruthless tyrant. He even stopped doing business with him."

"He was always nice to me when we visited. Why do they all hate him?"

"First, the man really was ruthless. He was tight in Italian politics and all the corruption surrounding it. He put all those skills into his international real estate business, and the guy was good at what he did," she explained, repeating the rumors and assumptions always made about Ettore Salvaggio. "Second, he really was the tyrant Letty described in how he treated Rafe. He may have hidden his sociopathic side from you, or maybe you just couldn't see it, but it was there. None of us know why Rafe practically worshiped the man. He was horrible to her."

"How?" asked Eden. "How was he horrible? He seemed so generous. Rafe said he gave her his car when she moved out here, and he sent me jewelry for my birthdays and Christmas.

They were always working together, and she never mentioned any problems."

"I'm not saying he was horrible to her all the time," she backtracked, "but there were times." She shook her head. "You know her mother died when she was twelve, and she practically saw it happen, right?"

"Yes, Letty told us. It must have been so horrible for her."

"But Rafe never told you about it?"

"No, she just told me her mother was in an accident and had died." She had never pressed Rafe to talk about her mother. She learned early on Rafe shared what she wanted to share and some subjects were off-limits. Eden thought little of it since she didn't talk about her own parents often either.

"Every time Rafe did something wrong," Julia stopped and shook her head, "well, got in trouble with a teacher. If she made him mad somehow or when he was just pissed off about something, and Rafe was around, he would bring up Rafe's mother and her death in some way. He would feed the guilt she felt over her mother's death. I think, in a way, he blamed her. I know she blamed herself for some reason, and her father used it against her when he was angry."

"She was just a child, how could he blame her?" It was hard for her to believe Ettore was as bad as Julia and Letty portrayed.

"He just did," Julia said emphatically. "I heard him. The first time I heard him, we were caught ditching school, and he was yelling at her, half in Italian and half in English, but I got the gist of the conversation. He was saying her mother died taking her to school, so the least she could do was go to class. Like she had dishonored her memory by skipping, and if she weren't a troublemaker, she would still have a mother. It was horrible and scary, but she just stood there and took it. She didn't even cry."

Eden shook her head stunned. "I had no idea," she said softly.

"I think it's one reason she was so adamant we never get caught on our adventures," Julia said thoughtfully. "I asked her about it once, and she told me not to worry about her papa. Her mama had defined her, and she was exactly what her mother told her she was—her wild child. She would just look at me with this crazy smile and laugh. Then we were soon off on another adventure. I think she truly used everything in her to be a wild child. From our adventures to challenging her father in business, and sometimes with women. I know Letty thinks the competition between them led to Rafe moving here, and I think she's right."

"I don't understand. Why would she hide part of herself from me?"

Julia laughed condescendingly. "During her wild-child stage, you wouldn't have lasted a minute with her. She would have had you the first night she met you and forgot about you before she left your bed. Come on, you saw how fast she got those girls to come home with her. She got three in one night, for fuck's sake! Do you think she called them again? The answer is no, she didn't. I was actually hoping she would. One of the women, Jillian, was actually nice and very interested in

Rafe. I can't tell you how relieved I was when Rafe started spending time with Greer. When I thought you were out of the picture, I was trying to convince her to stay with Greer." She hesitated, not revealing, in the beginning, she hadn't been happy with Rafe's choice in Greer and how serious they became so quickly. "Honestly, there were times I felt like she should give up on you and be with Greer, but she insisted she loved you and had to be with you," she said throwing up her hands.

Eden looked up at Julia, unhappy at the mention of Greer. She had come to like Greer, but still worried she might lose Rafe to her. "What are you saying? You think she should be with Greer?" she asked shakily, wondering if Julia was really being a friend.

"No, I'm not saying anything of the sort," she said seeing Eden becoming upset at the possibility Greer would return. "If you really do love each other, I hope you stay together."

"I do love her," she said desperately, "I can't help myself. Even when I was away from her, I was in love with her. I just had a lot of anger at her and myself that I had to work out. I'm so in love with her. Seeing her like this, and hearing the things that she's been saying to me, it's killing me. I know she's right. I made mistakes, but I didn't do those things to hurt her. But clearly, I did."

28

JULIA HAWTHORN NOTED Eden Kingsley was palpably upset. She imagined it was hard to hear certain things when you were the wearer of newly purchased rose-colored glasses. Since Eden returned to the fold, it seemed like she had forgotten all of Rafe's past transgressions. It was not her intent to upset Eden but just educate her.

"I'm glad you love her. She needs you to love her," she said to console and placate Eden, "but this is not just about the mistakes you made," said Julia firmly. "I'm telling you, Rafe was a match to her father in ruthlessness in everything she did. She studied at his feet. All the complaints published about her were nothing compared to how she was with everything she did, including women, in New York, Italy, England, France, Spain—wherever she was going to school or working. I don't even think you know how close to the truth the article was about their company and the properties and contracts they acquired."

Eden frowned as she sat silently remembering how angry Rafe was about the article. "Why wouldn't Rafe tell me all of this about herself?"

"She didn't tell you because she literally changed who she was," said Julia pointedly. "I think she changed the definition of herself and how she acted because she wanted to be with you. My father said it was as if she had suddenly grown up. Rafe didn't want you to know her as the person she was before—the one Abby is always harping on about. I think she knew she couldn't be with you and be the way she was then. Something about you, or how you met or, I don't know what, but something made her decide to become the Rafe you know."

Eden tried to take in everything Julia was saying. The person she was describing was not the woman she knew. Rafe was uncompromising at times and determined. She sometimes had little patience with people in certain situations. She could be controlling and definitely knew how to get her way. But criminal or ruthless, as Julia had described—not her Rafe. Rafe was kind and good. She was fair and sometimes had an idealistic sense of justice. With Bronte, she was so gentle and caring with everything from teaching her new things to teaching her to share with the others in art class. Her Rafe was full of passion and humor, and her Rafe loved her. She wanted to have her love again. She didn't understand how everything Julia was telling her was going to help with their problems.

"I don't know what you expect me to do with this information or how knowing it is going to help Rafe," said Eden. "You're telling me Rafe's a different person with me, so I might not be able to stay with her. Rafe's telling me she's changed, and I might want to leave her. I'm just not sure what to do or where to go from here." She looked up at Julia. "Last night, I tried talking to her again. I was hoping she would forgive me and we'd still be good."

"Wait a minute," Julia interrupted, "you asked Rafe for forgiveness?" she asked, remembering Eden mentioning this kind of thing once before, but she had shrugged it off.

"Yes." Eden nodded. "I've been asking her since she got back. I told her we needed to forgive each other. The other night, I told her I forgave her for the things she did, and it didn't go over well. She told me she didn't need my forgiveness."

Taking a deep breath, Julia leaned back in her chair then let the breath out slowly. "Did she give it to you?"

"I'm really not sure," said Eden remembering the argument. "She did what she always does and told me there was nothing she could forgive."

"So, in the past, when you asked for forgiveness, she just told you there was nothing to forgive?"

"Yes, and every time, she was always very sweet. I was always amazed at how she could make everything okay."

"Oh, Eden." Julia shook her head in disbelief. "I don't think you and Rafe have the same definition of forgiveness."

Eden wrinkled her brow. "How many definitions are there? Forgiveness is forgiveness."

"No, not in Rafe's world," said Julia. "You have to remember where she's from, and the life she's had. I'll bet you were taught forgiveness absolves all, and you believe all the 'ask, and you shall receive' stuff running along with it coupled with all those very American notions all tied into religion."

"I was taught if you do something wrong, or you hurt someone, you ask for forgiveness to show you know you did something wrong and you're truly sorry. If the person forgives you, they understand you're sorry and that you know you were wrong. This way you can both heal and learn from the mistake."

"So, you were taught forgiveness is like a learning tool then, and it somehow also helps with healing."

Eden thought about it and shrugged. "I guess."

"Well, I hate to tell you this, but Rafe has never actually forgiven you for anything."

"What?" Eden said in shock and feeling hurt.

"Not by your definition. You said she always tells you there's nothing to forgive. Well then, she's not giving you forgiveness. She has never said the words *I forgive you?*"

"No, I guess not. But she did forgive me because then we would fix things and we were always okay."

Julia rubbed the back of her neck then smoothed down her silver blond hair. "You may think she's given you the forgiveness you want, but she hasn't given you what you think is forgiveness—because, she can't, or won't, give you forgiveness in the way you understand it."

Julia realized Eden had no idea what she as talking about so tried to explain further. "When we were at school, we had philosophy together. Rafe got into a heated argument with the instructor about the concept of forgiveness and its modern usage. Rafe was really quite brilliant, still is actually," she said as she picked up her glass to take a drink, wetting her throat in preparation for talking about herself and Rafe.

29

WALKING INTO THE classroom, impeccable in her school uniform and her silver hair pulled back in a long French braid, Julia Hawthorn smiled when she saw Rafe had made it to class. Students had sat in the dark paneled room for over a hundred years, but Rafe made it her mission to be there as little as possible. Making her way to her seat, Julia sat next to Rafe. Rafe was disheveled, missing her jacket again, and her sleeves were dark from pencil lead. Julia stopped herself from suggesting again Rafe's father hire a maid to help at least get her out the door looking presentable. But she knew the problem wasn't with Rafe's father and the lack of a maid. Rafe just had no interest in how her school uniform looked or how she looked in it. More than likely, Rafe would get a demerit from one of the instructors, and she wouldn't care about demerits, either.

Julia's nemesis, Rebecca, had watched her walk into class and sit next to Rafe. Even after two years, she still made fun of Julia's English boarding school accent. Since Rafe was there, Julia could risk speaking without being teased and criticized. Rebecca felt intimidated by Rafe so would never say anything or make a scene if she knew Rafe would find out.

"You made it," she observed quietly as Rafe drew in her notebook.

"I've been informed the library is out of bounds to me for a month during class period. Plus, the copy machine is broken, so there's no volunteer work to get me out of class."

"How do you find all those ways to get out of class? Are you really volunteering?" Julia asked in disbelief. She never knew Rafe to do anything without some sort of ulterior motive.

Rafe looked up at the clock, ignoring Julia's questions. "Late again," she remarked. "Useless."

Julia hid her smile. She knew how much Rafe hated their philosophy instructor. Her constant tardiness was maddening to Rafe. The rest of the class didn't care as it was less time listening to the old daft cow.

It wasn't long before the instructor flounced in and demanded everyone take their seats and quiet down.

"Please forgive my tardiness," said the rather large woman at the head of the class.

Julia snickered as Rafe groaned and the rest of the class mumbled under breath. The instructor said the same thing every time she was late, which was quite often. Rafe tried to control her temper, but there was always a point where she could no longer hold in her flames of anger, and Julia would listen to her tirade with amusement during lunch. She suspected it would be time to hear Rafe's opinions on the matter again soon.

The instructor smiled as the students settled and waited for her to continue. "An interesting thing, forgiveness," she segued into what she hoped would be a lively philosophical discussion about the concept of forgiveness. "It will be the subject of today's discussion." She wrote the word 'forgiveness' on the blackboard. "Who would like to start the discussion?"

Rafe stood, and Julia mumbled, "Right, here we go then." She could see the tenseness in Rafe's body and knew it meant she was gearing up for a confrontation.

Rafe waited to be recognized and received the nod of acknowledgment. "I... and possibly everyone in the class," she began, and her volume grew with each word, "would like to know which form of forgiveness you require to feel better about being continuously late for the class you were hired to teach. Which form of forgiveness are we required to give for your decision to continue to be a poor instructor? Which form should be granted for a instructor who persists in wasting the time of her employer and her students, not to mention the wasted money of parents and any other entity giving money to this institution, in which we are all assembled and required to be subjected to your obvious disdain for us, along with your lack of knowledge of the subject you, somehow, have been granted leave to teach?"

Julia choked back her laughter and covered her mouth. You could hear a pin drop. Everyone thought Rafe had completely lost the plot.

It was clear the instructor was shocked at hearing the berating comment come from Rafe. The rest of the class was shocked into silence too because, one, Rafe rarely showed up for class, and two, when she was there, she usually ignored everything and everyone.

Rafe continued. "Would you like us to bestow upon you religious forgiveness, legal forgiveness, psychological forgiveness, medical forgiveness, social forgiveness, or some other personal characterization of forgiveness you will explain to us?"

"Which do you think would be most appropriate?" the instructor asked with a tolerant smile.

Julia shifted uncomfortably in her seat along with several other students. The instructor thought she was being smart by asking Rafe such a question, but Julia knew it was the wrong road to take.

Rafe remained calm. "None," she said firmly. "Personally, I won't be giving you any kind of forgiveness based on those categories or any other. If you really think you deserve some sort of forgiveness, you'll just have to give it to yourself."

The instructor turned a ruddy shade, angry at Rafe's impudence. "You're not very kind, Ms. Salvaggio."

"No, you're the one not being kind by constantly asking for something you don't deserve and is impossible for your students to give," Rafe argued.

Julia looked from Rafe to the instructor as all hell broke loose. The instructor started yelling at Rafe about how she was being purposely belligerent, and she was to go report herself. Rafe said if she has to report herself for being belligerent then so did the instructor.

It was a standoff as the instructor tried to stare Rafe down and intimidate her. Then the instructor got up her nerve. "Ms.

Salvaggio, you're being purposely disruptive and rude in this classroom."

Rafe very calmly pushed her book off her desk. It landed on the floor with a thud. Julia swallowed as Rafe stared at the instructor with the look she got when she was about to take someone down.

"That is the only thing I have done purposely in this classroom. The rest you invited me to say by asking for my forgiveness," said Rafe not breaking eye contact with the instructor.

The students murmured around Rafe. Julia and everyone in the class witnessed in awe as Rafe slagged her off.

"You've proven by your actions you've relegated the concept of forgiveness to nothing more than a way to not take responsibility for transgressions and wrongdoing, when, in reality, a punishment would be more appropriate," Rafe lectured. "Forgiveness is a corrupted concept created to guilt people into not taking appropriate action against transgressors. It should be left only for those people who continue to live in the mindset of the dark ages. The modern concept of forgiveness has been marginalized into a commercial concept to sell a product. The idea of forgiveness itself has been turned into a commodity to be bought, sold, and traded. The emotional currency of forgiveness is self-esteem, guilt, and shame, but it can also be traded out for very real cash."

It was all Julia could do not to cheer Rafe on when she got into one of her arguments. It was not long before Rafe started digging into the instructor personally.

"By asking your students for forgiveness for your own intentional choices you're corrupting the minds and emotions of youth. It is clearly abuse and argues to the point you should be dismissed from this institution."

The class looked on as Rafe continued what was a very well thought out argument for the instructor's dismissal. Meanwhile, the instructor was not listening but was screaming at Rafe to be quiet and present herself to the headmaster.

"Get out of my classroom and report yourself!" she demanded shrilly as several other instructors and students visited. The instructor's screaming and raving had drawn them in.

Soon, the headmaster walked into the classroom. "Silence!" he demanded over the screaming, mostly from the instructor who was still yelling. Rafe just continued to stare at her unwaveringly.

"Ms. Salvaggio is inciting discord and being belligerent," she insisted. "I demand she leave my classroom and be taken to task."

The headmaster turned to Rafe. "What happened?"

She spoke very calmly. "Our esteemed philosophy instructor is unable to have an unemotional debate regarding the concept of forgiveness. It's clear the woman is unqualified to teach me anything." Rafe picked up her book and walked out of the room.

Julia grinned at the audacity as Rafe made her way out, stopping only to knock once on Rebecca's desk. Julia knew it was to remind the girl not to pull any of her bullshit while she wasn't around or there would be trouble. Rebecca scowled with the rest of her friends as they watched Rafe leave.

No sooner had Rafe walked out the door, the class erupted, and all the students came to her defense. The arguing and chaos continued for a week, and it all led to the dismissal of the instructor. All the students agreed it was to their benefit.

It was rumored, when Rafe's father found out, he supposedly bought her a diamond bracelet with a large blood red ruby in the middle. Rafe sold it and bought the instructor a bust of the philosopher Herodotus. Someone said when the instructor got it, she smashed it to pieces and cursed Rafe's name. But it was all just a rumor. Julia never admitted she was the one who started the rumor. She loved the attention being the friend of Rafe brought her in a place where she was ostracized otherwise.

30

HER EYES GLITTERING with the memory of her school days, Julia refocused on Eden. "The point is that Rafe doesn't think forgiveness fixes anything. She also doesn't feel it's something she, or anyone, should be asking for or be given in the sense it is some sort of a commodity to trade for mistakes or choices."

Eden was unsure what to think. "Okay," she said slowly. She glanced down at her plate then up at Julia. "So, do you think it means she's still holding everything I asked her forgiveness for against me? Does she not believe me when I tell her I forgive her?"

"No," Julia shook her head, "it's more like she feels like whatever you did, it's not up to her to forgive you. So, there's nothing for her to forgive. As far as you forgiving her, well, I don't think she will ever ask for forgiveness. If you told her you gave it to her, she might be insulted you think she would believe she'd need it."

"She never acted insulted. She acted like we were good."

"Well," said Julia with a shrug, "maybe, with you, she just lets it go. Like Abby says, she does treat you differently."

Eden looked down at her plate, wondering how they could fix anything if forgiveness was not part of the solution. "But she really didn't treat me different if she never gave me her forgiveness."

"Just the fact she acted like everything was okay was different," said Julia, "but the forgiveness is just one example of what I'm talking about, Eden."

"Just one example? What else did she do?"

"If you can think it up, she probably did it," said Julia adamantly. "She was a fifteen-year-old wild-child growing up in New York without fear, almost no real supervision, and a large allowance that included her own credit card." Julia hesitated. "I can tell you some things, but other things, I can never tell."

"Why," asked Eden nervously, "why can't you ever tell? How bad could a fifteen-year-old be?"

Julia laughed. "Fifteen? This stuff happened all the time until a continent separated us when she went off to college. She shipped off at seventeen, mind you because her father couldn't be bothered about getting her into another school in New York for her last year of high school. He bought her way into an intensive college prep program then somehow arranged for her to take college entrance exams. She passed them, of course, and started college in Milan. But her antics and adventures continued whenever we saw each other on breaks. I joined her less and less, but she found others to join her, and she just got better at what she was doing and more adept at not getting caught." Julia took a sip of her tea. "I can't tell you some things because she made me swear on my life I'd take our secrets to the grave. At first, I thought it was a lark, but I soon found out—it was dangerous to break those promises."

Eden swallowed hard. She had just made the same kind of promise to Rafe. "Dangerous?" was all she could force out.

"Yes," said Julia with certainty. "She had this way of making sure if she told you the consequences of revealing the secret, and you told anyone, the threat would happen. Anything from getting kicked out of school to bodily damage depending on the secret." Julia shuddered at the memories. "It wasn't ever pretty. She was like an Italian mafia boss sometimes." Julia saw Eden was pale. "Don't worry, she never killed anyone or anything. She never made those kinds of crazy threats. Just things she knew it was in her power to actually do and she knew would be something very convincing or even scary to the person keeping the secret."

"So," said Eden shakily, "she made those threats to you back then, and you're still keeping her secrets?"

Julia nodded. "Absolutely. Even if I know now there would be no way she could carry out the threats anymore, I still won't tell. It would be a betrayal, and who knows what she might do instead. She's been my best friend for a long time, and I'd like to keep her my friend. She's like a lover," Julia hesitated, hoping she had not given her real feelings away. She continued, eager to make sure Eden wouldn't catch her mistake. "More like a sibling, because my father adores her. She was there for me and helped me when I was in need of a friend."

"Does she still have you swear like she did in school?" asked Eden wondering if this was something Rafe did with a lot of people.

"Not anymore," said Julia with a wave of her hand. "Now, she'll say I have to swear, but never puts conditions on it. Like I said, she stopped the majority of her old behavior patterns by the time she moved to California and the rest of it about the time she met you." She wiped her mouth with her napkin. "Has she told you about her name?"

Eden looked up at her with a frown. "Her name? What about it?"

Julia grimaced. "Her middle name, Erodotie, has she told you about it?"

"No," said Eden with confusion She had just always assumed it was just an unusual Italian name.

"I asked her about it. She said it was the Italian adaptation and feminized name for Herodotus. She said it was her father's favorite philosopher."

"Like the bust you said she sent the instructor?"

"Supposedly sent," Julia clarified, just in case Eden ever talked to Rafe. She didn't want Rafe figuring out she was the one who started the rumor. "And, yes. When she told me about her name, I looked up the philosopher. It was strange, so one day, I asked her about it. The guy was called the 'Father of History' but also the 'Father of Lies.' I asked her why her father would want to name her after him."

"Why did he?"

"I still don't really know. She just cryptically said 'he wanted me to know who my father was' and laughed, and then got up and took off." Julia watched Eden look down at her hands and could tell she was having difficulty with hearing about Rafe. She decided to tell her something less disturbing about Rafe to balance the scale.

"It wasn't all bad," said Julia trying to sound upbeat. "Some things she did were outrageously funny." She smiled to reassure her. "She got in trouble one time for not bringing her dress-out clothes for athletics." Julia couldn't help her grin at the memory. "You have to understand, Rafe has always been beautiful. You remember the way she showed up for the obstacle course? Well, imagine it at sixteen."

Julia gave Eden a moment to get a picture in her head then continued. "The instructor told her she better find a way to come prepared or face reporting herself, so she came out onto the athletic field in just her bra and underwear. When she was asked what the hell she was doing, she said she found a way." Julia laughed with amusement. "Well, it got her escorted to the counselor where she spent athletic time for two weeks. But when she went, she changed her clothes in front of the counselor each day to be dressed out. Her dressing out antics apparently so unnerved the counselor, she turned in her resignation. Rafe said the councilor was enjoying looking at her body too much and couldn't handle the fact she was a closet lesbian, and she should thank her for setting her free," Julia divulged.

"When the HM got wind of what happened, he sent an official letter to Rafe's father saying she had crossed the line, and he needed to go to the school for a meeting. It's what made Rafe's father pull her out of school and put her in a fast track college prep school. Then he sent her to Italy where he got her into college right after she turned seventeen. It's how she graduated college before all of us and ended up continuing with school for her doctorates. She was really pushed by her father, but I think she was also just driven."

"So, you knew Rafe was gay in high school? She didn't keep it a secret?" asked Eden.

Julia scoffed. "Not only wasn't it a secret, but it was also a challenge to everyone. It was an all-girls school, and she did have a few girlfriends, but unacceptable behavior, between same-sexes, was frowned upon, more than frowned upon really. Anytime it came up, the faculty tried to handle it quietly. They didn't want paying pupils pulled or alumni to pull pledges. Rafe had this way about her. She was always unavailable, untouchable, and it seemed like it made everyone want to be around her. If she talked to you or smiled at you, everyone made out like it was a big deal. When, actually, she really gave no one else any thought. She was too busy keeping her father off her back, pulling in top grades, and planning adventures. Most adventures took place outside of school. She dated more girls who weren't in our school anyway." Julia shrugged off the hurt of the memory. "She said it was more of an adventure."

"She's still kind of untouchable at times. Especially for me right now," said Eden sadly.

"Eden, you have to know," Julia paused, "the reason I'm telling you these things is not to upset you or make you think badly of Rafe. It's to help you understand her better. To help you see, if you can't be as ruthless in keeping this relationship as she might become in pushing you away, you will lose her." Julia studied Eden for a moment, wondering again if Rafe splitting with her would be such a bad thing. *It would be so much easier to deal with Rafe if Eden was not in the way,* she thought then pushed the thought back down. She knew if they did ever break it off, and Rafe thought she had anything to do with it not even all the begging and beer in the world would be enough to get back into Rafe's good graces. "Right now, Rafe needs all of us, even though she'll tell you she doesn't need anyone."

Julia stopped short of repeating how Rafe had been a much different person since meeting Eden. Abby had said it enough, so there was no need to remind her again. "Of late, she's been nothing like her father," she said. "I know it's one thing Letty's afraid of—that Rafe will turn out like him, alone even though he was surrounded by people. I think the only people who really loved him were his wife and Rafe. Maybe they were the only people he allowed or demanded to love him. But Rafe, she has all of us. I know we all really love her." She noticed Eden wringing her hands anxiously. "You know, even Greer kept saying she was irresistible. But now, I can see her pushing us all away."

"I know she's been pushing me," said Eden sadly trying to ease her anxiety about everything Julia was saying and feeling the painful pinch in her nerves at hearing Greer's name again. She wished Julia would stop bringing her up. "I can feel it every time we're in the same room." She looked up at Julia. "How is she pushing you and everyone else?"

"It's little things," said Julia. "With me, she's been holding back and not telling me things like she used to, like what she told me in Canada. She never mentioned what was going on between you until she left the hotel." Julia watched Eden flush red but pressed on. "The other day, I could tell there was more on her mind, but she chose her words very carefully. So, she's not talking as much and not challenging me anymore," she said concerned. "With everyone else, it seems she's tolerating them but can't wait to get away from them. I think she's been spending too much time alone, too. I know you said you thought you were doing well, but I think you might be wrong."

"She's been going to therapy. When I ask her about it, she tells me it's going fine," said Eden with a sigh, feeling like she was failing. "I try to talk to her, but I get nowhere. How can I get to know her better if you're banned from telling me about her? Abby only knows crazy dating stories, and Rafe constantly rakes me over the coals with all of my mistakes and bad choices. How can I be ruthless when I just want her to love me? I don't want to hurt her anymore or be cruel. I just want her to be the woman I love and to love me back," she said anxiously. "What's the point of telling me all of this if it can't help us?"

"The point is," said Julia firmly, "I think she's regressing into the person she was before she met you. I'm afraid of what will happen because of the trauma she's been through recently. Add on top of it all the childhood things between her and her father and the way he treated her—frankly, it has me worried. This is why I keep saying you need to grow up and stop depending on her to take care of you. You need to step up for her and take care of her right now. This means not asking her to take care of your emotional issues and waiting for her to tell you everything's okay. You have to make them okay yourself. You have to fix the things she can't right now."

"I don't know what to do, Julia!" Eden couldn't hold in her frustration. "You're saying I don't have her forgiveness. She won't tell me she loves me, she will barely touch me, she gets angry and uses her words to tear me apart and push me away. Then sometimes at night, she panics if she can't find me. Sometimes, she looks at me like she does when she wants to make love, or says things to make me laugh, and I think she might just tell me she loves me soon. I told you, I just don't know what's really her or if all the stress is breaking through."

"This is why we have to watch her closely," Julia declared. "We have to spend more time with her, and, if necessary, we may have to find a way to get her placed again—even if it means calling Greer and her doctor friend. If Rafe decides to take off again, there may be no way to get her back, even with Letty's power of attorney, and especially, if she goes to Italy."

"Julia, I have to work. I've already taken off all the time I can for a while," said Eden feeling helpless and trapped by the limits placed on her. "I have to keep my job so I can stay in the house and not break the cohabitation agreement. I have to take care of Bronte. I want to help her, but it seems like the things I need to do to help will end up pushing me further away."

"I understand," said Julia as she nodded, knowing the situation Rafe put Eden in with the cohabitation agreement. "I've talked to my father and have taken some time off to see if I can help. I don't expect you to do this all on your own. I'll enlist the others too. Just give me some time to talk to them. I only hope we haven't put things off too long."

167

It may already be too late for Eden, but maybe not for me, thought Julia.

31

FOR THE REST of the day, as Eden Kingsley tried to work, she went over everything in her head that Julia had talked about. Apparently, Rafe was somehow changing back into who she was before they met. Eden was uncertain if she and the person Julia described could be together. According to Julia, it would not be possible.

As she drove home, she felt her old anger toward Rafe build inside again. She wondered if Rafe was untruthful about who she really was and if their relationship had been built on a lie. Maybe it was why Rafe cheated. Eden didn't want to be in a relationship where they would have to be ruthless and hurt each other. She wanted the relationship she thought they had when they first met, a relationship where they loved each other and were truthful.

Eden sighed because she knew trust was the biggest problem they were having. It was one Rafe had already pointed it out to her. She had even talked to Rafe about it before she moved back into the house. It looked like neither of them had been trustworthy and truthful with each other. Eden knew she kept secrets, and it was upsetting to Rafe. But now, it looked like Rafe was the one who had all the secrets. It didn't seem fair Eden was being punished for having had secrets and Rafe could keep all of hers.

It felt like she didn't know what or who she was going home to anymore. She wondered if Rafe had the same feeling about her. Maybe it was why Rafe said she didn't know what they were anymore. Eden shook her head, remembering telling Rafe she couldn't go back in time and be who she was back then. Now Rafe might not be the same woman she thought she was, either.

Eden pulled into the driveway and saw the garage was open. As she got out, she heard pounding coming from inside the garage and knew Rafe had started a new project in her workshop. She pulled her briefcase from the back seat, and as she started walking toward the garage, Rafe stepped out with Bronte in her arms and pushed the button to close the garage door.

Rafe was in her old work clothes. It had been a long time since Eden had seen her dressed to work on a construction site, and she couldn't help but smile at how great she looked in her jeans, sleeveless denim shirt, and old black work boots. The only things missing were her tool belt and the old hard hat she had to wear in hardhat zones. Both Rafe and Bronte were covered in dirt and sawdust, it looked as if they both had been working hard.

"Hey!" Eden said with a smile. "Looks like you two have had a fun day."

"Oh, we did." Rafe grinned at Bronte. "Right, B Girl?" Bronte clung to her mama's neck. "She got to wear eye and ear protection, and use all kinds of tools today."

"She looks worn out," said Eden. Bronte reached out her grime-covered hands toward her. "I see you got really dirty today," she said with a smile for her messy daughter. "I think I'll let your mama carry you in for a bath before dinner." She chuckled then realized she lost her anger at Rafe as soon as she saw her with Bronte.

"Bath time is our next stop, right, B Girl?" asked Rafe as she tickled Bronte, making her giggle. "Let's go," she said as she turned and walked to the house.

Eden watched Rafe walk away and had to close her eyes at the sight of her and how good she looked. *Why do I have to want her so much*, she thought. She shook her head to clear it of the image making her head spin before following Rafe into the house.

After changing, Eden went to Rafe's room and knocked on the door. "Hey, are you two all clean in there?" she asked through the door.

"All clean," called Rafe. "Here comes the naked baby. Catch her if you can!" Rafe laughed as Bronte ran out of the bedroom and into Eden's arms.

"I got you, naked girl," Eden cooed as she lifted Bronte and kissed her. "Let's go get some PJs on." She took Bronte into her room where she helped her open the dresser drawer. "Okay, babe, what do you want to sleep in tonight?" Bronte looked in the drawer and pulled out a princess nightgown.

"Okay, you picked a good one. Let me help you put it on." She helped Bronte with her pajamas then ran a comb through her hair for about three seconds. Once Bronte heard Rafe, she squirmed away and ran out of the room. Eden heard Rafe ask Bronte if she was hungry and knew they were on their way to the kitchen, so she headed after them.

"What shall we have for dinner, my girl?" Rafe asked Bronte as she looked inside the refrigerator. "A jar of pickles? No?" She laughed as Bronte giggled. "How about tomatoes and prosciutto? No, are you sure? Hmm, I guess this means we have to use the stove." Rafe sighed dramatically. "You know what this means," she said and put Bronte down. "*Corri!*[6] Run from the kitchen! The stove is about to be used!" She laughed and ran out of the kitchen behind the squealing Bronte.

Eden laughed softly as they ran out and Rafe helped Bronte get out a few toys. "You know, if you make her run out of the kitchen every time the stove gets turned on, she'll never learn to cook for herself."

Rafe walked back into the kitchen with a grin. "It's for her safety. Sometimes, I've been known to burn things."

"Oh, yes," said Eden. "I remember the infamous broiler incident."

"Yes and the flaming pan of death!" Rafe laughed and winked. "So, it's best if she's far away before I turn on the beast."

"Well, I'm here to save you both," said Eden and started getting out ingredients for dinner.

---

[6] Run

"Are you sure? I can make some pasta and some grilled cheese sandwiches with prosciutto and tomatoes in the toaster oven. You can go hang out with the B Girl and relax."

Eden smiled and shook her head at the dishes in the sink. She could see Rafe had made something for Bronte, but it did not look like Rafe had eaten anything. "Based on the dishes in the sink, I have a feeling it's what you made for lunch. We need to get a vegetable in her and something in you." She looked up at Rafe, and then she quickly pulled away from her gaze feeling guilty for having another secret—her conversation with Julia. "Go play and see if you can get her hair combed," she said. "You can make the salad later."

32

AFTER FINISHING DINNER, Rafe Salvaggio and Eden Kinsley played with Bronte until her bedtime and then tucked her in with a story and kisses. Rafe made her way to the kitchen and started cleaning things up and putting food away. Eden came in and sat at the counter, so Rafe poured the rest of the wine into her glass and served her. "Thank you for fixing such a nice dinner," she said and went back to cleaning.

"No problem," said Eden and sipped her wine, wishing Rafe had eaten more than a few bites. "What were you working on today?"

"Nothing, really," said Rafe as she filled the dishwasher. "Just a project to keep Bronte and me busy."

"Okay," said Eden as she nodded and held her wine glass. "How was your therapy session?"

"Fine," said Rafe shortly as she dried her hands.

Eden watched as Rafe finished with the kitchen then made herself a scotch. She was getting those short answers from her again. She knew there was more Rafe should be telling her. "You always say it's fine, but you never tell me if you think you're making progress or if you think it's helping you. Is it helping?"

"I guess." Rafe shrugged off the question. "I'm going to sit outside for a while."

Eden watched as Rafe took her scotch and walked out through the patio doors. She took a sip of her wine as she wondered if she should just go to bed and read over a few scripts she had brought home or go out to try to talk to Rafe again. She remembered Julia said they needed Rafe to talk and not leave her alone so much, but every time she tried to talk with her, Eden felt beat up or guilty for saying the wrong things.

There was really no decision to make. She needed to try to talk with Rafe. She took her wine out onto the patio and found Rafe in a lounger by the pool again. It was a nice night and clear enough to see the stars. She sat down on the lounger next to Rafe and put her glass of wine on the table.

"Rafe," she started hesitantly, "I'd really like to know how your therapy is going. Is the doctor telling you to talk to your friends or to me? Do you like her? Are there things I should be helping you with?" They were all the questions she had asked many times before but never got any real answers.

Rafe sat silently and sipped her scotch. All she wanted was some quiet time outside. She didn't want to talk or *think* about anything. She just wanted some peace tonight. She knew Eden would keep pushing like she did every night unless she could get her off the subject.

"I've been thinking of buying back into my old business."

Eden looked up in surprise, "Really?"

"Yes," said Rafe forcing a smile. "I found a property I like, and it looks like a great project to work on. It's an old art deco hotel someone tried to convert into a single-family home. They've done a very bad job, but I think I can fix all the things they've done wrong."

"Sounds like a big project."

"Pretty big," she agreed, feeling the excitement a new project could bring run through her. "But I think, if I buy it, I should keep it a boutique hotel. The renovations will mostly be making some of the rooms bigger, updating the kitchen, and making system updates. I'd like to keep the art deco design and just freshen up everything."

Eden could see the excitement for the project on Rafe's face. She knew Rafe wasn't sure about going back to the Conservatory. Maybe, with what happened there, it would be best she didn't go back. "It's good to see you happy about a project again," she said. "I hope it works out and you can buy back in. I know how much you loved your job."

"Thanks," said Rafe and took a sip of her drink. She hoped they could sit and just be quiet now and enjoy the silence.

Eden took another sip of her wine and looked over at Rafe. She knew Rafe had changed the subject to avoid answering her questions. She laid her head back and closed her eyes, taking a calming breath as she did. "You looked really good in your work clothes. Really hot," she said softly.

Rafe looked over at Eden and chuckled. "So, dirt turns you on, huh?"

"Only when it's on you," said Eden as she opened her eyes to look at Rafe in the low light. She was caught by surprise to see Rafe looking at her intently. She almost tore her eyes away but decided she didn't want to stop looking at her. She missed touching her and being close to her. It hurt not to be able to hold her and comfort her when she knew she wasn't doing well. It was so hard keeping the distance Rafe said she needed. The way Rafe looked at her, Eden wondered if she really wanted the distance or not.

Eden got up and stood over Rafe. Taking the drink from Rafe's hand, she sat it on the table. She sat down close to Rafe and then quickly held Rafe's hands against the lounger. "I see how you look at me with burning eyes," she said softly, like the gypsy girl under the bridge.

"What are you doing?" Rafe tried to ask as she felt Eden kiss her. She turned her face from her. "Eden, please," she said softly. "Don't."

Eden took Rafe's face in her hands and kissed her again, small kisses on her face and the corner of her mouth and longer ones on her lips. Rafe stayed still and closed her eyes.

"I love you, and I want to show you," said Eden between her kisses. Rafe had closed her eyes, and Eden decided she didn't care if Rafe responded or even kissed her back or not. She wanted to feel her face against hers, breathe in her breath again, and just be close to her. She moved her face against Rafe's and moved her body, so she was curled up in her lap like she used to do. The only difference now was Rafe's arms weren't around her, and she wasn't returning her kisses. Eden felt the difference profoundly, and it hurt. She felt like there was a hole in her soul, and she knew only Rafe could fill it again.

Rafe kept her eyes closed as she felt Eden rub her face against her, kissing her. She could feel the softness of her skin and the light flutter of her eyelashes against her cheek. Eden's scent surrounded her, and she could smell the sweet aroma of the wine she drank on her breath. She fought her body's natural response to wrap her arms around her and kiss her back. She fought to calm her heart rate and her breathing while she searched inside herself for the anger she had at Eden for everything she had done. She fought to keep the walls up she felt she needed to keep herself from giving into her. She was not ready to be close to her. She wasn't even sure she should be close to her anymore. She clenched her hands into fists to keep them from moving involuntarily and touching her.

Feeling Rafe's body stiffen under her, Eden sighed then ran her hand over Rafe's face and shoulder. "You shouldn't fight against your love for me," she said softly and kissed her cheek gently. "I fought against my feelings for you for a long time." She put her head on Rafe's shoulder and nuzzled into her neck. "It took me a long time to come to my senses, but I had to give up fighting my feelings for you because I love you and can't be without you." She ran her hand gently down Rafe's face and rested it on her shoulder then closed her eyes and hoped Rafe could feel she was telling her the truth.

Rafe sat unmoving as Eden lay against her. She remained silent after Eden's confession about fighting her feelings. She still wasn't sure Eden really knew what her feelings were no matter what she confessed. *Tomorrow, she may change her mind, or her feelings may change.* Rafe sighed with exhaustion at all she was fighting and dealing with. She just wanted to have a quiet drink and relax, and now she found herself being a pillow for Eden both emotionally and physically, and she felt a bit used.

It seemed like Eden always took, but she never really gave anything back. Eden always needed something or wanted something from her. Just like now. She wanted to be close, so she just took it. *What about what I want or need*, thought Rafe. *Time away, time alone, personal space, time to think, silence.* She needed those things right now, and Eden was making it hard to have them.

After working through her frustration and bringing herself back into a calm state of mind, Rafe could tell Eden was asleep. She wondered if she should wake her and tell her to go use someone else for a while—some stranger again.

Instead, she put one arm around Eden and the other under her legs and then sat up. She turned her body then stood with Eden in her arms. As she carried her inside, Eden wrapped her arms around her neck with a sleepy sigh.

Feeling Rafe's arms wrap around her, Eden began to wake. By the time they made it to the bed, she had realized Rafe had carried her inside and was surprised again at her strength. She had never carried her before. As Rafe pulled away, she reached out and held her hand to keep her close. "Thank you," she whispered. "Thank you for just letting me be close to you for a while. I love you."

Rafe pulled away gently. "Go back to sleep," she whispered, and then walked out of the room, hoping to get some dreamless sleep for herself.

33

JULIA HAWTHORN WALKED into The Kiki Bistro Saturday morning on a mission. She saw her friends sitting at a big table near the back of the restaurant and headed toward them. She had no doubt they would agree to help with Rafe, but how they thought they should help might be an issue. She also knew sharing too much of Rafe's life before California would put a strain on their friendship. She thought talking to Eden about it might have been okay, but she knew if she gave

Abby too much information, it would be all over town. She didn't want to risk a scenario where Rafe might go berserkers and take them all on a short ride for a long nap. She chuckled to herself then frowned, hoping nothing like it would actually happen. "Hey, girls," she said as she sat down.

"Finally," complained Abby. "What's the emergency? Did Rafe leave the country again?"

"Abby," said Jude with annoyance, "she hasn't left town. I saw her outside with Bronte yesterday."

"Well, she still had time to go if she wanted to go," said Abby with a smirk.

"She hasn't left for anywhere," said Julia dryly, "but it doesn't mean she hasn't been thinking about it."

"What do you know?" asked Abby suspiciously.

"I know there's been a significant setback with Rafe," Julia revealed. "They went to see Katheryn, and there were some things revealed." Julia paused. "Let's just say Eden didn't come out looking well in Rafe's eyes."

"What the hell did she do to Rafe now?" asked Stacey with disgust. "She really should just leave Rafe alone and let her have her life back."

"Stop it, Stacey," Flynn told the redhead angrily. "I know Eden loves her, and Rafe loves Eden too! It's all Jake and his stupid group's fault."

"Well, it is where the information came from, but Rafe's more upset at what Eden told them," said Julia. "She feels like Eden was keeping more secrets about what was going on before she even got pregnant, and now she may think the relationship would have ended no matter if Jake was involved or not."

Jude pursed her lips in confusion. "But they found each other," she said. "I mean, after everything, Rafe came home."

"She came home, Jude, but it doesn't mean they found each other," explained Julia. "Rafe's still in therapy, and they're still in separate rooms."

"What?" Abby screeched. "But I thought..." she stammered, "the way they looked at each other when Rafe came home, I thought they went home and, you know, made up."

Julia shook her head no. "Rafe will still barely touch Eden. She's just not doing better. It's one of the reasons I wanted to meet with all of you." She took in everyone's shocked faces. "Eden can't help her alone. We all need to help and be there like Greer suggested."

"How can we help?" asked Jude. "You know I'd do anything for her. She's done so much for me from helping with my business and signing up for classes to stocking the studio with supplies."

"Me too," said Flynn. "She taught me about restoring things and helped me with bulking up and a lot of other things. I'd do anything for her and Eden too. She means a lot to me as a friend."

"Well," said Abby, "you know I'm in. She's a pain in my ass, but I can't help wanting to be her friend. Plus, she did get me all kinds of interviews and things for my blog and articles. I'm sure Erica will help too when she's not busy with school."

"I'm in," Stacey declared, joining in. "Rafe talked to Eden about recommending me for a gig at her studio for all the zombie flicks, creating characters, and doing makeup. I've had a great run and made some incredible contacts."

"Good," said Julia relieved. "I know if we ask Letty, she and Ephraim will help too. Now, all we have to do is figure out what to do."

"Well, what are we supposed to be helping with?" asked Abby. "Are we working with the therapist? We don't want to do anything to hurt any progress she's made."

"I'll tell Eden to call the therapist," Julia assured her. "The problem is the therapist can't talk to us about the sessions with Rafe. We can only ask if we're helping or hurting. Even then, she may not work with us unless Rafe agrees."

"We have to get Rafe to agree," said Jude. "We need to convince her to let us be part of her sessions somehow."

Julia let out a laugh of frustration knowing it might be wishful thinking to get Rafe to talk if she didn't want to talk. "I have no idea if it will be possible. But, I agree, we do need to at least try to talk to Rafe. We need to start spending more time with her. She's alone too much, and it may be causing more problems."

"What about Eden?" Stacey asked. "Why can't she spend more time with her? It might help their relationship."

"No," said Julia as she shook her head, "she can't take off any more work time. Plus, Rafe has a clause in their cohabitation agreement stating Eden has to have a job, or she has to move out."

"What the fuck?" Abby yelled. "I knew signing that thing was a bad idea for Eden!"

"Actually, it wasn't a bad thing," said Julia. "It would be fine if all this wasn't going on." She sighed wondering if the best thing for Rafe was to be placed rather than them taking her on. She was confident she could always call Greer as a last resort. "What we need to do is make a schedule and make sure we stick to it. We also need a way to report to each other in case things start getting worse."

The group worked on a schedule to spend free time with Rafe and get her to talk with them about anything they could get her to talk about.

With the schedule figured out, Julia took a final sip of her coffee. "Okay, I'll talk to Eden tonight and go over the schedule." Since Julia had taken time off, she knew she would be spending a lot of time with Rafe. She and Jude would spend time with her Monday. She just hoped they were doing the right thing. "I'll see you Monday, Jude."

Jude nodded, anxious to help. "I'll be there."

"Right, I'm off then," said Julia. She got up from the table and started out the door, dialing Eden as she headed to her car to let her know the plan.

"I hope Rafe realizes someday what a pain in the ass she is," said Abby shocking everyone. "Well, it's Rafe. She's always been a pain to deal with," she said with a shrug. She knew helping Rafe would be better than Julia's idea of placing her. She didn't think having the stigma of being in a mental facility twice would be great for Rafe's image.

34

THE SOUND OF an electric saw was coming from the garage as Julia Hawthorn walked up the driveway to Rafe Salvaggio's house. She waited until she knew Rafe had been home a while from her therapy session before coming over to keep her company. She just hoped her surprise visit would be well received. In the garage, she saw Rafe holding up a piece of wood and using a nail gun to attach it to another piece of wood. It looked like she was making some sort of arched thing. "Making a sculpture in here or something?" asked Julia as she approached Rafe and her project.

Rafe looked up with a frown at the unexpected voice, and when she recognized Julia, she grinned and took off her safety glasses. "Or something," she answered as she put down her tool. "What are you doing here?"

"I'm here to visit the sick and infirm," she joked, "but it looks like you must be okay if they let you use power tools."

Rafe scoffed as she brushed the sawdust off her shirt and jeans. "Let me get everything cleaned up," she said and started covering her work with a tarp and putting tools away.

"I was hoping we could hang out," said Julia as she watched Rafe work. "I know things haven't been going well, and I thought you might need a sounding board again. Or," she added, "just someone to have an adventure with for a while."

"Well, an adventure sounds much more fun," said Rafe as she finished. "Just let me get cleaned up. Then we can figure out something to do."

Julia followed Rafe into the house and fixed a glass of water to drink while she waited for Rafe to change. She looked around at what used to be a pristine house with art and expensive rugs. Now it was adorned with toys and spill-stained replacement rugs. Everything was clean and orderly but had a more lived-in look.

It was hard to reconcile Rafe with what she was seeing. Having Bronte in her life and Eden moved back in seemed to change Rafe even more than when she started dating Eden. There were plastic character cups in the cabinets, for fuck's sake. Julia shook her head and laughed, she was sure Eden had brought those in because they weren't there when she was living in the house. The cups were stuffed far in the back where they could barely be seen—there was Rafe's touch.

She could see the marks from the vacuum cleaner, the cleaned counters, the dishwasher going, and the dust-free woodwork and knew Rafe had tried to get things as clean as she could. She could also see the little things telling her Rafe was rebelling a bit against the chaos. She still hadn't taken down the damn blue woman painting in the dining room, every dish and glass in the cabinets were perfectly aligned, her office perfect as usual, and the art on the walls were still being rotated.

Julia sat on the couch in the living room looking at the new art on the walls when she heard Rafe open her bedroom door. When she walked in, Julia's jaw dropped. "What the hell are you wearing?" she asked in shock.

Rafe looked down at herself in confusion. "My running clothes," she answered with a smirk, "obviously. I thought we could go run on the beach. I know you have your workout stuff in your car. You always do. If you get them on, we can go."

"You go running on the beach dressed in those? Does Eden know?" Julia shook her head at Rafe's outfit. She looked almost naked in the skimpy shorts and sports top, obviously only there to secure her breasts because nothing else was covered. "Is there more to your get-up you haven't put on yet?"

"I have a jacket, and I'll take a change of clothes in case we decide not to come right back to the house afterward," said Rafe. "Why does Eden need to know about my running clothes?"

"Okay, Rafe," Julia said as she laughed, "I know you're playing dumb and do realize you're half-naked, more than half. Are you telling me this is a regular thing?"

Rafe winked at Julia. "I've found whenever I go running in the morning like this, I'm usually invited for a drink or even lunch by someone." She smiled and winked again. "It's always fun to meet new people. It's an adventure."

"Right," said Julia, "an adventure." She saw another of Rafe's rebellious actions. The difference here was this rebellion could cause problems. "Are you picking up women? What about Eden?"

"What about her? She goes to the gym at the studio. I'm sure she meets all kinds of people there."

"Seriously, Rafe, you're being purposely evasive. Have you decided not to try to stay with her? Does she know?"

"Fuck it," said Rafe in frustration. "I thought you said you came over to go on an adventure. Obviously, you came over to talk about Eden. Did she send you over? Did she complain about the other night to you? Is she getting you tell me to do things I don't want to do now too?"

"No, no," Julia tried to assure her. "It's just that you came back here from Mexico instead of going to Greer, and you told me you loved Eden. I'm worried running half-naked on the beach means you're either sabotaging your relationship with her or you've changed your mind about how you feel."

"I'm not the one you have to worry about changing their mind about how they feel. I'm not the one who has feelings for every stranger who steps in front of me!" she said heatedly. "I haven't done anything wrong." She crossed her arms defensively. "I haven't picked anyone up or talked to strangers about my life. I just go for a run and, if I'm lucky, have a drink or lunch with someone and talk about nothing and then come home. Half the time, it's not even with a woman."

"Okay, I'm sorry," she said as she held up her hands in surrender. "I didn't mean to upset you. You know I'm just looking out for you because you're my friend."

Rafe dropped her arms and sighed. "Fine," she said and sat down. "I guess this means no beach and no free lunch."

"I'll tell you what, how about I buy you lunch for messing up the adventure. You just go put some clothes on, please."

"I remember not long ago, you wanted me to dress like this all the time when you went out with me," she said with a smirk. "What happened? Can't take the heat?" She winked roguishly.

"Oh, ha, ha!" Julia smirked back. "I will admit, you are eye melting, and I'm extremely jealous of those muscles, but my beauty is a soft and alluring mystery while you're still the hard, dark, smoldering smoke you've always been—just to the nth power now," she confessed with a laugh. "Get dressed!"

Rafe laughed and went back to her room to change into something Julia might find more appropriate. She came back out and stood in front of Julia presenting herself. "Will I do?"

Julia looked up at her and shook her head. "You'll have to. I don't think I can take what else you'll come out in." She was thankful Rafe was covered, at least—even though she still looked like a walking invitation to an orgasm party.

"Great," said Rafe and flashed her smile signaling she knew she had won. "Where are you taking me?"

Julia decided to take Rafe to an out of the way place famous for serving old-fashioned hamburgers, and they sat down at one of the outside picnic tables with their food.

"I guess you are jealous since you're feeding me junk food," Rafe joked as she ate a French fry.

"This is my American guilty pleasure." Julia laughed as she picked up her burger. "I just have to indulge once in a while." Julia took a bite of her burger and relished the taste. "So," she said after she swallowed her food, "tell me what's going on. Why do you think Eden sent me over? What's she complaining about and trying to make you do?"

Rafe took a drink of her iced tea pushing down her frustration. "She's just acting crazy again," she said tersely. "She's pushing into my space, and it's pissing me off."

"Pushing into your space? What do you mean?"

"Touching me and kissing me, and the other night, she decided I was her fucking pillow and climbed into my lap because *she* wanted to be close to *me*. She just takes and takes, no matter how I feel about it."

"And her being close to you was something you didn't want? Rafe, I don't understand."

No," Rafe said annoyed, "it isn't something I want right now. After reading the file Katheryn gave us, I'm not sure what I want anymore. I need space to figure it out, and she just keeps taking even though I hardly have anything more to give. I'm angry, I'm tired, and I'm just confused about where I should be and what we even are. Then she pulls her pathetic stuff, and it makes it worse."

"Well," she said with a laugh, "it's clearly all your fault!"

"Fuck you," Rafe grumbled.

"Look at you, Rafe. If you dress like this, show off your body and give her any of those looks you seem not to be able to control, she has to be going crazy for you. Then you complain when she answers your invitation. It's not very fair."

"Whatever. If I can control myself, she should be able to do it too."

"Since when have you been able to control yourself?"

188

"Believe me, I have to work harder at it," said Rafe with an arch of her brow. "I never take money to the beach, and I only leave with a few beers and maybe lunch."

"That's so fucked up," said Julia and laughed. "You only work harder because you put yourself in those situations."

"Sometimes, I just feel like I have to have a challenge. I'm so fucking bored." Rafe sighed as she picked up her burger. "I've got a bunch of different projects going, but none of them seem to help me burn off all this anger so I can think clearly," Rafe complained and took a bite of her burger.

"You have all day to think without her around. How much time do you need?"

Rafe looked hard at Julia. "As much as I need," she said evenly. "It's not just about being alone all day. It's about personal space when she's there. When I have to listen to her talk, ask questions, and go on about how she loves me, I can only take so much right now, and then I need a break from it. . . from her."

"Have you told her?" Julia asked as she took the last bite of her burger.

"Yes, I've told her I don't want her to touch me or kiss me. I try to leave the room, but she follows me. Then she just takes the touches and kisses she wants."

"Well, what do you do when she's taking them?"

"Suffer," she said annoyed by Julia's attempt to defend Eden.

"Come on," scoffed Julia. "I thought the fact she follows her heart and emotions was one of the things you loved about

Eden. You said you liked it she wasn't all logical and predictable when it came to showing her feelings for you and when she," Julia paused and looked around, "when she wants to have sex or just be close. She's just trying to connect with you."

"Well, I'm not ready to connect," said Rafe and threw her burger back into the basket. "I can't eat any more of this. I feel like grease is going to start coming out of my pours any second."

"Okay," Julia relented with a laugh, noticing Rafe only took about four bites of her burger. "Let's go walk it off and look in some shops. We haven't shopped together in a long time."

"Okay," agreed Rafe and followed her down the street. "So, if Eden didn't send you, why did you take off work to see me?"

"I had to get out of the office," Julia confessed. "Actually, I told Daddy I needed to take some time off, and he agreed to give me as much time as I needed," she said with a smile. "So, now I have to figure out what I want to do until he decides to drag me back in. I was hoping you could help me out."

"Your father actually gave you time off? Are you sick or something? Is he sick?" Rafe asked with concern.

"No!" Julia laughed and reassured her as she saw the worry on her face. "No one's sick. He just understands I need a break and knows I want to explore my options."

"Oh," said Rafe relieved. "My papa would never find it acceptable for me or anyone else to leave their job and save a place while they go explore options. But I didn't need to explore my options. I was doing what I loved."

"Your papa was awful to you and a tyrant," Julia said absently as she looked in a store window.

"Fuck you, Julia! You don't know what you're talking about! My papa was a great man and worked hard every day," insisted Rafe angrily. She hated it when people talked badly about her father.

"Okay, okay, I'm sorry I said anything." Julia cringed and chided herself for not thinking before she spoke about Rafe's father.

"I really miss him and my work," she said sadly. "I miss the travel and the detail work, even working with all the trades and the negotiating. Everything."

"It'll be okay," said Julia as she patted her on the back. "Now you get to spend time with Bronte and work on all your projects." Rafe frowned as they walked. "Do you think you're missing the work because you want to get away again?"

"I don't know." Rafe groaned, not wanting to talk to Julia anymore. "Let's go in here and look around," she suggested and headed into a shop.

Julia noticed what shop they were going into and shook her head. Leave it to Rafe to find a liquor store. She smiled and remembered their booze cruises from England to France and back when they were younger and in college. Those were some great parties and made better when Rafe joined in. Rafe brought along girls from around her school in France. Since she and Rafe were fluent in French, they had to translate a lot.

Julia was sure Rafe was helping the budding romances along when she was translating because there were a lot of intercontinental negotiations going on in the dark.

As they walked through the store, Julia watched Rafe pick wines, an outrageously priced scotch, and some different beers then take it all to the counter to pay. "We can't walk around with all of this," she complained.

"I know. We can just head back to my place," said Rafe as she paid for her alcohol.

35

CARRYING BOOZE INSIDE after arriving back at the house, Julia Hawthorn helped Rafe Salvaggio put everything away. They opened a bottle of wine for Julia and the scotch for Rafe, and then they went to hang out in the living room. Julia glanced at her watch and knew it wouldn't be long until Eden got home with Bronte. She was hoping to find out more about what was going on in Rafe's head, but so far, she really hadn't found out anything.

She watched Rafe swirl her neat scotch and get comfortable. "So, tell me what else is going on. Is it really just Eden trying to touch you and all, or is there something more?"

"It doesn't matter." Rafe sipped her scotch appreciating the floral undertones. "If I can just figure things out, I'll be able to get on with my life and know where I should go—with or without her."

"See, when you say those things, it worries me," said Julia as she sat her wine down. "I know you have the files from Katheryn to consider, but you also tell me your feelings for Eden haven't changed, but you have to figure something out." She frowned at Rafe. "What exactly are you trying to sort out?"

Rafe shook her head. "It's like I don't know her," she tried to explain. "I thought I did but I—" she stopped as she saw Jude walk in from the patio.

"Hey, Rafe," said Jude. "I saw Julia's car and thought I'd come over. It's been a while. I've been crazy busy. Those new marketing materials are working out well, and I started my classes you helped me with." She smiled and stopped, realizing she was talking too much. "Hey, Julia." She gave a small wave, and Julia lifted her wine glass toward her.

"I'm glad things are going well for you," said Rafe as she wondered what the real reason was everyone was coming out of the woodwork. "Let's get you a beer," she said and headed to the kitchen as Jude and Julia followed. She got Jude a beer and refilled Julia's glass as well as her own. "It's getting stuffy in here. Let's go outside." She headed outside, thinking this was going to be a hard day.

"What are you doing out here?" asked Julia inspecting a staked off and dug-out section of the garden.

"Just a little project," said Rafe waving away her question as she sat by the pool. She wished she had put on her swimming suit but didn't want to go change now.

Julia let the so-called little project go and sat on a lounger as Jude did the same. "We were just talking about the Eden issue," Julia told Jude.

"Oh," said Jude as she looked at Rafe. "You doing okay, Rafe?"

"I'm fine," she responded evenly.

"So," Julia began cautiously, "how are things going with all the therapy you're being subjected too?" Rafe just scowled at her darkly. "I just remember when you had to do counseling at school." Julia grinned. "Now, there was something!"

"Counseling in school?" asked Jude with concern.

Julia was tickled at the memory and laughed. "Yes, she was a counselor's nightmare. She ended up resigning after dealing with Rafe for two weeks."

"Whoa, really?" asked Jude in surprise. "What happened?"

"You know," Rafe said as she sighed, wishing Julia would stop talking, "she ended up okay."

Julia turned to Jude, excited about telling a Rafe story. If she told it to Jude, then it would not be a surprise Eden knew the story. "She got in trouble for not dressing out properly for athletics," she explained. "She walked out onto the field practically naked in just her very skimpy underthings," she chuckled, "so she was sent to counseling."

"I was told to find a way to make it to the field in something other than my school uniform, and I did."

"What happened to the counselor?" Jude asked as she laughed with Julia imagining Rafe's antics.

"Well," Julia started, "Rafe was furious about being sent to the counselor for two weeks. In protest, she took her dress-out uniform in every day, stripped out of her clothes, and changed into the uniform. Apparently, the strip routine became," she paused knowing she was telling more about what happened than she had told Eden, "more exotic," she grinned, "each day." She winked mischievously at Jude. "Soon, it drove the counselor to distraction, so she ran out of her office and resigned on the spot!" She laughed, and Jude joined her.

Rafe smiled as she remembered what happened and watched Julia and Jude laugh. "Actually, I stripped twice, once when I got there and once to put my regular school clothes back on. She didn't resign until the two weeks were over, and I was fully dressed for the last time," she said and chuckled softly. "I knew she was a closet lesbian, and I just helped her along." Rafe shrugged with a small grin. "I saw her several years later at Harriot's in New York. She was dancing in a cage with her girlfriend—Dusty, I think it was. She came up to me and was actually happy to see me. She had opened a therapy office specializing in LGBT youth counseling and was a volunteer at the community center and some other places. She looked much better and happier than she had working at the school."

"You should know, Jude," Julia confided with a laugh. "Rafe is a very good dancer. Very sexy. She does this incredibly sexy, sensual dance. When we were younger, we did a dance competition with a bunch of other girls, and it was awesome!"

"Really?" Jude asked excitedly. "Did you win?"

"Of course, we did," said Rafe as she was pulled into the memory. "We called our dance *The Dark's Seduction of the Light* and blew the crowd away."

"How old were we, Rafe? I think we were twenty-one," said Julia answering her own question. "We were in New York during a school break. What were the songs?"

"Yeah, I had just finished my undergrad work," Rafe recalled watching Julia roll her eyes. Julia was still annoyed Rafe had shipped off to Italy and started college a year earlier so graduated first. "There were three songs for the main part then we did another after we won," answered Rafe. "It was 'Bring Me to Life' by Evanescence—it was a new song. Then 'Pretty Woman,' and then 'Drive' by Melissa Ferrick, which was popular with the family crowd but not a lot of other people knew it then."

"Oh, right, and you actually sang 'Pretty Women' so we would have all three songs done by women." Julia laughed as she winked at Jude. "Can you imagine her singing? It was brilliant!"

"I think the crowd was more impressed with you and the other girls than my singing." Rafe chuckled because she was lucky her friend Gabri had given her impromptu singing lessons over the years. "You were good."

"Jude, don't let her fool you!" Julia winked as her Mediterranean blue eyes sparkled with the memory. "Imagine the twenty-one-year-old Rafe jumping and spinning around moving around the stage like sex unleashed. She was stripping her clothes off in her seduction of the light... which was me, by the way, and then switched up to sing 'Pretty Woman.' I danced around her and brought in the other dancers for my own seduction dance. Then 'Drive' came on in the mix, and Rafe completed the total seduction of the light, stripping off my white outfit until I was all in black leotards and a bikini top. Both the men and the women in the crowd went crazy." Julia laughed at the memory. "Doing those things with Rafe was like being on drugs!"

"Don't forget, when we won, we did the 'Back in Black' routine," added Rafe with a smile.

"Oh, my god!" Julia laughed at Jude's wide-eyed face. "We had all the dancers, including one girl Rafe had totally entranced, dressed in white, and Rafe and I were in black. We danced around and pulled the white outfits off the dancers until they were all in skimpy black outfits and practically having sex on stage. It was crazy!"

"Hannah," said Rafe grinning at the memory of how her dark ebony skin contrasted with her white outfit. "I met her after I got kicked out of school for the striping incident."

They dated for a while before Rafe left for Italy. Over the years, they would see each other when they were in New York or when Hannah traveled with her dance company to wherever Rafe was going to school.

"She was an amazing dancer and a good sport for letting me and Julia take the leads." Rafe sighed wishing things were as simple again.

"She couldn't be a lead because it was an amateur show, and she's a pro," Julia reminded her.

"You should do the dance at the bistro sometime," said Jude imaging those two dancing around half-naked. She could feel her face turning red and took a drink of her beer.

"No," said Rafe, "it was a long time ago in a different life. I'm not the same person anymore."

"You've probably lost your moves by now anyway," Julia teased then got up and spun into one of the dance moves. "I've still got it, though."

Rafe glowered at Julia through squinted eyes. "Is that a challenge?"

"Oh, I think it is," dared Julia as she laughed.

Rafe grinned then got up and went inside to put in the CD with a song from their old mix. Then she turned on the sound system outside. "Okay, let's see who is the best dancer," Rafe challenged as she rushed back out excitedly and the 'Evanescence' song came on. "Jude, you can be the judge. When I win, she goes in the pool!" Rafe declared mischievously, and they started dancing around the patio wildly.

Jude laughed as she watched the two spin and move their bodies sensuously around to the song. Their dance was kind of the story of the song, but it was clear from the dance moves in the interpretation that the singer was being saved from herself and the denial of her sexuality. As Jude watched, she noticed movement inside the house and saw Eden standing at the patio door.

36

EDEN KINGSLEY WATCHED as Rafe Salvaggio and Julia Hawthorn danced and touched each other sensually with intimate moves. She had no idea what was going on and trembled as she held Bronte. Julia was supposed to be helping, not seducing Rafe in her own home. Eden followed Rafe with her eyes as she danced and moved her body to the music. She had never seen Rafe move her body in such a way before, and she was entranced. She stepped further out onto the patio, not sure what to do or say.

Rafe spun and saw Jude look up toward the patio doors. Following her gaze, she saw Eden there with Bronte. She smiled and danced over to Eden and took Bronte from her arms. Bronte laughed as Rafe spun around with her and danced back over toward Julia.

As Rafe continued to dance, Julia saw Eden and stopped at the look on Eden's face. She was glad she had been dancing, so the blush on her face looked like it was from exertion and not from the thrill of being so close to Rafe again.

Rafe spun with Bronte and noticed Julia had stopped dancing. She smiled because she had won. She danced over to Jude and handed Bronte off to her then danced over to Eden. She took her hands, pulling her out where she and Julia had been dancing. She danced around her, moved against her sensuously and wildly, and began striping her already skimpy clothes off to the music. When the song was over, Rafe was standing close to Eden, wearing just her bra and underwear. Rafe smiled then gave a little bow, and a wink then turned toward Julia.

She ran up to Julia, caught her, and then lifted her up and carried her to the edge of the pool, with Julia protesting the entire way, as Jude and Bronte laughed.

Rafe stopped at the edge of the pool. "I win again!" she declared and threw Julia in the pool where she splashed and sputtered. Rafe gave a conquerors laugh then dove in next to Julia. As she came up, she splashed Julia in the face. "Who still has all the moves?" she asked playfully.

Julia wiped the water from her face and caught her breath. "Okay, I give! You still have moves." She laughed and made her way to the edge of the pool and pulled herself out.

Rafe followed her out of the pool. "Right, so don't forget," she said with a knowing smile as she took Bronte from Jude. "*Ciao, bella, ti piace ballare?*"[7] she asked and then spun around with Bronte. She danced her over to the table for the remote to turn down the music and switch the player to a mix list.

Eden watched, still fighting for her voice, as Rafe danced with Bronte on the patio and talked to her in Italian. She turned and saw Julia blush. "What the heck were you doing?" Eden asked crossly.

"They were showing me the dance they used to do when they were younger," Jude volunteered. "They won a contest with it."

---

[7] Hello beautiful, do you like to dance?

"I was just trying to loosen her up," explained Julia, hiding her guilt as she wrung out her hair and clothes. "I wasn't getting anywhere." *Well, I might have gotten somewhere if you hadn't shown up*, she thought.

"It looked like you were getting somewhere to me," Eden started angrily as Rafe walked up to them with Bronte.

"B Girl and I are going for a quick dip in the pool," she announced cheerfully. "Eden, would you mind getting us some pool towels, please?"

Eden just stared at Rafe's half-naked form as she carried Bronte to the stairs and then descended into the pool. She nodded as she saw Rafe had Bronte stripped out of all her clothes. She watched for a moment as Bronte laughed and splashed with Rafe, and then she turned to Julia. "You see what she does to me? I'm just dismissed unless she wants something," she seethed and stormed into the house.

In shock, Julia watched Eden walk away. "Keep an eye on Rafe," she said to Jude. "I'll go smooth things over with Eden."

Julia went into the house, trying not to drip too much water, and found Eden as she was pulling pool towels from the linen closet. "What the hell, Eden? She just asked you to get towels. Don't you think you're overreacting?"

"I don't know, maybe. I just. . ." she started then sighed in frustration. "I come home, and you guys are out there doing some kind of sex dance, and I've been worried sick all day about what was happening and what state of mind she would be in when I got here," she explained. "Then she dances around me like she did, and then cuts me off by asking me to go get towels. She didn't invite me to swim or explain what was going on. It's like I don't count."

Julia held her hand up to stop Eden. "Hold on, try to calm down. I didn't see the same thing at all. She saw you and included you and Bronte, dancing around, and when the music stopped, she took care of the music and Bronte. She didn't tell you not to swim. You can change into your swim clothes and swim. She's not stopping you."

"She didn't say a word to me until she asked for towels, Julia. No hello or greeting of any kind."

"She did acknowledge you, though, and showed you her dance moves. She didn't just stop and ignore you. I think you're on a fine line here."

Eden ran her hand through her hair in frustration. "Fine, we'll see how things go tonight and see if you're right," she relented. "Did she talk to you at all about anything?"

"She did, a little, but we can talk later. Let's get back out there. Are you changing into your swim things?"

Eden frowned. "No," she said angrily, "if I decide to get in, I may do a strip too, and see how she likes it!" She pressed a towel into Julia's hands. "Try to get all the water off the floor before Rafe sees it," she said then pushed past Julia with more towels in her arms as she headed back outside.

"She might like it," mumbled Julia as she cleaned up the water then followed her out.

Stepping outside, Eden took a breath to calm herself. She walked to the edge of the pool where Rafe was playing with Bronte, and Jude was sitting with her feet in the pool. "Here are your towels," she said trying to be happy as she sat the towels down.

"Thanks," said Rafe and smiled up at her. "I bought some of the wine you like today. It's in the wine rack." She kissed Bronte then spun around with her as the little girl laughed.

Eden felt struck with guilt. "Thank you," she said softly. "I think I'll go open a bottle and start dinner." She turned toward Jude and saw Julia had come out of the house. "Are you guys staying?"

"I can't," said Jude. "I have a date." She got up and slipped her sandals on.

"I'll stay," said Julia. "Why don't I help you?" She turned to Rafe. "Hey, will you two be okay out here whilst I help Eden with dinner?'

"We'll be fine," said Rafe. "Won't we, B Girl?" she asked as the spun in the water again with the laughing toddler.

Jude made her way out the back gate, and Julia followed Eden inside the house. As they walked into the kitchen, Eden burst into tears.

"What's wrong? Why are you crying?" asked Julia dismayed by Eden's sudden outburst of tears.

"Because I don't know what I'm doing," she said shakily. "I don't even know when she's cutting me off or being nice! Did you hear her? She bought wine for me, and I'm complaining about her to you."

"You have to look at this as positive," Julia said encouragingly. "She was upset when she was talking about you today, but she still thought about you and bought you something she knew you'd like."

"So, is she canceling out a bad with a good?" asked Eden as she pulled out the bottles of wine Rafe bought then opened one to breathe. "What are you saying?

"No," said Julia, "I don't think so at all." She pulled her sopping shirt from her body. "Hey, can I borrow some dry clothes?"

"Sure, come on," she said and led her into her room. "Just get whatever you need."

"Thanks," she said and took out a shirt and pair of yoga pants and put them on quickly as Eden looked away. "Sit down for a second," Julia said and sat on the bed.

Eden hesitated then sat down on the ornate chase lounger Rafe had restored and gave her when she moved in. "What did she say to you?" she asked with worry.

Julia sighed knowing Eden was not going to like what she had to say. "She says she still needs space. She needs you not to touch her or kiss her right now."

"Did she say why?" Eden asked softly trying to hold in her emotions.

"Not really. She just says she can only take so much talking and then she needs space from you. She's upset you follow her everywhere, and you used her as a pillow the other night."

She could see the tear well out of Eden's eye and knew she was hurt. It was difficult because of her own doubts about Eden, and her opinion that Rafe should move on, but Julia knew she had to double down on the friendship. Like Greer said, Rafe had to think it was all her idea to leave.

"Listen," said Julia, "we're going to keep talking to her. She's just having a hard time with everything raining down on her. She has a lot of anger at everything still, and her anger has been flamed by the file Katheryn gave her." She kept to herself the other things Rafe said about not knowing what they were anymore. "It's been over a month, and she doesn't seem better. And really, you can't expect her to be fine with the file. Maybe you should give her time to process this new situation before expecting her to get close again. Just take it slow."

Eden leaned over and put her face in her hands. "I wish we had never seen the Stewards file. I wish I never talked to those people." She sobbed. "I don't know if I can keep living like this. I'm feeling lost and shut out. Rafe barely speaks to me," she complained. "When she does, I feel like she's pushing me away." She looked up at Julia. "The only reason I sat with Rafe was that she kept looking at me. I thought it was what she wanted, so I went to her. Then she told me no, but I was already there. I couldn't help myself. I needed her. I needed to be close to her."

"See, this is what I was talking about," said Julia in frustration. "You can't depend on her for all your emotional support right now. She needs your help much more than you need hers. She's the one who needs you to be strong, not the other way around. You have to be able to live without touching her and everything else right now. I know it's hard." Julia sighed in frustration at Eden but still sympathized a bit because she knew well how it felt to wait for Rafe. "She makes it hard with the way she dresses and the things she does."

"I know," said Eden with a shuddering breath. "The dance she did," she shook her head at the memory of Rafe's body moving against her so sensually, "where did she learn it?"

"It's something she's been able to do since I met her," she said with a smile remembering the first time she saw Rafe dance when they were fifteen and in her room. She was sure it was then she fell in love. She shook herself from the memory. "We altered it for a contest we entered, and it just got better." Julia gave a short laugh recalling how much fun they had when Hannah helped them take the dance to the next level. She refocused on Eden. "Look, I know this won't be easy but, if you love her, you have to be the one who's strong and give her what she's telling you she needs. She's not keeping it a secret from you, but you don't seem to be listening to her."

"So I just let her walk away from me and stop talking? She's supposed to be talking about things. She's supposed to be telling me what her therapist recommends. I have no idea what things she's supposed to be doing or talking about, and her therapist can't talk to me. I just have to live with her in silence?"

"Some days, you might," said Julia. "She has a lot to process. She has to work through her PTSD from the hostage situation at the school as well as everything with Jake and what he did to you. Now there's the Stewards file, and she feels she has nothing left. Oh, and don't forget all the childhood trauma Letty told us about and how she grew up. I'm surprised she's functioning."

"Well, what am I supposed to do?" asked Eden angrily. "She looks like she's functioning fine. She was out yesterday tearing up the yard and digging holes. I have no idea what she's doing in the garage, and I have no idea what she does or where she goes all day. I call, and she ignores me unless she is in the mood to answer her phone. She never used to let a call go, and now she avoids the phone almost all the time. Maybe she just avoids it if I'm calling. I have no idea!"

Julia sighed and went to sit next to Eden. "Calm down. This is why I've enlisted help. I know you worry, and I know Rafe is doing some confusing and sometimes hurtful things. But you have to stop complaining and start helping find a solution. If we want her back, we have to help her get through all the problems we can. I'll try to find out more about her sessions, but knowing what goes on in them may not be any help at all as to how we handle her. Just do me a favor," she begged, "give her the space she needs right now, and we'll all work on helping her, okay?"

Eden hoped Julia was right. It was going to be hard, but she just wanted Rafe and their life back. "Okay," she said softly, "I'll try my best."

Julia smiled reassuringly. "Good."

They both looked up at the sound of Rafe's voice yelling out that Bronte was on her way inside. Eden went quickly to the bedroom door just as Bronte showed up trailing her towel behind her looking for her Mommy and making the sign that she needed to potty.

"Hey, baby, it looks like you need some clothes." Eden smiled and noticed her sign. "Let's hurry to your bathroom," she said and led Bronte away.

Julia went into the kitchen to help start making dinner. She hoped Eden would take their talk to heart and start handling Rafe better. For the first day of her mission, she was happy with how things had gone. Rafe was engaged and talking a little, and she was being playful, so it was a plus. And now, after talking with Eden, maybe she would give Rafe space, and they could start getting along again. Knowing Rafe was teetering on the edge about Eden and not doing anything to tip the scales was difficult. Even if she did tip the scales, Julia knew there was no guarantee Rafe would decide to change her mind about being in a relationship together. Rafe may even go to Greer. Greer could definitely handle Rafe, but Julia would rather have Rafe here with Eden than the Greer scenario.

Eden quickly walked into the kitchen. "Julia, take Bronte! Something is wrong with Rafe," she said in a rush as she handed her Bronte.

Julia took the toddler in surprise.

"I need to go check on her." Eden rushed over to Rafe's door and knocked. "Rafe? Rafe, I'm coming in," she announced as she pushed into the room. She found Rafe on her knees in the bathroom. "Are you okay? What happened?" she asked with worry.

"Fucking Julia," Rafe groaned as she stood and flushed the toilet then got out her toothbrush. "I'm fine now," she said then began brushing her teeth.

"What happened? Why were you sick again?" Eden asked as she watched Rafe finish brushing her teeth and wipe her mouth.

Rafe, with a sickly appearance, held her hand to her queasy stomach. "She fed me grease on a bun for lunch." As Eden followed, Rafe made her way into the bedroom and lay down on the bed. "I should have eaten something else," she groaned in pain.

"Let me get you some medicine," said Eden and went back into the bathroom. She came out, poured some medicine into the dosage cup, and sat on the bed next to Rafe. "Come on," she said softly, "sit up, and take this." Rafe took the medicine then handed the cup back. "I'm sorry you don't feel well, babe," Eden said as Rafe lay back down. She pushed Rafe's hair back from her face then stroked her head wanting to comfort her. With uncertainty, she pulled her hand back, remembering what Julia said to her.

"Thank you, Ede," said Rafe weakly as she curled into a ball. "Fucking, Julia," she groaned.

"Just rest, babe," she said softly, her heart leaping with hope again at hearing the name of endearment Rafe called her again. "I'll come back to check on you in a little while." Eden closed the bedroom door then went into the kitchen. Julia was letting Bronte help make a salad. "What did she eat today? She was in there throwing up and cursing you."

Julia looked at Eden in surprise. "We just had an American hamburger and fries," she said innocently as she handed Bronte to Eden. "She didn't even eat it all!"

"Julia!" yelled Eden in frustration. "She's barely eating because of her medication, and you feed her junk? Look at her!" she said as she motioned toward Rafe's bedroom. "Can't you see how thin she's got? She barely eats! The only time I can be certain she's eaten anything is if Bronte is here, or I'm watching her."

"What? She told me she eats out and has drinks sometimes when she goes to the beach to run," Julia revealed. "I know she looks thin, but I just thought it was from the running and weightlifting."

Eden shook her head as she took Bronte to her toys in the living room and Julia followed her. "You believed her? She tells me she eats all the time. I know she doesn't," insisted Eden. "She may drink, but it doesn't help because she is not supposed to be drinking, and I can't stop her. She hasn't kept a lot down. She won't tell me half the time, but I can hear when she's sick if I'm in Bronte's room when it happens because the bathrooms are next to each other. Then she's up half the night, trying to get back to sleep unless I get her to take some medicine for her stomach. I've been trying to make sure she gets a small amount of chicken or fish and a vegetable or salad at least once a day. I thought she was starting to do better, but clearly, I was wrong."

"Eden, I think you need to tell her doctor she has all these side effects," Julia said with concern.

"What side effects? She's been this way the entire time she's been home."

"Well, don't you think she's acting strange? You're the one complaining," said Julia in frustration. "She doesn't want to have sex or even touch you," she began counting off side effects on her fingers, "has insomnia, and when she does sleep, she's still having nightmares, she's not eating, but she's vomiting and losing weight." Julia frowned. "You and Rafe both told me she's angry all the time and can't work through it," she revealed. "What's worse are her manic episodes, when she does those crazy stunts and the way she drives her father's car. Who knows what else has been happening when she's alone. She needs to either change her meds or get a different dosage." Eden's jaw dropped in shock. "You've just been too close and couldn't see it," said Julia. "This is why I'm telling you the things I am. You can't depend on her right now. She needs you to look out for her."

Eden sank to the couch despondent. "Oh, god," she said softly and leaned into her hands. "You're right, you're right. I've been trying to fix side effects and not helping her at all. I feel so stupid."

"Don't beat yourself up," said Julia sympathetically. "You've been completely scattered and may not have been able to take it all in. Now we know what's happening, and we can tell the doctor."

"I'll call her," said Eden trying to hold back her tears. "I'll call her first thing in the morning so she can talk to Rafe at her next appointment."

37

HEARING MUSIC COMING from the garage Friday afternoon, Julia Hawthorn stopped walking up the steps to Rafe Salvaggio's front door. She turned around, walked back down the stairs, and headed toward the garage. She could hear the sound of a power tool under the loud music, so she knew Rafe had to be inside. She tried the door, and it was locked, so she pounded on it with her fist. The sound of her knock was nowhere near loud enough to be heard over all the noise coming from inside.

"Rafe!'" she called, without result.

She walked around to the side of the garage and went up the two steps of the deck making her way to the garage window. She tried looking inside but found the window covered, so she knocked on the glass. Hoping Rafe had gone to the door, she went back to the front, but the door remained closed and locked.

"Bugger," Julia said as she flipped back her silver hair in frustration.

She stood in front of the overhead door and waited for a lull in the music, then banged on it with both her fists. Rafe yanked the door open, and Julia was rewarded with the appearance of Rafe wearing her old work clothes, safety glasses, and big green ear protectors over her head.

"Hey, Rafe," said Julia with a small wave.

"What the fuck?" Rafe asked angrily as she pulled off her ear protection and glasses, disheveling her dark hair. "Why are you beating on the garage door?"

"I wanted to get your attention," explained Julia. "I tried knocking, but I don't think you could hear me over the noise."

Rafe pointed to the button next to the door. "This is a buzzer, and it also flashes a light. You don't have to beat the shit out of my door."

"Oh." Julia grimaced. "I guess I just didn't see it. It's not like I make a habit of entering your garage."

"What do you want?" Rafe asked tersely.

"I just thought I'd come over and see how you were doing. You missed dinner when I was over Monday night because you were sick, and I wanted to say I'm sorry about the bad food. Maybe I can make it up to you by getting you a better lunch today."

"I'm not in the mood today," she said and started to close the door.

"Wait! Wait, Rafe," she said as she held the door. "What's wrong?"

Rafe glared at her then turned away without answering. She went back into the garage and could feel Julia following her closely. She wished she would go away. She was trying to work off the anger burning on a low flame inside since her therapy session Wednesday. So far, the burn was not cooling, and it pissed her off even more. It was bad enough to try to control things on a regular day, but now she had to do it with people interfering with her sessions and calling her doctor.

She sighed and threw her glasses and ear protection on the workbench. She picked up the shovel she had been sharpening with the grinder and hung it back on the wall. Then she began putting away all the tools and debris from the other small projects she had been working on this morning.

Trying to avoid any dirt, Julia watched as Rafe worked and could see she was angry about something. The trick would be finding out what without making her angrier.

"Well, why don't you tell me what's wrong? Maybe I can help." She watched as Rafe sighed, dusted herself off, and then headed for the door. "Rafe!" Julia called following her as she headed into the house.

When they were inside, Rafe made for her bedroom and slammed the door on Julia. "Shit," Julia hissed softly then pulled out her phone and went into the kitchen. "Eden Kingsley, please," she said into the phone and waited to be connected. "Eden, it's Julia. Hi, yeah, I'm here at the house with Rafe. Did something happen between you two to upset her? No, no, she's fine. Right now, I think she may be in the shower. So, you don't know if anything's wrong? She hasn't talked to you about what's on her mind? Okay, well, maybe she's just in a bad mood. No, don't worry. I'll let you know what I find out if it's even anything. All right, bye," she said disconnecting the call.

She went back over to Rafe's bedroom door and could hear the shower running. Trying the door, she found it locked. Julia shook her head, unhappy because Rafe was not supposed to be locking her door. She would give her a pass this time because she was in the shower, but she hoped it didn't turn into another problem. She went to the living room and sat on the couch to wait.

Finally, Rafe came out of the bedroom. She sat in the chair across from Julia then crossed her arms defensively. Julia was relieved to see she was dressed in something normal, and it actually covered her body. Looking at her closely, Julia could see now what Eden was saying about her being thinner, and she also looked sleep deprived.

"What's going on?" Julia asked, Rafe's glare boring into her. It was clear she was angry about something.

"Why are you here?" snapped Rafe. "I'm not in the mood to help you figure out your life today."

"I told you," she said, ignoring her flippant comment, "I wanted to make sure you were okay and maybe take you out for lunch."

"Really?" asked Rafe with a low growl. "Are you sure you're not here as a fucking spy for Eden, so you two can interfere with my life?"

"What? Spy?" Julia shook her head in confusion. "What are you talking about?" Rafe stared back at her with the hard look she got when she thought someone was lying. Julia realized this had to be about Eden's phone call to the doctor. "Are you just going to stare at me, or are you going to tell me why you're so angry?"

"Don't act all innocent," Rafe said accusingly. "I know it had to be you, or her, or even both of you! You called my doctor, and now she's taken away my medicine!"

"Eden can't make the doctor take your meds away," said Julia evenly trying to be reasonable. "If the doctor changed your meds, it's because she thought it was the best thing to do."

"I need my medicine!" yelled Rafe as she got up and paced the living room. "Kate said I have to take it so I can start working things out! Now, how am I supposed to figure anything out if I don't have it!" Rafe turned to Julia. "I know it was Eden! She keeps calling my doctor—*my* doctor! She keeps calling and telling her things, and she needs to stay out of it!"

"I'm sure if she did call, it was because she was worried about you. She wants you to get better too."

"Really? She wants me to get better?" Rafe asked argumentatively. "Then why is she pushing me and making things hard? Why is she calling my doctor and making her take my medicine away? I need my medicine!"

"Didn't the doctor give you a different medicine?" Julia asked concerned. "Maybe you should tell me what your doctor said, or maybe I can be an advocate for you, and you can let me talk to the doctor and help you," she suggested.

"Oh, you'd like that!" Rafe snapped angrily. "I don't need an advocate. I need people to stop messing with me and calling my doctor! Now I may have to go longer! I know she was going to sign off so I could stop going so much and get back to work. Now it's all up in the air again! Fucking Eden!" she cursed and sat down angrily.

"How do you know someone called?" asked Julia calmly.

"Dr. Conrad told me Wednesday she got a call from one of my 'friends' Tuesday morning," Rafe revealed. "Because of the call, the doctor decided to take me off my medicine and wait on changing my sessions. This isn't the first time she got a call, either, so someone is spying and reporting things to her."

"Rafe, if Eden did call the doctor, she had to have a good reason. From what I saw Monday, I think she may have been right to call."

"You just don't understand! I need my medicine!" she said desperately. "It's what's helping me figure things out!"

"Well, maybe you were just on the wrong medicine. Maybe she'll give you another one. The medicine you think you need may not have been helping at all."

"What are you talking about? It was working fine! I was so close to being able to go back to work and getting back to my life!"

"I don't know about how close you were to getting back to work, but I don't think you were close to getting your life back," said Julia to Rafe's clearly wrong assessment of the situation. "You've been pushing Eden away, do you realize that? You've been pushing us all away, but especially her. I don't think you have any idea how close you are to driving her away! Do you want her to leave? Do you want her to take Bronte and move out? It sure seems like you do! Look at what you've been doing to her!"

"I haven't done anything to her!" fumed Rafe. "I've had things under control! I've been good! I've been taking care of everything! I've been faithful! I've stayed even when I felt like running from everything!" she yelled as tears dared to form in her eyes. "I need my medicine," she said desperately. "I need it so I can stay, so I can figure everything out." She could not tell her or anyone how close she was to buying a ticket to Italy and leaving everything behind.

Julia examined Rafe, thinking she must not understand the side effects she was having from the medication and the impact on her relationship with Eden. She also realized they handled the situation wrong. Along with reporting Rafe's symptoms, they probably should have just suggested the doctor lower the dose or give her something else. Rafe was clearly attached to the notion she needed to take medication to get better based on whatever happened with her therapy in Mexico.

"You don't need to go anywhere," she assured her. "I'll help you. What if I call the doctor for you?" Julia offered. "What if I call her and tell her you need your medicine, maybe just a different one. The one you had, Rafe, I'm telling you, it wasn't helping you." She watched Rafe sit quietly but could tell she was still angry. "Let me see if I can help. Okay?"

Rafe observed her suspiciously. "I thought you said Eden couldn't make the doctor take my medicine away."

"I did."

"Well, then how the hell can you make her give it back to me?" Rafe asked angrily. "Are you the one who called? Why are you doing this to me? I thought you were my friend!"

"I am your friend!" Julia insisted. "I may not have made the call, but maybe I should have! Look at what you're doing right now! You can't even see when someone's trying to help you!"

"Then fucking help me!" demanded Rafe. "Make her stop calling my doctor and spying on me! Make her stop pushing me to do things I don't want to do! Make her stop just taking and taking from me! Make her call and tell the doctor to give me back my medicine!"

"Fine!" Julia yelled back. "So, you want me to call Eden right now? Do you want to listen while I talk to her?" Julia pulled out her phone. "If I do this, you have to let me help you all the time. You have to talk to me about your sessions and about everything going on. I'm not going to do a half-assed job, Rafe. If you want me to help you, then you have to actually let me help!" She looked on her phone at Eden's number then at Rafe. "You have to swear, Rafe. I'm not doing anything unless I know you agree. Do you swear?"

Rafe glared at her angrily. "I'll swear, but you have to swear you won't be telling everyone my business! I don't want you telling everyone I'm crazy and calling my doctor and telling Eden things!"

"No, Rafe," said Julia as she shook her head. "You can't put conditions on my help. I won't tell anyone you're crazy, but I need to be able to talk to Eden and your doctor. Eden is living here with you, and she'll need to know things sometimes. She loves you and worries about you. So do I," she confessed then continued quickly, "I'd like to help you, both of you. Don't you think Eden might need some help sometimes? Plus, how can I tell her to stop pressing you if I can't talk to her?"

Leaning forward into her hands, Rafe felt pushed into a corner. She needed her medicine, and Julia was using it against her to get her to do something she didn't want to do. She and Eden were obviously the cause of the problem, and now they were pushing her even more and trying to fuck with her. She looked up at Julia angrily. "Fuck off, Julia! I don't need your help! Stop talking to my doctor and stop fucking with my life!" She got up and stalked out of the house angrily.

"Fuck all," Julia said softly and followed her out to the patio to try to reason with her. She immediately saw Rafe was not there and ran for the gate, thinking she may be taking off in her car. When she got there, Rafe was already in another argument, but this time it was with Abby.

"Get your car out of my fucking way!" Rafe screamed at Abby because she was blocking the driveway.

"What the fuck, Rafe? What the hell is wrong with you?" asked Abby offended. "I just came over to see what was up!"

"What's up is I need to leave right now, and you're in the way!" Rafe fumed.

"Rafe, come on," said Julia as she made it to the driveway. "Don't leave, I'm sorry."

"What the hell is going on?" Abby asked Julia.

"You people need to stay out of my fucking life, that's what's going on!" Rafe yelled then turned to go back toward the house. She stormed through the gate to the backyard, just wanting to get away from them.

"Hey," said Jude as she came out of her house. "What's all the yelling?"

Abby turned to Jude. "Rafe is fucking crazy!" she said heatedly.

"Abby, if you say 'crazy' in front of Rafe, she will explode, so knock it off!" growled Julia. "You know it upsets her, and she is already pissed!"

"Well, what the hell did I do?" asked Abby perturbed. "She didn't have to bite my head off."

"She was obviously trying to leave," said Julia annoyed with Abby and frustrated with Rafe. "It's probably a good thing you were blocking her in. Otherwise, no telling where she would go or what she would do." She bit her lip then looked at Abby and Jude. "The doctor took her meds, and she's angry at Eden and me about it. We need to go talk to her and try to get her to let us help her. Come on," she commanded and led them into the backyard. When they didn't see Rafe by the pool, they headed inside.

38

IN THE KITCHEN, Rafe Salvaggio was filling an ice bucket with ice and had pulled out a new bottle of scotch and a glass. At the moment, she needed a strong but cool drink. She picked up everything and then turned to take it outside and saw the women intruding on her again. "Are you still here?" she snapped. "I told you to fuck off!" She pushed past them and went out to the patio where she sat her drink station up on a side table and sat on the lounger.

Julia led the group after Rafe in frustration. "What the hell are you doing?" she asked as she stood over Rafe and watched her pour scotch into her glass.

Rafe scowled angrily. "I'm medicating myself!" she spat then took a drink and sat back on her lounger.

"Drinking isn't going to help things!" Julia argued and threw her hands up in exasperation.

Jude could see they had backed Rafe into a corner, and she was trying to escape by drinking. It was something she was very familiar with and knew it could lead to more problems. Sometimes, the best way to handle people was to be on their side. "I think Rafe has a good idea," said Jude softly. "I could use a beer. Rafe, can I get one from you?"

Rafe felt a wave of appreciation for Jude and knew she understood. "Sure, just get what you want," she said and took another sip.

Julia followed Jude into the kitchen. "What are you doing? We can't let her get drunk. Eden will kill us."

"You need to relax. I've dealt with Rafe before when she's been upset," Jude explained. "If you keep nagging her, she's just going to drink more. When Eden nagged her about the pot, she smoked more to defy her. She had me leave her a couple, but she ended up not smoking them once Eden left her alone."

"So, what are you suggesting?"

"Just leave her alone and give her some space," said Jude. "Plus, the alcohol may even calm her down. Maybe after a few drinks, we can take the bottle from her, and she won't get drunk." She pulled a beer from the refrigerator, and with a smile, she said, "She always has the good stuff." Then she took her beer outside.

Julia groaned in disagreement as she watched Jude leave but hoped she was right. She opened the cabinet and got out wine glasses for her and Abby. She then opened a bottle of wine and carried it all outside. She walked over to Abby and handed her a glass. "I think we can all use a little something to help us relax," she said and poured the wine.

"Thanks," said Abby and sat down on the edge of one of the loungers and Julia sat in another. "Looks like we're having a piss party," she said still miffed about Rafe yelling at her in the driveway.

Rafe was happy to enjoy her drink in silence but wished all her babysitters would leave. After a while, she looked over at Jude and saw she had finished her beer. "You need another?" she asked softly.

Jude sat up and put her bottle on the table. "Here," she said and took Rafe's glass, "let me pour you another." She put more ice in the cup and splashed scotch over the ice. "Here ya go," she offered, handing Rafe her glass. "I'll go get another beer."

She left, and Rafe took a sip of her drink then laid back and closed her eyes.

Jude came back with a beer and sat down close to Rafe who had her eyes closed. Jude looked over at Julia and raised her eyebrows, signaling 'I told you so,' and Abby rolled her eyes.

"So, Julia, what's going on," Jude asked tentatively. "What'd you do to Rafe?"

Julia sighed and shook her head. "I just showed up at the wrong time, I guess. I was going to take Rafe out for lunch, but she was mad when I got here."

"Oh." Jude nodded. "Well, there's a lot to be mad about." She looked over at Rafe. "Was it the file thing from Katheryn?"

"No," said Julia. "Her doctor took her medicine away."

"Seems like a good thing, Rafe. It may mean you don't need it," said Jude hopefully.

Rafe opened her eyes and frowned at Jude. "I need it," she said flatly.

"Why?" asked Jude with a shrug. "I hate taking meds."

"I need it," said Rafe in frustration, "because I haven't figured everything out yet, and it was helping."

"What do you need to figure out?" asked Abby. "Maybe we can help."

Julia watched as Rafe turned her head away and knew she was not going to answer Abby. "She has to figure out things about Eden, and she apparently isn't making it easy," Julia revealed. "Eden's been pressing in on Rafe's space again, and Rafe isn't ready to have her close yet."

Jude nodded her understanding. "Sometimes you need space to figure things out."

"Apparently, Eden's telling Rafe she needs some comfort, and Rafe just isn't ready to let her touch her yet," Julia informed them.

Abby gawped at Rafe in disbelief. "Rafe, I thought you loved her. The way you were looking at Eden when you came home," she said haltingly, "I just thought you would be past all of this and be back together."

Julia watched Rafe take a sip of her drink then look out over the pool, ignoring Abby. "Do you still think you two would have split even if Jake and his group hadn't been involved?"

"I think," Rafe paused, thinking about everything going on at the time they were dealing with the insemination process, "I think, if she were having those feelings about men, and she actually told me about them back then, we would have broken up before we had a child. We probably wouldn't be together now."

"Why did you come back here, Rafe?" asked Julia with empathy. She shook her head, thinking that maybe Rafe was better off with Greer after all. It was disappointing because she was once again missing the possibility of being with Rafe. *I should be used to it by now*, she thought. She pushed those notions from her mind, reminding herself she was just there to help Eden until Rafe did whatever Rafe did.

"Wait, what?" Abby screeched, at Rafe's shocking revelation. "No, you can't think she shouldn't be here!"

Rafe just stared at Abby for a moment then ignored her. She leaned her head back to look up at the blue sky. "You know the answer, Julia."

"Abby, she clearly isn't happy," said Julia as she nudged her. "I know you need the therapy, Rafe, but you could have gone to Greer, even if you just went as a friend."

Rafe looked over at Julia with a frown. "You have no idea what you're talking about. You should just leave me alone."

If Rafe was feeling this way, Julia did not understand why she was treating Eden so abysmally. "So, how long are you going to punish Eden," asked Julia as she sat back on the lounger.

"I'm not punishing her," Rafe said evenly. "I am just trying to figure out things, like if I can trust her not to leave me again."

"I don't think she will," said Jude calmly. "I think she wants to stay. She was really worried about you."

"Yeah," said Abby, "the week you were away in Mexico, we came over every night, and she worried about whether or not you would come home to her. She barely ate or slept the whole time because of her anxiety."

Jude took a swig of her beer and waited to see if Rafe would respond. "She really cares about you," Jude added hoping to get a response.

"Sounds like she cares about herself," said Julia sarcastically. "She was worried about you coming home to her, but not about you," she said, hoping maybe Rafe would defend Eden like she usually did. Then she would know if Rafe really did feel the same about her.

"She was worried about Rafe," insisted Abby, not understanding what Julia was doing. "She was upset she had to leave her there, Julia, and was sick because she didn't know anything about how Rafe was doing."

Jude saw Rafe was not going to respond. "Well, I'm still just wondering what happened with the file thing Julia told us about. I guess I just don't understand what was so bad in the file."

"Yes," agreed Julia as Rafe sat silently, "what happened, Rafe?" she asked, changing tactics. "I mean how bad could what she wrote online be?" Rafe glared at her. "What are you so angry about?"

"I'm angry she didn't say any of it to me," she said evenly remembering how Eden could suddenly talk to her if she pretended she was a stranger. "If she had, maybe some of this stuff wouldn't have happened."

"Well, are you more angry about what she said or who she said it too?" asked Julia.

"I'm mad about it all," said Rafe annoyed with her questions. She sat up and peered at Julia forcefully, deciding if Julia wanted to know details, then she would fucking tell her exactly why she was angry. "I'm pissed that she told strangers about our life. She kept things from me and lied to me. She thought she had to protect me from the Stewards group and Jake," she ticked off the reasons furiously. "She's cost me my job and possibly my reputation in business. She didn't trust me. She touches me and kisses me when I ask her not to all the time. She's thoughtless, she took things from me I can never get back, she thinks I need a mother, she thinks I need her forgiveness, and she made the doctor take away my medicine.

The list could go on and on. There is so much I had to fucking write it all down, so I didn't forget anything!"

"Come on, Rafe. You've made mistakes too, and she isn't holding them against you anymore," said Julia. "Plus, some of those things she had no direct control over, and you know it."

"Are you sure?" Rafe asked skeptically as she forced herself not to rub her aching temples. "What is it you think I did to her that compares to any of the things she's done? Oh, and you don't get to count my fuck up in New York because, for the past three years, I've been paying for it."

"Yes, I'm sure," answered Julia wryly and took a sip of her wine, considering her other question.

Abby frowned with concern. "Rafe, you know she had no real control over the whole Stewards thing, even if she was talking to them in a chatroom," said Abby. "She had no idea she was targeted or how far they would go to succeed at their mission. Katheryn showed us all the things they were doing."

"So take everything they and Jake did off your list of things you're angry about, including the stuff in the file," said Julia haughtily.

"Why should I?" demanded Rafe. "She caused it all by her choice not to talk to me or anyone she knew. She made a choice to leave, and the choice to push me, you, and everyone else out of her life for a year! Now she wants to walk back into a life with us," she said pointing heatedly to herself and the others, "and then expect us to just forget the trail of pain and destruction she caused, and you all are just fine with it?"

"She hasn't asked us to forget," said Abby. "She knows what she did and the fact she made a monumental mistake. She's apologized many times over to all of us."

"True," said Julia with a nod to Abby. She looked back at Rafe pointedly. "So, are you going to punish her for years like you think she's doing to you over Lauren?"

"She was hurting a lot then, too," said Abby feeling like Eden needed an advocate. "When she," Abby hesitate then blurted on, "when she left you, she was dealing with the things Jake was doing to pull her away from us. Then everything after she left him and he was messing with her. Remember, she did start seeing a doctor and getting the help that she needed. I think she punished herself a lot, so maybe you should stop punishing her."

"I'm not punishing her," Rafe said evenly. "I'm trying to figure things out."

Julia sighed and shook her head. "Really, Rafe, after you take away all the Steward chaos, what's left to be angry about?" she asked with a shrug. "Let's see, protecting you and keeping things from you, acting like you need a mother, pushing into your space. She wants you to forgive her or she wants to forgive you, or whatever, the time you missed with Bronte," she listed then stopped to think. "Oh, yeah, calling your doctor and the meds, maybe, anything else?"

"Trust," said Rafe. "She doesn't trust me anymore, and I don't know if I can trust her."

"Wait, wait," said Jude making a time-out sign. "Why does her asking you to forgive her make you mad?"

"Rafe doesn't believe in giving forgiveness as a resolution tool," Julia informed her. "It serves no purpose except to excuse punishable behavior. Right, Rafe?"

Rafe glared at her with annoyance. "Something like that," she said to Jude. "Really, Jude, there is nothing for me to forgive." She could see Jude didn't understand and needed more clarification. "I just don't think I should be called on to bestow forgiveness for every mistake someone makes," she explained. "People should just forgive themselves and not put the burden on anyone else. Because, really, is forgiveness for the forgiven or for the forgiver? Usually, I think it's for the person who wants to receive the forgiveness and does much less for the person giving it to them. I think it is much healthier to forgive yourself, no matter if others forgive you or not. This way, forgiveness is not a commodity. It's just part of your inner strength of character no one can take from you."

"Well, what about her forgiving you? Or if you want to forgive someone?" asked Jude puzzled.

Rafe shrugged and finally had to give in to rubbing her temples. "If people can forgive themselves, they shouldn't need your forgiveness. If you're forgiving someone, then you should just do it for yourself and not worry about making some production about it," she said through her pain. "I wouldn't want someone coming up to me telling me they forgive me for something they think I need forgiveness for doing or saying. It would just send the message they've judged you, and they're your judge and jury, deciding whether or not you're worthy of their forgiveness. If you think you have to forgive someone, you should think about why you're doing it. Are you really doing it for them or for yourself? Who really benefits? If they're asking for it then what will they gain by having it? Most times, they just want you to excuse their behavior, and they're making you be the judge and jury so they can feel better about themselves. It's not my place and, if they feel bad, then they need to resolve their issue without involving me."

"You see, Jude!" Julia laughed. "This is what you get when you read your child books on philosophy at bedtime. But you've never told your views to Eden, have you, Rafe?"

"Why would I have to tell her?" Rafe took another soothing sip of her scotch.

"Well, so she would know not to ask you for forgiveness," Julia said and raised her eyebrows.

"Julia, you know her background," said Rafe with a short laugh. "She was taught forgiveness is just a word and something you just give out like candy. For her, it's been all tied up in self-worth, religion, and all the rest—just like most people. So, I just tell her there's nothing to forgive, and it satisfies her need for what she thinks is a cure for whatever problem she's having. Then I leave her alone to work through it on her own so she can forgive herself if she thinks she needs it."

"Some people actually think forgiveness is more than a commodity and plays an important role in relationships," said Julia. "What about those people? What if Eden is one of those people?"

"She's not," said Rafe gritting her teeth. "She already told me her definition of forgiveness, and to her, it is a commodity to be traded for mistakes, bad choices, or bad behavior."

"Maybe Eden thinks it's a tool to show she has learned from her mistakes, and it helps people heal from the pain of those mistakes," Julia offered.

"That's what an apology is for," said Rafe as she swirled the ice in her glass, "so if forgiveness is an apology to be given and received, then it's not really forgiveness, is it? There are a lot of definitions made up for forgiveness, but I don't think an apology is one of them."

"Well, Eden has apologized," said Abby as she shook her head at Rafe's logic. "Are you saying you don't or won't accept her apology?"

Rafe looked menacingly at Abby. "Whether or not I accept her apology has nothing to do with being able to trust her! And apologies mean nothing if you keep repeating the offense!"

"Repeating the offense?" said Abby confused. "What the hell?"

39

JULIA HAWTHORN KNEW Rafe could argue her case for both forgiveness and apologies all night if they allowed it. It was just another way to push them off the topic and control the conversation. She had to get Rafe talking and thinking about Eden and what she was doing to her. She felt Rafe had to stop blaming Eden for everything, or Eden would never be able to get anywhere with her. Plus, if Rafe really was thinking about leaving Eden, maybe hearing some hard truths would push her into action other than tearing everyone down. She decided to change the direction of the conversation.

"I just think Eden has more growing up to do," said Julia and then took a sip of her wine.

Rafe frowned. "More growing up? What do you mean?"

"Yeah," Abby piped in, "she's grown up."

"Come on, Rafe," said Julia with a short laugh and ignored Abby. "You remember back when she first took time off work and had to take care of all the household stuff. She totally messed things up."

Rafe gave a short laugh. "Yeah, she did."

"Why *did* you make her start taking care of it all?" asked Abby.

"I didn't make her. She said she wanted to help and said she could take care of things for the house," said Rafe and poured another drink.

"Why do you think she didn't tell you she was having a hard time when she was taking care of the house while staying home," probed Julia.

Rafe sipped her drink. "I don't know."

"Maybe she was afraid of disappointing you," offered Julia.

"Disappointing me?"

"Yeah, because you just dropped everything on her. You expected her to know about everything and how to do it," Julia pointed out.

"I didn't expect her to know everything. I expected her to learn it, just like you'd learn to do any job," said Rafe defensively.

"She was used to coming home and being a little *dogsbody*, just cooking then maybe putting dishes away and vacuuming. Then, suddenly, she had to know about all the bills and maintenance schedules and whatever other bloody lists you have that needed tending to," quipped Julia and laughed. "On top of the lists, you have different bank accounts for different things she had to figure out."

"So?" said Rafe annoyed. "Things need to be tracked."

"Rafe, you have a household account for food and supplies, a home maintenance account, a car maintenance account, and two personal accounts. Why you can't track it all from one account, I don't know. I remember Eden being terrified you were spending too much money because one of the accounts was almost empty." She looked over at Jude and Abby. "She had been using the wrong account," she explained, and then looked back at Rafe. "I remember, after she left, you were complaining about how bad she fucked up the accounts. Did you even give her an overview or a clue about what was what?"

"It was pretty obvious," said Rafe through gritted teeth. "If she would have spent as much time on figuring the accounts out as she did online, she would have had no problems!"

Julia could see Rafe was getting angry, but she kept pushing. "So, you agreed she would quit her job so she would be under less stress, and then you caused her more stress by making her go through a trial by fire on the finances?" Julia asked with a sarcastic laugh. "You could have taken the time to help her. Every job has some training to it." She scoffed at the fact Rafe was being so obtuse. "As a matter of fact, you could have just had someone in our accounting office take care of everything temporarily so she wouldn't have had to worry about anything."

"She needed to learn it all," said Rafe evenly. "It wouldn't have been stressful if she had actually taken it seriously. She needed to know what was going on with the finances, and what things cost, and how to take care of things. At the time, we were only living on what I made, so having your office do the finances wasn't an option, and you know it." She wondered why they were ganging up on her again. *They always defend Eden*, she thought. *Maybe she would just leave her to them.* "It wasn't like we would starve, but we cut off a quarter or more of our income when she stayed home. All I wanted her to do was cut out what we didn't really need, and she started cutting out everything. It was all because she couldn't find the time to figure out the accounts."

"It does sound reasonable," said Jude hesitantly. "Knowing your finances is important." She glanced at Julia and shrugged, knowing she really had not helped. "But it may have been less stressful if she had some help when she first started," she added, hoping to get back in Julia's good graces.

"Rafe, we were already doing your business accounts, so adding those would have been negligible," said Julia with a sigh. "I really don't think you cared if she messed them up. I think you're more upset you think she failed."

"What?" Rafe laughed. "I would never have let her do them if I thought she would fail. She's a very smart, college-educated woman. She could have figured it all out. As a matter of fact, if I had thought they would have been so stressful, I may have just kept doing them myself." She held her glass tightly trying to hold in her anger. "I trusted her, Julia, and she was fucking strangers on the internet!"

Julia knew better than to defend Eden for that indiscretion right now, so she ignored it. "You're right, she is a smart woman," she said, trying to change tactics, "but, like I said, she needs to grow up."

"I think she's pretty damn grown up," said Rafe. "She's done her best to prove she doesn't need anyone."

"You think she was being grown up?" Julia asked with a laugh of disbelief. "She was used and manipulated like a child, and you know it. She has never grown up because you never really let her."

"What the fuck are you talking about?" asked Rafe angrily.

"You told me the other day you were mad because she said you need a mother, but really, you've treated her more like a mother would, and she doesn't need a mother, either," said Julia pragmatically.

"I've never treated her like a mother. She has a mother! One she chooses not to see," said Rafe annoyed. "If Eden's not grown up, it's her fault."

"Rafe, you met her the year before she graduated college, and you've never let her spread her wings," Julia paused, "and now she has spread them, without you," she said pointedly, "you're angry with her for growing without you. You were the one stopping her from growing."

Rafe shook her head as she glowered at Julia. She could not believe what she was saying. "I didn't stop her from anything," she said confused.

"Think about it, Rafe. You can barely let anyone be in charge of planning something as mundane as a dinner party, including Eden," she said insistently. "When was the last time you let Eden be exclusively in charge of anything?"

"She's in charge of herself," said Rafe crossly. "I don't even know why we're talking about this or what this has to do with anything!"

"You said you want a partner, not a mother or protector," answered Julia. "Well, a partner is there when the other person in the relationship falls and helps them stand back up. A partner allows the other to grow and encourages them."

Rafe clenched her fist angrily. "A partner doesn't shut you out, Julia! A partner doesn't lie and take the trust you give them and destroy it! A partner," she fought her anger, "a partner doesn't leave you without saying goodbye!"

Julia shook her head at Rafe and her unjustified righteous anger and wanted to strangle her for her blindness. "You're right," she said softly. "I guess you aren't a very good partner since you did all those things to Eden."

"What the fuck are you talking about?" raged Rafe as she slammed her glass on the table spilling the contents then jumping up and standing over Julia.

Julia could feel the heat of Rafe's anger, but she stood her ground. "You did all those things," she said calmly. "You shut her out while she was going through the hormone and insemination process. You were so busy being angry and working, you didn't see she needed you. I know you're mad she told a stranger, but she shouldn't have had to feel like she had to talk to them. You should have seen she needed you and made sure you were there for her!"

"I was working! I was making sure we had a fucking roof over our head!"

"Bullshit! You went because your father insisted you oversee things when you could have had someone else to go!"

"You have no idea what you're fucking talking about! My father was sick! He had nothing to do with the projects I was working on, and if I wasn't there, we could have lost millions! I fucking saved my company by being there!" Rafe said indignantly. "Were you there? Do you know what was happening in my company on those sites? Did you know what was happening with Eden?"

"No, I don't know what was happening, but I know you made a promise to Eden you would make a family together. And I know, instead, you chose to take on huge projects that took you away and left everything on her shoulders," Julia shot back, "and now you're punishing her for having problems when you knew she couldn't function well under pressure sometimes because of her anxiety."

"I'm not punishing her!" Rafe raged. "Stop fucking saying that!"

"She showed me the files. I could see what she was going through!" Julia informed her hotly. "I remember what was going on back then. I didn't see you going to very many appointments or helping her when she was taking hormones, and they were changing her in all kinds of ways. I didn't see you picking up Eden and helping her when she was devastated by the failures in the insemination process. She was alone for all of it and walking on eggshells because of you!"

"I am not a fucking mind reader!" fumed Rafe as her anger pressed out of her in waves of heat causing her skin to begin to glisten with sweat. "None of those things is an excuse to not call me or email me, and to go talk to strangers instead! She's the one who shut me out! I would have been here if I'd have known and you know it!" Rafe growled. "She could have told one of you! None of you can keep your fucking mouths shut about anything and are always telling me what I'm doing wrong and how I'm hurting Eden! So where were you? Apparently, you have no problem telling me what a fuck up I am!"

"You're not a fuck up," said Abby wanting to calm her. "We love you and knew your business kept you busy. We just want to help Eden sometimes because you can get," she paused, "distracted."

"Yeah," said Jude, "but Rafe is right, Eden didn't tell us about the problems she was having."

"Why would she?" asked Julia with a harsh laugh. "She was having feelings for men, and we're all Rafe's friends. She may have thought we would tear her apart. She may also have been afraid of what her feelings meant for the promises she made to Rafe and the child she was trying to conceive. We have no idea what was going on in her mind back then. It all may have just been happening because of the extra hormones and the stress."

"So, really," said Jude trying to mediate, "they're both to blame for what was going on." She was concerned as she watched Rafe who was sitting down with her hand clenched against her head as a drip of perspiration ran down her cheek. "You can't be mad at her if you share the blame, Rafe."

"Oh, no," said Julia, "she doesn't get off so easily." Rafe looked up at her with a murderous look, but she pressed on. "You're shutting her out again right now."

"How am I shutting her out?" asked Rafe with her eyes blazing. "It looks like she's doing just fine to me!"

"I didn't see you helping her after her ordeal with the Stewards. You just beat her down and punish her like an insolent child," said Julia as Rafe glared at her. "Don't you think she deserves a little comfort after dealing with all she's been through? Rafe, even when she was trying to get some kind of comfort from you after Jake tried to take Bronte, you couldn't be bothered with holding her or even giving her comforting words."

"Fuck you, Julia," Rafe fumed as more streams of sweat ran down from her temples. "Just add another entry to your list of my fucking faults and reasons she should leave me! It's what you all think any way, right? That she should just leave me again?"

"No, Rafe," said Abby, horrified with what Julia was saying. "We don't think she should leave you. We know she loves you and you love her and Bronte."

Julia stared up at Rafe as she stood over her seething with anger. She had to make Rafe see what was happening and hope her words would make it past her anger so she would see reason. She knew she was making her mad, but she was already angry. Eden and the others treating her with kid gloves wasn't helping anything. "I know you think it should be off-limits, but when you cheated on her with Lauren, you lied to her! Not just about the affair, but about her importance to you! You're the one who destroyed the trust you feel you can't find with her!"

Rafe clenched her fists in a fury. "I know what I did, Julia! I know, and I've paid for it over and over again! I'm still paying for it right fucking now!"

"You're still paying because you're the one who destroyed the trust between the two of you," Julia said evenly. "And now you're beating Eden up with all the reasons you can't trust her when you're the one who broke the trust in the first place! A little hypocritical, don't you think?"

"Julia, stop," said Jude worried about the state Rafe was in as she watched the sweat pour out of her from her anger, making her dark hair curl against her face. "I don't think this is helping."

"You go ahead and hold the one," Rafe forced through her clenched teeth, "one thing I did in all of this over me! You go ahead and beat me over the fucking head with it! It doesn't change the fact she fucking shattered the trust between us with all the things she did! She broke the fucking trust long before I did with her online strangers and her cyber fuck! So fuck you, Julia!"

"Come on, Rafe!" Julia yelled in frustration. "We just went over the fact she was having problems back then with anxiety and the hormones and the inseminations and the loss her body was going through when they didn't work! If you weren't cut off from her, she might not have had those issues! She didn't plan to have emotional issues and the feelings she had. She may have got a cyber fuck, but she didn't go find an actual man until you pushed her away!"

"Well, I didn't plan on fucking Lauren! I was pushed away too! She just left me there and cut me off!" fumed Rafe as sweat ran down her back.

"Just like what you did to her!" said Julia trying to make Rafe see the common thread. "You can't put everything on her, Rafe! She was under a lot of stress too! On top of everything else, you, the person who is supposed to love her, didn't help her when she was failing at everything from conceiving to taking care of the house. You didn't even encourage her to ask for help from you or anyone else either," said Julia firmly. "As a matter of fact, she was so afraid to let you down, she wouldn't ask you or anyone else for help!" Julia stood up and faced Rafe down. "So how could she grow and not fail? She couldn't, and she's still acting like a child who needs to be told what to do because of you and how you treat her. And now she has to deal with you dragging her over the coals for things she had no control over!"

"Julia, maybe this is too harsh," said Jude uncomfortably.

"Maybe it's another reason why she should leave," said Rafe evenly, barely holding in the anger with threadbare control.

"Maybe," said Julia as she smirked at Rafe. "Why do you think she's staying?"

Rafe didn't answer, and Jude couldn't hold in her words. "Because she loves you, Rafe," she said, "that's why. She doesn't need another reason, does she?"

"Why are you doing this, Julia?" Rafe asked in confusion as she wiped her hand over her sweat-covered face and through her dark hair. "I thought you were my friend."

"I am your friend. You just have to see the truth about Eden and this whole Stewards thing, including those files."

"The truth?" she asked mystified. "I think I see what happened pretty clearly."

"So you realize this is the first truly traumatic thing to happen to Eden since leaving her parents behind because they couldn't accept she was gay?" asked Julia and watched Rafe try to understand what it meant.

"She's bisexual," Abby piped in, and Rafe glared at her making her stop talking immediately.

"Rafe, Eden hasn't had any real tragedy in her life," Julia continued trying to get her to see reason. "She was never thrust into a new world when she was young and had to fight her way through life practically on her own like we were. She never saw death up close like you have. She never had to fight for anyone's love or acceptance like we all have. Everyone in her life, including you, Rafe, has protected her from tragedy. But no one, including Eden, can be protected forever. Do you really think she wanted to be beaten and shot at or manipulated away from the life she chose when she chose to be with you?"

Rafe closed her eyes at the memory of Eden's bruised body. Blood red waved through her vision at the thought of Eden being an inch from death. The pain seared through her mind sparking her fury. "Julia, those things happened because of her choices! Her choice not to talk with me or anyone. It was her choice to leave in the dark of night with someone she barely knew. She could have stopped it if she had wanted to stop!" Rafe seethed, infuriated at Julia and the others and their continued defense of Eden.

"She did stop," Julia said trying to hold back her frustration at Rafe's inability to see things clearly.

"No, she didn't really stop! She thinks she did by telling me that she was trying to protect me. But really, she was still just lying!"

"So, she took over as protector and was trying to grow, and you're pushing her away because of it," Julia accused her. "Maybe she was wrong to try to handle it on her own, but I think you or I would have done the same things. We're just better equipped," Julia insisted emphatically.

"It's true," said Jude trying to de-escalate the situation. "We would. I tried to protect her from being hurt when you were angry, Rafe. So did Flynn and Abby. We all protect her from a lot of things. So maybe she learned her behavior from all of us. Can we blame her for doing what she saw us do?"

Rafe shook her head at Jude and Julia's words. "Maybe, she needs to learn to think first!" she snapped. "Maybe, she should think about how her attempt to protect really ended up causing problems for herself and everyone else! Protecting is more than taking things on alone. It's thinking about the people you're protecting and how they will be affected by your actions. Sometimes, protecting is telling people what's going on and getting help. Sometimes, giving up things for yourself and letting others handle things is a better way to protect someone. Especially, if you haven't done it before," she said heatedly.

"I think she's learned her lesson the hard way, don't you?" Julia watched Rafe and knew she was getting way past her boiling point, so she redirected. "If she never learns how to fight and stand up for herself, she'll never grow," Julia said softly. "Someday, she may need to handle it on her own again, especially if you decide you can't stay with her. Now she's proven she can handle things. But she has a long way to go yet," she said and took a deep calming breath. "If you decide to stay with Eden, you need to accept she'll be making more mistakes, and she'll need you to help her sometimes until she can actually do it all on her own."

Rafe sat on the edge of the lounger shaking and wiped the sweat from her face again. She looked up at Julia feeling betrayed and confused, feeling pain from pressure building around her chest and head. "I need my medicine," she complained. "I need you to leave! I—" she said and couldn't find the words to express all of the emotions rolling inside of her.

"If you're mad at her for calling your doctor, you need to talk to her about it rationally. If you think you need medication, you need to just tell your doctor or let us help you and give us permission to talk to her." Julia sat next to Rafe. "Part of Eden growing up is you letting her know when you're pissed off or when you need help and letting her handle it. Let her help you. Don't take away her chance to deal with it by storming off or fixing it yourself and leaving her out of the process. She wants to help you, Rafe, but you have to stop and look at what you're doing to her. If she's pushed too far, you already know what will happen. She'll leave again, and I know you love her. I know you want to keep her here or you would have made her move out when you got home."

Abby came out of the house with a glass of water. "Here, Rafe," she said and handed her the water. "Maybe this will cool you off."

Rafe took the glass of water. The three women now surrounding her made her feel suffocated and beaten down. They were the ones doing the punishing. They were the ones always protecting Eden and telling Rafe she was the monster. She took an angry breath and stood up. "I get it," she said evenly, "I'm still the fucking monster!" she said as she dashed the glass of water onto the ground shattering it. "Fuck all of you!" she forced out through her teeth. "Maybe I should be the one to leave!" she growled then walked away from them into the house.

"Rafe!" screeched Abby. "Rafe, you're not a monster!" she called then faced Julia. "What the hell are you doing?"

"She has to see reason," said Julia as she shook her head in frustration. "She has to see the truth of things. She still isn't seeing it, but maybe some of it will get through."

"Don't you think pushing her so hard was kind of a harsh way of doing it?" asked Jude with concern.

"I don't know," admitted Julia. "I just know no one is putting the truth in front of her, and she's carrying around a lot of wrong thoughts. If either if you have any better ideas, please, feel free to let me know," she said in vexation. "I better go check on her."

40

WALKING INTO THE house, Julia Hawthorn was sure her little push would get some sort of action from Rafe. She was pleased she could help manage to get Rafe thinking about doing what she should have done long ago—walk away from

Eden. Figuring Rafe would be in her bedroom, she headed straight to her door and knocked. "Rafe," she called, "Rafe, I know you're mad, and I'm sorry. I'm just trying to help you see the truth." She tried the door handle, and it was unlocked, so she opened the door. Rafe was kneeling on the floor with one hand holding her head and the other pressed against her chest. "Bloody hell," Julia hissed under her breath. She knelt next to Rafe and pulled her up so she could see her face. "Rafe, are you okay? Are you feeling the phantom pains?"

Panic filled Rafe, and she felt sick to her stomach. "I need my medicine," she said shakily. "I—" she started but couldn't speak.

"I'm sorry," said Julia and put her hand on Rafe's head as they were instructed. "This is my hand, okay? You're feeling the phantom pain. It's not real. Are you feeling the pressure in your chest?" Rafe nodded her head, her clothes soaked with sweat. "Okay, let's get up and get out of here," coaxed Julia. "Maybe, in a minute, you can go take a shower and put on one of your racy outfits, then we can go to lunch or something," she offered, trying to get Rafe's mind off her phantom pain. "You want to go drive around? Maybe we can go test drive some really expensive cars after lunch. How does that sound? I'll be driving, though," she tried to joke as she got Rafe to her feet. "Come on." She led her into the living room.

"What's going on?" asked Abby when she found Julia leading Rafe from her room.

Julia sat next to Rafe on the couch. "At the moment, she thinks her best friend is an asshole. Right, Rafe?"

"Shit, Julia," hissed Abby as Rafe leaned over with her hand against her chest again. "What the fuck! Look what you did to her. You made her sick!"

"Calm down," said Julia to Abby as she rubbed Rafe's back. "Sit up, Rafe," she said as she pulled her up and put her hand over Rafe's hand that she had pressed against her chest. "It's okay. Just breathe and know you're okay. You're safe with me. See, it's just my hand against you. I'll always take care of you, okay? You know that right? We're a team."

Rafe leaned into Julia's shoulder. "I need," she said shakily, "I need my medicine."

"Okay," said Julia managing the panic she felt at Rafe's condition. "I'll call Eden, okay?" She felt Rafe shaking against her and glanced up at Abby. "Abby, come and sit with Rafe so I can talk to Eden." She let Abby take her place, and as she walked to the kitchen, she pulled the phone out of her pocket and dialed Eden. "Hello, Eden Kingsley, please," she said into the phone. "Eden, listen, I think you should call Rafe's doctor."

"What's wrong? What happened? Is she hurt? Do I need to come home?" Eden asked with worry through the phone.

"No, no, she's going to be fine. She's having a problem now, but Abby, Jude, and I are here so she'll be fine."

"Why do I need to call her doctor?" asked Eden nervously.

Julia sighed into the phone. "She thinks she needs her medicine."

"What? Didn't the doctor give her something new?"

"Apparently not. Listen, I don't know what kind she needs, but it certainly can't be what she had before. Maybe she can give her a placebo unless she can give her something real."

Eden was silent on the phone. "I don't understand. A placebo?"

"I just know she seems to believe she has to have something to help her think," said Julia.

"She was just taken off a medication," Eden said shakily. "I don't know how soon she can start another."

"Maybe she'll have to let what's in her run its course," said Julia with frustration. "I don't know. Maybe she'll realize after a few days she doesn't need it. All I know is, right now, the reason she's angry is because she thinks you took it away."

"Great," said Eden and was silent. "Fine, I'll call and see what the doctor says."

"Good. Sorry about this. I'll talk to you later." Julia hung up and rubbed her temples then went back into the living room and sat next to Rafe. "Okay, I talked to Eden, and she's going to call your doctor. She'll tell her what you said about needing meds. But it can't be the one you had before, Rafe. It really wasn't helping you."

41

GETTING THROUGH WORK was difficult for Eden Kingsley after Julia called about Rafe. She was nervous and worried as she arrived home and pulled her car into the driveway. After Julia's call, Eden phoned the doctor and told her everything Julia had said including how Rafe was telling them that she needed medicine. The doctor listened but didn't reveal her thoughts on the matter. Eden would have to wait to see what the doctor would decide to do until Rafe went to her session on Monday.

Apparently, the conversation Julia and the others had with Rafe didn't go well, and she had a setback. Julia said they stayed with Rafe until she was better, and Abby went and got them lunch. Rafe didn't eat much, but it wasn't surprising to Eden. They tried to get Rafe out of the house, but she wouldn't leave. Instead, she told them she needed to be alone and went to her room. Julia waited around for a while, but it was soon clear Rafe wasn't coming out. She checked on Rafe before she left. Rafe was curled up in bed and wouldn't answer her when she tried talking to her so she couldn't tell if she was asleep or not.

Eden was nervous about what shape she would find Rafe in when she walked into the house. She took a deep breath and got out of the car, grabbing her briefcase from the back seat. Abby stormed over from Jude's house, and she didn't look happy. "Hi, Abby," Eden said trying to be calm as Abby approached.

"Did Julia call you about Rafe today?" she asked hotly.

"Yes, she called and said she had a setback," she answered tensely.

"She didn't just have a setback," complained Abby. "She was practically driven into it by Julia. What the hell is she doing?"

Eden wasn't sure what to say. "She," she stammered, "she said she was telling her some hard truths so she would start understanding what was really happening with everything. She said she was trying to help her move forward."

"Well, I don't think raking her over the coals until she has a breakdown is the best way to do it!" Abby complained hotly. "She could have at least waited until Rafe was completely off her medication and was thinking better, and not so angry."

"Dang it," Eden said under her breath. "I don't know why she had to do it now." She looked toward the house and sighed. "I have to get inside and make sure she's okay. I'll talk to Julia," she said as she closed her car door and then headed to the house.

"Jude and I will be talking to her too. This whole thing is so fucked up!" Abby called out and then headed back over to Jude's house.

Eden walked inside and went straight back to Rafe's room. She opened the door quietly and saw the bed was a mess but Rafe wasn't there. As she closed the door, she heard a noise coming from the direction of the patio, so she headed outside where she found Rafe using her shop-vac around the loungers.

"Hey," she said over the noise as she walked up to her, "what happened?"

Rafe turned off the vacuum. "Hi," she said as the noise receded. "I broke a glass. I'm trying to make sure I got it all cleaned up, so no one steps on the broken shards."

"Oh, okay." She was glad to see Rafe up and around. She had been afraid of how she might find her. "Are you hungry? I can make us something, or we can go out."

"Where's B Girl?" asked Rafe. She was looking forward to spending time with her and forgetting everything else.

"Oh, well," Eden started nervously, "Julia said you weren't feeling very well, so I asked Letty if she could watch her. I thought maybe we could have a quiet night." She could see Rafe's disappointment as the shine in her gray-blue eyes left. Even though she was up, Rafe looked like the setback had taken a lot out of her. "I can call and have Lydia bring her home if you want, or we can go get her."

"No, it's okay," said Rafe knowing that by not bringing Bronte home, Eden probably wanted to talk. "You're probably right about needing a quiet night. I don't want to go out, though."

"Okay." Eden smiled, trying to be positive. "I'm going to go and change, then I'll see what we have for dinner." She watched as Rafe nodded then turned on the vacuum. Leaving Rafe to her cleaning, Eden went back inside to change before making dinner.

Eden knew Rafe hadn't eaten much for lunch so she wanted to fix something she would actually enjoy eating even if she wasn't very hungry. Something not only to tell her she loved her, but she understood she needed something in her that she could keep down.

In the kitchen, Eden pulled things out to make dinner and decided to make comfort food. So she got out everything for a Caprese salad and some stelline pasta with a little garlic, fresh tomato, and olive oil. She also decided to make a chicken breast to add a little protein for Rafe. She had all of the ingredients out, the chicken almost done, and the pasta drained by the time Rafe finally decided to come inside.

Rafe walked into the kitchen to see everything Eden was cooking. "So, do you need any help?"

"Sure," said Eden happy Rafe was helping. "Can you get some basil from the herb garden?"

"Okay." Rafe stepped outside the patio door, picking some basil and then brought it to the sink where she washed it then dried it on a paper towel. "Do you want me to make the salad?"

"Oh, it's okay. I think I've got it. Why don't you open a bottle of wine and get out some dishes."

Rafe looked into the pasta bowl where Eden had just added fresh tomatoes. "You made stelline? That's for B Girl," she complained.

"I think Bronte will be okay with us eating it," said Eden with a soft laugh. "I think there'll be enough for her to have tomorrow."

Rafe said nothing as she opened a bottle of wine and poured a glass for Eden then got out the dishes for her. She sat at the island and watched Eden as she cut up the tomato for the Caprese salad, and then cut the chicken she cooked into two pieces and put them on a plate.

She wanted to tell Eden how mad she was about her calling the doctor, but she didn't know if she could take any more punishment from Julia and the others if she upset her. She would be happy if they just left her alone. This afternoon, she came up with a plan she thought was a good one for keeping away from them for a while.

"This smells really good," she said instead of confronting her. "Do you want to eat outside? I can start taking things out."

"Outside sounds nice," said Eden as she smiled at Rafe then took a sip of her wine. "I think everything's ready. I just need to get the bread."

Eden was worried about the fact Rafe was being so quiet and hadn't brought up the things that happened today or her medicine. She wondered if it meant Julia was right and Rafe needed to hear whatever she told her, or if Rafe was saving her anger for later. She could only hope Julia was right about it being the medication causing most of the issues Rafe was having. Hopefully, she would start doing better.

She picked up the last of the things they needed and took them out to the patio table where Rafe was already sitting down. "Okay, I hope you like everything," she said as she joined Rafe and started eating her salad.

Rafe hoped they could eat in silence. She felt drained and really didn't have anything left worth offering to a conversation. She picked at her food. She knew it would be good, but it was hard to eat it. She took some small bites and then sipped her wine, hoping Eden wouldn't get upset again over the fact she couldn't eat all the food on her plate.

Eden watched Rafe hold her fork but not take a bite of food. She saw her hand shake as she put the fork down and pick up her wine glass. "Is the food okay?" she asked gently.

"It's fine," said Rafe shortly then gave her a half smile to make up for her tone. She picked up her fork and took another unwanted bite, hoping it would satisfy her.

They continued to eat in silence, and when Eden was finished, she noted again Rafe had only eaten a few bites of the salad and her pasta but hadn't touched the chicken. It took everything in her not to tell her how worried she was about her not eating, and how thin she had become over the last month. She was trying to be strong about things like Julia said she should. She was glad she was getting help from their friends, but sometimes, she felt like she was failing at being strong.

"Are you finished?" she asked and watched Rafe nod. "Okay, I'll get everything taken inside."

"I'll help," said Rafe and began gathering things to take inside. After they carried everything in, and Eden put away the leftover food, Rafe poured the rest of the wine into their glasses. "I'm going out to relax," she said as she picked up her glass. "Do you want to come out too?"

Eden looked up in surprise at Rafe's invitation. She was usually mad when she followed her outside. "Sure," Eden answered, putting the last of the food away. She picked up her glass of wine and followed Rafe outside.

Rafe sat down on a lounger next to the pool and waited for Eden to get settled. "Thank you for making dinner. I'm sorry I couldn't eat very much."

"It's okay. I know it's because the medicine is still in your system. I think a lot of things have been happening to you because of it. I'm sorry I didn't see it sooner," said Eden softly.

"I need my medicine," said Rafe quietly. "I know it has side effects. I've read the information from the pharmacist. I've been doing everything I can to manage them. I'm sorry I haven't done better. I just," she paused, "it really did help with a lot of things. I wish you hadn't called my doctor."

Eden fought down her guilt and sighed. She was relieved Rafe didn't seem angry. However, she was worried about how calm she seemed. Sometimes, what Rafe was controlling would break out into an even more intense anger. "I know," she said softly then paused, "I know you're angry about me calling. I didn't know you were trying to manage things. If I had known, maybe I could have helped you. After I talked with Julia, and she pointed out all of the side effects you were having, I just got really worried and wanted to help you."

"I can help myself," said Rafe with annoyance.

Eden rubbed the back of her neck and her temple, not knowing what she could say to Rafe and not sound argumentative. "Is it why you have so many projects going? Are they how you think you're managing?"

"It's one way," she answered and sipped her wine.

"I noticed you don't take your camera out anymore," she said softly. "I thought you loved doing photography."

"I can't focus on it right now. I tried."

"I think," Eden started cautiously, "if you can't focus on something you love doing, then maybe, trying a different medicine could be a good thing."

"It's not about what hobby I can focus on," said Rafe her voice rumbling with frustration. "I need to get through my sessions and finish them so I can get back to work and figure out things so I can get back to my life. I was so close," she said with a groan wanting to make her understand, "and now it may be all up in the air again."

"I'm sorry." Eden toyed nervously with her wine glass. "I didn't know."

"Now you do," said Rafe evenly then looked at Eden firmly. "Now you can tell Julia I talked to you rationally. I'm going to my room." She got up and went inside, leaving Eden alone with her glass of wine.

Eden leaned her head back against the lounger and closed her eyes. At least all Rafe's anger wasn't only directed at her. It looked like Julia was at the receiving end of it now too. She wasn't sure if it was a good thing or not, though.

Eden got up then went inside and found her phone. She dialed and held it to her ear. "Julia?" she said into the phone.

"Hello, Eden," she answered. "Is everything all right?"

"Yeah, it's fine," she said softly and looked to make sure Rafe was still in her room. "I just wanted to let you know Rafe's okay. For some reason, she wanted me to tell you she talked with me rationally."

Julia sighed into the phone. "Well, I hope that's not the only thing she heard from me today. Did she say anything else?"

"No, and she barely ate again. I guess all we can do is see how things go over the weekend and let the doctor know if things look better with her or not."

"Right, well, goodnight then," said Julia.

"Goodnight," Eden answered softly and disconnected the call. She looked over at the closed door to Rafe's room, wishing she could go inside and hold her. Help her somehow. *I don't know what I'm doing*, she thought as she wiped her hand over her face, feeling the fallen tear. *I just want her back.*

42

THE GATES OF hell are beautiful. They are not dark and ominous as normally described in fairy tales. They are inviting, welcoming, and full of promises of bliss. The works joining the bars of the gates are sculpted into the most beautiful shapes and lines in nature. Representations of plants, animals, humanity, and strange beings and creatures never before seen by living human eyes are depicted. The gates are made up of gold holding within its secrets hidden from the naked eye. Encrusted with pearls and precious gems shining so brightly the gates blind all that approach from what lays in wait down the golden path behind them. Mysterious whispers flow out of the gates to entice wanderers to come closer. A triumphant arch, engraved with ancient symbols and images embraces the gates, telling the story of creation and the glory the gates and arch were built to celebrate.

Rafe looked up at the imposing mendacious gates in wonder. They were brilliantly beautiful and very finely done. She wanted to get closer so she could hear the secrets and to make the glare go away so she could see more details. As she walked forward, she saw a familiar shape from her past approaching. She stopped in her tracks and stared at the girl with dark hair, dark skin, and dark eyes gliding toward her.

"Maria," she exclaimed with a laugh. "It's been so long," she said in Italian. "Where have you been? Why did you leave and not tell me goodbye? I looked for you for months."

"You always ask those questions." Maria smiled patiently. "You know the answers if you think about it. You figured it all out long ago."

"I imagined I saw you looking at me one night, but I blinked, and you were gone," said Rafe as she rubbed her head trying to remember when it had happened.

"I am always with you," said Maria as she smiled patiently, "even when your eyes are closed."

Rafe was in awe as she marveled at Maria, her first kiss. "You look just like the day I last saw you."

Maria laughed and took Rafe's hands. "You shine like a night full of stars," she said, looking at Rafe with curiosity.

Rafe looked down at herself and saw Maria was right. Her skin sparkled as light flared and faded from somewhere deep in her skin. She looked up at Maria with confusion. "This is strange. I don't know how this is happening. Am I really here?"

"It doesn't matter," said Maria and kissed her on the cheek. "You must have walked a long way to be here. I have not seen you in a while."

Shaking her head in confusion, Rafe surveyed the area around her. "I don't know where I am." She pointed to the gate. "I was just going to get a closer look at the beautiful gate over there."

Maria followed Rafe's gesture and shook her head sadly. "Why are you trying to go there again? It is not a place for you to go."

"Why?" asked Rafe. "It looks so beautiful. Is it the gate to heaven?"

"No," said Maria with a soft laugh. "It is not the gate to heaven. I have seen it, and this is not the one."

"You've seen the gate to heaven? Is it at the *Palazzo Pitti*? Was it so close and I couldn't see it? It looks like it could be the gates to heaven everyone describes."

"No." Maria laughed at Rafe's words again. "They don't describe the gate to heaven. They describe this gate. Most people see this gate, so they think it is the gate to heaven."

Rafe furrowed her brow in doubt. "Well, where does this gate lead?"

"Nowhere you want to go," she said firmly. "Do you really think a benevolent god-like being would make a gate like this, from earthly things, for his fortress? It is the Fool's Gate."

Rafe studied the gate then looked back at Maria. "If this is the Fool's Gate, what does heaven's gate look like? How can anything be more beautiful?"

Maria giggled and took Rafe's hand again. "You are so funny and full of questions every time you come here."

"I've been here before?"

"Look at your footprints. You have walked through this place many times."

Rafe looked down and saw it was true. "Why do I come here?" she asked herself.

Maria pulled on her hand. "Come away," she said, and Rafe allowed herself to be led away from the gate. "If we are seen again, it won't be good."

They followed Rafe's footprints, and soon, they were back on the streets of Florence.

"This is where you belong," said Maria with a smile as she led her into the *Boboli* Garden behind the *Palazzo Pitti*. "Italy is your home—you should come back to us."

Rafe looked around and felt her heart shudder with homesickness, and for all she left behind in her childhood home. Then she smiled as memories of her childhood filled her. "I miss being here," she said softly. "I remember drawing with my mother in this garden. We would come home covered in black charcoal and sticky from the gelato we got on our walk home." She laughed at the memory. "Sometimes, we were covered in pastels and sugar from zeppole."

Maria joined Rafe's laugher and winked. "I remember the grotto."

Rafe remembered her fondly with sadness in her eyes. "I remember too. I can never forget."

"Who would you take to the grotto now?" she asked with a sly smile.

Rafe looked away then shrugged. "No one," she said softly.

Maria smiled patiently. "What about the golden one?" she asked. "You always come here to find her and take her to the grotto." She laughed at the look on Rafe's face. "Don't worry. I'm not jealous. We have to love and be passionate. It is life."

Shaking her head, Rafe didn't understand. "The golden one? You mean Eden? I've never taken her to the grotto. Never."

"No, but you try," said Maria and skipped off into the garden.

Rafe watched her skip away and started to follow but stopped as her surroundings suddenly changed and the garden disappeared. She looked around and tried to get her bearings. She looked back, thinking she could return to the gate, but the Fool's Gate was gone.

Everything was gone.

She was left in the dark.

The only light came from the stars flaring and glowing within her skin. She looked down at herself then looked around feeling as if she were on display. She wondered if there really was someone out there in the dark watching her. She took a step forward in the dark and called out in Italian. "*Ciao? Dove sono?*" When there was no answer, she called out again, "Hello? Where am I?" But the silence remained.

She walked forward, holding her glowing arms before her, hoping to find a way out of the darkness. It seemed like she had walked for hours, and she could feel the sweat running down her back as the temperature in the dark went up, and her frustration grew. Finally, she stopped and knelt down to rest. She closed her eyes and breathed deeply to calm herself. Rafe opened her eyes and found herself on her knees with a gun to her head.

"Death is here," said a mocking voice, and Rafe could feel the hot breath in her ear. "I hope you haven't been waiting long."

Rafe shivered as the familiar voice let out a deep laugh. "This is not real," she whispered hoarsely.

"Not real?" the voice growled angrily, and Rafe was pulled back by her hair. "I'm very real. Look at me!"

"No," said Rafe defiantly as she turned her head away and closed her eyes as she fought her body's need to shake as the gun pressed into her temple.

"Rafe, look at me," said Julia's voice. "Open your eyes."

Surprised at hearing Julia's voice, Rafe opened her eyes and found Julia standing in front of her. "What are you doing here? You should leave!" Rafe warned her. "He has a gun!"

"I have the gun now." Julia laughed and brandished the gun then put it under Rafe's chin. "It's time for our game. Who can find the golden girl?" The laughing voice changed into the mocking tones from before.

"You're not Julia!" Rafe choked as the gun pressed into her neck. "I don't know where Eden is. Just leave her alone!"

"She's the last one now," said the thing in the shape of Julia as it dissolved back into a black form. "I'll have them all soon. I already have the small one. The golden one gave her to me."

Rafe looked up in horror at the shadow. "Bronte? No! No, you don't have her! Eden would never give her to you!" Rafe cried and tried to push the dark form away.

The dark form laughed softly and put its face up to Rafe's ear. "Go look for yourself. She's not in her room. She's better off with me."

Rafe lurched forward and found herself standing in her room. She yanked her door open and ran to Bronte's room with fear pulsing through her veins like fire. She opened the door and ran to Bronte's bed. She tore at the sheets and blankets tearing them off the bed.

Bronte was gone.

"Eden!" she screamed with fury. "Eden, where is she?" Rafe looked around the room, in the closet and bathroom, but Bronte was gone.

"It told you," Death said with a taunting laugh. "Now, come with me, and we will start. Remember how close I am to her now. She's giving me things and wants to give me more, including herself."

Rafe shook her head and ran her hand through her hair trying to think. "No, no, please just leave her alone. Leave all of us alone and bring Bronte back to me."

"No one comes back from death," said the dark form in her father's voice, "and you should know this better than anyone."

Blackness surrounded Rafe again, and when she thought she had come to her senses, she found herself in her classroom, looking out over the desks. Shaking as she looked around, taking in the familiar room, she saw her mother was there and so was her father. She looked behind them and saw Bronte, Brettito, and Maria.

"How…" was all she got out as she was slammed in the chest and fell to her knees struggling to breathe.

"My collection," said Death as he stood over her, "and yours too, of course. We're only missing one to make the set complete."

Rafe gasped for breath at the pain searing in her chest. She looked up and saw Eden with her golden hair and shining eyes standing just outside the door. "Eden," she choked out, "Eden, run!"

Eden smiled at Rafe. "It's okay, babe," she said happily. "I want to be here with you and Bronte."

Sobbing from anger and pain, Rafe pulled herself up and leaned against the desk. "Why did you give her to him?" she demanded with tears in her eyes. "How could you?"

"Because she doesn't love you," said the dark form in a gravelly voice. "She is a liar! Why else?"

Rafe looked from Death to Eden, who was standing just outside the room. She pushed the desk back and ran to Eden grasping her shoulders. "Do you love me?" she asked her frantically.

"I think the real question is, do you love me," said Eden sadly. "You haven't told me."

Dark laughter filled Rafe's ears, and she held her hands over them.

"She will leave you," said Julia's voice. "You're pushing her away. You are so close to driving her away! She is going to take Bronte with her! Look at what you've been doing to her!"

"No," said Rafe and kept her eyes on Eden. "You have to understand," she said desperately. "Death, he's taking everything!"

Tears came down from Eden's light brown eyes, magnifying the golden specks at their center. "I can't live this way, Rafe. I need you to love me. He promised he would love me," she said looking at the black form longingly.

"No, no, you can't believe him," she said frantically. She took Eden's hand and pulled her down the hallway. "Come on. We have to get away before he takes you too." Laughter followed them, and as Rafe looked back, Eden was taken away in a swirl of blackness. "No!" Rafe screamed as she tried to hang on to her.

"You have a long way to go if you want to keep her from me," Death said teasingly and pushed Rafe back with the gun, shoving it into her chest until she was against the wall.

Rafe closed her eyes so she couldn't see him. She turned to face the wall and tried pulling herself down the hallway clinging closely to the wall. *I have to find Eden,* she thought desperately. She felt the air change and become warmer as the texture under her hands changed. She opened her eyes and found herself against the base of a large rock formation. She turned around and saw she was alone again. She climbed up on top of the rock to see if she could tell where she was. As she looked around, she saw something gleaming in the distance, and after a while, she realized what it was. The Fool's Gate. She was back where she started. She looked up at the gray sky. "Eden!" she called loudly. "Eden, where are you?"

She looked to her left where she thought she saw movement then jumped down off the rock and ran to see what was there. It took her a moment to comprehend what she saw.

A golden-haired woman was standing on top of a large flat rock, and there was a target behind her full of bullet holes.

Eden.

As she walked along the flat rock, Eden threw something out to the hazy black crowd below her, making them cheer and laugh. Rafe ran through the crowd to the edge of the rock, and as she got closer, she could see what Eden was throwing. One of her pills landed at her feet. She bent to pick it up and looked at it then up at Eden.

"What are you doing? Don't throw these away! I need them!" she yelled frantically as the pill dissolved in her hand. "I need my medicine!"

As Rafe climbed up the rock, she heard an explosion come from behind her and then familiar chilling laughter. She stopped, gripping the rock until the echo of the explosion faded away.

"So close," the dark voice gloated and laughed.

Above her, Rafe saw a new hole in the target, and Eden happily throwing her medicine to the noisy crowd. She scrambled over the edge and ran to Eden, not bothering to brush the dirt from her skin and clothes.

"Ede," she said as she caught her. "Ede, we have to leave." She pulled Eden to the edge of the rock so they could get away.

"Let me go, I'm helping you!" Eden said irritably as she pulled away. She flung the last of the pills out to the crowd and smiled happily at Rafe. "See, now you'll love me."

Tears of frustration were dried instantly by the heat of her anger as sweat streaked down Rafe's face. "No! I needed those!" She wiped the sweat from her cheeks then clutched Eden's hand. "Come with me. We have to go before he comes for you again!"

Rafe pulled Eden down from the rock as several short bursts of deafening gunfire rang out and peppered the target behind them. As they ran across the hot crusty terrain, Rafe pulled Eden along, desperate to outrun the bullets chasing them. She looked straight ahead and saw the Fool's Gate getting closer. She stopped as she remembered Maria telling her she should not go there. She looked around and could find nowhere else to go.

She looked back from where they had come from and saw a line of people walking toward them. It was everyone from the classroom. They were bound together with golden shackles. Even Bronte had a golden shackle. Rafe wasn't sure why Death would put one on a child, and it infuriated her.

She felt Eden pull against her as she tried to go to them. "No, Eden we can't be with them."

"I see Bronte," Eden said excitedly. "I'm going to be with her. Please, just let me go," she pleaded and pulled against her.

Rafe kept a firm grip on Eden as they watched the people coming toward them. Beyond them, she saw the black form of Death pick Bronte up and put her on his shoulder.

"She needs a real family," he said in Jake's voice. "I'm her father now."

"I need a man," said Eden as she struggled for release. "Look how Bronte loves him."

"He doesn't love her! He doesn't love anyone!" Rafe screamed and pulled Eden back, making her fall to the ground. Rafe fell on top of Eden and held her down, looking into those eyes she knew could mesmerize her if she allowed it. "How could you give her to him?"

"Look at all the people you love, Rafe," said Death mockingly. "All shackled by secrets that brought them to me. Secrets you made them have because of your actions." He laughed at the pain on Rafe's face. "It's amazing how one little secret can lead to me having all of this for myself."

"Eden knows!" she told him hotly as she stood to face him. "She knows my secret now! I'm not alone!"

Death laughed again at the new information. "So, that's how you found her so fast. Well, it doesn't matter because she really doesn't understand. She'll give herself to me. She wants to come to me and be with her little one."

Rafe screamed with fury at his words and gripped Eden's hand, dragging her up from the ground roughly. "Run, Ede!" she said as she pulled Eden with her. "Maria says we need to try to get to the grotto. We have to find it!"

"Do you love Maria now too?" she asked with tears in her eyes. "You love everyone but me!"

Rafe could feel Death daring her to deny Eden's words. As soon as she did, Rafe knew Death would take her. She could not say those words. She stopped and looked at the ground in front of her for anything to help find the grotto. Eden pulled on her hand as she sat down heavily in exhaustion, and Rafe sat with her.

"Look at your skin," she said in amazement. "Is this why you can't love me because you're not real? You aren't really here?" She touched Rafe, feeling her warmth as she marveled at the spiraling lights and the blooms of bright colors flowing over Rafe's body.

"Don't look," said Rafe softly. "I don't know what it means. I'm here Eden," she said desperately. "I'm here as much as I can be. I'm real but something's missing. I don't know what it is yet."

"I think I know," said Eden huskily as she leaned in and kissed Rafe on the mouth. "You need me," she whispered. "I'm part of you."

A gunshot rang out, and the dirt beside Eden exploded. Rafe pulled her up and stood in front of her as she looked for the dark form she knew had to be close.

"She's a liar!" barked Death, laughing in his dark voice. "You can't trust her! I will always be just an inch away! The closer you get to her, the closer I will be too!"

Rafe reached behind her and took Eden's hand as she backed away. She looked down and saw her footprints along with a set made by Maria. Hope surged through her as she spun around and pushed Eden in the direction the footprints led.

"This way!" she said and ran with Eden.

Rafe didn't know how long they had run through the wide open space, but they were both exhausted. Wiping the sweat from her eyes, Rafe looked up and laughed manically. "We're here," she said. "We're in the *Boboli* Gardens!" She pulled Eden along the garden path. "The grotto is this way!" She laughed as she ran.

The *Buontalenti Grotto* announced itself with its imposing entrance, adorned with stalagmites and stalactites and flanked by the statues of the gods, Ceres and Apollo. Relief flooded Rafe as she got closer. She wasn't sure why she had to be at the grotto, but Maria said she always tried to take Eden there, so she hoped the reason would reveal itself.

At the entrance, Eden scanned the grotto and then looked with wonder at Rafe. "It's beautiful," she said in awe, "but why are we here?"

Looking around, Rafe ran her hands through her dark hair anxiously. "I'm not sure," she said honestly. Holding onto Eden, she started for the entrance and saw Maria come out of the grotto.

"You came at last!" said Maria with a smile. "Now the golden one can come inside. Follow me," she encouraged Eden.

Eden let go of Rafe's hand and followed Maria. "Who are you?" Eden asked as she passed between the pillars and crossed the threshold.

Rafe watched as Eden followed Maria, not understanding how Maria escaped or how Eden knew what Maria was saying in Italian, but she moved after them. Before she caught up, a black void covered the entrance, and Ceres stepped down and blocked her path.

"There is nothing for you here," the goddess Ceres said and pointed Rafe away. "Mothers are protected here by me," she said firmly.

"What?" Rafe asked as Ceres took her place again. She went to the dark void and tried to cross, but she always ended up back where she had started. "I don't understand," she said and sat down on the ledge next to Ceres and put her head in her hands. "I need to go inside," she pleaded. Maria was inside with Eden so she didn't understand why she couldn't go too. When she looked up, fear rose in her again, seeing the darkness had overtaken them. "Please," she begged the goddess, "please, I need to get away! I need to go inside!"

Rafe could feel the darkness ooze over her and begin to cover her skin slowly. *It's covering the light in me*, she thought as she tried to scrape it away.

"I told you she would leave you!" Julia's voice came from the dark form. "She left you behind. All of them left you behind," she chortled. The voice slid into a growl. "I will have her soon now. You're alone again." Rafe felt the gun against her head. "Say the words and let her go. It's easy, you've done it before." Death pulled Rafe's head back by her hair and pushed the gun to her throat. "Even the goddess doesn't want you. She will protect your golden one from you, but even she can't protect her from me."

A tear escaped from Rafe. "Why," she choked out, gagging from the pressure of the gun on her throat. "Why can't I go in with her? I don't understand."

Laughter rippled through the air. "She doesn't understand! Let me explain," hissed Death as its darkness continued to cover Rafe's skin slowly. "You have killed your mother, you have caused the golden mother pain, and you have driven her to give her child to me, a stranger. The goddess would have you take her pain away. And when you do, she is mine!" He laughed, and the sound cut painfully through Rafe.

"No!" sobbed Rafe. "I didn't know! I didn't mean to hurt anyone!" She felt herself slammed back against the sun-warmed stone of the grotto and pain shot through her chest.

"You hurt everyone!" said Abby's voice.

"Just tell her," Jude's voice encouraged her. "Tell her you love her."

"Say the words and take her pain away," commanded the goddess.

"Yes," said Death with sadistic happiness, "say the words, and then let her go. She doesn't love you, so it should be easy," he whispered. "She lies to you, so letting go should be even easier this time," he said louder. "She wants you to let her go!" he growled. "She wants to be with me!" He laughed mockingly. "I'm the stranger who she gave her child to because of you," he reminded her again, "and now she wants to give herself to me! Say the words!" he demanded venomously.

"Eden!" Rafe screamed out in anguish.

43

EDEN KINGSLEY SAT straight up in bed at hearing her name screamed in terror outside her door. "Rafe." Her heart skipped as she pushed her sheet back and jumped out of bed. She rushed in panic to open her bedroom door at the sound of Rafe screaming her name. She found Rafe sitting against the hallway wall shouting in her sleep and shaking as she held on to Bronte's blankets. She knelt down and took Rafe by the shoulders. "Rafe, Rafe, are you okay?" she asked in distress.

Deep in her nightmare, Rafe knew Death wouldn't stop this time. She had nothing left because he was covering her with his darkness. Eden threw away all her medicine so she couldn't hold him back anymore. She released a low mewling whine of despair. The only thing she could do now was to warn Eden to stay in the grotto. "Eden!" she screamed in panic, "Eden, don't come out! I won't hurt you. I won't say it! Eden!" she screamed and shook. "Eden, I'm disappearing. There's almost nothing left! Eden!" she choked. "Help me," she sobbed softly as she pleaded with the goddess. "*Salvami!*" she cried desperately.

"I'm here," said Eden alarmed at seeing Rafe in terror, her hair plastered to her face, and her body covered in sweat. "Rafe, you're okay, you're okay." Rafe looked at her, but Eden knew from her glazed eyes that she wasn't awake as she spoke.

"You have to go back into the grotto!" Rafe begged her in her sleep. "I don't have any medicine, and he's taking me! I won't let him hurt you!"

Eden ran her hand over Rafe's hot sweat-covered face. "Rafe, wake up. It's okay," she said trying to be calm. "Wake up," she swallowed back her anxiety. "Please, wake up."

Rafe leaned forward and got to her knees, struggling with Eden as she tried to push her back into the room. "Go," she sobbed, "go back inside."

"I'll go," Eden said softly. "You can come with me." She pulled on Rafe, hoping moving around and getting her in a new place would wake and calm her.

Rafe shook her head, looking at something in her dream. "She won't let me. She can't keep him away if I go inside." Eden watched as Rafe looked down at her hands and arms.

"The light, the light is going away. Do you still see it?" she asked Eden.

Eden wasn't sure what to do so she hoped she guessed right. "I see it, Rafe. I see the light. You can come in with me."

"No, he has Bronte," she said and held Eden's shoulders. "Why did you give her to him?" she asked in anguish.

"Who?" Eden asked, not understanding and thinking she may mean Jake. "Who did I give Bronte too?"

"She's not in her room!" Rafe roared as she shook Bronte's blankets she had compulsively held onto and could not let go. "You gave her to Death! He said you just. . . gave her to him!" she said in misery. "How could you? How could you do it?"

Eden shook her head, and tears burst out of her at seeing Rafe suffering in her sleep. "Rafe, it's okay. Bronte is with Letty. She's fine and just went to play with her Zia Letty. I told you where she was when I came home." She pushed Rafe's wet hair back from her face. "Rafe, wake up. It's just a dream." Rafe looked around like she was listening to something and Eden couldn't understand what she was saying in Italian in her sleep to whoever was in her dream. "Rafe, look at me," said Eden as she took Rafe's head in her hands. "It's just a dream. Please, wake up."

"You have to go back," said Rafe shakily. "You can't let him shoot at you again. He is only an inch away!"

"Who, Rafe?" asked Eden with worry. "No one is here. We're safe in our house." Rafe's eyes opened, and it seemed to Eden like she had focused.

"Death," Rafe said shakily, her gray-blue eyes glazed with her nightmare. "You're only an inch away. He can't make me say it. I'm fighting him. If I say it, he can get to you through me. When I disappear, then he can't get to you!" She pushed Eden's hands away from her face and tried to push her to the grotto. "Hurry and go back into the grotto. Maria is there. She can tell you everything."

"Maria?" asked Eden not understanding who she was talking about. She resisted Rafe's push toward the bedroom and held onto her hands. "Rafe, you're safe. Come with me. I'll hold on to you, and everything will be okay." She pulled Rafe gently through the bedroom door, and Rafe fell heavily to her knees. "Rafe, get up. Come on," she said softly and lifted her back up. "Come sit on the bed." She sat Rafe down and sighed as Rafe leaned over and put her head in her hands. Eden knew Rafe was feeling the phantom pain in her dream because of her shaking and the way she held her head and chest.

Rafe shivered. In her dream, Eden had pulled her into the cool grotto. "Eden, we can't be here. I can't be here," she whispered. She looked around, her mind trying to figure out where she was because the grotto was gone. She realized they were in Eden's room. She didn't understand how they got there and wondered if it was safe. "Eden, everything's changed again," she said softly as she looked around. "Do you see it?"

"What changed," she asked softly.

"We're in the house again," she tried to get up, but Eden held her down. "I need to check the house," she said and tried to push Eden's hands away.

"You already checked it, babe," said Eden and held her down. She could see Rafe wasn't awake yet but hoped she was close. "We're safe here," she tried to reassure her. "Nothing can hurt us now."

Rafe shook her head. "Please, don't lie. He said you're lying."

"No," said Eden as tears fell again, "I'm not lying."

Rafe felt anger surge inside her as the walls of the room wavered. "It's changing again," she whispered. "Try to keep me here. *Salvami!*" she begged as she looked at Eden wildly. "I'll let you go, I promise. Just help me stay in one good place for a while."

"You don't have to let me go," said Eden as her breath shuddered. "I want to keep you here. Will you wake up? If you wake up, you'll stay in one place. I'll be right back," she said softly. She then went to the bathroom to get a cool washcloth.

When Eden came back in the room, Rafe was on the floor again and leaning against the bed. Eden sat down next to her with the cool cloth in her hand. Before Eden could put it on her neck, Rafe lashed out, pushing her backward, and the cloth flew from her hand.

"Don't lie!" she hissed to the Eden in her dreams who she had pushed in her dream and who was telling Rafe she was never leaving. "I know you're leaving again. Julia told me! She said I was pushing you and Bronte away," she shook her head slowly, "but I am just trying not to disappear right now." She looked at her arms and could see the darkness moving up them slowly. "Look at me! Look how much is gone!" she demanded. "You just keep taking! I can't stop him! You've thrown all my pills off the rock, and they all took them! How can I fight without them?" Rafe looked over and saw Ceres appear and look at her with disapproval. "*Mi spiace*," she said. "*Non costringermi a lasciare, per favore,*"[8] she begged and closed her eyes, pressing out the tears holding on to the edges of her eyes. "Don't let her make me leave, please!" she said to Eden in her dream.

Eden scrambled up, taking Rafe's face in her hands. "Rafe, look at me," said Eden wiping Rafe's tears with her thumbs. "You don't have to leave. Julia is wrong. I'm not going to leave you." She picked up the cool cloth and gently wiped Rafe's face. "There, babe. You need to cool down. Will you wake up and look at me? It's okay. Wake up," she said and pulled her close then kissed her forehead and cheeks.

Rafe gasped and snapped her eyes open, and they shifted from side to side as she woke. She found herself looking into Eden's brown eyes. "Eden," she swallowed. "What—" was all she could think to say as she shook uncontrollably.

"It's okay," said Eden. "You've had a dream." She felt Rafe's body shake as the tension in it was releasing. "I think it was a pretty bad one. I'm sorry," she said and kissed her on the forehead again then ran the cool rag over her face.

Rafe felt herself coming out of the fog from the dream. She remembered some of it and shuddered. She could hear Eden telling her she was safe, and as her mind cleared, she let Eden

---

[8] Don't make me leave, please,

take control of her. She was exhausted and felt sick. "I'm sorry," she said and could say nothing more for the moment.

"It's okay, babe," she said softly. "I'll take care of you." She helped Rafe stand and sat her on the bed again. "Just lay back, babe. I'm going to cool the washcloth off again. I'll be right back."

Rafe could feel the tremors racking her body caused by the effort to stand and get in the bed. As she lay back, she lifted her arm. It felt like it wasn't attached to her body as she put her hand on her head. She knew what was happening. The nightmares were coming back. She hadn't taken a pill for three days, and the dreams were back. Her body shook as she fought the hot tears running down her face.

She hadn't locked her bedroom door, so her nightmares brought her out of her room. Now Eden saw her. She saw her beaten and weakened by her own mind. Now Eden would never see her in the same way again. Now she would be someone to pity. Eden would use her like she used the letter Rafe had written to her mother. Rafe did not want her love to be from pity. She didn't want her to think about her in this state and use it as an excuse to stay where she might be unhappy.

Eden came back with a cool cloth and climbed into bed next to Rafe. She wiped her face and neck. "Babe, your pajamas are soaked with sweat. Do you want to take a shower and change? You might feel better."

"I can't," she said weakly. Meaning to tell her that she couldn't feel anything, but her mind couldn't make her voice form the words yet.

"I'll help you. It's okay," she said softly.

Eden got up and started the shower. Then she went to Rafe's room to get fresh pajamas. When she got back to the room, she found Rafe was in the shower. She put the pajamas on the bathroom counter. "Let me know if you need help," she said but got no response.

Eden paced while Rafe was in the bathroom. After a while, Rafe came out. She had her pajamas on, but her shirt was unbuttoned. "Here," said Eden as she walked up to her, "let me help you." She buttoned her shirt noticing again how thin she had become before she led her over to the bed. "You can sleep here tonight if you want to, babe." Rafe lay down shakily without a word, so Eden covered her up and got into the bed next to her. She held herself up on her elbow over Rafe. "I love you," she said softly and kissed her forehead. "I'm so sorry."

Rafe turned her head to look at Eden and tears welled in her eyes. "I can't go back to sleep."

Eden's heart ached for Rafe. She wanted to do more to help her, but she did not know what to do. She was so tired of failing her and not understanding what she needed. She took a breath to calm herself. "Maybe, if you let me, I can hold you for a while. This way you can feel me and know you're home and safe. Then maybe you can sleep. Do you want to try?" She looked into Rafe's eyes and saw her nod slowly. She could tell by her desperate look and the way she was shaking that, at this moment, Rafe would probably try anything. Eden wrapped her arms around Rafe and pulled her close. She put her face close to Rafe's and whispered gently to her. "I love you. You're safe at home. I won't leave you. I love you."

44

IT HAD BEEN a long night, but Eden Kingsley was up and out of the house to pick up Bronte. Letty was taking her in to work at The Kiki Bistro, and they agreed to meet there. She left a note for Rafe and let her sleep because she had been awake most of the night just looking at the ceiling and saying nothing. She knew Rafe was thinking about something, but she didn't share her thoughts. Eden was awake worrying most of the night herself, wondering if she and Julia had made the right decision in calling Rafe's doctor. Finally, sometime early in the morning, Rafe went to her own room and fell asleep again. Eden checked on her several times before leaving, and it was clear Rafe's sleep was not peaceful.

She walked into the bistro and hoped Julia was there like she agreed earlier this morning. She didn't want to leave Rafe at home alone very long right now. As she scanned the tables, she found Julia and went directly to the table where she was sitting with Abby and Jude.

"Good morning," said Julia as Eden sat down.

"Hi," said Eden unhappily. "I can't stay long. Ephraim and Letty should be here soon with Bronte, and I need to get back to Rafe."

"Is she okay," Jude asked concerned.

"No," Eden said flatly, "no, she's not okay." She turned to Julia in frustration and anger. "What the hell did you say to her? Did you tell her I was leaving her?"

"Eden, I—" Julia started then sighed. "I told her she was pushing you away, and she is. I just told her some hard truths."

Anger swelled up in Eden like she had never felt toward her friend before, and she lashed out at Julia. "Don't you ever, ever say that to her again! Do you understand me?" she demanded as she looked into Julia's shocked face. "I fought so hard to get us back into each other's lives, and you're making her think I'm going to leave again! How are you helping? How could you be so cruel?"

"I'm sorry," said Julia softly, surprised at Eden's uncharacteristic outburst, "but you have to understand—"

"We're all sorry," Abby interrupted, happy Julia was being taken to task for yesterday.

"We are," Jude agreed as she shifted uncomfortably and felt ashamed.

Julia sighed and took a sip of her coffee. She wasn't expecting Eden to be angry. Worried, yes, but not angry. "Eden, I was just trying to make her see things from your perspective. She never talks to you about anything and blames you for everything."

"I know," Eden said sadly and ran her hands through her hair. "I know, and it's hard. I'm trying to deal with all of it, and you just made it harder. Please," she said imploringly, "just don't give her a reason to think I'm leaving."

"What about all the things she does and says to you, though?" Abby asked with concern.

Eden couldn't hide her distress about everything. "I don't know, I don't know," she said throwing her hands up. "I just need you not to upset her again. Last night," she said uneasily remembering the fear she felt run through her, "last night was scary. I've never seen her so," she hesitated, "so sick. I know she's come and told me she had dreams or was feeling pain, but I've never seen her in the middle of one of her dreams."

Julia sat up with concern. "What happened?"

"No," said Eden shaking her head, "no, I'm not going to talk to you about it now. I need to talk to Rafe and maybe her doctor first. If you slip up and mention something, it'll make things worse for me." She turned her hard gaze on Abby. "She hates it when you talk about her and call her crazy. I know you're only joking, or she upsets you, so you say it, but it upsets her more than she'll tell you."

"I'm sorry," said Abby with a grimace. "I'll watch myself, I promise."

"We all will," Jude said with a nod.

"Do you want me to come talk to her?" asked Julia. "Maybe I can help smooth things over."

Eden and held her hand up in protest. "No. Not today. She needs rest, and she needs to stay calm. I don't want her upset to the point you drove her again," she said looking at each firmly then directly at Julia. "If she sees you right now, I don't know what she might do. I don't know how much of what she said last night she even remembers." Eden saw Letty carrying in Bronte. "I'll call you later," she said dismissively and went to meet Letty.

Abby watched Eden walk away. "I knew the whole thing yesterday was fucked up."

"We still need to help Eden," said Julia as she frowned. "She may be angry, but I think it's just because she's so worried. Rafe will probably keep doing things, saying things to her, and punishing her, and we have to help her. I'm hoping it will all have been the fault of the medication, but we won't know for a while."

"I don't think I've ever seen Eden so angry before," said Abby as picked at her food.

"I think she may finally be growing up," said Julia with a raised eyebrow.

"What do you mean?" asked Jude.

"It means, instead of *asking* us what to do, she *told* us what to do," Julia pointed out. "It may be small, but she's taking a step in the right direction."

45

EARLY SUNDAY MORNING Eden Kingsley left the house and made her way to Julia's condo. She left Rafe and Bronte at home having breakfast together with plans to work on another project. She told Rafe she was going to meet Julia and run errands to the grocery and drug stores. Rafe wasn't pleased with the fact she was going to meet Julia and didn't try to hide it. It was very clear Julia was not in Rafe's good graces after Friday. It seemed no one was in her good graces at this point.

Eden needed to know what had happened between Julia and Rafe. She felt like since Julia and the others started getting more involved, she and Rafe had taken a step backward. Rafe was still angry, and now she not only avoided talking but, sometimes, she wouldn't even be in the same room.

What set Eden off the most was Rafe telling her she was 'free to go anytime' and walking away. It was clear whatever Julia said had Rafe thinking she would leave. Eden knew her assurances she wasn't leaving were met with doubt. The feeling that Rafe was the one thinking about leaving again crept up on Eden and the thought terrified her.

Between fighting against Rafe and her reasons they should not be together, and the ones Julia and the others were creating and adding on top of everything, Eden was having a hard time holding it all together. Julia was telling her to grow up and take care of Rafe, but then she tells Rafe things that send her into a tailspin. A tailspin so terrifying, she wasn't sure Rafe would recover. Eden wasn't sure *she* would recover herself from the memory of the terror on Rafe's face and the things Rafe said and did in her dreams.

She wanted to talk to Cathcart about it, but decided to wait to see if Rafe's doctor gave her a new medication first. If it worked, she would try to talk to Rafe. She called and left another message for Rafe's doctor and would call her again first thing Monday morning. She didn't know if new medication would help Rafe's dreams or not, but she knew she did not want Rafe to have another nightmare like the last one. She would call Rafe's doctor as many times as she had to if it meant keeping her from going through that terrifying experience again, even though she knew Rafe wouldn't like it.

Right now, though, she really needed everyone to back off Rafe and give her time to recover, let her start her new medication, and give them both a chance to calm the storm Julia and the others had stirred up.

Eden rang the bell outside the condo, and Julia opened the door with a cup of tea in hand. "Good morning," she said groggily.

"Late night?" asked Eden as she followed Julia into her kitchen.

"Yes, another night chasing the dream," she said sarcastically, and she sat down and poured a cup of tea for Eden. "So, are you here to slap my hand again? I was only telling her those things for her own good."

"I'm not here to slap your hand, but I do want you to tell me what you said to her," said Eden as she put her hands around the warm teacup. "I thought you were taking time off to help her, not upset her and make her have nightmares."

Julia furrowed her brow, wishing she hadn't agreed to meet Eden this morning. She was sure if Eden opened her eyes, she would see she was trying to help Rafe—and Eden by association. "Okay, I'll admit I may have gone too far. But at least we have proven some of what I said sank in. She's so stubborn, and sometimes I just want to wring her neck."

"What, exactly, were you trying talk to her about?" Eden asked anxiously feeling like Julia was evading.

Julia shrugged. "Everything," she claimed. "Everything from before you were pregnant to what she's doing to you now."

"Before I was pregnant?" Eden repeated, worried her online activity was part of the discussion again.

"Yes," said Julia as the oven timer went off. She went over to take the chocolate scones she had made out of the oven. "I told her I read the Stewards file, which I skimmed most of. I told her you wouldn't have had to go online if she had been paying attention to you and what you were going through." She put the scones on a cooling rack and sat down. "There are two people in a relationship, and she should have been paying more attention. She should have known you might have some issues with your anxiety and shouldn't have put so much pressure on you."

Eden looked into her teacup and could not help blushing with guilt because she knew she was not easy to be around sometimes back then. "It does take two," Eden agreed. "I wasn't exactly innocent," she said, knowing she had been having anxiety problems. She was very thankful she had started seeing Dr. Cathcart for help. "I may have put more pressure on myself than she put on me." She met Julia's gaze. "What else did you say? There had to be more to make her so upset."

Julia took a sip of her tea and tried to remember everything she said that she thought was important. "I told her she'd never let you spread your wings, and now, since you have, without her, she's angry with you for growing as a person." She sat her cup down. "I told her she was the one stopping you from growing."

Eden was confused. "What do you mean by 'spread my wings'?"

"I mean she never let you take care of things or go out on your own to do things so you could grow," Julia said pointedly.

"I don't know if that's true." Eden shook her head because she knew it was just easier to let Rafe handle things because she had certain ways she wanted things done. If anything, she felt she stopped herself from growing, or at least contributed to the problem by just standing by and letting it happen. She never said she wanted to be in charge of anything, or even offered, and Rafe never complained. She thought that maybe she should have tried to have a more active role in things. It's not like Rafe would have said no. Rafe was fine with her doing things when she took time off from work. "I don't think she had any doubts about me until I messed everything up," she said knowing there was a lot more happening that led her to fail.

"Well, you have to admit she never let you be in charge of anything," she said as she got up to get scones for them. "She never lets you, or anyone else, be exclusively in charge of anything."

"She is better," said Eden as Julia sat a plate with a chocolate scone in front of her. "She's trying so hard, and I understand it's part of her personality. She wants things to be perfect."

"No, she wants to control everything," said Julia with a scoff.

Eden looked down at her scone then picked up her fork and used it to take a bite. She never felt like Rafe was controlling until after she started talking to people online. It had felt comforting when she heard other people talk about how controlling Rafe was, and she felt people were on her side. Now she realized she was justifying the opinions and thoughts put into her mind. Even if Rafe was controlling, it had nothing to do with what was really happening. Dr. Cathcart helped open her eyes. Looking back now, she could see Rafe's controlling behavior may have been a coping mechanism and not something she did just to piss people off. "What else did you tell her," she asked softly.

"I told her a partner is there when the other person in the relationship falls and helps them stand back up," she said and could see Eden was not happy with her. "I had to tell her those things, Eden. She needs to see she wasn't there for you."

"If she's guilty, I am too." Eden rubbed her forehead. "I'm trying so hard to help her stand back up, but I'm lost. I don't know what to do for her. It seems like everything I do is wrong or makes her angry."

"But you're there for her," said Julia feeling a small wave of guilt. She knew she complained to Rafe a lot about Eden, but at the same time, she didn't want Eden to belittle what she was doing for Rafe.

Sometimes, Julia thought Eden sounded just like Andrea, her ex-girlfriend. Julia began dating her not long after Rafe tossed Andrea aside. Andrea would never say anything against Rafe, even though Rafe treated her badly when they dated. It was frustrating because Julia liked Rafe, and still had hope, after all these years, of being in a relationship with her, but she didn't like Rafe treating Eden with the same disregard she dealt Andrea. Anger at the memory of the pain Rafe caused Andrea swept through her.

The only good thing out of Rafe's break up with Andrea was she and Andrea found each other. Julia only wished it had lasted. It seemed, since their break up, and since Rafe met Eden, Julia had poor luck with finding anyone special. It was one reason she kept thinking about dating Rafe again. She knew Rafe, and it meant Rafe couldn't get away with the things she did with Andrea, Eden, and all the rest.

She forced herself not to think of Andrea, and what might have been, and to focus on Eden. Sometimes, she wished Eden had stayed away from Rafe. If she had, then taking care of Rafe would be easier, and she wouldn't have to deal with Eden being in the way. But for now, she would just try to steer her in the right direction.

"Look at what was happening back then," Julia said trying not to show her exasperation. "She wasn't there going to appointments with you and helping you when you were taking hormones, or when you were devastated by the failures in the insemination process. She shut you out and walked away."

"I don't know if she shut me out. She did try." Eden sighed knowing the real problem was her shutting Rafe out by all the irrational things she was doing and saying at the time. Maybe that was all it was—hormones, and the insemination process, and the stress of the failures she was feeling along with her anxiety. Rafe knew how she could get when her anxiety was bad and sometimes walked away rather than fight. Maybe Rafe just thought, if she left her alone, she would work through it like she had worked through other things. "I'm not trying to lay the blame on her for everything," she said softly.

"I know, I know," said Julia as she ate her scone. "But she thinks she shouldn't shoulder any of the blame, and we both know she's responsible for a lot of the things happening back then by her actions, or inaction, and more recently with what went down with Jake."

Eden flinched at the mention of Jake. "I think she knows we both did things wrong," said Eden unhappily. "She had an affair, and I made choices leading to us both being hurt."

"The difference is you were trying to get pregnant, and she made a promise she would make a family with you. Instead, she was gone all the time working and left everything on your shoulders. Now she's punishing you for having problems when she knew you had anxiety issues."

"She had to go," said Eden feeling like she had to defend Rafe even though she had complained about the same things. She couldn't believe Julia had actually said those things to Rafe. Of everyone, she thought Julia would be on Rafe's side and understand Rafe's father was sick, and she had to pick up the slack. Looking back, Eden knew Rafe didn't have a choice at times. Now she didn't think it was fair to hold her work against her.

"Well, I told her you shouldn't have felt like you had to talk to strangers, and she should have made sure she was there for you. She could have had someone else to handle things at work. Because she was so busy being angry about things and working, she couldn't see you needed her."

"I've been thinking about what I did and what she's been telling me. I have to admit she is right about some of it," confessed Eden. "I should have sent her those emails, and I should have said something."

Eden knew Rafe as much as Rafe was supposed to know her. Well, sometimes it seemed Rafe knew more about her. Rafe was hyperfocused on getting those jobs done so she could finish everything overseas and just start concentrating on projects here and helping her father get well.

It was the plan Rafe had, and she knew it, but she still complained about her being gone. She also knew deep down, if she had told her what was going on, Rafe would have dropped everything. She also knew how sick Rafe's father was and how important the projects were. Rafe would come home and tell her about mistakes costing hundreds of thousands of dollars. She knew Rafe had to go, and she didn't tell her about anything going on at the time.

So Rafe was right when she said she chose not to tell her things and told strangers instead. Eden knew the blame was on herself. "I try to tell her I'm sorry and explain," she said dejectedly. "It seems like I can never talk to her when she'll listen and not be angry."

Julia knew what Eden was up against. "She does have a stubborn streak. I informed her she's shutting you out again right now," she said then sipped her tea. "You might just need help after the ordeal with the Stewards too."

Eden looked up at Julia and shook her head in confusion. "How can we expect her to help me right now? Even you say I can't depend on her for comfort or anything. You do know I still see Cathcart, right?"

"I didn't, but I'm glad you are," said Julia. "Still, Rafe could give you some comfort.

"I admit I need it from her," said Eden feeling the pain caused by the distance between her and Rafe. "But I can see how she just can't. I try to comfort her, and she pushes me away. I try to talk with her and sometimes it feels like she cuts me through the heart. But I know I just have to keep talking to her until she sees, no matter what, I love her. It's all I know to do."

Julia could see the pain Rafe was causing Eden. "She doesn't want to get close because she thinks she can't trust you. I told her she was the one who destroyed the trust between you two, by having an affair, and she's being hypocritical."

Eden put her fork down and looked up at Julia in disbelief. "I think she knows she shares the responsibility for breaking the trust between us," she said firmly. "We both agree trust is a big issue. I told her that I forgave her. I know, I know, she may not have wanted my forgiveness, but I said it, and I have forgiven her. I still have a lot of questions about why she did it for her to answer, though, and I don't know if she ever will. I just want us to be able to get past it so we can be happy."

"You may be past things, but she brought up your online encounter," Julia said rolling her eyes. "I told her if she weren't so cut off, you may not have felt the need to find comfort somewhere else. I told her you didn't plan to have emotional issues. Then she got mad and said she didn't plan on having an affair. She said you pushed her away and just left her there. But it's still no excuse for her behavior, and she can't put everything on you. I reminded her you didn't find a real man until she pushed you away."

"Wha—" Eden choked on the tea. "You said that to her? That she pushed me away and it was the reason I found a 'real man,' as you call it? Now you're blaming Rafe for me leaving her for Jake? Julia—" Eden shook her head in despair.

"No," Julia backtracked, "no, not what I meant." She hesitated, but only for a moment as she tried to hide the lie in her statement. "I just meant if she were there for you, maybe you wouldn't have, you know, had feelings about men."

"That's just as bad!' snapped Eden upset. "None of what I did was her fault, and there is no way to know if her being there would have changed things." Eden could feel the flush of heat run through her at the thought of how the Stewards and Jake manipulated her, and how she was so blind, she couldn't see what was really happening. "I feel like such a fool every time I look through the file and see what I wrote to them and the things they were telling me. I can see it clearly now, and I just can't believe I couldn't see it then. If I had, we might not be where we are today."

"That's why I told her she should stop dragging you over the coals for things you had no control over," said Julia. She put her hand on Eden's to calm her. "You were doing your best to deal with the first truly traumatic thing to happen to you since the ordeal with your parents. I tried to explain to her you didn't have the experiences in life she had, so you were bound to make mistakes. You had a very protected life," she said with a shrug, "so you made a lot of mistakes, and she should just accept you did your best."

Eden frowned. She pulled her hand away feeling like Julia was being a little condescending. It is true she was doing her best, but Julia made it sound like she was a child, or worse, stupid. "I don't think my choices had anything to do with having a protected life," she said trying to hold in her annoyance. She was sure it was more the fact her chronic anxiety had taken over her mind, and all the manipulation and other things battering against her just made it worse. "Rafe asked me all the time if there was anything more I wanted to tell her, and I didn't tell her what was going on," she reminded Julia. "I even convinced Flynn to keep things a secret. Rafe giving him a black eye was completely my fault."

"You were trying to protect her," she said sympathetically. "She can't fault you for having good intentions even if your reasoning was wrong."

"But I didn't really protect her, did I?" she asked knowing the answer. She could see now she should have told Rafe everything, and she was right. "I try to apologize, but I don't know if it will be enough for her to stay with me."

Again, Julia was reminded of how Andrea talked about Rafe. Maybe Eden would soon see life would be easier without Rafe. The sooner, the better in her opinion. Then Julia could remind Rafe of all the things they had in common and could show her they would be better off with each other in the end. "She's just angry at the situation," Julia said with certainty, knowing she just had to bide her time. "She just needs to get over it."

"Get over it," Eden repeated. "How can she when you and everyone else are beating her over the head with it?" she asked in frustration. She saw Julia bristle and knew she saw things differently. "I have to go." She braced herself, knowing Julia may not like her next words. She stood and took a calming breath. "Just give her some space and don't upset her. You can't help either of us if you're just going to make things worse."

Julia saw Eden out then went back to the kitchen to get another chocolate scone. "I could help Rafe much better than her," she mumbled to herself. She pushed her jealousy down and ate the scone to soothe her frustrations.

46

IN THE BACKYARD, Rafe Salvaggio was banking a fire in the pizza oven she had built. Rafe had pre-built all the forms, dug out the area in the yard where she wanted to build the oven and gathered a few key materials before she began building the oven. With Flynn's help, it only took a little over a week to get all the other materials together, build the oven, and get it to the point where they could use it.

Rafe was proud of how the oven turned out and hoped everything went well with the inaugural use tonight. She was also glad the project kept her too busy over the last week for Julia and the others to bother her. It gave her something to focus on so she wouldn't think about all the things going on in her life all the time. It also used up a lot of her energy, so when she did think about things, she could think clearly. She added more wood to the oven then stepped back to see if there were any heat cracks.

The oven was a dome Rafe created by making a form from wood she covered with painstaking precision using red fire bricks and heat resistant mortar then covering them in turn with an insulator and a decorative mosaic. Below the oven was a base made of cinder block doubling for the storage of wood and was faced with a small ornate plaster mantle from an old fireplace. The sides and back were covered with Italian tiles. There were also slots included in the base for the storage of utensils, pizza paddles, ash broom, and the ovenware Ephraim brought over. Everything looked good, and the fire had been burning at increased temperatures for about four days to help cure everything. Now it was getting to the right temperature for cooking.

Rafe saw Flynn unloading wood and bringing it into the backyard. "I think this load will fill up the storage space. We can put the rest in the garage on the wood rack," she instructed him with a smile for a job well done.

"I didn't realize we'd need this much wood," said Flynn as he dropped the wood he was carrying next to the oven. He stood up and admired the oven with a grin. "I can't believe I helped make this," he said proudly. "We could probably go into business making these!"

Rafe laughed as she helped stow the wood. "I don't think you'd make as much money making these as you do at your day job," she said. "But I'm glad you had fun helping."

"When we first started and were carrying all the brick and tile back here, I never thought we would end up with this. I think the girls will be impressed."

"They will be impressed—if it works. This is why Ephraim's testing it out this morning. It should be well cured now, so we just need to make sure the temperature doesn't get too high or too low when we're cooking. We need it to be about 370° Celsius or 700° Fahrenheit for pizza. We can use this inferred gauge I bought." She showed Flynn the temperature gauge. "Otherwise, it'll have to be done by feel, and you have to be extra careful, especially if you want to make some bread or cook in the crockery."

Ephraim was in the kitchen making pizza dough. He brought over all the utensils and pizza making things he ordered when Rafe told him she was building it. He even ordered a small metal prep table with wheels to set beside the oven so they could make the pizzas outside.

Wheeling out his table with dough, sauce, and toppings, Ephraim made his way to the oven. "Okay, how's it going out here? I have everything ready for the test run," he said excited about the new toy.

"The fire is banked, and it looks like the temperature's good. We just need to make sure most of the ash is swept back off the baking tiles and make our pizzas," said Rafe as she looked over the ingredients and ate some of the mozzarella cheese. "This looks great, Ephraim."

"I gotta tell ya, Rafe, I was doubtful about you getting this done as fast as you said you would. But you're right on schedule," said Ephraim excitedly. "I'm glad I went ahead and made the order for all the supplies. What's Eden and Bronte think of all this?" he asked with a chuckle.

"Well, I think Eden thinks I'm cracked, and Bronte just liked playing in the cement. I let her put her handprint down in the corner of the pad for the base," she said and pointed to Bronte's tiny handprint. "I hope they'll like it."

"They will," Flynn assured her.

"I think you're right," Ephraim said to Flynn as he stretched out the pizza dough. "I know I was impressed when I came over this morning. Makes me wish we had a house instead of an apartment so we could have one."

"You can use this one anytime," offered Rafe with a grin. "Just leave some pizza for us!"

"No problem," Ephraim assured her happily. "So what time is everyone coming over? I have more ingredients and toppings at the bistro I want to bring over."

"Eden and Bronte should be home in a couple of hours from running errands." She worked to hide the irritation Eden was probably out somewhere with Julia. They had been meeting and talking a lot over the last week, and Rafe didn't like it. "I guess everyone can come about three o'clock if they want to swim and stuff before dinner. Then we can just cook as everyone creates their pizzas."

"Great," said Ephraim as he nodded and looked the oven over and got out the ash broom.

"I was wondering if you'd be willing to do something else for me," Rafe asked Ephraim.

Ephraim shrugged as he swept the ash off the baking area. "Sure, what do you need?"

"Well, I was hoping you might teach Eden how to use the oven and make different things," she said as she sampled the pizza ingredients. "I built this for her so she and Bronte can make pizzas, and I just thought you could show her what to do. She's a really good cook, so I'm sure she'll catch on fast. She's very smart."

"I'd love to show her the ropes." Ephraim smiled at Rafe. "You know, I knew you would come home to her. They were all worried, but I've seen how you look at Eden. The look has never changed, even when you were apart and with other people. I know Letty has had problems with Eden, but I told her, your love for Eden ran very deep and would always be there no matter what happened in your life. You still look at her that way, and now, you're doing this great thing for her and Bronte."

Rafe shifted uncomfortably. "I just want them to be able to do something fun together," she said softly not sure how to respond to his observation.

"It's a great way to show how much you care," said Ephraim then slipped the pizza paddle under the pizza. "Let's get this in the oven and get it cooking!"

47

PUSHING THE STROLLER down the sidewalk, Eden Kingsley wheeled Bronte toward the small café in the middle of the shopping square. She saw Julia was already there waiting. She maneuvered Bronte inside and got her some juice, and a coffee for herself then went to Julia's table. "Good morning, we made it," she said as she sat down.

"Good morning," said Julia with a smile. "It looks like you've already been to a few shops."

"Yeah, Bronte needed new shoes. She's growing so fast," she said as she gave Bronte her juice. "I also found some good deals on a few outfits for her. She ruined some of her good clothes helping Rafe with her project."

"So, is she finally finished?"

"Yeah, everyone is invited for pizza tonight. Come earlier if you want to swim." She looked at Julia anxiously. "So did she tell you anything yesterday?"

"Not really," Julia said with a roll of her eyes. "She's avoiding me. Probably still angry we called the doctor," she said wryly. "I hope since they took her off the original medication, she'll be better now that it's out of her system." She sipped her drink. "I know you want things to happen fast, but they just can't. Did you get a look at the new prescription yet?"

"Yes, it's Prazosin. I looked it up, and it's just to help with her nightmares and help her sleep. I don't want to see her go through that again," she said nervously at the memory. "She must be doing just therapy for the rest," said Eden and sighed heavily. "She's still not telling me much, no matter how many times I ask."

"Well, it's good she got something new, anyway," said Julia with optimism. "I'll try again to see if Rafe will start to talk to me about the therapy. I'll suggest we try to talk about whatever they aren't covering. I have a feeling she's not telling them everything. Have you still been giving her the space she needs?"

"Yes," said Eden and sat her cup on the table. "It's been really hard." She looked at Julia sadly. "I hate feeling like this, Julia. I hate feeling so far away from her when I could just reach out and touch her."

"You have to do this for now," Julia encouraged her. It seemed like she was now Eden's cheerleader. It took a bit, but she was now back on Eden's good side. She knew Eden needed a lot of support to get through this, and knowing Rafe, it might get harder for them both. Plus, it was the best way right now to stay close and keep an eye on Rafe. "Have you been watching her? Is she still having side effects or are they going away?"

"I've been watching her," Eden confirmed. "She's been working with Flynn on the pizza oven most of the time. Flynn says she doesn't talk much except to talk about weird things like the history of concrete, the construction of domes and similar things. Apparently, she's giving Flynn lessons in construction materials." Eden shook her head. "I don't think she trusts him because of the secret he kept from her, so she won't talk about anything important with him."

"Well, it makes sense," said Julia as she nodded. "She really wanted to hurt him. He's lucky he just got a black eye and that Stacey dragged him out of the waiting room. What about the side effects?"

"She hasn't been throwing up, and she's been eating a little more, but it's been more snacking than meals. It seems like her nightmares are better. She hasn't come into my room looking for me or anything. It does seem like she's slowed down a little too. She's not doing so many projects and is concentrating mostly on the oven. It seems like everything else is the same, though."

"Well, that's positive," said Julia as she looked at her watch. "I have to go. I'm having a fitting for a new outfit before going over. I'll see you tonight, okay?"

"Okay," said Eden as she got up with Julia. "We have a few more errands to run then we're heading home. See you later." Eden watched as Julia walked out. She gathered her shopping bags. When she had everything ready, she pushed Bronte out of the café. She hoped Julia was right and Rafe would be better soon.

Eden was amazed at the oven Rafe had made and was glad she was doing a project keeping her home most of the time. She had no idea what made her want to build it, but watching her let Bronte help and seeing her so happy was worth the ruined clothes and all the extra baths. It was priceless really. These last few days she watched as Rafe stayed outside burning wood in the oven. She said she was curing it, but Eden had no idea why it took so long. She thought it might be a way to have the alone time Rafe said she needed.

The girls had kept their promise about not upsetting Rafe, and with the new medication, it seemed like things were going better. She couldn't get Rafe to talk about her nightmare or much of anything else. It was not surprising so Eden just kept letting her know she wasn't leaving and she loved her and hoped it would help.

Eden saw the store she wanted up ahead and pushed Bronte inside. She wanted to get something for Rafe to go along with the oven from the specialty kitchen gadget store. She looked around the store unsure of what to get because there were so many things. Finally, she decided on practical things, a rocker knife for cutting the pizza, some serving trays and a table stand for the pizza. She smiled when she saw the chef hats and decided to get one for Rafe and one for Bronte. She hoped Rafe like what she picked out.

48

ABBY VAN FALKOV HAPPILY led her date inside Rafe's house. She had been dating her for about three weeks and was excited to bring her to Rafe and Eden's pizza party because she wanted to introduce her to the gang. Darcella was a beautiful French girl with dark eyes and short dark hair, adorned with blue dye artfully streaked through it. She worked as a freelance travel writer and was sexy, fun, and mysterious. Abby couldn't resist her. She was hoping things would go well tonight and maybe things would progress to the next level with them. She saw Julia in the kitchen and took Darcella up to her, trying to contain her excitement.

"Julia, this is Darcella," said Abby as she introduced her date. "She's French," she said as she looked knowingly at Julia. "Darcella, this is my friend Julia,"

"*Salut, ah, 'ello,*" said Darcella shyly. "It is good to meet you," she said in her heavy French accent.

"*Bienvenue,*"[9] replied Julia as she reached out her hand toward Darcella.

"*Ah, tu parles français?*"[10] asked Darcella as she shook Julia's hand.

"*Je me débrouille,*"[11] Julia answered with a ripple of laughter. "*Mais Rafe est très couramment. Mais Rafe parle couramment. Elle a étudié en France.*[12] She's just outside."

"Ah, well I look forward to meeting 'er," she said in her accented English, intrigued.

Abby frowned and shifted uncomfortably, not following the conversation. "So, let's go meet everyone else," she suggested and led Darcella out to the patio where everyone was either admiring Rafe's pizza oven or sitting at the table after having made pizzas for Ephraim to cook.

---

[9] Welcome,

[10] Ah, do you speak French?

[11] I can hold my own,

[12] But Rafe is very fluent. She went to school in France.

"Hey, everyone, I'm here," she announced as she held Darcella's hand.

"Hey, Abby," said Eden. "Who is this?" she asked motioning to the girl Abby was leading.

"Everyone, this is Darcella," she said proudly. "She's a travel writer."

"'Ello," said Darcella in her pronounced accent and smiled at everyone returning her hello.

"Hi, I'm Eden," she said as she shook Darcella's hand then started pointing around. "I'm sure you probably know Erica since she works with Abby." She pointed at Jude. "This is Jude and her date Cara. This is Flynn and his date Robbie. Stacey, and over there by the oven is Ephraim, Letty, and Rafe, who is holding our daughter Bronte."

"Oh, yes, Rafe," she said with interest, "the lady inside says she speaks *Français*," said Darcella as she looked over at Rafe.

"Julia," Abby reminded her.

"She does," confirmed Eden with a smile. "You guys go on over and make a pizza," she said then went inside to help Julia.

Abby led Darcella up to the pizza making station Ephraim had set up. "This looks great Ephraim," she said as she looked over the prep table.

"Thank you," Ephraim said with delight. "Just take a ball of dough and spread it out then add your sauce and toppings. When you're ready, I'll slide it in the oven for you."

"He and Rafe really outdid themselves," said Letty proudly as Ephraim put her pizza in the oven.

"Hi, Abby," said Rafe as she brought Bronte over to the prep table. Bronte reached for Letty, and Rafe released Bronte into Letty's arms. "Who's your friend?" she asked as Letty took Bronte over to the patio.

Abby was excited about introducing her date. "This is my date, Darcella," she said with a huge grin then looked at Darcella. "This is Rafe," she said and motioned toward Rafe.

"Enchantée de faire ta connaissance,"[13] said Darcella sweetly as she offered Rafe her hand. *"On m'a dit que tu parlais français."*[14]

Rafe looked at Darcella, taking her all in, and smiled as she took her hand and kissed it gently then looked into her eyes charmingly. *"Tout le plaisir est pour moi,"*[15] she purred and stepped closer to her. *" Bienvenue chez moi. J'espère que tu passeras une bonne soirée en notre compagnie."*[16]

"Te regarder et parler avec toi a déjà fait mon bonheur,"[17] said Darcella as she looked Rafe over. *" Tu es la première Américaine à m'embrasser ici,"*[18] she said with a smile, *"tu auras donc une place à part dans mon cœur."*[19]

Rafe gave a small laugh. *"Je serai ravie de vivre dans ton cœur,"*[20] she said with a wink. *"Abby et toi ne vous êtes pas embrassées?"*[21]

---

[13] A pleasure to meet you,

[14] I was told you speak French.

[15] The pleasure is mine,

[16] Welcome to my home. I hope you have a good evening in our company.

[17] I already found joy watching you and speaking with you,

[18] You are the first American to kiss me here,

[19] so there will be a special place for you in my heart.

[20] It will be my pleasure to live in your heart

"*Juste bonjour et au revoir. Rien à voir avec l'amour.*"[22] She smiled at Rafe. "*Ça fait du bien de parler à quelqu'un qui me comprend et comprend l'amour à la Française.*"[23]

"*Je comprends très bien,*"[24] said Rafe softly and let go of her lingering hand. "*Abby, en revanche, ne comprend que l'amour à l'Américaine, nous devons donc prendre soin de son cœur.*"[25]

"Okay," said Abby, only understanding her name had been mentioned. "I hope you're saying good things about me." She laughed nervously at the intense looks Rafe and Darcella were exchanging and the way they had held hands.

Rafe looked at Abby and smiled. "Only good, Abby," she said then looked at Darcella. "*Amuse-toi bien. Je te reverrai à table,*"[26] she said with a sight bow of her head. She turned and walked over to the patio table.

Darcella watched Rafe walk away. "She is very beautiful, your friend," she said to Abby. "She is not really American, is she?"

"Who, Rafe?" asked Abby as she looked over at her dark-haired friend. "She's half Italian," she revealed. "She's always saying things in Italian we can't understand." She laughed to hide her discomfort. "Let's make our pizzas," she said and began making her crust, and Darcella joined her.

---

[21] You have not shared a kiss with Abby?

[22] Just hello and goodbye. Not for love,

[23] It is good to talk with a person who understands me and French love.

[24] I understand very well,

[25] But Abby only understands American love so we must guard her heart.

[26] Enjoy. I'll see you again at the table.

Julia and Eden brought the plates and salad out and had watched Rafe's exchange with Darcella. As Rafe walked to the table, Julia could see the emotions of hurt, disbelief, anger, and jealousy crossing Eden's face from watching Rafe talk to Darcella and hold her hand much longer than necessary.

"*Tu dragues les femmes devant tout le monde, à présent?*"[27] Julia asked Rafe softly making sure Eden did not hear.

"*Va te faire foutre,*"[28] Rafe said with a dark look, " *Je n'ai rien fait de mal.*"[29]

"Nice," said Julia under her breath and shook her head then turned toward Eden and smiled. "Thanks for your help with the salad, Eden. Do you want me to help you get the wine and the glasses?"

Eden looked at Julia with wide eyes, holding in her emotions. "Sure," she said when she found her voice. "Rafe, would you like a glass of wine?" she asked as Rafe sat at the table.

"More would be nice." She smiled at Eden. "Thank you."

Eden broke her gaze away from Rafe and smiled weakly at Julia. "Come on," she said, "let's bring some bottles of wine out for dinner." She made her way inside and started setting out bottles to open.

Julia put glasses on a tray and watched Eden. "I'm sure it was nothing," she said, knowing it could be a lie because Rafe

---

[27] You make love to women in front of everyone now?
[28] Go fuck yourself,
[29] I have done nothing wrong.

had treated Andrea and others exactly the same way. "She was probably just being nice."

"It's fine," said Eden shortly as she opened a bottle then turned to Julia sharply. "You know, I don't know why I'm even trying. Maybe you were right about her pushing me away."

"She's definitely pushing, but she's pushing everyone, though," said Julia in frustration.

"I thought things were going well, but she clearly doesn't want me here," Eden said as she ran her hand through her hair anxiously.

"I doubt that," said Julia trying to be reassuring, but secretly hoping it was true. "It's just the meds and what she's going through. You know it isn't true."

"Do I? If I weren't here, she would have already stolen blue-streaked-hair-girl from Abby, and she would probably have her in bed tonight." She worked the corkscrew angrily to open another bottle of wine. "She probably wouldn't even have to wait that long!"

"You can't think this way," said Julia. "Plus, believe me, French girls are not as easy as everyone says they are. They flirt terribly and suggest all kinds of innuendo, but it's all they do most of the time. They won't even kiss you half the time unless they're very serious about you."

"She looked like she was serious," said Eden as she opened a third bottle of wine.

"I'm sure it's just the love of the game," she said and picked up the tray of glasses. "Let's get this out there and try to have a good time tonight."

"I'm sure some people will have a good time," she said heatedly as she opened another bottle and then followed Julia outside with the wine.

49

WHEN THE PIZZAS were ready, Ephraim Holden started bringing them over from the oven and placing them on the table. When the last pizza was delivered to the table, the wine glasses were filled, and everyone was sitting, Rafe stood up and to speak. "Everyone," she said over their conversations and held up her wine glass, "thank you for coming to help us use the pizza oven for the first time."

"No problem. You know we can't pass up free food," Jude wisecracked, and everyone laughed in agreement.

Rafe chuckled and then continued. "Every day, when I worked on this project," she began, "I thought about Bronte and Eden. I hope they'll have fun making pizza and other things together with the oven. Eden is a wonderful cook," she said and smiled at Eden. "This is why Ephraim has graciously agreed to teach Eden how to use the oven so she can enjoy her gift and so she and Bronte can make pizza together all the time." She looked across at Eden again. "I really hope you like it." She lifted her glass and looked around the table. "Now," she said, "here's to pizza and friends," she concluded and took a sip of her wine, and the others followed her lead. Rafe sat down and began helping Bronte get some small pieces of pizza on her plate.

"I just love this," Abby said as she ate her pizza. "Rafe, I had no idea you could build something so cool!"

"I had a lot of help from Flynn and some from Bronte too," she said with a smile at Bronte. She let Letty take over feeding Bronte as the little girl deconstructed her pizza, making quite the mess.

"It was fun helping," Flynn declared. "When Rafe showed me the plans, I had no idea how we were going to get it done, but Rafe had everything really organized. The hardest part was waiting for the concrete to dry," he joked.

"How'd you do the tiles on the dome?" asked Erica.

"It was a design already on a backing, and we just had to lay it on," answered Flynn, "then it was grouting and cleaning it up."

"Cool," said Cara, Jude's date, as she sipped her wine.

"I really like the ornate piece on the front," said Robbie, Flynn's date. "It looks like a fireplace mantle."

"It is," said Rafe as she ate a small bite. She looked at Eden who was frowning and looking down at her pizza but never looked up at her. Rafe turned her attention back to Robbie. "I found it in an architectural salvage yard. I made the base so it would fit perfectly."

Julia leaned toward Eden, who was silently eating a piece of her pizza. "See, she does want you here," whispered Julia. Eden frowned then got up and went inside without a word.

Julie wiped her mouth and cleared her throat, trying to hide her surprise. She caught Abby glaring at her, so she shrugged.

"She must have forgotten something," said Abby then followed Eden.

Abby found Eden in her bedroom sitting on the edge of her bed. "What's going on?"

Eden looked up wiping her eyes. "She's pushing me away, and maybe I should listen to her."

"No, she wants you here," she assured her gently with understanding because she was thinking of scratching Rafe's eyes out herself over Darcella not long ago. "She practically built you a monument."

"I know," said Eden feeling miserable. "I just did it again."

"What?"

"I was angry and complaining about her, and then I find out she is doing all of this for me. She must be right."

"Right about what," asked Abby confused.

"Well, I must not trust her," said Eden shakily. "I got angry when I thought she was flirting, but Julia was right, she probably wasn't. I didn't trust her. The same thing happened the day when she was dancing with Julia and had bought me wine. I'm screwing up," she said sadly.

"No, you're not. You're not screwing up, Eden," she said sympathetically. "You just can't take so many things personally, and you have to remember she cares about you no matter how things might look."

"Right," said Eden. "You mean, trust her, which is just what I said I apparently can't do."

"It's hard. No one expects you to be perfect, but when you find out you're wrong, you can't just run off. You need to acknowledge it to yourself then show Rafe you hear her because she may not even know she's telling you she cares through her actions if not through her words."

Eden sighed and pulled herself together. "Okay," she said. "I bought something for Rafe today and maybe giving it to her now will show her I appreciate her and what she made for us." She went to her closet and got out the bag with the things she bought at the kitchen supply store. "Let's go," she said and headed out of the room.

Abby followed her. "Just let me get more wine," she said and grabbed a couple of bottles and the corkscrew then they headed out.

Eden walked outside with the gifts. She sat beside Rafe and put her hand on her shoulder. "You did a great job on the pizza oven," she said with a smile then removed her hand, not wanting to invade her space. "When I was out today, I got you some things," she said and handed Rafe the bag. "I hope when Bronte and I are making pizzas, you're there too."

Rafe smiled slightly then looked in the bag. She pulled out the chef hats and put one on Bronte and then one on Eden. "This looks good on you," she said cheerfully. She looked in the bag again and pulled out the rocker knife. "A mezzaluna." She chuckled and handed the knife to Ephraim. "This will come in handy." She pulled out the two large boxes and looked at the pictures. "This will make serving the pizza much easier," she said as she looked them over and nodded. "They'll go well with the oven." She sat the boxes to the side of her chair. "I think you got some great things," she said, her lips flashing a slight smile then took a drink of her wine. "It looks like pizza night is a success," she said cheerfully to the table, and everyone agreed and continued talking. Rafe looked over at Abby and Darcella. "*Que penses-tu de ta pizza, Darcella?*"[30] she asked politely, and they began a conversation in French to Abby's chagrin.

Confused by Rafe's actions, Eden took the chef's hat off her head. She got up and went to sit in her original chair. Trying to control the flush of anger, she turned to Julia. "What the heck just happened?"

"I'm not sure," Julia admitted uncomfortably. "Just hang in there. I'll talk to her about it later," she promised.

50

THE TABLE CONVERSATION was lively, and soon, everyone had eaten their pizzas and finished drinking their last glass of wine. Julia Hawthorn tried to pull Rafe away from her conversation with Darcella because she could see both

---

[30] How is your pizza, Darcella?

Eden and Abby were getting frustrated. As far as Julia could discern their conversation was completely innocent but their laughter and interaction made it look—not so innocent.

Julia sipped her wine as she watched Rafe get up from the table and walk to the pizza oven. She shook her head with concern as Darcella got up soon after and followed Rafe.

"Well," said Jude as she stood, "we have to go. Thanks for inviting us, Eden. I'll see you soon."

"Bye," said Cara.

"Yeah," said Flynn as he and Robbie stood, "we're going out to Bab's tonight."

"It's going to be a fun night, and there'll be a surprise performance later," said Erica with excitement.

"Will you guys be there?" asked Stacey.

"I don't think so, but thank you all for coming," said Eden as Jude and the others gave her a hug then headed out the back gate toward Jude's house.

Abby moved to the chair next to Julia. "Well, Rafe sure is getting along well with my date," she said disgruntled. "I have no idea what they're talking about, but Darcella keeps smiling at Rafe and touching her hair then touching Rafe on her arm."

"Don't worry about it, Abby," Julia tried to reassure her, "it's harmless. It's just typical French flirting, and it doesn't mean anything unless they start snogging." She forced a laugh as she watched Darcella flirt and stand very close to Rafe. She hoped Rafe didn't start kissing the girl.

"Hey, Eden," Letty said as she carried Bronte over, "Rafe did a great thing for you!" She smiled and shifted Bronte on her hip. "It looks like this B Girl needs to be cleaned up," she said and passed Bronte to Eden.

Eden took Bronte and gave her a hug and kiss. "Did you get enough to eat?" she asked the messy little girl. "You certainly got a lot of pizza on you." Bronte kissed her back and they laughed and then she took the messy girl inside to get her cleaned up.

"What's going on with Eden?" she asked Julia. "She looked angry."

"I think she's upset because Rafe didn't thank her for the gift and ignored her again," revealed Julia with a sigh.

"I'm going to go see what they're talking about over there," said Abby as she watched Rafe and Darcella. "I'm not sure I like dating girls I can't understand, no matter how sexy their accent is. I should have learned my lesson with Rafe," she complained.

"It's been my experience French girls don't date," said Julia with a roll of her eyes. She had learned her lesson in college.

"What's that supposed to mean?" asked Abby with irritation then got up and walked over to her date and Rafe.

"I swear," said Letty with frustration as she watched Abby walk toward Rafe, "I'm beginning to lose patience with Rafe. I know she's sick, but she is acting just like her father. Eden has been nothing but good to her lately, and I can see Rafe's hurting her. Now she's flirting with her friend's date."

"I'm sure it's nothing," said Julia hoping it was true and Rafe hadn't decided she had possibly found a new paramour.

"She's probably just enjoying speaking French to someone and making the girl feel welcome."

Eden came back outside and sat down. "Ephraim has Bronte, and they're playing with her kitchen stuff. She's really cute in her hat," she said then lost her smile as she saw Letty's angry look. "What's wrong, Letty?"

"I'm sorry Rafe's treating you so badly," said Letty sorrowfully. "I've seen her father do the same thing to women, to people in general. Just doing and saying things to hurt them," she said getting angry. "He even did it to Rafe, so I can't understand why she would do it to you."

Julia nodded in agreement. "My father said the same," she said and stopped as she looked up to see Rafe standing near her.

"What did your father say?" asked Rafe as she smiled and pulled out a chair then sat down.

"We were just talking about how my father gave me time off and said I need to be happy with what I do," said Julia trying to save them from drama.

"Oh," said Rafe as she nodded. "Abby and her friend Darcella left. I think Abby is taking her to Club La Femme tonight. She's a really nice girl. Smart." She reached across the table for her wine glass. "I think the others are going to Bab's."

Letty couldn't hold in her anger. Rafe discussing flirting with another woman in front of Eden was too much. "Rafe, what the hell are you doing? You're turning into your father! The worst part of him!"

"Letty, no!" exclaimed Eden, frightened at how she was talking to Rafe.

Rafe furrowed her brow, understanding the women had been talking badly about her father. Her anger flared. She stood looking at Letty darkly. "You have no idea what you're talking about," she said in a low growl.

"Oh, really?" said Letty angrily. "I know he was a horrible, cruel man and treated people like shit, including you!"

"My father was a great man who worked very hard to provide me with everything," said Rafe calmly. "You know nothing about him, so I'd appreciate it if you stop fucking talking about him." She glared at Eden and Julia then walked into the house.

"Oh, I knew him!" Letty shouted after Rafe angrily. "You're turning into him, Rafe!"

Eden stood up along with Julia. "What are you doing, Letty?" asked Eden fearfully. "We can't challenge her like this. It may make things worse! You know what happened when Julia upset her."

"I'm sorry, Eden, but she can't be allowed to do this and get away with it," she insisted.

"I'll go check on her," said Julia and went after Rafe.

"She's been doing so well," Eden said despondently, wishing Letty had not upset Rafe. "It's hard, but we can't challenge her and yell at her. It affects her terribly now. We have to be able to talk to her calmly," she said and shook her head trying to hold in her anxiety of what might happen. "Please, just stay out here for now and let us talk to her," she said and went inside to find Julia and Rafe. As she walked in, Ephraim carried Bronte toward her.

"Eden, something is going on with Rafe and Julia," he said with concern.

"I know," she said anxiously, "can you take Bronte outside with Letty?"

"Sure," he said and took Bronte to the patio.

Eden walked toward Rafe's room and could hear Julia and Rafe talking. Rafe was speaking in French, but Julia was answering in English.

"No I won't do it," Julia yelled. "I won't, Rafe! You need to just trust me and talk to me," she insisted.

Walking into the room, Eden saw Rafe scowling at Julia angrily. "What's happening?" she asked with worry. "What's she asking you to do?"

"Get out of my room!" yelled Rafe. "Both of you leave!"

"No," Julia yelled back. "I know you're angry but don't cut us out. Don't make me promise on my life not to tell. That's the old Rafe, it isn't you anymore," she said trying to reason with her. "Just talk to me."

"*Tu ne sais rien de moi ni de mon père,*"[31] she said heatedly, "*Je ne veux pas te parler de lui!*"[32]

"I do know you, Rafe," insisted Julia, "and I knew your father. I'm not going to make some crazy promise to you so you'll talk to me!"

---

[31] You don't know me or my father,
[32] I will not speak to you of him!

Eden hesitated only for a moment and made a decision. "I'll do it," she said firmly.

"Do what," asked Julia as she turned to Eden.

"I'll swear," she said and swallowed nervously and meeting Rafe's eyes. "I'll swear whatever you want so you'll tell me about your father."

"No, Eden," said Julia, "you can't swear to anything with her in this state. What if she tells you something you have to tell someone? What if it means her life if you don't tell when you need to tell?"

"*Allez-vous en, toutes les deux,*"[33] said Rafe angrily. " *Je ne veux pas te parler de lui!*"[34] She waved them away.

Julia looked at Eden then back at Rafe. "Please, Rafe," she begged, "don't make her swear on her life and tell her something terrible will happen if she tells. You need to talk to her or me, without threats and demands."

"No," said Rafe evenly and pointed to the door.

"Come on, Eden," said Julia. "Let's give her time to calm down." She took Eden by the arm and led her out of the room. "You can't make those kinds of promises. I'll come and talk to her again tomorrow."

Eden looked back at Rafe with the knowledge she had already made the kind of promise she had been warned about.

---

[33] You two need to leave,

[34] I will not speak to you of him!

51

LETTY CARVER HELPED Julia and Eden get everything cleaned up while Ephraim took care of everything around the pizza oven and then played with Bronte. She felt bad about getting on to Rafe, but she didn't want to see the wonderful girl she used to spend so much time with turn into someone like her father. Rafe was always full of energy and curiosity. She was such a bright and happy child, and it broke her heart to see the changes she was going through. When they finished cleaning up, Letty sat across from Eden and Julia at the kitchen island with their glasses of wine while Ephraim held Bronte and played with her toys on the toddler table.

"She's not coming out," said Eden with worry.

Letty shook her head in disappointment. "She's stubborn just like her papa."

"This has always been a sore point for her, Letty, and you know it," said Ephraim. "You shouldn't have said those things to her."

"I had to say something," she insisted. "I can't stand seeing her doing those things to Eden, or anyone else. You know I never saw her father after I came to California because of the things he did." She shook her head at the memory. "I just don't understand why Rafe can't see how he was. She always says he was a great man, but he was terrible."

"But Letty, if you upset her, it makes it harder for me," said Eden. "Now I have no idea what she'll do. What if she thinks we're ganging up on her and decides to leave again? Or what if she has another setback and goes through one of her nightmares? It was scary, Letty." She ran her hand through her hair anxiously at the thought. "I can't take it again."

"Do you want me to stay with you tonight," asked Julia. "I can help if she has an episode."

"Maybe we can take Bronte," suggested Ephraim. "This way you don't have to worry about her if something happens."

"I'm sorry, Eden," said Letty sympathetically. "I really am. I'm just so worried about these changes in her and the problems with her medicine. I thought this new one would help."

"I know," Eden said and patted her hand. "Really, though, the new meds are helping with a lot of things."

"Not everything she does is because of the medicine," said Julia. "Some of it is just her wrong thinking right now."

Eden sighed and closed her eyes. She hoped everything would just blow over tonight, but knew it might be wishful thinking. "I think Bronte going with you is a good idea," she said as she looked at Letty. "Maybe I'll be able to get Rafe out to the bistro in the morning to pick her up. She hasn't been there in a while."

"Sounds good," said Ephraim as he stood. "Come on, Letty, maybe we can stop and get Bronte a treat."

They gathered Bronte's things together, and Eden kissed her goodbye. "Do you think I should tell Rafe?" she asked. "She might want to say goodnight to her."

"If she hasn't come out, maybe we should just leave her alone," suggested Julia. "If you don't think you need me to stay I'm going to take off too. I'll come by tomorrow," she promised. "If you need anything, just call me."

"I'll be fine," said Eden waving away their concerns. "It started out to be such a good day," she said with a sigh as she hugged Julia goodbye.

52

EDEN KINGSLEY WATCHED as everyone got into their cars and drove away and then she went to the kitchen to rinse out the wine glasses and put them in the sink for the next dishwasher load. After locking all of the doors and turning out the lights, she went to her room. She took a shower then put on her pajamas and wondered if she should try to talk to Rafe. She decided she should at least check on her to make sure she was okay. She went to Rafe's door and knocked.

"Rafe?" she said and listened. "Rafe, everyone's gone now," she said into the door. "Bronte went with Letty and Ephraim. They're going to get a treat and take her to their house for the night."

She listened, and again there was no response. She hesitated and then opened the door. Rafe was sitting in her meditation position with her back to the door. "I'm sorry about what happened," she said as Rafe roll her shoulders. "I'll be in my room if you want to talk," she said softly. She started to close her door then stopped. "Thank you for today, for what you did for Bronte and me. I don't think I said it to you."

Rafe leaned forward and put her face in her hands. "I'm nothing like they say my father was," she said softly then turned and looked up at Eden. "But I might be getting close."

"No," said Eden, "you're nothing like they say your father was. I thought your father was good. He was always good to us when we saw him."

"Would you really swear," she asked cautiously.

"Yes," Eden said nervously. "I'll swear. I trust you."

Rafe stood up and walked over to Eden. "They don't know what they're talking about," she insisted feverishly. "They didn't really know him."

Eden could see Rafe was still upset and saw the pain on her face telling how the subject made her feel. She wanted to hold her or touch her, but she was afraid to do anything to make her stop talking. "Do you want to go sit in the living room or go outside? Everything's all cleaned up out there." She watched Rafe thinking about if she wanted to go out of her room or not. Eden took her hand gently. "Come on," she said encouraging her to follow her into the living room.

Rafe looked at her hand as Eden gently pulled on it and decided going to the living room would be a more comfortable place to talk. "Okay," she said, and let Eden lead her to the couch. She sat down next to Eden. "I'm sorry I didn't say thank you for the kitchen things, but I thought you didn't really like the pizza oven. You just left without saying anything, and I was mad."

"I'm sorry I left. I love it," Eden assured her. "What made you think of making it?"

Rafe shrugged. "You told me you hadn't made pizza here with Bronte, and I wanted you to be able to make it."

"Rafe," Eden laughed softly, "I made pizza with Bronte and just used the kitchen oven."

"Oh, well, now it'll be better," she said with a frown. "Ephraim said he could show you how to do bread and casseroles and all kinds of things."

"It will be better," agreed Eden, touched by her thoughtfulness. "I think learning to use it will be fun. I really do hope you'll help us use it. Maybe you can wear the chef's hat I got you." She smiled but saw Rafe wasn't in the mood to joke. She waited to see if Rafe would talk, but she just sat on the edge of the couch like she might get up and leave. "Do you want me to swear now?" she asked quietly.

Rafe studied Eden and wondered why she wanted to swear. Most people don't want to swear unless they thought they had to do it for some reason. She wondered why she thought she had to do it. Eden didn't need to know about her father. No one did. It was the reason she told people they had to swear because she knew they wouldn't do it just to hear about a man they did not know or really did not like. She kept thinking about her dreams and wondered if she told more secrets to Eden if they would stop. It was so hard to think about everything again. "Are you sure you want to?" she asked giving her a chance to change her mind.

"I'm sure," said Eden softly. "Tell me the words you need me to say."

"You know the words," she said and frowned fighting the urge to press into the bridge of her nose to quell the pain forming. "What you don't know are the conditions."

Eden nodded slowly. "What are the conditions?"

"They're the same as before," she said softly. "You will never be able to gain my trust again, and you will never see me again—ever."

"I understand," said Eden anxiously.

"And, after you know, you'll have to defend him because he can't defend himself," she added.

"Defend him?"

"Yes, you can't let them talk about him badly again," she insisted. "You have to tell them to stop and tell them he was a great man who took care of me and gave me everything. I wouldn't be where I am without him."

Eden nodded her agreement. "Okay, I can tell them."

Rafe wondered if Eden really could. If she could find the backbone and the strength to defend someone everyone else hated and didn't know, without telling the secret. If she could stand up to the ignorance of people who couldn't or wouldn't see the truth about him. "Okay," she paused. "Swear like you did before," she said challengingly.

Eden cleared her throat. "I, Jayne Eden Kingsley, swear on my life, I will take this secret to my grave," she swore for the second time. Rafe helped her with the Italian, and she swore again in *Italiano*. She could tell Rafe was still on edge. "Do you want me to get you some wine or some scotch?" she offered. She hoped it would help calm Rafe even though she wasn't supposed to be drinking. She didn't think one more drink would hurt since she had already been drinking wine today. "Maybe it will help you relax."

"Sure," she answered softly. "Scotch, the good bottle since we'll be talking about my father."

"Okay," said Eden and went to make their drinks.

When Eden returned, she handed a tumbler to Rafe containing a small amount of the caramel colored liquor. She knew not to put ice in this particular scotch. It was the one Rafe and her father liked served neat.

Sitting down, Eden prepared herself as best she could for whatever Rafe was about to reveal. Though Eden had told Rafe everything about her own childhood, they had only talked about inconsequential things in Rafe's childhood. It never really occurred to Eden that Rafe had never talked a lot about her childhood or her father very much. But she did know Rafe's mother had always been off-limits. "Why don't you sit back and relax, babe? Then you can tell me when you're ready." Maybe it was because, since her own parent's rejection, Eden stopped talking about her childhood and had put it to the back of her mind. Since meeting Rafe, none of it seemed to matter anymore.

Rafe sat down at the other end of the couch and tried to get comfortable. Looking into her glass, Rafe thought about the first time she had really begun to see her father. She had to see him because her mother was dead, and he was all she had left. She cleared her throat and began to tell someone for the first time about her father.

"My father had always been in the peripheral of my life," she started. "He worked hard and was gone a lot on business. But, when he was home, my mother always made sure we did things together as a family. Sometimes, he would read to me at night. He never read typical children's books to me. It was poetry or philosophy and sometimes history. I remember thinking he must think I'm smarter than I was."

She smiled sadly and continued. "So, sometimes I would get the books and have my mother read them to me or read them myself so I could always have a good question to ask him and impress him." She looked down at her drink feeling like her lungs were not filling up as they should. "The day I really began to see who he was, I had been taken to the hospital after seeing my mother lying in the street. I didn't understand what had happened. I just knew she was hurt, and I was going to see her. My teacher had led me inside, and we walked down the sterile hallway as she tried to find out where we needed to go. I looked up and saw him sitting in a chair with his face in his hands, and he was crying. I had never seen him cry before. I called out as I ran up to him, and he clutched me and hugged me to himself. He was thanking God I was safe.

"I remember he had so many tears. They soaked into my clothes and moistened my skin. I asked him about Mamma, and he looked at me with his dark eyes, wet and red-rimmed, and there was something unfamiliar in them that I couldn't name. He told me we were alone now, my mamma, his wife, was gone. She was *morto*—dead.

"As understanding came to me, I could feel tears leaving me, but my mind had shut down. I could hear myself telling him I was sorry, that I didn't mean to be bad and to please bring her back and I would do better. Then I heard the teacher and a doctor telling him my mother had to drop me off at school, and the reason she was there was because I had been skipping again. My father just looked at me sadly and shook his head then told them to take me away. I didn't want to leave, so I fought against them, crying and calling for my mother. I thought, if I could just see my mother, I could tell her I was sorry, and she would come home, but they dragged me away, and I never got to see my mother again.

"After they took me away," Rafe hesitated and rubbed between her eyes, "everything was a blur. I don't remember a lot. I know I was upset because I was sure, if she hadn't had to take me to school that day, she would still be alive. I could hear everyone telling me I should have been better. I shouldn't have planned to skip school. I didn't know how my mother knew I was going to skip, but she did, and it was why she insisted on taking me to school. To make sure I went. Once I came out of the dark fog I was in, I decided, since my father had sent me away, I wasn't wanted. So, I ran away. I ran as far as I could to get away. I had very little money at the time, so I couldn't get on a train, but I could follow the tracks. I thought I would go to the ocean. I really had no concept of how far away the sea was on foot, but I didn't care. Soon, it was dark, and I just kept walking."

Eden watched Rafe fight to control herself as she talked about her father. She could see the pain in her gray-blue eyes at the memories stirring inside her. She wanted to reassure Rafe but knew, if she interrupted, Rafe might change her mind and stop talking.

"I don't remember how far I got," Rafe continued, "but at some point, my path was lit up by a light. It was my father in his car. I had no idea how he found me. I found out later Gabri and Brettito had told him about how we talked about going to the ocean. He pulled over and walked up to me, picked me up, and then carried me to the car where I collapsed in exhaustion. We drove home in silence, and I was glad of it. I couldn't tell him she was gone because of my adventures. Because of me and the secret that Mamma had found out about. I needed him to still love me."

Rafe rubbed her head and cleared her throat. "The next thing I remember is my father crying over the *affisso* someone brought over for my mother's funeral," she said with the vision in front of her.

"*Affisso?*" asked Eden softly.

Rafe nodded. "Yes, it's like a small poster. They're posted everywhere to tell of her death, and the time and date of her service," she said but didn't tell her she still had a copy hidden away. "I remember all the people bringing food and all the telegrams delivered," she continued, quickly glancing at Eden then down at the drink in her hands. "They're like sympathy cards in Italy. Our neighbors and my father were always on the phone answering questions and talking about Mamma. The whole time, I knew they all could see my guilt and knew it was my fault she had died. So, I avoided them and stayed in my room as much as I could."

Rafe took a sip of her drink, unable to taste the floral and honey notes she knew were there and continued. "I remember the funeral and the priest who talked like he knew her, but he was a stranger," she said sounding offended. "They carried her casket up the isle and then covered it with flowers. There were so many flowers for her. I looked at my father, and it was like he wasn't there. He was with her in his mind, and I knew she was telling him what I had done. I knew because, when he looked at me, his eyes held nothing I could recognize.

"There were so many people there who wanted to speak about my mamma. She was an American who, through her marriage, became one of them. They loved her and would miss her terribly. They spoke of all the good she had done and all her talent, and how much she cared, and how the world was less now without her. I knew they were reminding me if I had been better, the world would have been better because then she wouldn't be dead."

Eden waited patiently as Rafe sat in silence until she could continue.

"I remember walking through the cemetery to the mausoleum and holding my father's hand in the rain as he held the umbrella over us with his other hand. Inside, I remember looking into the dark empty vault as water dripped off us onto the marble floor. They carried her casket over and slid it into the hole in the wall. It was at my eye level so I could see inside it as the bricklayer closed it up, brick by brick, and then he covered the bricks with a layer of concrete. He pushed a paper sign into the wet concrete, and it served as her headstone until the one Papa ordered replaced it. All the time the mason worked, I held my father's hand. I could feel him tremble as he watched as they shut his wife away from the world all because of me. Sometimes, his grip was so tight, the tears in my eyes were from pain instead of grief, but I still didn't let go," said Rafe with a feverish glow in her eyes.

"Finally, we went home to silence where we were alone again. From my room, I could hear him cry for my mother. You see, he loved her deeply and was *il cuore spezzato—* heartbroken. I didn't really know what the concept meant back then, to be heartbroken, but now I know."

She looked at Eden, who had wiped a tear from the corner of her eye. Rafe wanted to tell her not to cry because it didn't matter anymore since her father was dead. Instead, she looked away, took a sip of her drink and then continued. "It took two weeks for him to walk out of the house again. It took me longer because of the shame I felt. Even after both of us were able to leave the house, it was a strange existence. We were both there, but separate. I went one direction, and he went another. He poured himself into work, and I poured myself into my adventures. Soon we were at odds with each other. He made demands intended to control me, and I exceeded his demands out of guilt and continued my adventures."

"He would not speak about her for a long time." Rafe hesitated because it was painful to think about her past, and it was hard when the pain came flooding back. "A few months after her death was the first time he said the words, 'if not for you, she would still be alive.' I almost didn't recover," she paused and felt the hurt again. "He finally said out loud what I knew he was thinking, and it was devastating. Then, he had to go on a business trip, so I was left with the *au pair* as I dealt with my guilt again.

"I would wander around the city alone in a daze a lot, and one day, a friend saw me and took me to her home. She and her Nonna fed me and took care of me all day. At some point, I was talking to Nonna about what happened, and she showed me the truth about my father. She told me the reason he cried and said the things he did was because he was in pain and was hollow because his heart, the thing he lived for, his wife, was taken from him. I knew she meant I took her from him, even though she never said it.

"She said his tears and angry words were the only way he could tell me right then how much he missed her and still loved her. She said they were words of grief, a type of grief I had no real understanding of at the time. She said when I heard those words I should listen, not to what was coming from his mouth, but what was coming from his heart. I should listen and see him for the man he is now—a man who is alive but without his heart, without his love. She said someday, it may change and he wouldn't say those things, but until then, I was his only witness to the love he had for my mother.

"Later, Gabri came and got me. I thought about what she said as Gabri walked me home, and I knew she was right. Whatever words he said to me about my mother came from a place of heartbreak, and the blame for his heartbreak was on me. Whatever anger he had was rooted in heartbreak, and it was also my burden. He became angrier over her death as the years went on, and soon that, and any other anger became directed at me because I was the closest target."

Rafe looked at Eden intently. "So, I know he said hurtful things, and I know he could be cruel, but he wasn't angry or cruel before she died. So I took the punishment I usually deserved without flinching, knowing when he used words about my mother, he was still missing her and heartbroken." She took a sip of her drink, thankful Eden was quiet. "It was the least I could do for taking her away from him."

Eden looked at Rafe as she fought the tears for her on the brink of falling. She didn't understand how someone could say those things to a child. How they could blame her and excuse her father for saying those things, even if he was grieving.

This was just so wrong in her mind. To leave a twelve-year-old to deal with grief and guilt alone and fill her head with such wrong ideas was incredibly cruel. She didn't understand how Rafe could continue to carry such obvious wrong thinking. She was smart and so logical in her thinking, and this guilt she held and the excuses for her father made no sense.

"Rafe," she said softly, "you were twelve. It doesn't matter how heartbroken he was. He shouldn't have been saying those things to hurt you or punish you."

Rafe could see the look of horror on Eden's face. "I know it sounds bad, and maybe a little illogical, but I was twelve, and after a while, it became a habit, then it became a challenge, and finally, a competition. It was how we lived in those moments," she said and took a sip of her drink. "Anyway," Rafe shrugged, "it doesn't matter anymore because he's dead now too." She could see Eden didn't understand. "Just remember your promise, and you have to defend him."

Eden nodded sadly. "Can I ask you a question?" Rafe nodded yes. "He was so nice when we went to see him. Why? It seems like he said or did things to other people, and it made them not like him. Why was he nice to me?"

"He was better," she said with a smile. "Around the time I started my graduate work, he told me he finally realized he could be happy if he let himself. He knew Mamma would want him to be happy, and she would want me to be happy too. He compared himself to a bridled stallion finally able to remove the bridle and be free again. He started dating and enjoying life again. He wanted us to get along better, and we did. He wanted to be thought of as good again by people. You thought well of him until Letty and Julia started talking about him."

Eden could see the shine in Rafe's eyes as she spoke about her father. "So," she said hesitantly, "he apologized for saying those things to you? He told you he was wrong?"

"He wasn't wrong," Rafe insisted. "It was my fault she was there that day."

"But she was your mother. It was where she was supposed to be. She was taking care of you."

"Yes, but if I weren't skipping school, she would have been at home."

It was clear to Eden she wasn't going to get anywhere with Rafe on this subject tonight. She needed time to think about how to talk to her about this and help her see she should let go of the guilt she obviously still held. Maybe Dr. Cathcart could help figure out how to approach the subject without upsetting Rafe. The problem was she had promised not to tell anyone. "Well, I'm glad you were getting along better." She had to ask another question. "So, was your skipping school the secret your mother was keeping? She knew you were skipping school? I thought you said your first kiss led to her death."

Rafe frowned then drank the last of her scotch. "I think that's all I have for now," she said shortly. "I don't want to talk anymore." She got up and stretched. "I'm going outside."

"Would you like me to bring you another scotch or something else?" asked Eden hoping to have an excuse to go with her.

Rafe thought about it for a moment. "I am kind of hungry for some reason," she said, "so maybe something to eat with something to drink."

Eden smiled and was glad she was feeling hungry since she was on her new medication. "Okay, you go out, and I'll bring something to you," she said and got up then went to the kitchen as Rafe went outside.

53

WITH HER HANDS full, Eden Kingsley carried the food she had made for her and Rafe to share out to the patio. She arranged the plate of fruit and cheese, with a little bit of dark chocolate, along with a bottle of wine and two glasses on the table beside Rafe.

"Here you go, babe," said Eden as she poured them each a glass of wine. "I just made something light, but if you need more, I can get you something else."

"This looks good," said Rafe as she took her glass of wine from Eden and picked up a piece of fruit to eat.

Eden sat down with her glass of wine and watched Rafe eat. "So, did you enjoy speaking French to Abby's date?" she asked, trying to mask her jealousy.

"I guess," said Rafe as she picked up a piece of chocolate to eat. She sighed at the flavor of the mixture of wine and chocolate as the chocolate melted in her mouth.

"What were you talking about?"

"Lots of things," she answered with a shrug. "How different things are here, about France, her work, different things."

"It looked like she was flirting with you," Eden said as she raised her eyebrows.

Rafe laughed softly. "It's hard not to flirt when you're speaking French," she said and winked. "Most of the time, I was trying to tell her not to flirt too much with Abby if she didn't want more. I told her Abby didn't understand the game."

"The game?"

"Yes, the game of love and flirting. In France, it's kind of expected you flirt a little, and it doesn't always mean you want to have a relationship. But for Abby, all the flirting means something. To Abby, it means they might be hooking up or worse—be in a relationship. Abby falls in love with everyone she has sex with," she said with a sigh, "so, I just told Darcella to be careful with Abby's heart."

Eden remembered when Rafe had told her the same thing about Abby when she was stoned. She looked over at Rafe as she took a sip of her wine. "So you learned all about the game when you were going to school in France?" asked Eden with a smile.

"Well, we *Italianos* are no slouches when it comes to *amore*." She winked at Eden. "You could say I got my extra credit course while I was there."

Eden looked at Rafe and could not help wanting her. *She's so beautiful*, she thought, and her heart thumped in her chest. "I remember when you used to flirt with me." She smiled at the memory of when they were in a better place. "Your presence was overwhelming at times. It still is," she said softly and took a sip of her wine.

Rafe just looked at her with a small smile for a moment then sat back as she ate more food and sipped her wine in silence. She knew Julia had been upset when she was talking to the French girl, and it was probably because of Eden, but she hadn't done anything wrong. If they wanted to think the worst of her, there was nothing she could do about it.

"How do you do it?" asked Eden suddenly.

Rafe looked at her in confusion. "Do what?"

"Just get people to like you and want to be around you, touch you, flirt with you," she paused, "want you?"

"I don't get people to do anything," she answered, not understanding Eden's reasoning for such a question.

"You did it with Darcella, Abby's date."

"What? No," she said with a laugh and shook her head.

"She came out of the house and asked about you. Then, when I pointed you out, she took one look at you, and she changed, she became focused on you. She walked up to you, and suddenly, she couldn't keep her eyes off you. Then she was touching you and laughing too much at what you said, and playing with her hair. What did you say or do to make her so into you so fast? She's not the only one who's been into you so quickly, either."

"Eden," Rafe hesitated, "you know it's just... no, it's on her, not me. She was probably focused on me because she missed speaking to someone in French. I didn't do anything but be nice."

"Right," she said slowly, "I think there's something else. Even when you act all cut off when you were going to the bar with Julia, they all flocked around you."

Rafe shook her head. "It's just how the bar scene is when anyone walks in who might be available," she said and waved her away.

"I don't know," said Eden. "I never got hit on like that."

"Really? I would think you'd have been hit on a lot. You're so beautiful." Rafe winked. "Maybe you intimidate people with your beauty and intelligence."

"Right," Eden laughed and could feel herself blush.

"Or, maybe, you just need Abby and Julia to spread sordid rumors about you," Rafe said sarcastically.

Eden smiled at Rafe as she remembered Abby and Julia talking about Rafe in the clubs. "So how did you get three women to come home with you?"

Rafe shrugged. "I just asked."

"Come on," Eden protested. "You're telling me you got all those girls, and Greer, just because you were suddenly available and you asked?"

"Pretty much," Rafe muttered with a nod. "Listen, all that stuff, I'm not doing it anymore if it's what you're worried about. I'm not picking up girls or cheating on you."

"No, no, I didn't mean to suggest you were," said Eden realizing Rafe thought she was accusing her of being unfaithful. "I was just asking because I never saw you doing those kinds of things before, and I was curious."

"Okay," said Rafe and watched Eden as she nervously played with the stem of her glass. "Sometimes, you have to ask for what you want," Rafe said with an arched brow and a wink. "You have to be brave for *amore* and not just wait for everything to come to you. It's a lot harder to work up the nerve to ask someone, and risk them saying no, than to tell those who ask you no. I don't think people appreciate it like they should when someone takes a risk and asks."

Eden looked at her thoughtfully. "It was hard to tell you no," she said with a small nervous ripple of laughter.

"I guess it's because, apparently, I'm so irresistible," she said wryly.

Eden gave a small laugh again then sobered. "So, what about Greer? Did you just have to ask her?" she queried softly.

Rafe sighed and drank the last of her wine. She figured Eden was taking a roundabout way to find out if she was thinking about leaving and going to be with Greer. It was kind of a strange way of doing it, but there it was. She knew Eden was worried about it. Everyone kept telling her how worried Eden had been about where she would go after Mexico. "No," she said, "I didn't ask her. She asked me."

"Oh," said Eden and nodded as she looked out at the pool.

"You don't have to worry about her," said Rafe as she poured more wine into her glass then refilled Eden's. "She's not a threat to you," she paused, "or to us if we decide to stay together. She wouldn't be a threat even if we weren't together."

Eden looked over at Rafe and shifted nervously. She did not like Rafe's use of the 'if' word. "Why?"

Rafe sighed and closed her eyes for a moment then looked at Eden again. "When I called her to help me, she was already seeing someone else. Someone who could love her the way I just couldn't. I think she's happy, and I wouldn't want to ruin her happiness, just like she didn't want to ruin mine."

Eden continued to look straight ahead so Rafe couldn't see the tears coming from her eyes. It seemed like Rafe was so close to saying she loved her. She wanted her to say it so badly, but she knew it probably wasn't going to happen anytime soon. Suddenly, she felt very hot as her emotions boiled inside her. She got up, went to the edge of the pool, and began to strip out of her pajamas.

As Eden slid her pajama top off, Rafe tried to look away but found she couldn't take her eyes away from her. She had not seen her body since her first day home. She shifted in her seat as Eden slid her pajama pants off and stood naked at the edge of the pool. In the dark, she couldn't see if the bruises were still there or not. It didn't matter. They were there in her mind.

Eden threw her clothes on to the lounger then dove into the pool. She swam to the end of the pool and back then held on to the edge of the pool and looked up at Rafe. "Your turn," she said with a smile.

Rafe gave a small laugh. "Are you challenging me?"

"Only if you think you can handle it," Eden purred. "I am kind of intimidating with my beauty and intelligence."

Laughing, Rafe stood up and stripped off her clothes, and then dove into the pool and swam her lap and back. As she came up out of the water, she smoothed her hair back and looked around for Eden. She caught sight of her walking out of the pool.

Eden grabbed her pajamas then stood naked in the soft light looking at Rafe. "Goodnight," she said then turned and walked toward the house.

Rafe watched her walk away and grinned, shaking her head. When Eden was in the house, Rafe laughed out loud. "I deserved that," she said to herself and swam another lap in the heated water.

To be continued in Book Eight - Traditorè. . .

Salvaggio's Light

Book Eight
TRADITORÈ

C.L. Cattano

NOTES

Translations: For translations of Italian, French and Spanish use: www.Babblefish.com

The chapters in this book were arranged with the intent of saving paper. This chapter style saved 28 pages. Original Total Book Pages 387 — Final Pages 359.

Music mentioned in this book.

No financial incentive was given for the mention of the following artists in this work. The author is a fan and felt mentioning them worked in the story. For the use of their name, credit is given, and links to their work are below.

Enjoy!

Melissa Ferrick

Website: http://www.melissaferrick.com/
Facebook: https://www.facebook.com/melissaferrick
Twitter: https://twitter.com/melissaferrick
Instagram: https://instagram.com/melissaferrick/
YouTube: https://www.youtube.com/user/melissaferrick

ABOUT THE AUTHOR

C.L. CATTANO LIVES in the Midwestern U.S. with her partner and their dog somewhere between the city and the forest. With a joy for traveling, she and her partner have visited many countries and have a love for meeting people and learning about the places they visit. When possible, she likes to include references in her work about the things she has learned, the places she has been and people she has met while on her travels and in her everyday life.

Cattano has a variety of creative interests including, but not limited to, creating fine art, writing, photography, and supporting women in the arts. She considers herself a 'Jack of All Trades' dabbling in what she terms the 'whimsies of her soul' that pull her toward happiness and fulfillment.

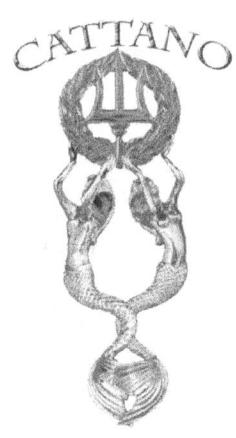

OTHER BOOKS
By C. L. Cattano

Cursed Hearts is a love story that transcends time and gender. Separated from by a gift from a bored demon on All Hallows Eve two souls connected

by the power of love have been searching through time for each other and incarnated as both men and women.

Over time, the gift became a curse and a game for the demons.

Now the souls have finally met again, and they must fight for a life together.

Will love prevail? Will they finally be able to live together again for a lifetime? They have one night to figure out the riddle and get it right to break the curse.

NOTE: 18+ Lesbian Romance. Some light erotic moments.

Available on Amazon <u>Cursed Hearts</u>

Salvaggio's Light Series
Available on Amazon

<u>Shattered Paradise</u> – Book One
<u>Blue Inferno</u> – Book Two
<u>Secrets & Rivalry</u> – Book Three
<u>Wildling's Claim</u> – Book Four
<u>Sowers of Discord</u> – Book Five
<u>Fire of Wrath</u> – Book Six

REQUEST FOR REVIEW

Thank you for reading **Salvaggio's Light** — An Epic Contemporary Romance Serial.

I hope you enjoyed book seven, **Confronting Darkness**, and will consider leaving an honest review. It only takes a few minutes, so I encourage you to go now and leave a review!

Check out the Salvaggio's Light Facebook page to join in the discussions and fun! www.facebook.com/pg/SalvaggiosLight

Join the CL Cattano Mailing List www.clcattano.com

I love getting fan mail, and you can contact me at clc@clcattano.com

www.ingramcontent.com/pod-product-compliance
Lightning Source LLC
Chambersburg PA
CBHW070623260626
47161CB00007B/2557